ALSO BY NEIL RUSSELL

Rail Black Novels
Beverly Hills is Burning
Wildcase
City of War

Non-Fiction
Can I Still Kiss You? Answering Your Children's
Questions about Cancer

NEIL RUSSELL

BEVERLY HILLS IS BURNING

A RAIL BLACK NOVEL

ROTHINGTON HOUSE

An Imprint of Site 85 Productions, Inc.

Copyright © 2014 by Neil Russell
ISBN 978-0-9915991-0-3

Beverly Hills is Burning / Neil Russell
Mystery Fiction. Suspense Fiction. Hollywood Fiction.

First Rothington House printing: March, 2014 z
Second printing: January, 2020

Rothington House is an Imprint of Site 85 Productions, Inc.
Trademark application pending.

Printed in the United States of America.

For more Neil Russell books visit www.Neil-Russell.com.

2 3 4 5 6 7 8 9 10

For Harold Robbins.

A NOTE FROM NEIL RUSSELL

I was born into a theatre-owning family that goes back to my grandfather and sawdust-floor nickelodeons. In our house, it was always *theatre,* not *theater*.

My birth was announced from the stage of one by Desi Arnaz who was just a bandleader then. Desi and my impresario father had spent the previous night singing and tap dancing their way through after-hours clubs celebrating my impending arrival. At sunrise, still clad in tuxedos and bearing champagne, they arrived at the non-air conditioned hospital where my mother lay in August-hot discomfort awaiting her call to the delivery room. I'm told the Sisters of Mercy (the nuns, not the rock band) loved the impromptu hallway show, and the monsignor came by for an autograph and a glass of bubbly. Family legend has it my mother held her applause.

Conversations around our dinner table were about grosses, holdovers and which stars were touring and might be coming to dinner. From the time I was old enough to sit upright, I saw every motion picture released, whether in a conventional theatre, drive-in, screening room or someone's home. Looking back, I can't believe how lucky I was. I loved everything about the movies and the dark, smoky rooms where grizzled movie men ran new pictures and made sarcastic remarks far funnier than anything onscreen. Those experiences turned out to be more important to my future than my college degree.

As a kid, I met many of the original moguls: Zanuck, Zukor, Cohn, Goldwyn, two Warners and both Schencks. (Regrettably, I never got to meet Mr. Mayer.) Walt Disney used to send birthday presents to my sister and me. I also met some of the major producers and directors of the time:

Howard Hawks, Sam Spiegel, Otto Preminger, Stanley Kramer, Hal Wallis and a host of others. What struck me was that the studio bosses and moviemakers spoke more about material and rights than about stars.

I have worked for some exceptional people. Frank Yablans and Barry Diller were the smartest and toughest. Kirk Kerkorian, the shrewdest. Mario Kassar would have been right at home with the original moguls. On the other side of the ledger was David Begelman. A deeply flawed man who left demons in his wake.

I have had the privilege of negotiating against some of the brightest minds in the business and working alongside one-of-a-kind talents. I've traveled places, seen things and met people who shaped history. When I set off on this journey, I could never have imagined what a remarkable life lay ahead. I am grateful to those who provided me with the opportunity.

When I left theatres after college to join Paramount Pictures, the term intellectual property was not in common usage, but because of my upbringing, I knew it was the lifeblood of the business. I actually bought my first IP the summer before I graduated. Later, I spent every free moment poring through the archives of Paramount and each subsequent studio at which I worked (Columbia, MGM, United Artists, Carolco) reading contracts and picture P&Ls. For better or worse, I can tell you Gable's *Mogambo* location package— which is interesting but not important—and the James Bond deal at United Artists—which is both interesting *and* important.

Eventually, I began buying IPs for studios and later for myself. In the past four+ decades, I have purchased thousands, including the life story rights of commandos flying out of a hot zone (bought while they were still on the plane), bestsellers by world-class authors and manuscripts from first-timers. I have also acquired screenplays, television formats, trademarks, song and magazine titles and documents found by a researcher working inside an Iron Curtain country's secret police archive—a phone connection that I'm sure awakened the night shift at the NSA. I've also acquired scores of stories from the victims of crimes (I don't buy rights from criminals), the cops who brought the perpetrators to justice and the prosecutors who put the bad guys away.

I've purchased large and small movie libraries to obtain television and remake rights and commissioned reporters, private investigators, civil servants, housewives and taxi drivers to chase IPs I thought would make good filmed entertainment or entertainment brands. Sometimes, I picked right.

Once, I also audaciously attempted to buy a portion of a major studio's IP. As an executive at the studio at the time, this did not have the dealmaking ending I'd envisioned. It did, however, change the trajectory of my career beyond anything I could have blueprinted. Sometimes you *can* fill an inside straight.

Hollywood is always changing, yet always the same. And it is always seemingly on the verge of disappearing because of some new technology, radical shift in audience behavior or the ebb and flow of capital. Not once in all my years in the business have I ever sat in a meeting where the collective opinion about the industry was upbeat. It's always doom and gloom. I believe this insecurity is why we adapt so quickly. If the wildebeests move to new grazing lands, it's in our interest to already be there.

In recent years, the fanboy surge has sidelined many previously highly-regarded filmmakers. Not since the conversion from silents to sound have so many commercial producers, directors and writers been involuntarily "aged out" of the mainstream. And United Artists, once the place where the best from all creative walks could turn, is little more than a hollow logo inside a company that in the past quarter-century has had more owners than hits. Yet, last year, there were just as many pictures made, grosses were up, and I am certain every single company raised the book value of its library. Hollywood is alive and well. It's not going anywhere.

But for all that's written about the entertainment business, very little of how it really works is ever seen by those who are not part of it. The following novel may pull back the curtain a little. It is fiction, of course, but people in the industry will have little trouble recognizing the machinery—old and new—including things that are only spoken of in hushed tones: sewing circles, hedonistic predators, sophisticated hustlers, financial corruption, blackmail and occasional self-destruction. For if there is one thing Hollywood knows how to do, it is to live lives as extraordinary and dramatic as the ones it puts onscreen.

However, unlike professions where the less ambitious can garner a degree, a license or a title that allows them to coast through life with no requirement to stay on the cutting edge or even pretend to, there is no slow current in Hollywood. Those without creative, legal, financial or executive talent—and more importantly, an insatiable hunger and immunity to rejection—would be wise to have a cup of coffee at LAX and take the next plane home. Heartbreak and poverty haunt every street corner.

But if you're good—really good—the men and women who prowl those corners to pluck brilliance out of obscurity will find you. Your eccentricities will be celebrated and your past failures forgotten. Here, only money matters.

It can be an exhilarating life, but keep your celebrations short, or they will be few. Sleeping with one eye open is also recommended.

On the other side, Hollywood also gives birth to friendships that last a lifetime. Honor your handshake, remember *everybody's* name, reach out to colleagues going through a difficult time and, most of all, learn how to graciously accept a no. You will be welcome back to any office.

This book is not for the timid or the sanctimonious. It contains raw language, graphic violence and sex—the kind, that as a kid, you read under the covers with a flashlight. All the things that have been a part of books and movies—in fact, all storytelling—from the beginning. And always will be.

However, society lurches, slides and grinds its way through its relationship with fiction, so I offer my gratitude and dedicate this novel to Harold Robbins and his seminal lawsuit for making it possible for this story and so many others to appear in print.

Neil Russell
Beverly Hills, CA

The biggest sin in life is to have leverage and not use it.

Frank Yablans, 1972
President, Paramount Pictures

CHAPTER ONE

Diamonds and Parachutes

It was just after midnight when the girl in the blue diamond necklace fell out of the sky.

I was sitting on the flybridge of my Benetti, seven miles off the ritzy hills of Newport Coast, drifting without power on a dead calm, starlit sea. Sam Cooke's "Another Saturday Night" was adding just the right smoothness to a perfect California evening, while I put a dent in a tall Japanese beer and a good cigar.

After a trying few weeks among my land-dwelling brethren, I was enjoying a meteor shower and looking forward to a long weekend of snagging fish without enough IQ to avoid the world's worst angler. Mostly, though, I just wanted to be alone. Not that I don't revere my fellow man, just that I hadn't seen the best of him lately—with the exception of Geraldo, the Dolphin Bay Yacht Club bartender, who had packed my cooler with 22-oz cans of iced Sapporo Reserve.

A 102-foot cruiser is not a one-person boat, however, I grew up around much larger ones and can handle the *Sanrevelle* alone when I need to. She'd been custom-built for a well-known, NBA big man who was having some acute alimony trouble, and when you're my size and find a doorway you don't bang your forehead against, you buy what's around it. Tonight, the ocean was so serene a four-year-old could have run something twice her size.

I was just about to open another Sapporo when I heard the unmistakable, firecracker-like staccato of popping nylon. The sound every

1

special operator and skydiver dreads. The one a parachute makes when it's not all the way open.

I was running dark except for emergency spots at the bow and stern, but when the woman rushed past me, she was so close I could see her tight black dress was ripped up the side, and she was wearing only one silver high heel. You couldn't miss the necklace either, but flashy as it was, the terror in her eyes outshone it.

I also recognized its wearer. Valentine Jones, the movie star, who I'd just seen on some awards show, sullenly applauding whoever had beaten her for best actress. I couldn't remember the name of her picture only that it wasn't one of the smash-and-crash, special effects flicks she was known for, but something arty that was supposed to make this nomination *the one*. Luckily for the tabloids, she'd missed again and treated them to turning over a table and pulling the winner's hair at a fashion magazine's after-party.

Then Miss Jones was gone in a whoosh of spray, her tangled orange and green chute following her into the deep. I hadn't heard a plane, but a couple of minutes earlier, there'd been a noticeable splash in the distance off my starboard side. I'd assumed it was a sounding gray whale. Maybe not.

I probably should have climbed down to the deck before diving in, but instinct took over, and I grabbed a pocket-sized Maglite off the chart table and went. It seemed like a week before I hit the water, then, adrenaline notwithstanding, the shock of the cold Pacific wrenched away my beer glow and reactivated the Delta Force part of my brain.

The first rule of sea rescue is to never leave an untended boat without a static line. The second is to angle away from an emergency until you can assess the situation. I ignored the first because there wasn't time. I remembered the second when my dive carried me into the chute's rigging, and I became ensnared like a tuna.

Fortunately, the Maglite came on underwater, and though it only took a few seconds to untangle myself, they were precious seconds of breath I wouldn't get back. I kicked hard downward and quickly came to the girl. She was fighting like a wildcat, which was accomplishing nothing, but there was no getting her back from blind panic.

I came in from behind, grabbed the right side of her slender neck and squeezed my fingers tight. Sleeper holds are more effective if you use a forearm, but despite the disparity in our sizes, I didn't want to get into a wrestling match. Powerful men have lost their lives underestimating the hysteria-induced strength of smaller victims. Miss Jones was at the point where she had no idea my hand was even there, and I got a good enough grip on her carotid that ten seconds later, her head lolled, and I could unclasp the harness.

As I did, she slipped out of my grasp, and I had to grab her by the hair, which I used to pull her upward behind me. The drag from the chute had kept her from sinking like a stone, but with Murphy's Law timing, the canopy had now opened fully, and without her weight, it was spreading with the current. I had to swim laterally to escape being bundled into it, which not only took me further from the *Sanrevelle* but used up the rest of my oxygen.

By the time I broke the surface, I was choking seawater, and it took several seconds for the pulsating red flashes behind my eyes to fade. I used to do this kind of thing for a living, and I'm still in pretty good shape, but I was suddenly conscious of no longer being twenty-five.

Miss Jones had a heartbeat, but she had stopped breathing. I put her on her back and turned her chin toward me. After checking her throat for obstructions, I squeezed her nose shut, clamped my mouth over hers and blew a long breath into her lungs. I then drove my open palm up under her ribcage—not textbook and not recommended, but when time is critical, sometimes effective.

I had barely disengaged when she ejected something sickeningly sweet and rancid. Jagerbombs was my guess, laced with stomach acid. Tomorrow, if she survived, her head wouldn't be anyplace you'd want to visit.

Then, without warning, she raked my face with her nails and sank her teeth into my shoulder. When I tried to push her away, one of her thrashing knees caught me in the solar plexus and hurt like hell. Worse, I dropped the Maglite. I grunted something unintelligible, released her and dove after the light.

I caught up with it after a few feet, but when I resurfaced, Miss Jones was gone. I went back below to a spot where I thought she should be, but she wasn't. I was furious with myself. A long time ago, I'd tasted the same fury. It had been a different sea, a different woman, but I'd been tested and found wanting. It wasn't going to happen again.

The light didn't penetrate very far, so I had to make a guess. About fifteen feet further down, I caught a glimpse of a bare foot. I grabbed the ankle it was attached to and headed back to the top.

She didn't make it easy, kicking at me every stroke of the way. I reevaluated my earlier forensics. Probably some Cartel Charlie in there along with the booze—maybe a couple of huffs of meth to top it off. The way the best actresses are partying these days.

I wondered how cool they'd think it was if they could see the filthy hands and sore-covered skin on the creeps who handle the stuff on its way to their spa-pampered, organic-only bodies. Maybe watch some drug lord piss in the cocaine mash as a commentary on the DEA. Or a hepatitis-infected mule roll a wad of crystal in a leaf and stick it up his unwiped ass. It's safer to lick a toilet at a truck stop. But with this crowd, nothing matters but the moment.

This time, when we broke the surface, I didn't take any chances. I clipped her on the chin with a hard right—maybe a little harder than I had to—and she went goodnight. I looked around for the *Sanrevelle*. She was a hundred yards away, but the Pacific was just as calm as I'd left it. Mr. Cooke had moved along to "Chain Gang." I knew how he felt.

I floated Miss Jones on her back again and removed her necklace so it wouldn't bite any further into her neck. The choker of large blue diamonds was impressive but rendered inconsequential by the enormous marquise-cut stone hanging pendant-like against the hollow of her throat. It was massive enough that my thumb and forefinger would barely have encircled it, and I couldn't help but notice how heavy it was as I buttoned the piece into one front pocket of my cargo shorts and the Maglite into the other.

After sliding the lady's shoulders up on my left hip, I cupped her chin and began taking long, smooth sidestroke pulls toward home. I hadn't gone twenty yards when I heard a powerful engine coming fast. The likelihood of being run down was remote, but in the last few minutes, remote had become my middle name. I stopped and turned to check, and as I did, I heard yelling, then a pair of searchlights swept over us.

The Orange County Sheriff's rescue boats are the same kind the Coast Guard uses to interdict drug traffickers. They look like miniature red tugs, only they can do seventy and make a U-turn into their own wakes with enough g's to leave your tonsils on the window. This one had three deputies strapped into fighter jet seats wearing lifejackets over their bulletproof vests.

The fourth seat was occupied by a civilian—an ultra-skinny dude the glamour industries seem to have an endless supply of. He had a sheriff's department blanket over what was left of a tuxedo and was the one doing the screaming. "There she is! There she is! Oh, Dear Jesus, she's dead!"

The patrol boat throttled back, glided past me and stopped. As I came up on its stern, the pilot cut the engine. The guy in the tux was out of his seat and standing at the transom. "Don't just sit there, motherfuckers! Help her! That's Valentine Jones!"

I got a look at the face of the deputy nearest me, and he wasn't particularly moved. The one who joined him had a slightly different take. "Shut the fuck up, *sir*. Miss Jones looks like she's in capable hands." SoCal law enforcement doesn't get a rod-on when they see a celebrity. They do, however, have an aversion to being called motherfuckers. Especially by hysterical twits.

Miss Jones's dress had ridden up high enough in the boat's wash that her Full Brazilian was now on prominent display. I noticed for the first time a delicate stream of tiny tattooed stars beginning somewhere within her bare V and running down the inside of one leg, apparently to give the appearance they were falling out of her.

My first thought was ouch. I'm not a big ink fan, and the few times I've asked for an explanation of a particular one's symbolism, I've come away wishing I hadn't. With women, since I don't think we're going back to granny skirts and high boned collars, I have yet to see work the owner will be proud of when she's fifty. Miss Jones was no exception. But she was also an actress, so foresight was likely a concept she kept in the same storage locker as her manners.

I eased her close enough so the pros could grab her, and as she was being lifted aboard, something flashed in the glare of the searchlights. It was a tiny, silver flying bird on a matching ankle chain. I was surprised it had survived the impact of the fall, let alone our duel in the deep. Right about then, she came to. Refreshed from her nap, the thrashing she'd been doing earlier had only been a warm-up. And cocksucker was the word she seemed most comfortable with.

Despite all she'd been through, she'd maintained that one high heel, and she got it under the chin of the easygoing deputy, drawing blood. He didn't coldcock her like I had, but he did manage to bang her head on a chrome cleat with enough of a clunk that she came back to the real world. "Are you trying to kill me, cocksucker?" Then she threw a right that just missed.

This earned her plastic restraints around her wrists and ankles, and she went wild. The second deputy casually took out his Taser, and Tux-Man lost his mind. "You can't use that! She's the biggest star in the world!"

"How about I warm it up on you?"

All of a sudden, everybody rediscovered their gentler side—at least until Miss Jones put her hands to her throat and got her second wind. "Oh, my God, my necklace is gone! I had it when I jumped!"

Tuxedo came back to the transom and glared down. "You stole it, didn't you?" His screeching was now high enough to call dogs. He turned to the cops, "That necklace is the Star of…" He seemed to catch himself. "It's a Benedict Crown *original*, and it's priceless! I demand you arrest this man!"

The person I'm trying hard to overcome wanted to shrug his shoulders and feed Mr. Crown's—whoever he was—diamonds to the squid on my way home. My inner Dalai Lama, however, unbuttoned my pocket and passed the sparkles up. He grabbed the necklace with manic satisfaction. "See, I told you!"

Valentine immediately started bucking against her makeshift cuffs and screaming again. "That's mine, goddamn it! Somebody take it from that asshole!"

The guy forgot about me and the cops and turned on the new assault on his dignity. "Why you lying piece of shit! I just let you…"

Practiced in such matters, the deputy with the 50,000-volt attention-getter grabbed the necklace. "We'll sort this out at the station. Now both of you shut up… please."

The mellow deputy looked down at me, amused by the scene as only a cop can be. "You're Rail Black, aren't you? The rich guy who's on trial?"

This really *was* my lucky night. I didn't bother correcting him that it wasn't my trial. I was just a witness.

"My brother's a deputy too. Up in Santa Monica. He's working your courtroom. Monday's your big day on the stand, right?"

"So they tell me."

"Good luck, man. I wish you'd killed that little creep. If it matters, so does every cop I know. That your boat over there?"

"It is."

"Climb aboard. We'll run you home."

"I'm fine," I answered. "What you can do is leave my name out of your report."

The deputy thought about that. "I don't see a problem. The screecher here is Archibald Hatt, a local real estate hotshot. He says the plane was his, and him and Pussy Galore was the only ones aboard." He broke into a wide grin. "Besides, this is Newport Beach. Second marriages, third mortgages and Fletcher Jones. Nobody gives a shit about LA assholes."

I smiled back. "This LA asshole says thanks. Where were they headed?"

"Apparently, nowhere. Mr. Hatt says they was partying at his place in Laguna Beach when Miss Jones decided she wanted a ride in his new King Air. According to him, the hangar's supposed to keep it gassed up, and he didn't check the gauge. When things went to shit, he got her out and managed a couple of maydays before he put it in the drink. We was nearby, so we told the coast guard we'd check it out."

You never want to get in a plane with me at the controls. I might be the worst pilot on seven continents. But even drunk on my ass, I wouldn't take off without checking my fuel. High-end actresses wearing five figures of outfit and who knows how much in jewelry don't go looking for parachutes to climb into—especially over water only a couple of miles from land. "I don't believe it," I said.

"Neither do we," said the deputy. "We're hopin the girl can fill in the blanks."

I thought about what she'd regurgitated. "Don't hope too hard."

"Well, once we do a tox on him, Hatt's problem's gonna be his insurance company. He's upright, but he's asked me for a menu twice, so I'm bettin he slammed a lot more than a couple of appletinis. Add in the tab for our little bus ride, and he'll be writing checks for a while. Maybe it'll smarten him up."

"Don't bet on that either," I said. I waved, then turned and swam around the patrol boat toward the *Sanrevelle*. Five minutes later, I hauled myself over my own transom.

As I stood under a shower hot enough and long enough to wash away Miss Jones and her necklace detective, I was torn between calling it a night and starting over with a fresh Sapporo and a new cigar. Not surprisingly, alcohol and nicotine accompanied by Mr. Cooke won, and when I finally resumed enjoying the meteor debris from my flybridge, I committed myself to letting the next parachute fend for itself.

Unless, of course, Sofia Vergara happened to be dangling from it.

What I didn't know at the time was that for somebody who goes out of his way to avoid show business, I was just getting started.

CHAPTER TWO

Cypriots and Caddies

Matthias "Matty Aspirins" Papadopoulos turned onto Sepulveda Blvd. out of Pinkie's high-rise garage a half-mile from LAX. In the old days, this running around bullshit wouldn't have happened. He'd have walked out of United, crossed a few lanes and slipped into his wheels at one of the four-hour meters in the short-term lot. Ten minutes later, he'd have been rolling north.

But the falafels had fucked that up along with everything else. Now, everywhere you looked, there was a cop with a bomb dog or a flak-jacketed soldier running an electronic sniffer over your trunk. So you waited half an hour for a shuttle then stood with a bunch of assholes and their bad breath and puking babies while some *pousti* jitney driver with a five nose rings whiplashed your spine and screamed on his cell phone.

The signs on Pinkie's walls said vehicles were subject to a check there too, but just because you gave a guy a badge, a mutt and an assignment didn't mean he was going to work any harder than some lazy-ass sewer worker who goes on break while the toilets on your block are blowing turds at the ceiling. Once the cop's supervisor is out of sight, he and the dog are a cinch to head up to Randy's with the other union assholes to shoot the shit under the big donut.

Pinkie's was owned by a Korean, which guaranteed no security cameras. Matty's old man, Stavros, who loan-sharked out of his restaurant supply business before the cancer ate him, used to say the K's always paid, but if shoes didn't come with laces, they'd go barefoot. Koreans didn't buy extra anything. Matty didn't know about shoelaces, but he did know what cameras cost, plus if you had one, there was always a chance it might catch something. Then you'd have to jerk off for months with some Deputy D.A. who couldn't spell "earn a living."

Guys like Matty usually didn't drive themselves, but he'd ridden with one too many nervous dickheads who could attract a cop passing out communion wafers. He hadn't been to LA in six years, but nothing had changed, except maybe the traffic, which was worse. It was still hot, the air tasted like ass and nobody seemed to give a shit about anything.

He didn't like the car either, a black BMW 650. It was fast enough, but anybody who knew anything about this kind of work wouldn't have ordered up a 2-door. He was going to have to make a stop.

The Cypriot's shop was on Pico, a couple of blocks west of Hauser. The sign said Papazian's Auto Body, but if a guy named Papazian existed, he took orders from the Cypriot. Papazian's was an old four-bay gas station with the windows painted out and cars in various stages of damage and repair parked wherever there was room. But if you took your insurance company a quote from Papazian's, they fell out of their chairs laughing.

The Cypriot's business was tagging stolen luxury cars with clean VINs, greasing some guy at the DMV with a bad smack habit to issue new paper then running the sheep-dipped vehicles down to Long Beach for an ocean cruise. Most went to China, but Matty had heard the hot new market was Afghanistan. Afghanistan? What the fuck? He was glad he was in services, not P&L.

"Jesus Christ, if it ain't Matty Aspirins. I heard you might be in town." The Cypriot came out of an open bay, wrapped his thick arms around Matty and hugged him. "Motherfucker, you never put on a pound."

Matty watched the tight gold Greek Orthodox crucifix around the heavyset man's neck dance over his Adams apple. "You could maybe get a longer chain."

"Reminds me not to order a third Whopper," the Cypriot laughed, his whole body shaking. He looked at the BMW. "I assume you want to get rid of that."

"I need two more doors."

"I can give you a Caddie or a Benz."

"Fuck the Germans. Which Caddie?"

"DTS, silver."

"I gotta move some stuff over."

"You want one of my boys to help?" The Cypriot jerked his head toward the shop where two dark-haired young men were working on a yellow Vette.

"You and I can handle it."

"Pull around back. I'll get the keys."

The four dive bags clunked when the men handled them, but the Cypriot didn't comment. Matty slammed the lid. "You know who to bill."

The Cypriot shook his head. "You were never here. Plates are legit. Reg and insurance are inside. Everything's in the name of Elite Rubber. That's reclaimed tires, if anybody should ask. Real place, up in Fresno. My brother-in-law owns it. I'll call him soon as you leave."

Matty nodded and got into the Caddie. The Cypriot held the door. "You been at this a long time."

"That supposed to mean something."

"You gotta start thinking about slowing down before you find out you already have. Maybe at the wrong time."

Matty didn't like hearing it, but the Cypriot was right. These last couple of years, every job seemed like an ordeal. He was starting to hate airports— and adrenaline. "And do what?" he asked.

"You and me, we got someplace to go. Not like the working stiffs in this country who're gonna die in their own piss."

"Shit, Mykonos costs more than New York."

"Fuck Mykonos. I'm talking about Cyprus. I bought a building in Pyrgos. Five floors, just up the street from the water. I got a long-term tenant on the ground floor, and the top two are for me. You can have either of the others."

"Jesus Christ, I came for a car, not a real estate pitch."

"Four hundred grand. Furnished. Walk to everything. You got enough stashed away to live like Rockefeller there."

"What am I supposed to do at night? Watch you eat?"

"Man, you been out of circulation too long. The Med's liberated now. Women from all over go to Pyrgos to get laid."

"No shit?"

"No shit. Think about it. Four hundred large."

"Okay to leave the Caddie at the airport?" Matty asked, changing the subject.

"Just let me know where. Toss the keys. I got another set."

"You don't hear in a week, report it stolen." Matty fired up the big V-8, and the fat man closed the door. Just before he pulled away, the Cypriot held up four fingers and mouthed the price again.

One of the Cypriot's sons came out of the garage. "Which VIN you want on the Vette?"

"We got a new batch from the Armenian. Use one of them."

Matty burned rubber as he turned onto Pico.

"Who was that guy?" asked the son.

"An old friend. Matty Aspirins."

"Aspirins?"

"Somebody gets a headache, Matty makes it go away."

CHAPTER THREE

Gardenias and Additions

Cocoon ambiance is the hallmark of a new crop of high-décor, high-VIP hostelries that have sprung up along the expensive stretch of neon and valets known as the Sunset Strip. None more protective than the twenty-story, black and glass monolith, Hotel Innuendo, known to the glitterati as simply the I, which is fast becoming the newest backdrop for moneyed merriment and misbehavior. For well-heeled sybarites who are shy-of-camera and predatory surveillance, this is the place you want to lay your head. However, if you're a tourist hoping to see a famous face, it is advisable not to test the I's security. It bites.

Matty used a remote from his briefcase to open the underground parking garage of the Gardenia, a twenty-unit apartment building directly behind the Innuendo. He parked the Caddie in the rear slot of a tandem space marked 203, locked it and took the elevator to the second floor.

The apartment had been redecorated since he'd last used it, but it was still devoted to comfort, not vogue. He dialed the A/C down to sixty-eight and did a walk-through, closing the plantation shutters in each room. Several changes of clothes in his size were hanging in the closet along with a bathrobe. In the dresser, he found fresh underwear, socks, the remote for the flatscreen and a pair of expensive Brunton Epoch binoculars. He put the binoculars in his briefcase, located a cable music channel playing some Jack Jones then went back out, double-locking the apartment door behind him.

As he walked up the steep drive to the Innuendo's main entrance, he nodded to the uniformed doorman, who scrambled over to trip the electronic door. In the lobby, he followed the sign to the rooftop pool elevator.

Back in the day, Matty would sometimes skip the apartment and check into a five-star hotel near the beach so he could spend his afternoons in one of the cabanas. He liked to have a couple of ladies sent in for a blowjob and a girl-on-girl show, and most of the time, he could have had them do it on the diving board, because he had the entire pool to himself. Matty could never figure it out. LA douchebags didn't go out in the sun. That's why he liked Miami. Everybody, even guys a half-step from the worms, took their shirts off and baked. Just like Greece. The hotter the better.

Today, the Innuendo's roof looked like a Riviera cruise ship. Thirty people crowded around the water, each more tanned than the next and wearing all the gold that wasn't still in the windows at Bulgari. Matty caught a few words of Italian and French, and some old broad, who should have thought twice about a thong, was yelling at the pool boy in Russian—which Matty recognized because he'd once spent time in Sheepshead Bay, setting up a guy to disappear.

In his East Coast street clothes, he got some stares, but when he stared back, those stopped. Jesus Christ, were there any fuckin Americans left? Matty made his way past a spa and waterfall beyond which some designer had created a maze of hedges and ferns. He liked that because once he was on the other side, no one could see him.

At the corner of the roof, he took out the binoculars and swept an arc around Sunset Blvd. It was like taking a tour of past jobs. The ex-cop with the meth habit on Doheny, the witness protection cocksucker in the alley behind the Viper Room, and up in the hills, the pretty little brunette singer with the barbed wire nipple rings.

Matty didn't like killing women. He felt it was beneath him. He also thought any guy who let a broad get in a position to fuck up his life should mean the guy had to go, not her. But Matty didn't make policy. His aversion didn't apply to women who got mixed up in business. There was just enough Old World left in him to be disgusted by chicks with bigger balls than the guys who let them get that way. Ordinarily emotionless on the job, he enjoyed watching them die. Double when the guy was included.

New York and Chicago had been doing LA work since the beginning. It was better that way. The few made guys on the coast were mostly Vegas errand boys or union bag men. You'd hand one a piece, and he'd look at you like, "Where the fuck am I supposed to put that? It'll ruin the lines of my Tommy Bahamas."

When the bosses wanted a big job done right, they called the Greeks. Lucky Luciano had started that. No goomba bullshit like dressing up in shiny suits and waving cash around some nightclub so everybody remembered you. Greeks flew in, popped the right guy and went home to get laid—most of the time, anyway.

Matty had never even been arrested. He had a nice little chain of flower shops that paid the bills and kept some of his lesser relatives employed. He didn't know much about bouquets and boutonnières, but some guy he'd whacked fifteen years ago had owned the business, and when he found out the family was selling because their old man was in the ground, he had one of his cousins make an offer.

The Colosseum Pictures building was two blocks east and ten stories below, but the binoculars brought it close enough to identify the Prada crest on the rooftop guards' sunglasses. Matty'd been told that the rest of the security staff were the usual ten-bucks-an-hour Mexicans and moonlighting LAPD who worked for a company owned by Charlie "Big Bush" Busalacchi in Jersey. They'd be no problem. These two, however, and two more like them inside were professional *jabones* brought in strictly for next week's meeting. Matty would have to deal with them himself. The good news was that they were there, so everything was still on.

The men were standing under a temporary awning set up next to the building's air conditioning units, which probably made it noisy as hell along with the heat. Regardless, both were in black: black silk shirts, black slacks, black loafers, no socks. They were also carrying Uzis, which they probably thought looked cool but told Matty they were jerks. Unless you shoved one down somebody's throat and he choked on it, all an Uzi could do was get you killed. You sure as shit weren't going to hit anything with it. Maybe when he retired, he'd start a real security company. He used to think it would be in Miami, but maybe he should check out Cyprus.

Matty focused on the TV under the awning. Andy Griffith. With Spanish subtitles, which meant the guys had been brought in from overseas, probably Sicily, and were trying to find something almost-Dago to watch. But Jesus Christ, did you need SAP to figure out Aunt Bee?

He shifted the binoculars back to the street just as a stretch limo slipped to the curb. It deposited a leggy redhead along with two young men in dark suits a head shorter than she was. An actress and her agents for sure. He dialed down on her face but didn't recognize her. He wasn't surprised. Lately, the people they put on magazine covers were strangers. Fuckin superhero movies and reality television. John Wayne showed up today, they'd stick a Halloween mask on him and let some pimple-faced emo kick his ass.

What he did recognize was the bulge under the guy's suit who came out to meet them. The bulge and the shoes. Black Nikes, like umpires wear. Umpires and cops on their off-duty job. When the four disappeared inside, the limo pulled around the corner, out of sight. Matty knew that's where the garage entrance was.

A week from now, he'd make that same turn, but first he had another job to do—a last-minute assignment. Normally, Matty wouldn't have accepted two hits on the same trip, especially when the big one was complicated by having to manage other shooters, but the bosses in New York said the late-addition was an emergency, and there wasn't anybody else available who could be trusted to do it right. They also said it paid double, which meant it was more than serious.

Apparently, some mob bookie was getting ready to take a powder to Nicaragua. Matty didn't know the whole story, but it had to do with using his girlfriend to fix basketball games. Word was the Feds had her wired up.

Okay, you gotta run, you gotta run. But Nicaragua? Jesus Christ, he'd been there. Between the death squads, people starvin in the streets and the fuckin humidity, the place was worse than Jersey. He was doin the guy a favor. He deserved to be dead.

16

Now that he was out here, Matty was glad he'd taken the second job. He could do the guy then relax the rest of the week and get the feel of the town again. Adjust to the time change and go over everything with the Tata brothers a few more times just to make sure. In the meantime, he'd call a couple of broads. It'd been a while since he'd had a blowjob. They always helped ease his jet lag.

CHAPTER FOUR

High Walls and Cinnamon Pills

My house was built by Howard Hughes's personal attorney, J.C. Stinson. Most people think of Neil McCarthy as Howard's legal mouthpiece, and he was. Stinson never appeared in court for H.H., never spoke to the press, never willingly had his picture taken. He just gave the big man advice he wouldn't have listened to from anyone else. Without Stinson, Hughes would have eccentricitied himself into bankruptcy or a rubber room— maybe both.

The house is on Dove Way almost at the top of Beverly Hills. It's a 17,000-sq. ft. Spanish hacienda that during a series of post-Stinson owners had some frightening things done to it. I've spent more money than I care to count restoring it, helped along by an army of craftsmen and artisans, most imported from Europe, because fewer and fewer of America's young people will apprentice in the calloused hands trades.

They'll hunch over a computer for chump change rather than knock down a heavy six figures being physically creative and going home exhausted instead of wired. I blame teachers. They're the voices that are supposed to expand imagination. Instead, when they're not on strike, they're assigning *Fast Food Nation* for literature credit.

Hughes occasionally hid from the press and lawsuits in Stinson's pool house, so the estate's buffered isolation is superb, even by today's standards. J.C. was his own kind of eccentric, and Mallory, my often-mystical British houseman, as well as some of my occasional guests, claim to have seen him walking the grounds in his trademark white linen suit, Panama hat and long, black cigarette holder tipped skyward. For some unknown reason, they also report him to be barefoot, and though I haven't had the pleasure of an encounter, I have smelled tobacco smoke where there shouldn't be any.

The house is rumored to have a hidden room where J.C. kept his Hughes files, and every now and then, when I'm bored, I tap a few walls. One thing he didn't hide is a salaciously decorated, soundproofed elevator with only two stops: the underground garage and the master bedroom. Having heard about Stinson's reputation as a swordsman, I suspect it saw its share of Hollywood's famous faces. Some might have even made it all the way to the bed.

The reason I was in court was because of that bedroom. How Paulie Stuben had been able to get over a 12-ft. wall topped with broken glass, evade the sensors and cameras, then slip past Mallory, was something my security experts were still mulling over. The bottom line, though, was that he had, and when I got home from a boring dinner and took the elevator up to what I hoped would be a good night's sleep, I didn't expect to see anyone, let alone a naked, barely-out-of-her-teens, Wind Fortune passed out in my bed with Mr. Stuben positioning her for shots. A framed photograph of me, standing on the deck of my yacht, was half-gripped in her hand, apparently to make it appear as if she'd fallen asleep daydreaming over it.

Wind Fortune is one of Jake Praxis's most important clients. She's also Hollywood's biggest, baddest, bad girl star, which comes hand-in-hand with being one of the world's most damaged people. I was close to her late parents, and she was crashing in my guest wing while those of us who care about her tried to wrestle her back from yet one more self-destructive precipice.

I don't think the intruder could have been any more surprised than I was. The difference was that I was trained for the unexpected. That, and two of him might not have made one of me.

I held him by the hair while I got a sheet over Wind. He thrashed around a good deal and caught me in the neck with a wild swing of his camera. It didn't really hurt, but it pissed me off, so I did a quick grab-and-twist of his nuts, and he settled down.

Wind was breathing regularly, but very deeply. I guessed she'd been given something, but with most paparazzi, their dick is their camera, so I didn't think it was to rape her. Just to be sure, I asked the man who knew. He shook his head no, but it wasn't convincing, so I asked him again, suggesting he was about to go out the window—unopened. He shook his head vigorously and swore he hadn't touched her.

"What's she on?" I asked.

He reached in his pocket and came out with a couple of lint-covered tablets the color of cinnamon. Ambien. She'd sleep for eight and get up without a hangover. No paramedics necessary.

"You flying solo?"

He seemed to have lost his command of English, so I twisted his arm up and behind him until I heard his shoulder pop out of the socket. He went white and fainted. A couple of slaps across the face brought him back. His voice was shaky, but he got it out. "Just me, honest. When I told my agent whose house she was in, he said a picture in your bed could be worth fifty grand."

I nodded at the photograph I had put back on the nightstand. "And that was what you were going to use as proof?"

"I got some shots downstairs. Nothing really good, but enough for some of the bottom feeders." He was trembling now, and his teeth were chattering, which meant he had gone into shock. "Look, Mr. Black, I don't want any trouble. How about you let me go, and we'll both forget this, okay?"

It was a thought, but people breaking into my house and terrorizing my friends—in particular, fragile ones—had elevated it out of the nuisance category. Mr. Stuben needed a lesson, and those with similar ideas needed something to consider.

To dislocate a man's elbow, you twist his forearm inward and simultaneously chop just above the joint. Paulie Stuben's bones were like a sparrow's, and as the elbow on his good arm went, I heard a second snap.

Probably the ulna. Too much torque. My bad.

He passed out again, so while he was anesthetized, I broke both his wrists. It was going to be a long time before he clicked a Nikon again. He probably wasn't going to be working his own zipper for a while either, but looking at the widening wetness on his jeans, that wasn't an immediate issue.

After I took the memory card out of his camera and found some others in his pocket, I called the cops. He started to come to, so I got him on his feet, and we went down to the gate to wait together. Welcome to the California justice system, where the victim gets to spend as much time in court as the perp.

CHAPTER FIVE

Little Man and Little Augies

AUGUST 3, 1926
LOWER MANHATTAN

The rabbi didn't like being so far from home. He didn't like to drive either. Was terrible at it, in fact. Any of his congregants would have gladly loaned him a car and chauffeur, but then someone would know where he had gone and whom he had seen.

The one they called the "Little Man" was not long out of his teens, but his reputation had already reached anyone in New York who mattered. It would not be in an Upper East Side Man of God's interest to be confirmed in such company.

The rabbi wheeled the heavy, dark green Pierce Arrow along the rough bricks, its white tires occasionally throwing up horse droppings. Twice, he had to swerve to avoid ragamuffins who ran into the street, hurling catcalls at a rich man's touring car rarely seen in this neighborhood. The Grand Street docks were straight ahead, and the fetid smell of dead fish, rotting fruit and human excrement swept around the Pierce's windshield and into his nostrils. This far south, the East River was more sewer than waterway.

The rabbi had been told to look for a small office between the rows of riverfront warehouses, but with so many trucks loading and unloading, he nearly drove past it. Finally, he spotted the weathered sign

Ralph Wannamaker & Sons Ocean Freight
New York, Philadelphia, Liverpool

There was a wide, macadam apron in front, and he pulled the big Pierce over the curb onto it. When he stepped from the vehicle, a bull-faced man wearing a trench coat in spite of the heat came out of nowhere. "You lost?" he snarled.

"I'm here to see…"

The man held up his hand. "No names. You the priest?"

"Rabbi."

"Pay attention, padre, I walk fast." With that the man turned and moved quickly between the warehouses, threading his way up one row and down another amid a sea of dollies, handcarts and shouting stevedores. The rabbi found himself huffing to keep up. Several minutes later, they came to an unmarked door only feet from the water. The big man nodded then left without another word.

The rabbi knocked tentatively, and when no one answered, he entered. Inside was a comfortable office bullpen where no outside noise penetrated. Two rows of high, rolltop desks were occupied by men in shirt sleeves toiling over ledgers. No one paid any attention to him.

Momentarily, a diminutive young man, immaculately attired in an expensive blue suit, perfectly knotted yellow tie and corresponding yellow pocket handkerchief, appeared through a door to his left. His smile was open, his handshake warm. "You're a long way from 72nd Street, Rebbe. And not just in miles."

The rabbi smiled back. "You'd be surprised what goes on in some of those mansions up there."

"I doubt it. Let's go where we can talk."

The rabbi followed, noticing how surely 24-year-old Meyer Lansky moved. Not cocky… comfortable. As comfortable as any of the respectable uptown power brokers who played at piousness on Friday evenings.

Once inside a private office, they took seats in a small sitting area. The desk across the room was mahogany, the floor covered with two, thick Oriental rugs. Had the rabbi arrived blindfolded, it could have belonged to a prosperous merchant or attorney. "Nice place," he said.

"A friend's," Lansky answered flatly. He poured each of them a tall lemonade from a pitcher on the coffee table. While the rabbi sipped, his host shook a Lucky Strike from a dark green pack, lit it and inhaled deeply. "So tell me about this man, Benedict Crown."

"His father is Mordecai Crown, a member of my congregation for as long as I've been there. Mordecai runs a successful business repairing jewelry for the carriage trade and an occasional museum. Benedict is actually Avram, but when he chose retail instead of repair…"

"I understand. They weren't Crown in Russia either."

"Zubkovskaya," said the rabbi, and both men laughed. "Benedict is about your age. Very smart and ambitious. Not in any way handsome, but with great presence and a marvelous singing voice. He worked the nightclub circuit for a time with some lesser bands, but Benedict is not one for second billing."

"Instead he chose diamonds."

"He can glance at a pile of rough stones and know exactly what each weighs and its value. Only one man in ten thousand is born with such a gift, and he's developed a following. Benedict has been assembling a collection of perfect gems to open his own shop where he intends to cater to only the extremely wealthy."

"Fifth and Thirty-eighth. In the teeth of the Goyim."

"You're well-informed. The Blaine Building."

Lansky's eyes narrowed. "Pioneers sometimes get eaten by wolves."

"Yes, but the wolves could have simply banded together and leased the space themselves and chose not to. God knows Allen Blaine tried."

"I am familiar with Mr. Blaine. Too soon Zubkovskaya, not long enough Crown. Why not the others? Keep the street Jew-free?"

"Mordecai. He's irreplaceable with certain kinds of repairs. The white shoe firms can't run the risk of losing access. Some even went so far as to speak to Blaine on Benedict's behalf. Also, the space had been sitting empty for a year, and that's not a look anyone wants in a high-end retail district."

Lansky picked up his lemonade but did not drink. "Then as soon as Blaine makes the deal with Crown, another prospect appears. Probably at twice the price. So our greedy landlord hires somebody to steal Benedict's inventory, and like magic, more rent and no smell of gefilte fish."

The rabbi nodded. "Since it happened after signature, Blaine's got him both ways. Mordecai can bail his son out on the lease, but he doesn't have the kind of money it would take to replace the diamonds. Most are on consignment, so if Benedict defaults, he's dead in the business, forever. No second chances in that world."

"*Clever, this Blaine. How many stones are we talking about?*"

"*They're flawless blues, the most valuable of all diamonds. You could hold most in your left hand, but you would need your right for the largest. One hundred and four carats. It's been appraised at a million by itself. With the others, the total is at least three times that. Benedict is designing a necklace that will include all of them. His signature piece, as it were. It will be the only thing in his front window.*"

"*What's he going to do for his second customer?*"

"*That necklace will never be sold,*" the rabbi said gently. "*He's going to call the large stone the Crown Star, and if he's right, it will become an attraction. He has another several million in gems on reserve for actual orders, but that's academic at this point.*"

Lansky lit another cigarette. "*Sometimes the worst predators aren't wolves at all, but one's own kind.*"

"*I don't follow you.*"

"*It's not important. Men like the Crowns should be grateful to have you as a friend, Rebbe. I appreciate your showing such respect by coming all the way down here.*"

"*Thank you for seeing me.*"

Meyer Lansky walked his guest to the door. As the rabbi stepped back into the sunshine, Lansky said, "*Tell young Benedict to be more careful in the future. He may be able to look at a diamond and know its value, but others can look at a room and know where it's hidden.*"

The rabbi turned to say something, but the door had already closed.

———

The newspapers covered the deaths of four little-known thieves with a relish usually reserved for higher phyla of the criminal class. Fuchs, Bloom, Greenberg and Weiss all had records dating back to their childhoods and were smalltime at best. Ordinarily, their passing would have merited little in the way of ink.

But finding them on a Sunday morning hanging by their necks from the highest reaches of Brooklyn Bridge had a certain panache even the staid Times *found irresistible. That they had connections to the Little Augies, a notorious*

Jewish street gang also revved up the creativity of some of the city's more literate headline writers, none more so than the New York Journal, *whose grabber could be read as either superbly witty or inferentially anti-Semitic.*

FOUR FOR THE KEYVER

The disappearance of Allen Blaine made the papers too, though with no connection to the Little Augies and considerably more snickering in tonier neighborhoods. The wife of the well-to-do owner of several Fifth Avenue buildings did not report her husband's disappearance for a week, then seemed only mildly interested in the investigation. As it turned out another wife in Queens felt the same way. Then a third Mrs. Blaine arrived from Buffalo, and the circus shifted to the courthouse.

Benedict Crown knew much sooner than the authorities that his new landlord would not be returning home. The cube-shaped strongbox containing Mr. Blaine's head was delivered to his new shop by a man who did not introduce himself. A pouch containing the blue diamonds was tucked into Blaine's mouth.

Alongside the head was an envelope with a new lease, signed and notarized by both Crown and Blaine a month earlier. In it, the shop's rent had been reduced to one dollar a year for ten years as "compensation for a future favor." The substance of the favor went unmentioned.

So, the diamonds went back to the workbench; the lease into a safe, and the strongbox into the Hudson. The message and the favor due stayed with Benedict.

It goes without saying his gift to the rabbi was generous.

CHAPTER SIX

All Stars Aren't in the Heavens

NOVEMBER 22, 1932
HOTEL NACIONAL
HAVANA, CUBA

Meyer Lansky asked for a phone, and before the words were fully out of his mouth, a white-coated Cuban waiter handed him an ivory receiver and held the base in position for him to dial.

Eight floors above, in the Excelsior Suite, two short rings followed by a long pause awakened Benedict Crown. He'd missed his airline connection, so he'd taken an excursion ship from Miami, and the remnants of a tropical storm had pitched and rolled the shallow-hulled craft the full ninety miles. Benedict had spent the last hour of the voyage on his knees alternately dry-heaving and praying to die.

As the phone began its second cycle of rings, Benedict groped for the handset. "Crown," he croaked.

"The manager said you looked like shit when you came in. Sound like it too." The New York-accented voice was friendly but businesslike.

Benedict squinted at his watch, but before he could focus on the hands, Lansky said, "After breakfast, we'll take a ride." His tone left little doubt that the excursion wasn't optional.

"Give me twenty minutes."

A hot shower, half a grapefruit and three demitasse cups of Café Cubano later, Benedict was feeling almost normal. Real normal would have been having it in his suite at the Sherry Netherland back in New York, but that had not been on the menu.

The small man occupying the semicircular booth with him had read the newspaper while Benedict ate. Now he folded it neatly and put it on the table. "I come to this joint, I'm relaxed soon as I walk in."

Benedict couldn't disagree. It was vastly better than the supposedly upscale places in Miami where a stiff breeze rattled windows, and humidity caused the veneers to pull loose from the cheap, reproduction furniture. Just then, Benedict saw a sweaty man in a rumpled tropical suit striding across the dining room toward them. When he reached the booth, he extended his hand. Lansky took it but without enthusiasm.

"Señor Lansky, the architects have completed the drawings. Perhaps you could look at them before you leave."

"Not now, Gómez, but tell the colonel I appreciate him moving things along."

The man smiled and seemed relieved. "He will be most pleased to hear that."

When the rumpled man was gone, Lansky looked at his guest. "They're adding a casino and want my opinion."

Benedict Crown knew a lot about diamonds, but he knew something about people as well. What he had just witnessed wasn't about casinos. It was one dangerous power dealing with another, and it was eminently clear who inspired the most fear. He reminded himself to get free of his obligation to the Little Man as quickly as possible.

As deft as Lansky might have been in a business transaction, he was the exact opposite driving. The big, maroon, Lincoln 12-cylinder coupe wallowed and yawed as he braked too hard, accelerated in the wrong places and generally disregarded all traffic conventions. The driver's seat had been modified to accommodate his stature, but he had no feel for steering five thousand pounds of machinery along even the widest boulevards.

After their first stop at a nightclub called Caliente!, Benedict suggested he take over the car, and Lansky didn't argue. Following some seat adjustments to accommodate the six-foot jeweler, his host gave him directions. As they pulled into traffic, Lansky said, "Sing for me."

"Excuse me?"

"The rabbi said you have a voice. I like music. Entertain me."

Benedict had a vague feeling of unease. Lansky had not asked. He had simply told him to sing. No, not told... ordered. Like an employee. Benedict thought about it for a moment then saw Lansky staring at him. Clearing his throat, he eased his clear baritone into the Marion Harris hit of a decade earlier, "It Had to be You."

Lansky nodded his head along with the lyrics. "Louder," he said. "I like my music loud."

And Benedict obliged.

They stopped at two more places, Tradewinds and La Mariposa. All three were closed at this time of day but still beehives of activity inside as cleaning crews polished and swept, bartenders loaded coolers, chefs prepped kitchens and cashiers and dealers organized the heartbeat of each club—the casino. Benedict took note that, as they walked the rooms, no one spoke to Lansky. In fact, no one made eye contact.

Benedict had no idea why he was on this tour, so when they pulled away from La Mariposa, he politely observed, "Impressive operations. You've done well."

Lansky stared straight ahead. "Not mine. I just keep an eye on things. When the Cubans was in charge, these places was nothin but clip joints. Me and my partner brought in our people and established some discipline."

Benedict didn't need a guide. The Manhattan papers had more reporters covering Charles "Lucky" Luciano than President Hoover. In their defense, Lucky was a better executive and knew how to pick up a tab. It was no secret Luciano, Lansky and Cleveland's Mayfield Road gang had feasted on Prohibition with their "carpet clubs" catering to high-end gamblers throughout the East, Midwest and South. Cuba, however, hadn't been mentioned.

"Drive out the Malecón," Lansky said, pointing to an unmarked turnoff. Half a mile later, the two-lane road began running parallel to the beach, bordered by a wide, concrete esplanade rimmed with a seawall. Fifty yards beyond lay the Caribbean.

Except for a few taxis, there was no other traffic, and Benedict accelerated past people strolling the walkway or lounging on wooden benches. Leaving the highrises of beachfront Havana behind and circling around a large bay, the now-empty landscape ran to the horizon, unbroken except for sand grass and transient dunes.

In time, they came to a construction site on the right side of the road. The nearly-completed structure was twice the size of the clubs they'd seen earlier, but the long, palm-lined entry, circular valet area and two-story windowless exterior left no doubt what it was. "Looks like it can handle a thousand," Benedict said.

"Fifteen hundred," said Lansky. "The owners bought half a mile of oceanfront. Someday, there'll be a hotel and shopping with only the best stores."

Benedict parked, got out and listened. Nothing but surf and gulls. He tried to imagine the place in action and was surprised to feel goose bumps. The excitement of big money at risk did that to him sometimes, but this was the first time it had happened when it was somebody else's money.

He paused at the entrance. The imposing steel-plated door had been engraved in script so elegant it took Benedict a moment to decipher it.

We Only Close for Revolutions

"At first, the colonel didn't appreciate my sense of humor," Lansky said. "I told him his job wasn't to laugh, just make sure it stays a joke." The undertone wasn't lost on Benedict.

Inside, the club was still being decorated, but it already wasn't like any nightclub Benedict had ever seen. The high ceiling was regally domed and painted like the night sky. Stars twinkled, and he quickly picked out the Big and Little Dippers. Brass and glass were everywhere, making the place almost glow.

"What are you going to call it?" asked Crown.

"The Star of Havana," said Lansky.

"Very classy."

"I think so too."

The Little Man led him across the vast space to a wide hallway that Lansky said would connect the three dining rooms with the casino. Unlighted, it looked like the tunnel of doom. Fifty feet in, in pitch black, Lansky stopped. Squinting *to his left, Benedict could make out a wide revolving door flanked by two display windows. Lansky touched a switch somewhere, and tiny lights blinked to life, outlining tasteful, silver-block lettering above the door*

BENEDICT CROWN DIAMONDS
NEW YORK AND HAVANA

Moments later, the interior of the shop was bathed in a soft glow, revealing a sales floor immaculately dressed in Crown's signature midnight blue and silver. The empty display cases were elegantly crafted from deep-grained mahogany, their trim in polished chrome.

Benedict couldn't remember when he had ever been speechless. Even after the theft of his inventory seven years earlier, he had been resolute, not paralyzed. Now, words deserted him.

Lansky turned back to the corridor. Benedict did likewise, and instantly a spotlight in the ceiling came on, illuminating a four-foot, Corinthian pedestal rising from a wide base cut into the floor. Atop the pedestal, a massive, circular, dark blue marble display case was affixed at a forty-five degree angle. Weighing at least half a ton, its empty black interior was fronted with inch-thick, security glass. Benedict thought it looked like a tower clock in search of a face.

Soundlessly, the pedestal began revolve. "In there," said Lansky," will be that necklace you keep on display on Fifth Avenue."

Benedict looked at him dumbly, finally stammering out, "The Crown Star?"

"That was the old name. From now on, it's the Star of Havana."

CHAPTER SEVEN

Flashbulbs and Alligators

For the past half-century, the section of the Constitution guaranteeing a speedy trial was optional in SoCal. The fifteen million people of Los Angeles and its subsidiary cities are served by fewer courthouses than Mercedes dealerships, which worked out fine because we're much fonder of brisk steel than brisk justice. Also, the courts were closed on Fridays—no kidding—producing the added bonus of paralyzing beach parking.

As a result, no-profile criminal cases and civil suits arrived at jury selection almost as often as you found a Norwegian cutting your lawn. Media-intensive cases moved even slower because they were heard in only two locations: downtown and Santa Monica, where there are protocols for satellite trucks, pressrooms for spin-doctoring and full-length mirrors in the restrooms to check your outfit before wading into the lights.

Then Warner Bros. gave us what the Founding Fathers could not. TMZ. All of a sudden, lackadaisical defense attorneys and sloth-slow prosecutors found themselves riding a docket rocket piloted by camera-hungry judges with an eye on million-dollar second careers at dispute resolution firms. After all, what CEO doesn't want his patent-infringement case heard by a guy with enough face time on Fox to be asked for his autograph at Nobu? They still don't work Fridays, so scratch relief on the boardwalk.

The time elapsed between Paulie Stuben's arrest in my bedroom and his B&E plea bargain was a hypersonic six weeks. Now only a month later, we were in civil court as Jake and his partner pursued a monetary judgment that would take Mr. Stuben out of the paparazzi business for the next several centuries.

But even Harvey Levin can't infuse two courts with that kind of velocity unless one of the litigants is someone as famous—and as relentlessly pursued—as Wind Fortune. Then, new Armanis are purchased, robes pressed, hair shaped, eyebrows plucked and suddenly, more media vans appear at the courthouse curb than vegans at a plastic shoe sale.

"Please state your full name for the record."

"Rail Sheridan Black."

"And your city and state of residence?"

"Beverly Hills, California."

"Mr. Black, in rereading your testimony from the criminal proceedings, I see you were born somewhere called Clarissima, but for the life of me I can't find it in my atlas."

That was a load of shit. He'd spent half an hour making an issue of it during my deposition. Not to mention weeks of news coverage. "It's an island. In the Caribbean."

He wrinkled his forehead like he'd just been told his Amex Platinum had been declined. "Really? And I thought I had a very good atlas. Perhaps it's out of date."

"Clarissima is private."

"My goodness, how exotic. And it's yours?"

"At that time it was my father's. But yes, it's mine now."

"It must be wonderful to be you. Do you have any others? An archipelago perhaps?"

I waited while he basked in his moment. "No, just the one."

"Then should I presume you are Clarissimanian, or is that even a word?"

"I'm an American. My father was British and my mother was Brazilian. I was sent here for high school and fell in love with everything about the United States."

"Well, welcome to our shores. I hope you're doing a job some homegrown American won't."

The judge's gavel almost beat the gallery's laughter, but not quite. "Knock off the lounge act, Counselor."

"My apologies, your honor. Are you married, Mr. Black?"

I was prepared for the question. No, that's wrong. I was aware it was coming; I'm never prepared for it. Watching your wife and unborn child disappear in a burning sea only an arm's length away can never be erased, only dealt with. I can still feel the engulfing heat as the yacht burned behind me, and I dived until I could dive no more.

"Mr. Black... Mr. Black?" The attorney's voice brought me back to a courtroom that now seemed to contain too little oxygen.

"Widowed," I answered. "Her name was Sanrevelle." I don't know why I added the last part, except it seemed right to put her on the record too. With me.

The guy was a prick, but he was a good lawyer. Even if he hadn't been, the look on my face would have been enough. He made the correct decision for his orthodontia and slipped his rapier wit back into its holster. "My sympathies for your loss."

I've been on a witness stand a few times in my life, and it wasn't fun then or now. At the defendant's table, the dirty-haired creep, Paulie Stuben, winced when I looked his way and slunk further down in his chair. Despite his having shoulder-high casts on both arms, I still wanted to go down and choke the little fucker until his eyeballs exploded.

Across the aisle, my attorney, Jake Praxis, and one of his partners, Robyn Neece, flanked Wind Fortune, who cowered like the scared, young girl she was. I winked to give her a little confidence-boost, and as I did, a camera flashed in the gallery. Several of the deputies ringing the courtroom were on the offender before I could pick him out.

Judge Samuel Mayer, a gaunt-faced man with a receding hairline and no indication he had ever laughed, erupted, "Take that jerk into custody, and bring me the camera." A female deputy walked a tiny digital up to the bench while a scrum of khaki and olive dragged the would-be paparazzo out the back, giving him a little Welcome to Badgetown hair-pull along the way.

When the door banged behind them, Mr. Stuben shot a plaster-armed fist in the air and yelled, "Power to the press, motherfucker!"

Another deputy started toward him, but Judge Mayer held up his hand. Judges love a stage, and this gave ours a chance to show his stuff. He looked at the attorney questioning me. "How many more, Counselor?"

The lawyer's name was Walker Snive, which had cemented my contention that some people are designated at birth to be pissants. His slicked-backed hair was early Jersey Boys, his accessories alligator, and his clothes, more tight Italian swag than a *GQ* ad. "I swear, your honor, I had no idea anybody…"

Mayer cut him off. "That wasn't the question."

Snive went to his client, bent down and whispered something. The twerp apparently didn't appreciate the gravity of the situation, so Snive slapped him across the face, hard. The smile disappeared, and he held up two fingers.

Mayer surveyed the crowd. "Anybody with a camera or cell phone has ten seconds to vacate my courtroom. Otherwise, we're all going to sit tight while the deputies take you out one at a time for a strip search. You don't want to know what happens after that."

The judge started to count, and when he got to six, three men and a skanky-looking woman got up and left. So much for Mr. Stuben's math skills. The woman shot everyone the bird on her way out, but Mayer pretended he didn't see it.

"You may continue with the witness, Mr. Snive," the judge said. Then to me, "And Mr. Black, you wink again, and I'll have Mr. Praxis come up and slap you."

That got a laugh from everyone but me, and Snive went back to work. "What do you do for a living, Mr. Black?"

"I'm an investor."

I watched Snive's face twist into a sneer and waited to see which chapter of the Big Book of Cross-Examination he'd been practicing in anticipation of this moment. He took two steps toward the jury so they'd be sure not to miss his incredulity at my unadorned answer.

"Oh, please, Mr. Black, don't stand on modesty. Isn't it true *Forbes* lists you as one of the wealthiest men in the universe."

I thought Jake might raise an objection here, but he seemed busy jiggling one of his John Lobb loafers on his silk-stockinged toes and stifling a yawn. So I went with, "I don't subscribe to their intergalactic edition."

There were audible chuckles in the gallery and smiles in the jury box. Mallory was seated in the rear of the room, directly in my line of sight. He frowned and shook his head disapprovingly, his go-to move whenever I open my mouth.

Litigators live for wiseasses, and Snive grinned like a serpent. "Then let's limit ourselves, shall we. How much are you worth in *Earth dollars*?"

"I have no idea."

"Would it be over ten billion?'

"Perhaps."

"Fifty?"

Mayer was beginning to look annoyed, so with the point made that I was both rich *and* stupid, Snive moved on. "What do you invest in?"

"People, mostly. Brilliant ones when I can find them."

This seemed to confuse him. "Please explain."

"When my father, Lord Black, died, I inherited his company…"

Snive interrupted me. "For those of us still asking Santa for our own island, what company would that be?"

"Black Group, Ltd. Headquartered in London. Knightsbridge to be precise."

"We certainly want you to be precise. Go on."

"BG has interests in media, airlines, ships—numerous things. But early-on, I realized I wasn't half the businessman my father was, so I began investing in exceptional people then turning them loose to excel. It's been my experience that if you try to harness an extraordinary mind, all you reap is frustration."

"I'll keep an eye on Amazon for your book," Snive offered, but I don't think he meant it. "How many employees are there at Black Group?"

"Not many. It's a holding company. A hundred at the outside. The corporations it controls have many times that, naturally."

"Naturally. I'd ask you to estimate, but we know you're not good with numbers. It must be quite a rush being lord and master of even a hundred geniuses."

"I don't have a title at BG, and I don't exert any control over my managers' decisions. Once a year, they brief me, and if I want to know something in the interim, I ask. Otherwise, they're on their own."

"How has this utopian business style worked out, Mr. Black?"

I wanted to say it had doubled my net worth but looked at Mallory and went with, "Utopian indicates unvarying harmony. We demand excellence, and Black Group is a wonderful place to work if one meets our standards. It is a short career if one does not."

I saw a couple of heads nod among the only twelve in the room who mattered. Jake had moved from shoe tricks to what appeared to be a nap. It was nice to know that a thousand dollars an hour, plus expenses, provided peace of mind. Wind was using a pink felt tip pen to draw curlicues on a legal pad, and Ms. Neece was patting her shoulder. Apparently, I was going to have to be my own cheering section.

"Isn't it true, Mr. Black, that the real reason you hired others to run your firm was because, for many years, you were otherwise engaged as..." Snive paused to get his tone exactly right. "...a member of Delta Force?"

Jake finally decided to join the proceedings. His five thousand dollar suit rose, admirably concealing his Ruth's Chris bulge, and his baritone filled the courtroom with just the right inflection of Century City authority and why-must-I-suffer-assholes scorn. "Your honor, I thought we'd dispensed with this nonsense during pre-trial. Mr. Black's background, whatever it might be, has nothing whatsoever to do with Miss Fortune's suit."

Snive was ready for him. "I might agree if he hadn't nearly killed Mr. Stuben prior to calling the police."

"Killing somebody who's broken into your home is legal, even in this limp-wristed state," Jake shot back. "I think Mr. Black showed remarkable restraint. If he'd finished the job, the good folks of Beverly Hills would have pinned a medal on him, and we'd all be doing more important things this morning."

Somebody in the audience applauded and drew a sharp look from the bench.

Snive sneered. "His front door was unlocked. And we don't kill people for taking pictures."

"Send him up to my place and find out," Jake shot back, which got a bigger laugh than anything they've done on *Saturday Night Live* in a couple of decades.

The judge pounded his gavel for a while, and once everyone settled down, Mayer played the moment with the deliberation of Brando stroking a cat. "I'll allow the witness to answer defense counsel's question, but I should caution you, Mr. Snive, you are skating on the edge of a contempt citation."

Snive seemed unfazed by where his skates were and smiled so wide his gums appeared. "Do you need the question read back, Mr. Black?"

I did not. "I'm not aware of anything called Delta Force."

This time, Jake and Ms. Neece charged toward the bench at lightning speed, mouths open, objections pouring out. The judge banged his gavel, hard. "Bailiffs, please remove the jury and clear the courtroom. Mr. Black, you stay right where you are."

When the door closed behind the last Angeleno, Judge Mayer looked at the three attorneys assembled in front of him. "Ms. Neece, I don't see this little bit of theatre impacting your lawsuit, do you?" That made it clear that whatever his plans were for me, he wasn't going to let anything get in the way of nailing Scumbag Stuben for a judgment that would make his eyes water.

Robyn Neece was a pro. She got the message. "No, your honor, I don't."

"Excellent, then you and your client are excused. The deputies will arrange to have you taken out through the garage. They can run a decoy car to give the media something to chase, if you wish. But then, you've been through this drill before."

"We have. Thank you, your honor, but it won't be necessary."

He looked at the defense. "Mr. Snive, you now have the answer from Mr. Black you were hoping for. I'll be fascinated to learn how you intend to use it and not end up in a cell."

Snive reached deep for his stash of indignity. "Your honor, Mr. Black is rich, and Miss Fortune is rich. Meanwhile, my client is serving two years with a pair of arms that may never be able to hold a camera again—courtesy of a man trained by our government in the use of deadly force. Mr. Stuben has lost his freedom and maybe his profession, and now these people want to take away whatever pittance he's worth or might ever be worth. I ask, where's the equity?"

"If you're trying out your closing argument, Mr. Snive, you better have more in your man-purse than that." Maybe I'd been wrong about Mayer. That was pretty good. "In the meantime, I suggest you have a chat with Mr. Stuben and remind him that in his plea bargain allocution, he testified that he broke his arms when he fell off Mr. Black's balcony. If you're telling me he lied, I'm required to speak to the sentencing judge about vacating his deal."

The attorney squealed in protest. "He was terrified of this trained killer, your honor." The judge narrowed his eyes, and we all waited while Snive thought things over. "There'll be no need for you to have that conversation."

"I thought not. Please also remind your client that he is currently serving his sentence as a guest of one of our fine jails, which with overcrowding and the sheriff's penchant for early release, means he'll probably be home for Christmas. However, one more demonstration by him or one of his so-called supporters, and I'm going to tack on another year and have his butt hauled up to Folsom with a 'Hold for Full Sentence' recommendation. Capice?"

Snive wasn't looking forward to that commute. "Yes, your honor. May I at least..."

Mayer cut him off. "Unless you're about to ask to use the restroom, the answer is no, you may not. Now, go occupy yourself in the hallway, and don't wander away. I'll be calling you back in here shortly."

Snive looked at Jake then at me and became unnerved. "You can't meet with them without my being present."

"Watch me," Mayer shot back. "Hit the hallway…now."

Snive packed up his alligators and departed, making more noise than necessary. Judge Mayer then dismissed everybody but one deputy, a beefy guy named Sprankle who was stationed a few feet to my left. When the room cleared, Mayer turned to Jake and stared at him so long I thought he'd had a stroke. He hadn't.

"Mr. Praxis, I suggest you take five and call over to that I.M. Pei monstrosity I have to look at when I tee off every Saturday and have one of your sycophantic associates remind you that during witness prep you set yourself on fire, if you have to, to keep your client from perjuring himself."

"I don't think that call will be necessary, Your Honor."

"Fine, then would you please look up here at Mr. Black and ask him if he wishes to stick with the horseshit answer he just gave?"

Jake doesn't like to be told to do anything, even by a judge, and he seemed to be stuck in neutral, his neck getting redder by the second. So Mayer asked the question again, this time with a little more steam on it. Finally, the most important lawyer in Los Angeles muttered, "Yes, your honor," and turned to me, "Mr. Black…"

Mayer had proved who had the bigger set; he didn't need the full Monty. "Thank you, Counselor." He then swiveled in the direction of the root of the problem and didn't seem to be charmed by my wholesome good looks. "Mr. Black, unless you've been struck brain dead, I suggest you get on the phone with the Chairman of the Joint Chiefs or whoever else you have to and get leave to tell the truth—pronto. Otherwise, you and Mr. Snive may be having a pillow fight over at County this evening. You are excused until after lunch."

"Mr. Praxis, go get Mr. Snive and both of you hustle your butts back in here."

CHAPTER EIGHT

Maggie Dufree and Charlie Bronson

I'd known Wind and her parents long before her mother was killed by a wrong way driver on the 405, and her widowed father was murdered by a jealous girlfriend at his Malibu beach house. Back then, the Fortunes had owned a chain of high-end hair salons and lived around the block from me in the high hills of Beverly. We'd met after they'd rung my bell to ask for the name of the company that had installed my rather imposing front gate. Wind couldn't have been more than six, and when I invited them for a cookout, I said, bring swimsuits.

Because of my size, I'm sometimes mistaken for a professional athlete. Though the guesses range across the sports spectrum, my sport is swimming, and I was once good enough to almost make an Olympics. But even if your commitment is total, unless God breathes that little extra into your DNA or Lance Armstrong slips you a phone number, you can't ever train into it. Eventually, I found a better calling: the army, and, later, Delta Force, where I spent some of the most difficult and most satisfying years of my life. The SEALs would have you believe they're the only ones who work in, on or under the water. That's only because Delta guys never talk about what we do. We're better in a bar fight too, which we *could* talk about, but don't.

When I bought my home, I had a twenty-five meter lap pool added to one end of my main one, creating a fat blue "T" that never fails to elicit comment. I try to start each morning with a fast mile, half butterfly/half freestyle, which burns off the cobwebs from even the worst night. Wind had been swimming since before she could walk, and once she got a glimpse of the lap pool, her mother had to haul her out before she grew gills.

Mallory is slightly less cuddly than a wolverine, but his childhood was one of terror and loneliness, and there's something safe about him that kids sense and gravitate to. Wind was no different, and she followed him around, calling him Valerie and giving commentary on his dinner preparations. Then she found a box of my business cards in the foyer and went through the house putting one on every chair. And it's a big house.

I've seen people tied to a piece of lawn furniture and tossed over our security wall for less, but the prickly Englishman and his chatty shadow became instantaneous friends. When she started school, she would invite him to her swim meets and call for help with her homework.

Eventually, I introduced the Fortunes to Jake who became their attorney, and the three new men in Wind's life became Uncle Rail, Uncle Mallory and Uncle Jake. After her parents died, Jake persuaded the judge to permit her and her temporary, court-appointed guardian to live at my home while Wind's sole, surviving relative, a maternal aunt in Miami, finished out her contract as a cruise ship dance instructor and moved to California to assume custody.

That's when the trouble began.

Maggie Dufree was the kind of authority figure every girl thinks she wants until she gets one. Which translated, means no authority at all. Adding to the disconnect, there was plenty of money to take care of Wind, but the will provided Maggie with only a modest allowance and no access to the rest of the estate. Other than normal living expenses, everything had to be approved by Jake's office. Maggie and Wind continued to live in the big house in Beverly Hills, but if Maggie wanted an extra few bucks to hit the clubs, which she regularly did, she had to beg Jake for it—and he is not an easy beg.

Maggie may not have known much about parenting or budgeting, but she had a PhD in survival, and she quickly got one in custodianship. First lesson: if you order it, the lawyers have to pay for it. So out went swim teams and college prep, and in came dance lessons—from Maggie, of course, at a premium rate—acting classes, photography sessions, auditions and casting calls. If she couldn't loot the trust, she was well within her rights to grab fifteen percent of Wind's earnings as her manager.

I warned Jake to be careful, but he said he was playing the odds. "Screw the aunt. How many kids make it in show business, Rail? I mean really make it? She'll be back to algebra and Speedos in a year, maybe less."

Jake's a genius, but Maggie Dufree ate him for lunch. Then fate stepped in and had the rest of him for dessert. Wind not only *made it*, she blew Hollywood up. By the time she was twelve, she had starred in four films that cumed a billion and sold twice that in merchandise. By thirteen, she was earning twelve million a picture. A year later, she got her first Oscar nomination, and at fifteen, a star on the Walk of Fame.

Then Wind Fortune did something even worse—she became a woman.

Seventy-three-inch blondes, who move like flowing silk and speak like Bardot breathing *Je T'aime*, arrive in LA every day there's sunshine. Most fade to oblivion on their way in from the airport. A few join the parade of studio background candy or marry agents.

But every once in a while, one catches the public's imagination, and the world loses its equilibrium. Wind Fortune captured more than imagination. She awakened the abandoned magic and forgotten glamour that had been gathering dust since the last great golden-haired legend took her final ambulance ride. Without doing anything more than turning nineteen, she suddenly transcended the screen, stopping conversation in roomfuls of even the biggest stars and gracing dinners at the White House.

Not coincidentally, the wheels came off her personal life, and she accumulated more DUI's than people who cared about her, an equal number of stints in rehab and a couple of very unpleasant vacations in Orange Jumpsuitville.

One of the big talent agencies had long-since replaced Maggie, and Wind had graduated to handlers and handlers for the handlers. Maggie still hovered in the background, but her role had been reduced to finding bail bondsmen and negotiating tell-alls so she could blackmail her niece for cash.

Maggie had also become the housemate of B.B. Youngberg, the producer of a succession of low-budget slasher pictures, but equally well-known for being a violent, falling-down drunk. Once a month, like clockwork, he and Maggie announced B.B.'s next celluloid bloodbath, staring Wind Fortune, of course. And once a month, like clockwork, Wind's representatives scrambled to extinguish the resulting media firestorm.

In the ensuing years, Mallory and I made an effort to stay involved in Wind's life, but Maggie cut us out with the kind of anesthesialess excision invented in Hollywood. I felt sorry for both of them. Wind, for the childhood she'd lost, and Maggie, because she wasn't a bad person, just weak and out of her depth. Mallory wasn't quite as magnanimous. He would have happily strangled Aunt Maggie, then made himself a hot fudge sundae.

Then one night, a couple of years after we'd last seen Wind—except on the news—Mallory picked up the phone and found a good friend from the Beverly Hills PD, Capt. Dale Hunnicutt, on the line. "Couple of my officers just brought in a whacked out Jane Doe they found asleep behind the post office. She looks like hell, smells worse and's got no ID. But her clothes are Versace, and she had one of Mr. Black's business cards in her purse. We've got our hands full with a Persian New Year's party at the top of Benedict Canyon, and I don't want to mess around with a vagrancy that's maybe drugs, maybe isn't. So before I called County Services, I wanted to check with you."

Mallory knew right away who it was. He roused me out of a sound sleep, and we drove downtown to retrieve Miss Fortune. The good news was that the patrolmen had brought her in through the back, and Hunnicutt had her in his office, which had kept her out of sight of the camera slime who haunt Beverly Hills Central Booking, looking for something more interesting than Iranian D&D's.

Eventually, Wind was able to tell us she had walked off a picture in New York the week before and had no idea how she wound up snoring between two mail trucks. She showed none of the signs of a drug binge, so whatever was wrong, it wasn't just a matter of hustling her out to Betty Ford.

When I got Jake on the line, he reacted like I'd just told him his ex-wife was dating his accountant. "Jesus Fucking Christ, the studio's been looking for her everywhere! They thought she got high and took a header into the East River."

"I might not be up on my celebrity news, but I wouldn't have missed that," I said.

"No press. Bad for the picture."

"For a week? Bullshit, they're covering themselves. Where was their sense of responsibility for a fragile young girl?"

"Spare me. Actresses at that level don't disappear to die. They make a fuckin production out of it, like they do everything else."

"Maybe it's not too late to nominate you for the Albert Schweitzer Cup."

"Go down to the corner and look at the street sign. I'll save you the trouble. It says City of Beverly Hills. That's show biz, asshole. Something you like pissing on but, for some reason, also like living in the middle of. It was only a matter of time before Wind turned up. We're just lucky it wasn't married to a window washer with six kids and a parole officer. Now, get Miss Fortune on a plane before they sic the baddest motherfucker in town on her for the cost of the picture—plus damages."

"I thought you were the baddest motherfucker in town."

"Get her on a goddamned plane."

"Not going to happen. Whatever her problem is, work isn't the answer." I didn't think he could get any louder. I was wrong, so I hung up.

The next day, the president of the studio, the producer, two reps from the production insurance company, Jake and I sat down in Jake's conference room, gazed out over the LA Country Club and made a deal. The studio would issue a release that Wind had been rushed to an undisclosed hospital for emergency surgery. They'd be vague about the reason but hint that it was something female, which for people who can turn a heroin overdose into an allergic reaction to guacamole wouldn't cause them to break sweat. They'd also say that she was asking her fans and the press to respect her privacy.

So far, no one had reported seeing her in LA, so the story would send the media on an East Coast hospital canvassing frenzy and give us enough time to get another plan in place. In return, I agreed to cover the additional costs for the recast picture, which Jake would monitor to make sure I didn't end up buying Aston Martins for the producer's stable of Argentine underwear models. If the movie managed to hit a hundred million, I'd be paid back, but no more. Welcome to Hollywood.

It had taken two days for someone—probably the flack who wrote the release—to blow our cover and for the press to set up camp around Wind's home. How Paulie Stuben had determined she might be staying with me several blocks away is a tribute to his ingenuity, but not one he's likely to pick up an award for. Actually he did get a kind of award. And a police escort to the emergency room after the ceremony.

The Santa Monica courthouse is a long, low white affair that looks like it belongs on a studio lot. Dotted at lunchtime with employees lounging on a well-manicured lawn and protected by unobtrusive sheriff's deputies who actually smile, nothing about it says crime and punishment.

Across the street is the Rand Corporation, the much-revered think tank, where, in generations past, the brightest patriots among us dodged Soviet spies while applying their considerable brainpower to keeping America the world's great beacon of hope. Today, IQ still counts, but one is equally likely to find "social intellectuals" studying condom use among the homeless and the effects of global warming on pigeon shit. One of these days, the place will make a nice wind farm.

With Wind Fortune gone, the press had decamped, so Jake and I walked unmolested down the block to a roach coach, bought dogs and Cokes and grabbed the one bus bench that wasn't being used as motel by a bag lady. I was expecting a lecture, but instead Jake just chewed his Sabrett, watched the traffic and complained about how much it cost to tune his Ferrari.

I thought it might be useful to remind him where we were. "Am I going to jail?"

"Sometimes it might look like the set is decorated for David Mamet, but Tennessee Williams is in the wings."

"Meaning?"

"You're not even in the room. This is about me."

"Is that why you were sitting on your wallet while Snive was doing everything but waving his dick where he was going?"

"It was going to play out any way Mayer wanted it to."

"What did you do?'

"Fucked his wife... and some other things." He looked off toward the ocean with a smile on his face. "She's a prosecutor in Van Nuys. We used to have a thing. Guess we missed each other. Great head, lousy lay."

"What a heartwarming story. You should call Lifetime. Let me guess, Mayer had somebody following her?"

"No, he came home."

Wonderful, just wonderful. "Does Snive know this?"

"Everybody does."

"Everybody except me. Mamet and Williams, hell. This is *Death Wish*, and Charlie Bronson's on the bench."

"Jesus, could you be any more self-absorbed? Mayer doesn't give a shit whether you were in Delta Force or *Magnum Force*. He's as good a judge as there is, which is why I didn't ask him to recuse himself. He just had to get it out of his system. Couldn't look like a pussy in front of the rest of the black robe mafia. That big deputy will make sure word gets around about how he busted my balls but didn't let it get in the way of the case." Jake was still smiling, and he doesn't smile that much. The head must have really been spectacular.

"So now what?"

"You're off the hook. Mayer's not going to let Snive recall you. He's way more pissed about Stuben's groupies with the cameras, which he's convinced Snive helped orchestrate."

I had a vague sense of uneasiness. "Are you trying to tell me you had something to do with that?"

I didn't expect an answer, and I didn't get one. Jake rarely tells me anything, but he also rarely loses a case. "My compliments on your legal brilliance. What about the judge's wife?"

"I must be getting old. I decided the head wasn't worth the trouble, so I ended it."

I knew Jake, and he didn't decide that at all. Rubbing people's noses in his superiority is what he lives for. A judge made it all the better. Mrs. Mayer had obviously come to her senses. But like all good lawyers, ten minutes after Jake mouthed bullshit, he wouldn't make a ripple on a lie detector.

"That about it?" I asked.

"Pudgy Bernstein's shooting a picture in Asswipe, Cambodia or some other backwater and had to get vaccinated for plague. He can't get off the crapper, so there's an open seat at tonight's game. You up for a little Hold 'Em?"

Pudgy Bernstein's bowel report wasn't exactly responsive to my question, but I like Jake's game. "What time?"

"Eight, and remember, I lock the gates at eight-thirty."

CHAPTER NINE

Special Love and Special Deals

MARCH 11, 1935
HAVANA, CUBA

Since opening his shop in Havana, Benedict had spent more time in Cuba than New York. At first, it had been to establish the impeccable service Benedict Crown Diamonds was known for—and to nervously keep an eye on his inventory, especially his necklace. However, not a single gem had disappeared or even been misplaced—something Benedict had never been able to accomplish in Manhattan—and he had come to realize that the only security that mattered was the name Meyer Lansky.

The Star of Havana display had been a remarkable success. Whenever the club was open, long lines formed to pass by the revolving pedestal, its allure enhanced by the four armed soldiers posted conspicuously nearby. According to Lansky's figures, one in every twelve lookers went into the store and bought something.

Taking a page from Luciano's playbook, Meyer invested in an island-hopper airline and gave hefty points to Col. Batista, thereby guaranteeing it exclusivity into Cuba. Well-heeled travelers from South America, Europe and the States could now spend their days sunbathing in Nassau and Kingston then gamble until dawn in Havana.

And how this crowd did buy jewelry. With no regard for price. The bigger and the flashier the better. The kind of gaudy pieces Benedict could never sell on Fifth Avenue and at markups he could not have imagined. The steady stream of high rollers made his Cuban store wildly profitable. Even after Lansky's cut, it made Benedict very rich. If there were such a thing as a jeweler's paradise, Havana in 1935 was its epicenter.

Though Benedict never fully reconciled himself to having his signature creation on display so far from home, he did his best to enjoy the tropics. With his newfound wealth, he purchased a walled estate in the Miramar District where his neighbors were sugar and tobacco millionaires. And he grew fond of Cuban food, soon packing on an extra fifty pounds that did not flatter him. Benedict had never been successful with women, and once again, Lansky filled the void, providing a steady supply of girls who were as obliging as they were beautiful. The added bonus to this arrangement was that there were never any scenes, emotional entanglements or birthdays to remember.

But Benedict became captivated by one. Novi Montez was a large-framed, former showgirl who had aged out of dancing and opened a string of plush brothels above Havana cigar clubs. Here, scantily-clad girls sold well-heeled gentlemen their pleasure in flesh and tobacco then led them upstairs to enjoy both. The rest of their French-kissed Robustos could be picked up on the way out.

Novi had a mean streak that, combined with her size and a proclivity for sudden violence, made her effective at managing women who often had train wrecks for lives. Benedict found he liked watching Novi discipline her girls, taking pleasure in the many ways she had of handling even the most difficult ones.

He also got his first taste of heroin from Novi. Initially, just skin pops at parties. Then he tried snorting it, but it made his face swell. Eventually, he graduated to the mainline, and Novi kept him well-supplied and did most of his injecting.

Her cruelty combined with the heroin awakened a latent desire in Benedict to be dominated—both in business and the bedroom. At Novi's insistence, he made her manager of his Havana shop, and shortly, she was making most major decisions. Over time, Benedict stopped going to work altogether, and at some point—he couldn't remember exactly when—he married her, and she assumed control of his assets.

Benedict spent most days in his mansion in a heroin haze. Spikes in drug potency followed by periods of denial was one of Novi's tools for keeping him compliant. If he displeased her, she would handcuff him naked to the bathtub faucets and leave him with only a pillow and a blanket. Lying in the dark, shivering with need, he would pray for her to return and give him a jolt of horse. It was never enough, though, just a tiny jab to remind him of his transgression then she would be gone again.

This time, she had been away longer than ever before, and he was almost at his breaking point when the door opened, and Lansky and a pock-faced man with dead eyes entered. After so long in darkness, Benedict's pupils needed time to adjust to the bright bathroom lights.

The men were patient. Lansky leaned against the sink, smoking, and the pock-faced man rested a foot on the edge of the tub, one hand in his pocket, the other rotating a red topaz ring on his little finger. Finally, Lansky said, "Benedict, this is Charlie. He's been wanting to meet you."

At thirty-seven, Lucky Luciano was only five years older than Lansky, but violence had hardened his features and erased emotion from his voice. He looked at the naked man without expression. "Back when that rabbi come to see us, I was gonna look you up, but one thing led to another, and well… you know how it is. I'm glad we was able to fix your problem."

Benedict tried to shift position to see the man better, but the cuffs kept him in place. Luciano kept talking like they were sitting over cocktails. "I gotta tell you, Crown, you're a fuckin artist with diamonds. A real fuckin artist. Meyer tells me he's been takin good care of you."

Benedict tried to say something, but his mouth seemed full of cotton. Then he saw Novi in the doorway, holding a syringe, and he began to tremble. Suddenly, he felt tears on his cheeks and was conscious of a sob welling up in his throat.

"I want that necklace, "Luciano continued. "I got a friend who would really appreciate it."

Necklace? Benedict heard the words, but all he could focus on was the needle Novi was bringing closer. He needed what was in it then he'd be able to think.

Luciano was still talking, though the words kept getting farther away. "I'm not a guy who likes gifts, so I'm gonna pay you ten grand."

That seemed to penetrate Benedict's haze. He shifted his gaze back to the speaker and shook his head, trying to clear the cobwebs.

Staring into Benedict's filmy eyes, Luciano issued what passed for one of his smiles. "Plus my lastin friendship, of course." He let that hang a moment. "And don't worry about it fuckin up the business. I had the piece copied. Good job too. It'll be our secret."

Novi was now sitting on the edge of the tub. She had a length of surgical tubing, and she deftly tied it around his bicep. Benedict immediately forgot everything else and clenched his fist. He couldn't tell if a vein had appeared, but he prayed one had.

Luciano lit a Chesterfield and blew smoke at the ceiling. "As a token of our friendship, you're gonna try something special. From the mountains of Turkey, but processed in France. Same lab they make aspirin. Pharmaceutical grade all the way."

Jesus Christ, thought Benedict. When was this fuckin guy going to shut up and let him get right. Then they could work everything out.

But Luciano wasn't finished. "I want our deal to be kosher. That's the word you people use, ain't it?" He turned to Lansky who produced a sheet of paper and a pen.

Benedict couldn't see anything but the syringe. Lansky knelt, crowding out his vision of Novi, and spread the document's signature line along the ledge of the porcelain. "Standard bill of sale," Meyer said. "Your wife's already signed, but since we're all here together, let's get you on it too. Then she can get on with more important things, right?"

Benedict stared dumbly at the pen, trying to make sense of the strange instrument that had gotten between him and heaven. Lansky leaned back so Benedict could see the syringe then forward to block his view again.

This time, Benedict got the message, and ignoring the pain, stretched against the chain until he could grab the pen with his cuffed hands. He scrawled something approximating his signature then whimpered, "Can I have it now? Please, can I have it now?"

Lansky stood, and Luciano set a banded stack of bills where the document had been. "Ten grand. You can count it," Luciano said, "but you have my word, it's all there. We're square, right?"

Benedict was beyond hearing now. Luciano nodded to Novi, and she reached down and thrust the needle into the jeweler's arm. Benedict didn't think he had ever been happier. He was pretty sure he saw God.

In the mansion's driveway, a pair of white-coated attendants flanked a gurney, an empty rubber body bag draped across the sheets. The rear door of their ambulance was open, and a well-dressed man with a stethoscope leaned against it, drawing on a thick cigar. Luciano and Lansky stopped.

"Make sure Luis saws some chunks outta that fat fuck so the fish get the idea, Doc" Luciano said to the man with the cigar. "Tell him if anybody finds this guy, there won't be a next time."

"Si, Sr. Luciano."

When they got to Meyer's car, the Little Man opened his door. "You really gonna send the necklace to that drunk actress in LA?"

"Look what it did for us here. The more women dream, the more our handle goes up. Probably should send it on a tour of all our joints."

"We still gotta get that California D.A. in line."

"DiCicco says we're almost there."

"I know Pat's one of your guys, but if a whiff of pussy blows his direction, he forgets his name."

"I'm sendin Rollo this time. He's gonna have a talk with him."

"Well, that'll solve the pussy problem. Tough to get a hard-on when it's halfway up a gun barrel."

CHAPTER TEN

Seconal and Stolen Souls

MARCH 12, 1935
HAVANA, CUBA

Barrie Fontaine came awake well before dawn, sticky with the humidity of the tropics. She lay motionless and tried to remember where she was, a barely-caged barbiturate hangover residing just behind her eyes. Suddenly, the woman beside her moved in her sleep, and Barrie had a hazy vision of wrestling somebody out of a yellow dress followed by a tangle of arms and legs then very bright lights.

She turned and smiled when she saw the pair of smooth, mahogany shoulders, cascade of ebony hair and shapely derriere riding atop the chalk white sheets. The woman was almost twice Barrie's age, but she was fighting her forties with all the tools available to the rich. Though slightly thick in the legs, her ankles were delicate, and her sequined Ferragamos made a sexually exquisite picture.

Barrie had never slept with a woman this dark-skinned before, and she admired the way it set off the array of expensive gold bracelets and imposing diamond ring. She ran her hand between the woman's slightly parted thighs and felt the softness of the tiny triangle that barely contained its swollen prize. A small moan came from deep in the beauty's throat, and Barrie removed her hand, touching her damp fingers to her lips.

It had taken more Seconal than usual for this one to finally stop resisting and slip into that sweet twilight where a person will do anything and allow anything to be done to them. And they had done it all. Barrie couldn't remember when she had had so many orgasms—in so many ways—stimulated in part by how much money this Montevideo hotel baron's wife would soon be paying her.

The woman had still been trying to get at Barrie when Barrie pushed two more reds past her swollen lips and helped her down a final glass of brandy. The Uruguayan had passed out shortly thereafter, and Barrie had stroked her and kissed her until her own sleep came. It was likely the woman would be out until well into the afternoon, which was too bad because Barrie wanted her again. Maybe she wouldn't wait. Barrie enjoyed sex in these situations when her partners were fully compliant, conscious or not.

In the living room, Barrie's co-pilot, Woody Yates, snored away the quart of rum he'd tossed down, straight from the bottle. When he awakened, he'd be belligerent and have the shakes. Woody was at the end of his useful life in a cockpit, but he was still a passable photographer—even drunk—and that was where their bread was buttered these days. However, as she often did, Barrie reminded herself to look for a replacement.

Her own nakedness striking in the moonlight, Barrie swung her long legs over the side of the bed, swept her shoulder-length, chestnut hair away from her face and made her way out to where Woody sprawled, half on, half off the sofa. A photographer's lightbar and two cameras—one still, one motion—lay on the floor. Barrie ignored them and proceeded to the kitchenette. In the refrigerator, she found two spools of exposed 8mm motion picture film and several rolls of standard 35mm. Returning to the bedroom, she slipped them into a hidden compartment in her flight bag.

The silk sheers separating the cabana from the beach billowed inward. Barrie pushed through them and walked out onto the sand. The breeze was ocean-heavy, and her still-wet bathing suit draped across one of the chaises, uncomfortably cold. She gritted her teeth and pulled it on, shivering as the clammy material clung to her skin, and stray sand scraped her breasts and hips. A narrow strip of light appeared on the eastern horizon, and she ran toward it and dived into the bath-warm water of the Caribbean.

Half an hour of hard swimming later, Barrie was wading out of the surf, dreaming about an omelet, when she heard twin Evinrudes lumber up behind her. A familiar, high-pitched voice called out, "Señorita Barrie! Señorita Barrie!"

She turned and saw Luis Soto barefoot on the foredeck of his speedboat, grinning and waving while his cousin, Yappi, worked the throttles. Irritation rolled across Barrie's previous good disposition. She and Woody weren't scheduled to fly back to New York until Saturday and not being bothered with bullshit was why she'd taken a lease on the cabana instead of staying at the Nacional. That, and her own business needs.

"Señor Lucky say to bring you. No Señor Woody, just you. Pronto! Pronto!"

Barrie's annoyance was replaced by apprehension. Her boss was unpredictable, but never hurried. She always had the feeling her duties were planned until all contingencies were accounted for then handed to her with an inviolable schedule. Spur of the moment had never happened before.

"What's going on?" she shouted at Luis.

Luis held out his hands in ignorance. "He just say to bring what you need to fly. You not come back tonight."

If she had to, she could handle the bulky Ford Trimotor by herself, but there was a lot to do up there, especially if the weather got rough. "You sure? Without Woody?"

"I just repeat what Mr. Lucky say."

Wonderful, just wonderful. Well, the great man would have to sit tight until she showered… and if the woman in her bed still looked desirable, he might have to wait a little longer.

By the time Barrie returned, dressed in her navy blue flight suit, her well-worn flight bag slung over her shoulder, Luis had tilted his engines forward and let the surf back his speedboat onto the sand. Barrie climbed aboard in her bare feet while Yappi jumped out and pushed the boat into deeper water. But instead of swinging up to join them, Yappi turned and began walking toward the cabana. With his wet shirt sticking to his skin, Barrie could make out the distinctive outline of a revolver tucked against the small of his back.

Before she could say anything, Luis kicked the Evinrudes to life and threw the throttles forward. As the boat leveled out, Barrie bent to put on her shoes and noticed wide streaks of fresh blood smeared across the deck. Luis saw her staring and grinned his perpetual grin. "Me and Yappi catch much fish this morning. Luis very, very good fisherman."

Barrie felt her insides turn to ice. There wasn't a fishing rod anywhere, and she knew Luis didn't fish. Neither did Yappi.

She sat back and remembered…

———————

Barrie Fontaine and Woody Yates had gone to work for Lucky Luciano two years previously. They'd been limping along doing aerial surveying work when they could find it and humping private passengers and cargo when they couldn't. More often they were grounded—too broke to afford fuel… and sometimes food.

The plane was Barrie's, the last link to a bad marriage and a worse business. Earl Fontaine had been a former army pilot who'd dreamed of starting his own airline. Barrie worked three jobs to help him restore the ravaged, broken hulk of a 1926 Ford Trimotor that was sitting half-buried in a marsh off the south runway of Brooklyn's Floyd Bennett Field. The airport manager had been happy to give it to anyone who would get it out of his sight. Crashed aircraft did not make good advertising.

After the eight-seater was finally airworthy, she learned how to fly it alongside Earl, and in the process found she not only loved flying, she was good at it. Better even than her husband. She seemed to be able to feel the sky and make adjustments before they were necessary. Even Earl had to acknowledge that he had never seen anyone so natural in the air. When she certified, there were fewer than two dozen women on the East Coast with commercial credentials, and none who could also be mistaken for a fashion model. The couple's airline dream seemed close enough to touch.

But that was before Barrie found out you needed an airmail contract to make routes pay, and Earl copped to being a convicted bank robber only a couple of years out of Leavenworth. He couldn't pass a background check to fly seagull shit.

So they put everything in Barrie's name and hoped the postal inspectors wouldn't look too closely. Shortly afterward, she caught Earl sleeping with the chief mechanic's teenage daughter and discovered he'd blown what little savings they had on hotel rooms and slow horses.

The Trimotor was the one thing the creditors hadn't taken, which was only because Earl had hidden it in a hangar in New Jersey. Barrie got there first and found it packed with Earl's and Miss Jail Bait's getaway clothes. She kicked their stuff out over the Hudson and had a sitdown with the girl's father when she landed. Earl got an old fashioned ass-kicking followed by trip to Sing Sing, and Barrie cut a deal with the bank to refinance the plane. A few rounds of unconventional sex with a smarmy loan officer helped.

Woody Yates, a sometime-pilot, sometime-photographer, stumbled into her life shortly afterward, drunk as was his habit. But he also had a state contract to photograph potential dam sites, and she was down to her last ten bucks. More importantly, Woody had a valid pilot's license, and Barrie needed a right-seater to bid for long-haul jobs. Once the dam contract was fulfilled, Woody stayed on, sleeping on a cot next to the plane and hustling picture-taking gigs around Brooklyn when they weren't flying.

The two tried sex a couple of times but could have saved themselves the sweat. Woody liked whiskey better than women, and Barrie had come to the conclusion that if she was going to get undressed, there was going to be more to show for it than a cigarette and a nap.

Then one day, Mr. Luciano walked in. Barrie and Woody's first job for him was flying a planeload of flashy-suited, crude-talking characters around the North Shore of Long Island. The men didn't hide that they were looking for a place to establish gambling operations among the Gatsbyesque mansions of the very rich. They needed a vacant estate with maximum privacy that could be easily secured.

Woody took dozens of pictures, and later, Luciano came to the hangar and pored over them with a magnifying glass. The most feared man in America was terrified of flying, but before he left, he owned Fontaine Airways, and its two pilots were on generous salaries. He had no problem with a woman running things. Barrie knew because she asked. She also asked if she was going to have to sleep with him. "I'll let you know," he said.

The speed and efficiency of the aerial searches was soon extended upstate to Saratoga Springs then on to Kentucky, Arkansas, Texas, Louisiana and Florida. But gone were Barrie and Woody's gangster passengers, replaced by Meyer Lansky and groups of respectable-looking men. Men who spoke about overhead, profit margins, payoffs and silent partners.

Cuba was different. There, the clubs were already operating but being restaffed by Luciano and Lansky's dealers, pit bosses and food and beverage managers. Barrie loved flying those guys back and forth from the mainland. They partied hard and told great stories. She even dated a couple.

One was a craps dealer named Danny Dades. Because Cubans couldn't seem to master the intricacies of running a dice game, especially at high-roller tables where the demand for fast action and glib chatter flew in the face of laid back tropic attitudes and the locals' bewilderment of American slang, Lansky paid handsomely for top American pros. And Danny was maybe the best, with his own following of heavy bettors.

He could command his own price and live anyplace he wanted in the off-season, which in Danny's case was Laguna Beach, California. There, on a hilltop overlooking the Pacific, he built an ultramodern home that he named Highroller Hill, and it became the scene of some legendary parties among the Hollywood set—straight and gay—that had also discovered Laguna.

Barrie and Danny had been instantly attracted to each other, and she'd spent several weekends with him, riding Indian Chief motorcycles in the canyons during the day, raising hell with famous faces at night and having the best sex she'd ever had with a man whenever the spirit moved them. She loved California, especially the rocky, southern coast, and she might have gotten serious—Danny certainly wanted to—but he was so extraordinarily handsome, it unnerved her.

Barrie had never been insecure about her looks before, but when a roomful of people—men and women alike—stopped what they were doing to stare at her date, she didn't know how to compete. Worse, when she finally worked up the courage to tell Danny what was holding her back, he laughed at her, and she felt humiliated. So she'd let the relationship drift, and pretty soon, it drifted away.

But there was also something else. Something she'd only recently been able to admit to herself. Men left her unsatisfied. Even the most intense orgasm was just that: an orgasm. On a rare night, she might be able to find two before the guy snorted a couple of times, slapped his hips into hers whether she was in sync with him or not, then fell asleep. Unless he was one of those who rolled off, took a shower and went looking for something to do that didn't include the stinky thing he'd just left his load in.

She usually masturbated after sex with men, but that was pretty much like going shopping without money. The dress might look pretty in the window, but don't get your hopes up.

Barrie had never once felt fully used. The kind of used she read about in the magazines Lansky stocked on the Trimotor for his male clientele. Where some girl was getting banged until her eyes crossed, and she had to plead with whatever was on top of her to stop because she might die. Barrie died often under a hairy chest, but not once because she was out of climaxes. She'd never been close to feeling sated.

But what she missed in her sex life, she more than made up for in her professional one. Once the clubs were humming on all cylinders, and with the Trimotor newly decorated and its pilots attired in sharp-looking outfits, Fontaine Airways began ferrying high rollers from major cities to the gambling and partying, wherever it was. It was a seven-day-a-week undertaking, rotating geographically depending on each club's high season. Barrie knew she'd left her old life behind the day a group of Pan Am pilots dropped by Floyd Bennett to offer their services when she was ready to expand.

She and Woody also flew mountains of cash from the clubs back to Luciano in New York. Sometimes so much cash that Barrie would leave her copilot at the controls and just sit in the cabin and stare at it. She didn't know how yet, but she was going to have her own mountain someday.

————————

The heavyset man who boarded Fontaine Airways in the winter of 1933 was their only passenger to Cuba that trip. Carrying a double-strapped, hand-tooled, leather suitcase and matching attaché with gold fittings, the man permitted Woody to stow the larger bag in the luggage compartment but kept the attaché on his lap.

Smartly-tailored and polite, he did not appear much different from the other wealthy men they had flown to Luciano's clubs. Shortly after takeoff, however, he made a couple of long visits to the restroom, prompting Barrie to be concerned that he might be ill. She went back to check on him and noticed his hands were shaking. Without asking, she offered him a good-sized pour of Scotch, which he took down in a gulp.

"Lotta people get nervous up here," she said lightly, "but we haven't lost one yet."

The man held out his glass, and Barrie poured again. He drank a little slower this time, but soon asked for a third. "Please forgive my manners. My name's Benedict Crown. And I enjoy flying, always have."

"Barrie Fontaine." They shook hands.

"So this is your airline." It wasn't a question.

"I just work here," she smiled. "First trip to Cuba?"

Benedict shook his head no, and the trembling in his hands started again. This time, he spilled some of the Scotch on the attaché case, and Barrie helped him sop it up with his breast pocket handkerchief. As she did, she noticed the top of the case was inlaid with an intricate golden crown under which were the letters BCD, also in gold.

"Pretty fancy."

Benedict jerked around and looked behind him as if he were expecting to see someone over his shoulder. When he realized how foolish he must have appeared, he apologized. "How long have you worked for Mr. Luciano?"

Barrie smiled. "My paycheck comes from Consolidated News Services on Park Avenue. Long as it clears, I don't care what the news is or who's doing the consolidating."

Benedict seemed to think about something and make a decision. He handed the now-empty Scotch glass back to Barrie and unfastened the twin straps around the attaché. With a key from a ring tucked into his vest, he undid the lock and very slowly raised the top. As if on cue, a burst of sunlight crossed the window and struck the necklace inside. Set into its custom-built interior, the Crown Star and its sister stones became blue-white fire, glowing on darker blue velvet.

Barrie actually took a step back before coming forward again. Her eyes were so focused on the jewels, she dropped the glass. She didn't even notice it rolling up the aisle.

Benedict Crown's cheeks ran wet with tears. "Watch yourself, Miss Fontaine.

These people will take your soul." Then, starting at the beginning, he told her his story. All of it.

A month later, Barrie began her blackmailing business. She had been surprised how easy it was. In the course of shuttling Lansky and Luciano's dealers and croupiers to Havana—many of whom had Hispanic backgrounds—she had heard countless stories about the culture of macho. Macho, however, was a fluid doctrine, frequently dependent on a man's mood or the amount of alcohol in his system.

One indignity, however, was impossible to ameliorate. No Latin American husband could ever tolerate his wife's sleeping with another woman. An affair with a man was a loss of honor. One with a woman stripped him of his manhood.

In their deeply Catholic world, even priests turned their backs on such wives and granted annulments, dissolving marriages of decades. The law had its say as well, often stripping the women of their children and casting them out without recompense.

So with a built-in hunting ground of wealthy wives, Barrie had preyed. And the wives had paid. There seemed to be no amount she could demand that was too much.

For all but the one who had hanged herself.

CHAPTER ELEVEN

Pros and Lows

Hollywood poker games are the stuff of legend—usually bullshit. Since the first heartbeats of the motion pictures business, it's been a badge of honor to be considered a superior money player. But large amounts wagered do not a great gambler make. There are a few strong ones around, but, despite breathless tabloid stories written by people who have never witnessed a pro surgically remove a fortune from a pretender, none of them are actors.

There are two reasons: An actor's job is to let you know what he's thinking. That's why you watch him onscreen even when he's not speaking. He can't *not* act any more than Kobe Bryant can't *not* tear your throat out in a backyard pickup game.

Second, poker is not a once-a-week hobby. You either play it for a living, or you're simply a mark waiting to be undressed. Maybe a better-playing mark, but a mark nonetheless. A good player can beat other good players, sometimes regularly. But give a real pro—not one of the clowns on ESPN sporting a hoodie and earbuds—a week against the best player in Hollywood, and seven days later, the pro will be living in the guy's mansion and banging his wife. And that's only if he decides to stretch it out that long.

A few Hollywood agents have the right stuff to become top players, but poker is too slow for them. They can't stop checking their phones or stay engaged for the time it takes to keep track of every bet of every hand and still notice that an opponent's carotid thumps harder when he's got trips. That's why pros are pros. An hour into a game, they know who needs to take a piss before the guy does.

It's exactly like being the best after-work boxer at Gold's then getting in the ring with Earnie Shavers—even an old Earnie Shavers. You're going to die whenever Mr. Shavers says so.

I've known exactly three Hollywood players who could hold their own in the cold, hard world of high-stakes poker, played, not under television lights, but in private clubs in Europe, palaces in Asia, yachts on the Cote d'Azur and off-limits villas in Vegas. One is the CEO of a major entertainment firm; one is a music promoter and the third is dead. Most telling, though, is that even these three steered clear of genuine sharps. Poker is about money, not bragging rights, and clipping ego-players in Beverly Hills is a sure thing.

Pros also avoid other pros like a hooker with a rash. There's nothing to be gained bumping heads with a player as good as they are. So, for the slow learners: if you're knocking down $30 mil a picture and think you're slick enough to be the centerfold in *Hold 'Em Monthly*, if a real pro shows up in your game, cancel the photo shoot. You're not.

Jake lives in one of those iron-gated houses high on Sunset where a famous murder was committed, giving the place a certain Addams Family pastiche. A long line of show business types have lived there, which, coupled with the murder, attracts tour buses and sidewalk gawkers. More than one family has watched the gates open to let out a red Ferrari then gone home to Des Moines with a photograph of Jake giving them the finger. They don't have a clue who he is, but I'm betting they like telling the story at Thanksgiving dinner.

Jake has an extensive collection of Western art. Included are rare Russells and Remingtons and some of Bama's best work, but his pride and joy is a mammoth, nine-foot bronze of John Wayne, rendered from the final gunfight in *The Shootist*, the Duke's last picture. Big John stands in Jake's rotunda of an entry hall, hatless, wounded, snarling, revolvers blazing, passing gunslinger judgment on all who enter.

Like *Tom Horn*, McQueen's penultimate film, *The Shootist* puts an exclamation point on a giant's work. If there's a God—and I firmly believe there is—Steve, John and The Big Man are sitting in a screening room right now, listening to gunshots, knocking back Buds and sharing a carton of Camels. Maybe even planning an atomic wedgie for some of the recent crop of pretend successors more comfortable in spandex than a bar fight.

Jake's poker game is solid. The players all know their way around the block, and there are no conversations about movie deals or who's fucking who. Patsy Rocca and Irv Goodman used to be connected to the Chicago Outfit and were silent partners in a Vegas casino back when that was in fashion. Patsy and Irv don't get up in the morning unless they have an edge on the sun, so they're as close to pros as you'll find. They play against each other because they have a thirty-year running side bet: the guy behind at the end pays for both funerals.

Morrie Solo is a layoff bookie, which means you can't call him to get down on the Lakers. He only takes action from retail bookmakers trying to balance their books. Morrie's weekly handle runs to eight figures, but the last time he stepped out on a bet without the cards to back it up was never. Jake says he just invites him for the laughs, which, if you know any layoff bookies, makes that funny.

Dr. Cortez Detroit is a former veterinarian who is also black, something he points out every time he meets somebody new, as in, "I'm Dr. Detroit, and yes, your eyes are fine. The animals didn't give a shit, and no candy-ass hospital board ever says, 'We've got two of them already, let's see if we can find an Eskimo.'"

Half a decade ago, Cortez drank himself out of feeling horses' vaginas and started writing medical screenplays that nobody bought. Then, as happens in Hollywood just often enough to keep the incoming buses full, a panicked producer offered him a hundred grand and a couple of points to fix the script of a big-budget tentpole set in a futuristic space zoo. The rewrite took five days. The picture, *Escape from Dark Star 40*, grossed a bil. Suddenly, Dr. Detroit was back to healing—only this time, other people's screenplays instead of Thoroughbreds.

Guys who can make shit smell like Chanel work all the time and get paid more than the original writer. Way more. The only thing a screenplay shaman foregoes is seeing his name in the credits. Most soothe their ravaged egos by visiting a Lamborghini dealership. Cortez is no exception. He lives like a raja and uses his trade to bed whatever actresses will lie still. If he's on a bad run, the girl emptying the honey wagon is just fine too. Once you get to know him, he's a terrific friend, but he doesn't make the first part easy.

Marvin Oxford used to be Jake's partner and is now his only real competitor in the seamy underbelly of big-time Hollywood law. Jake's client list is probably longer, but he's ruffled a lot of feathers and fired more than a few high-income clients, including Valentine Jones. Most of the dispossessed moved down the street to Marvin's. Same prickly attitude, same first class results and, as a bonus, an equal dislike of Jake.

The only difference is that Jake works out of the spotlight, and Marvin would shove a baby down a stairway to get in front of a camera. Marvin also handles professional athletes—a category Jake recently cut from his practice for reasons he won't discuss but has something to do with a former girlfriend and an NHL enforcer. Marvin lives very, very well as a result of his willingness to watch guys shower.

The lone thorn in this otherwise congenial bouquet of pasta, pastrami and pussy-chasers is Nate Dovidio, who may be the best poker player on the West Coast but who has a longstanding issue with Patsy Rocca that will eventually end with one of them dead. More than once, Jake has had to take away guns they were holding on their laps, and they are required to arrive and depart a half-hour apart to avoid a Beverly Hills draw-down.

Though I'm friendly with several of the players outside the game, nobody cheered my arrival, and I got the undertaker stare from a couple. My father taught me how to gamble, and in his time, few were better. I leave assessments of my ability to others, but those who've played against me tend to get angry when asked. I assume that's a comment of its own.

Jake's game has its own catechism: First, everyone wears a tux, which in a couple of cases is a show in itself. Second, no booze—period. Jake's chef, Rodney, serves a sit-down steak dinner before the game, which ends promptly at nine when everyone adjourns to the card room. The strongest beverage available is iced tea, though I have seen the occasional flash of a flask.

Third, the buy-in is two hundred grand, and nobody is on the cuff. Bring cash or a certified check or don't come. There's also no borrowing during the game. You bust out, you're done, and you leave—immediately. No hanging around carping about your bad night. As a result, most players come with at least a quarter million. I brought twice that—cash—in a pigskin Prada satchel, which I opened and showed to Jake because he wants to nail me so badly, it affects his game.

Finally, Jake's game is eight-card, high-low Hold 'Em with a sixth up card after the river—in some circles called a spit or second window. So it's two down and five up like conventional Hold 'Em, followed by a sixth community card. Not only does this create another round of betting before the high-low declare, it changes the odds, card count and betting progressions to the extent you'd need Larry Ellison to get it right. This dealing unorthodoxy places a premium on watching tendencies because some otherwise smart players will routinely chase second-best lows.

It also builds exceptional pots.

Normally, I wouldn't walk across the street to play high-low because it's almost a guaranteed train wreck. But every now and then I watch a Jerry Jones draft too, so maybe I'm just a hopeless romantic.

Tonight, in honor of Jake's "big day" in court—which didn't seem like much of a day to me—he broke tradition and had Rodney open several bottles of Perrier Jouët during dinner. I stayed with one glass, but Morrie and Cortez made short work of a bottle apiece, which turned Morrie almost convivial. Nate, showing his usual good manners, declared that he didn't drink French piss, and Patsy countered that probably wasn't true since he'd seen him going down on a pool boy at the Paris Vegas.

After we got everybody back to a neutral corner, I decided to find out if Miss Jones had shared her previous weekend's water adventure with Marvin. Trying to ease into it, I congratulated him on his client's recent award nomination.

"Who, Valentine Jones?" he asked. "Fuck that cunt. I hope she never wins."

All agents and attorneys hate their clients, but not in public. And never in a bank-account-destructive way. Jake looked at Marvin and laughed. "I warned you, putz. I'm not taking her back."

"I didn't know your profession had a gag reflex," I said. "What gives?"

Marvin leveled his gaze at me. "Oh, I don't know. Maybe it's the calls in the middle of the night telling me to run out and pick up box of Kotex. Or maybe it's when she asks some storefront J.D. she happens to be fucking to review one of my contracts."

I raised my hands in mock surrender. "Sorry I brought it up. Maybe you'll get lucky, and somebody'll push her out of a plane."

That got no reaction from Marvin, but Irv weighed in. "Could be arranged, but it's better if she just disappears." No one at the table thought he was kidding.

"Don't get my hopes up." Marvin said.

I looked over at Jake. "Obviously, I haven't been demanding enough from my legal team. Keep your phone close tonight. I might want a sandwich."

"Call Marvin, he can bring your tampons too."

When we finally got down to gambling, the combination of Patsy and Nate glaring at each other plus the champagne, made for an uneven first hour, and I did pretty well. Eventually, though, everybody got his testosterone back in balance, and the game got tougher. Cortez, his usual luck holding, and I were the early winners.

It was closing in on dawn, and I was sitting with an ace/deuce of hearts. The flop gave me a perfect low, A-2-3-4-6. I was also four cards to a straight flush, but nobody bets the come on that. I had been raising the max without going all in and had lost no one. It was shaping up to be the pot of the night.

The turn brought a pair of sixes to the board, and Patsy, Irv and Morrie all raised. It smelled like two full houses and a low from Morrie. Jake called, and I booked him as a loser with a flush. Everybody else folded.

The river did nothing for me, but the second window filled my straight flush, six high. I looked like a lock on both sides. Timing is everything in life, and I pushed all the chips I had on the table forward. My buy-in had been only two hundred of my five hundred grand, so I wasn't able to bet the ranch. But with my current winnings, I was in roughly three hundred large.

Everybody had initially read me for low, but now, they had no choice but to contemplate the worst—a perfect low *and* a straight flush. It was a chip declare, meaning each player puts zero, one or two chips in his closed fist below the table, then everyone brings his hand up top again and simultaneously opens it. No chips means low; one, high; two, both ways.

High-low is designed as a split-pot game, but you can win the whole thing two ways: If everyone declares the same—high or low—and you have the best hand, it's all yours. The second way is to declare high and low and win both. But no ties. You have to win outright on each side or you lose both.

There's one more wrinkle: If you suspect the other players in a hand are going to declare one way, and you declare the opposite, it doesn't matter what your cards are, you get half the pot. In other words, the highest full house at the table could win low if that player is the only one declaring that way. If your attention span has you watching car chases with a channel-changer, high-low is not the game for you.

Patsy and Irv called my bet without hesitation. Morrie was slower, but he called too. Jake dropped. Patsy and Irv may have thought I was bluffing, but I didn't think so. They were gambling that Morrie had a perfect low too, which would take me out on a both-ways declare. One of them would then back into the high with his full house and split with Morrie's low. Either way, it took a lot of balls, and I had to tip my hat.

But something wasn't right. Morrie Solo wouldn't bet on the Kennedy assassination unless he owned the Zapruder film *and* the projector. He might have gotten a mild buzz on at dinner, but he was still Morrie. He'd just pushed almost a third of a mil into the middle of the table, which he'd most likely never done in his life. I took a moment and replayed the last round of betting in my head.

I don't care how much money you handle for a living, if it's not yours, it has the same emotional impact on you as your ex-wife's happiness. On

Super Bowl Sunday, Morrie wouldn't have flinched dealing with ten times what was in the pot. But this wasn't layoff dough from a herd of overstretched bookies. This was *Morrie's* cash.

Even so, if he had a lock low, he shouldn't have cared. He couldn't lose. At a minimum, he was guaranteed to split half the pot with me—a quarter of the total— three hundred grand. Break-even. And if I got greedy, went both ways and missed, he stood to pick up twice that.

But I now remembered his hand had twitched slightly on the push-in, which meant his small motor nerves were having trouble releasing the money. Translation: he didn't have a perfect low. So why was he there? He was too tight a player to be doing what Patsy and Irv were doing, and there wasn't enough champagne in Beverly Hills for him to have made a mistake of this magnitude.

That left only one possibility. He'd caught four of a kind, and he was dead if I had the straight flush, which nobody in his right mind thought I didn't. The Morrie I knew would have tossed in the hand, regardless. For some reason, this new Morrie was playing scared.

If I was right, he would try to force me into a high-only declare by making me fear a tie on the low. He would then go low himself with his four sixes and be there all by himself. I let everybody see me take two chips beneath the table for my declare and waited to see what Morrie did.

It wasn't subtle. He looked at Jake. "Rumor has it you're selling your Ferrari. After this hand, I might buy it for Connie."

"Who's Connie?" I asked innocently.

"Consuela, his Nicaraguan girlfriend," Jake answered. "Way too hot for this piece of shit." He turned back to Morrie. "You buy a fuckin Ferrari, Kia might have to cut back a shift."

Morrie's jaw was so tight he had trouble getting the words out. "I'm not kidding. Get the pink slip."

Mr. Solo might have been a first-string layoff bookie, but when it came to poker, he was strictly taxi squad. When I opened my hand, it held two chips. Both ways. Patsy and Irv showed high, and as I expected Morrie's hand was empty. Low.

I flipped over my cards, flashing the straight flush and the perfect low. Patsy and Irv looked at Morrie expectantly, but he didn't move as the color drained from his face. Suddenly, he was on his feet, and before any of us knew what was happening, he had his hand inside Nate's tux and had come out with a small automatic. It looked like a toy, but it wasn't. It was a Walther .22 and just as deadly at this range as it needed to be.

Cortez was furious. "Goddamn it, Morrie, knock off the shit."

I held up my hand to quiet him. He snorted but shut up. I glanced around. Marvin was nervous but under control; Jake was simply angry. But Patsy, Irv and even Nate were cool, obviously interested in where this was going. I turned to Morrie. "Is the trouble you're in that bad?"

"Fuck you, Black. If you weren't such a moron, I woulda won half that pot."

Patsy laughed. "If you mean that bullshit kibitz with the pink slip, that wouldn't have fooled my maid. You're out of your league, Morrie. Put the gun down and go home."

Nate spoke for the first time. His words were measured, but there was no mistaking their implication. "Morrie, money ain't gonna fix your problem."

Morrie looked like he'd been smacked. He pointed the gun at Nate. "You and your goomba friends can kiss my Yid ass, Dovidio." Over his shoulder he barked, "Jake, get me my half of the pot. In cash. No checks."

Jake looked at me. My eyes hadn't left Morrie. "Morrie," I said, "I'll make you a deal. You can take the whole thing if you walk out of here right now without doing something stupid."

Morrie tried to retain his command by turning the gun on me. "I can walk out with all of it anyway. But you got yourself a deal."

I nodded to Jake. "Give it to him."

"You're kidding."

"All of it," I repeated. "Including what's left in my bag."

Jake counted the chips in the pot. $1,220,000. Then he went to the credenza and after a long few moments came back with my Prada pigskin stuffed so tightly it barely closed. He set it in front of me. "You want to be a fuckin priest, have at it. I won't."

I pushed the satchel across to Morrie. He held the gun on me and grabbed it with his other hand. It was the obvious time to make a move, and I saw Nate tense up. I shook my head at him. He frowned and sat back.

"You can save the, 'stay-where-you-are speech,'" I said, "but do yourself a favor, Morrie."

He had sweated through his tux coat. "What the fuck you talkin about?"

"Only a guy planning to leave town would be this dumb, so don't wait around. Get out tonight."

He pointed the Walther at my forehead. "That a threat, motherfucker?"

I glanced at Nate and saw Morrie's future in his eyes. "Just the best advice you've ever gotten."

After everyone had gone, I stayed behind with Jake. "Leave this alone," I said.

"You're pretty casual about a mil and change."

"So do like I say, and leave it alone."

Just then, my phone rang, and I heard a voice I hadn't heard for a long time. "Rail?"

"Speaking."

"Teddy Chessman here. I need a ride."

Jake heard the voice through the receiver. "Want my advice?" he said. "Don't go."

"I thought Teddy was one of your clients."

"He's two years behind on his bill. Like I said, don't go."

I should have listened.

CHAPTER TWELVE

Hail and Holly

San Quentin isn't a place you want to spend an hour, let alone two years. Especially, if you're Teddy Chessman, a multiple award-winning producer who's used to private jets, personal chefs and champagne sunrises with an endless line of the beautiful, the ambitious and the willing.

The Q began as a ship anchored in San Francisco Bay. The Gold Rush seduced as many thieves, confidence men and murderers as it did dreamers, and when it became apparent that a few floating cells weren't going to make a dent in the pool of scum needing a heavy dose of iron bars, the early incarcerates were dragged ashore in chains to build a prison. The 160-year-old dungeon they constructed is still there, as is the newer, but not much more inviting Security Housing Unit.

The SHU makes the rest of the place seem like La Costa, and it's where a hardass Hollywood-type like Teddy had to be warehoused to keep him from becoming an addition to some lifer's tattoo collection. The silver lining was that there were also fewer ways to get high in the SHU, which was exactly what Teddy needed.

Ordinarily, his 24-month sentence for dousing a studio president's three-million-dollar Veyron with hydrochloric acid would have been reduced to restitution and a few weeks of house arrest. But throwing up a YouTube of his judge dancing at a West Hollywood nightclub dressed as Britney Spears wasn't the smartest idea Teddy ever had.

Even so, nobody gets shuttled off to San Quentin just because he pissed off a thin-skinned robe-wearer. At worst, he should have been sent to the minimum security section of the county jail with the child support deadbeats. But the day before sentencing, Teddy, Mossberg shotgun in hand, waltzed into the most revered talent agency in Beverly Hills, fired two blasts into the ceiling and announced, "I paid for this fuckin place, and I'm here to take it back."

The agency probably should have alerted the police sooner, but by the time they located someone who knew how to make an outgoing call, Teddy had slipped back into his Koenigsegg and headed home. Barricaded in a mansion once owned by Gloria Swanson, his two Best Picture Oscars sparkling under vanity lights above the Xanadu-sized fireplace, Teddy sat in the dark, swigging cognac from a decanter of Louis XIII and discharging buckshot into pieces of the décor that offended him. It took SWAT the better part of the night to drag him out, but they managed to do it without killing him, which disappointed a lot of people—especially at the studio, the talent agency and a certain Westside courtroom.

Unlike the movies, the Q doesn't just slide open a big gate the day your sentence is up. Release is a complicated, mind-numbing process that takes as long as the administration wants it to, followed by a cramped ride in a corrections department bus to downtown San Francisco for your final adios. Fortunately, Jake had a good enough relationship with the superintendent to have Teddy walked out through the visitors building—a plan destined to also piss off the hundred members of the media camped along the fence on the other side of the prison waiting for him.

Teddy and I weren't particularly close. He ran with the movie crowd I avoided, but I always liked him. He had a low bullshit quotient, and he knew what he did for a living didn't entitle him to tell others what to believe or how to vote. He also once did me an important favor. So when he asked me to pick him up—in a car, not my plane—because he wanted to talk about something that might take a while, I immediately said I'd be there. That kind of request is like loaning money. You either do it, or you don't, but you don't make the guy sweat through a slow answer.

I was still in my tux. I'd driven straight through and been waiting in the parking lot for a couple of hours, occasionally nodding off. Then, what had been an all-day rain suddenly turned to hail, and I awakened to the sound of icy BBs on my Phantom. I looked at the clock. Three-thirty, but in this weather, more twilight than afternoon. I squinted through the downpour. Still no activity.

My phone rang. "Rail, look, I'm sorry."

"Who's this?"

"Cortez. Jesus Christ, Rail, how many brothers you know who got your private number?"

"Just the ones who grew up in Hancock Park and wouldn't know Jay-Z from Tony Bennett."

"Fuck your honky ass. How's that?"

"About as street as a Connecticut suspender salesman. Okay, you're sorry. What about?"

"I should have told you this at last night's game, but I don't know… I…"

"Either spit it out or hang up. I'm busy looking at porn."

"I turned Teddy down, and I feel like shit."

"Because you didn't drive up here to pick him up? Relax, it's covered."

"I don't know what you're talking about. I turned down the writing job. I just won't work that way. Not even for Teddy."

Apparently, I'd come in at intermission, and Cortez figured it out too. "I might be a little ahead of the curve here."

"It would seem so."

"Well, when he tells you, I'm sorry."

"Say three Hail Marys and don't jerk off in the confessional. Can I go now?"

"Whew, I'm glad that's out of the way. I feel a lot better."

I shook my head, clicked on a dome light, cracked a bottle of Arrowhead and eyed the mountain of mail in the passenger seat. Since computers, the crap that comes from the post office piles up until I get tired of looking at it, or as happened this time, until my fussy houseman jams a load in a plastic laundry basket and sets it on my hood. I'd been riding around with it for days. I've come to accept that it's Mallory's world, and

I'm merely a guest. I took a deep breath and grabbed a handful.

As usual, it was mostly catalogues, Chinese restaurant menus and hearing aid coupons, all of which I tossed in the backseat. Near the bottom, Mallory had put a rubber-banded stack of first class envelopes with a note slipped on top.

TRY NOT TO GIVE IT ALL AWAY

These were letters from strangers pleading for favors, ninety-nine percent of which revolve around my sending them a check. Unlike some of my wealthy friends, I don't resent the requests. It comes with the territory. I have a great deal of money—money I didn't earn—and I don't consider it an imposition to read what people take the time to write.

To Mallory's scorn, occasionally, I even honor an appeal—though never directly. That's what lawyers are for. Jake complains such assignments are beneath him, but apparently not that far beneath him because he continues to bill me exorbitantly for the service. I pay without complaint because I worry about his bruised dignity.

I fanned through the stack. Some were addressed in a third-grade scrawl, others neatly typed. A few were perfumed. About halfway down, I opened one, and a lock of hair fell onto my lap. It was held together with a tiny pink piece of ribbon with a miniature bell dangling from the bow. Somewhere in transit, the bell had gotten mashed, but the metal was tissue-thin, and I squeezed it back into shape until I heard a faint tinkle.

> Dear Mr. Black,
>   This belonged to our daughter, Holly. She loved pink ribbons and bells in her hair. The chemo made her bald before she died. I collected as much as I could, and I'm sending it to people like you who have so much money nothing ever touches you.
>   You'll never know what it's like to hold your child while she dies, but maybe one day, the world will knock on your door, and you'll remember Holly.
>   Sincerely,
>   Audrina Subinski

I put down the letter and felt the emptiness in my heart that I struggle with every day and sometimes all night. Somewhere at the bottom of the Caribbean, my wife and the tiny life inside her that would have been our son or daughter, lie in a watery grave. Audrina Subinski was right about one thing, though: I never held my baby. I was there when my beloved was murdered, but I couldn't save her. I will never lay my head down again without thinking about that. Naming my boat after her serves as a constant, painful reminder that I'm alive, and she isn't.

I dialed Jake. His assistant, Stella, said he was in court. I read her the letter. It was all she could do to control her anger. "My God, how could anyone be so cruel? And to you of all people. If you'll give me permission, Mr. Black, I'd like to call her."

"There's no way she could have known or any reason she needs to. I understand exactly how she feels: heartbroken and powerless." I gave Stella the address on the envelope and told her to send a hundred thousand dollars to Children's Hospital of Orange County in Holly Subinski's name. "Then write a note to Mrs. Subinski and thank her for reminding me."

"Mr. Black, may I make an observation?"

"Please."

"Carrying all of this around isn't good for anyone. You need to put some of it down."

"Thanks, Stella. And I mean it."

As I clicked off, the door of the Rolls opened, and Teddy Chessman got in, the collar of his cashmere sport coat turned up against the rain. "Still with the black cars," he said.

"I think the silver hood makes a statement."

"No question: boring."

That was one of the reasons I liked him. We weren't going to waste time sentimentalizing over the last two years. He'd taken the state's punch and shaken it off in thirty seconds. "Next time ask for express checkout."

"Had a call to make."

I pointed to my phone. He shook his head. "You get one on the taxpayers on your way out. I figured I earned the motherfucker. You know Ross Dare?"

"Never heard of him."

"One of the town's young Turks. As of a few minutes ago, he works for me. Five mil a year, plus, plus, plus. The badges listening to my telephone tapes can think about that tonight while they suck on their Spam sandwiches."

I didn't bother to remind him that thanks to two doses of Jerry Brown, California prison guards make almost as much as studio heads. "Welcome back to the world."

"What say we put a few miles on this chariot before we shake hands? Highway 1 okay with you?"

I slipped Holly's bell into the glove box and started the car. Teddy fooled with the radio until he found a station playing Bob Marley's *Three Little Birds* then sat back and closed his eyes. "Let me know when this fuckin joint is out of sight."

CHAPTER THIRTEEN

Comets and Backseaters

MARCH 12, 1935
HAVANA, CUBA

"Meet Mr. Hughes and Mr. Stinson," said Luciano. "They just flew in from London." Barrie was standing only a couple of steps inside the door of the spacious, private lounge at Havana's new Rancho Boyeros Airport. Luciano, in a gray suit and no tie, was seated on a long, low sofa, holding a tall glass of something icy with an orange slice in it. Howard Hughes and J.C. Stinson occupied leather chairs opposite him.

Hughes, his black hair slicked straight back, was dressed casually in an open-necked white shirt with the sleeves rolled up, dark slacks and canvas loafers with no socks. Stinson, a Panama hat tilted back on his head, smoked a cigarette through a six-inch black and gold holder, ignoring the ashes making tracks on his white linen suit. Nobody made a move to get up.

Barrie didn't need introductions anyway. A few months earlier in New York, Hughes had called her out of the blue. He said he'd seen her picture in a flying magazine and wanted to take her to dinner and talk planes. At first, Barrie thought someone was playing a joke, but when a car rolled up at the appointed time, Hughes himself was behind the wheel. Then somewhere over steaks at Delmonico, he offered her five thousand dollars to be his arm decoration for the evening. He said he wanted to hit a few clubs where photographers hung out so he could make some actress jealous.

She didn't understand cash for a date she was already on, but, hey, the guy *was supposed to be eccentric, so let him be eccentric. Two hours later, she found herself in a hotel suite being choked and bounced off walls while Howard tried to get a hard-on. As he was fumbling his way out of his still-tentless pants, Barrie grabbed what was left of her dress and fled. To his credit—or maybe his survival instinct—Hughes sent his attorney around the next day with an apology and the five grand, plus an extra G for the dress, which had cost her forty dollars. The attorney was J.C. Stinson.*

An unintroduced fourth man sat at a small bar to Luciano's left, a line of empty beer bottles alongside him. His back was to the room, but the fact that he was wearing a flight suit made Barrie vaguely uneasy. The man swiveled on his stool, a fresh beer in his hand. Sunlight streaming through the floor-to-ceiling windows reflected off his mirrored sunglasses, causing her to blink.

"Rollo Tripoli," he said in southern-accented English, pronouncing it trip-HOLY. "I'll be your backseater to California."

Backseater? California? She could see him better now. A heavy, expressionless face under a mat of curly, black hair that needed a barber. "Apparently, I'm not in the loop, but if you're a pilot, I want you up front. That Trimotor can get quirky. I suggest you lay off the booze too."

"We're not gonna be in the Ford. And if you know what's good for you, you'll stay out of my business." To punctuate his point, Rollo took another long swig of beer.

Luciano finished his drink. "Rollo flies special cargo for Mr. Lansky. He's got some business to do for me in Mexico and Los Angeles, and you're gonna fly him. It's a hurry-up job, so Mr. Hughes here is loanin us a plane. A fast one."

Barrie didn't like any of this, and she forgot her earlier trepidation. "If this guy's a pilot, what do you need me for?"

Luciano ignored her and said something to Hughes. Barrie tried another tack. "Flying isn't like driving, Mr. Luciano. It takes time to get familiar with a new aircraft." She nodded toward Tripoli. "And I don't like being up there with people I don't know—especially ones with a bellyful of beer."

Luciano slammed his glass down on the coffee table so hard it shattered. "SHUT-THE-FUCK-UP!" He stood and advanced on Barrie with such menace she took a step back. But it wasn't her he was after. He jerked her flight bag off her shoulder, opened it and went immediately to the hidden compartment. He tossed the bag aside and held the rolls of exposed film in front of her.

"Now, listen close, you freelancing cunt. I know all about you clippin them old broads for eatin pussy. Brooklyn Commerce Bank sound familiar? Box Number 1076? You want the amount too?"

Barrie didn't think he was looking for an answer. She was also busy swallowing the vomit in the back of her throat.

Luciano tossed the film across the room, violently. "I'm only gonna say this once, and I ain't gonna fuck around with a lot of words. The reason you're not as dead as your fuckin drunk of a partner is because I need you for this trip. You got a slim chance for a comeback, but if I catch you takin a piss without permission, I'll turn you over to Luis and Yappi and let them feed you to the fish—after they have their fun. Have I got your attention?"

She wasn't surprised about Woody, but it still stung. Barrie managed a nod.

"Good." He turned to Hughes. "Fill her in."

Hughes leaned forward as if nothing had just happened. "You familiar with de Havilland?"

Barrie had to fight to make the transition in the conversation. It took a few seconds, but she got her feet under her. "The Brits don't have anything faster or with better range than my Trimotor. At least nothing I'd stake MY life in... yours maybe."

Hughes ignored the jab. "Except the DH.88."

"The Comet? Of course, but they only made three, and they're all racing in Europe."

Hughes smiled slightly. "Actually, there's a fourth. Built off the books with some refinements my engineers dreamed up." He turned and looked toward the windows.

It took Barrie a couple of seconds, then she made her way to the glass. Two stories below, sitting in the dazzling Cuban sun, was a royal blue de Havilland 88 that looked like it had just rolled off the assembly line. The canopy was raised, and Barrie could see into the front and rear cockpits. Both looked tight for a man the size of Hughes but no problem for her.

She thought it curious that there were no wing markings or tail numbers, only a narrow, canary yellow cheatline beginning behind the nose landing light and running the length of the fuselage. Inset into the line, in precise Hughes Aircraft Corporation font—also in yellow—was

--------- BEVERLY HILLS ---------

Barrie stepped out onto a railed balcony. A thick blast of morning heat swept over her, but she didn't notice. The lines of the 88 exuded both grace and power. Newsreels of the plane's winning last year's England to Australia race—the reason it had been conceived—hadn't done it justice.

"I figured since she's going to live among the stars, her name should say so. What do you think?" Hughes had come up behind Barrie without her noticing. He was standing close enough that she could feel his erection through his trousers. If she'd known that back in New York, she could have saved herself a few bruises by just taking him out to the airport.

"Why off the books?" she asked.

"She's going to be starring in new picture I'm producing, and Hollywood's not a town where you put your business on the street." He smiled and added, "I had some novel ideas for fitting her out that should make for great onscreen action. De Havilland's hoping I make the thing famous so they can roll out a few thousand."

Picture or no picture, Barrie couldn't imagine de Havilland being anxious to sell their most cherished achievement to a rapacious competitor like Hughes, but she'd learned to never underestimate the power of money.

"Why don't we take her up, so you two can get acquainted. I hate to give those tight-jawed limeys credit, but she's a helluva plane."

"So Rollo doesn't work for you?"

"Fuck that Greek marimbero. If I didn't owe Luciano a favor, I wouldn't let him near one of my planes. But Mr. Tripoli can't do anything up there unless you let him, and I suggest you don't."

"Marimbero?" It wasn't a word Barrie had heard before.

"He runs Luciano's heroin network. Charlie likes Greeks because they don't get bogged down in the bullshit that keeps the dagos whacking each other. That, and everybody's scared shitless of them—except the Turks, and that's a draw."

Hughes took her by the shoulders and turned her to face him. "Listen to me, Barrie. Rollo Tripoli has no humanity—none. He probably won't try anything because Luciano will have warned him not to. But if he can't contain himself, don't act like you've never seen a dick before, because he'll kill you and screw your corpse. You don't have to like me, but I know what I'm talking about."

"I believe you. Thanks."

"Okay, let's go flying. If I like how you handle my new toy, I might hire you for the picture."

Yeah, Barrie thought, I'm sure Lucky would be thrilled.

"You're gonna make two stops in Mexico. Matamoros and Tijuana." Luciano was standing over Barrie in the airport chart room. When he'd come in, the other pilots plotting courses had hurriedly left. "You don't go near the cargo, and you don't let nobody near the fuckin plane. For no fuckin reason. Understand?"

"That's going to make refueling interesting."

Luciano hit her so hard, she was on the floor before she could grab onto the table. He didn't wait for her to get all the way up. "And stay in Mexican airspace till you run out of it in Tijuana. Then you fly that fucker as fast as it'll go to San Bernardino. All they got there is sheep and crop dusters—no badges. We on the same page?"

"Staying in Mexico will add at least three hundred miles," Barrie said shakily.

"I don't give a shit if it adds three thousand. You keep the fuck out of the U.S. till you got no choice. You get forced down, you scream for the Cuban ambassador and don't stop screamin till he shows. Meyer's got juice with the president there."

If a crow has his act together, Havana to LA is 2300 miles. With these orders, weather detours, headwinds, imprecise maps and the other vagaries of transcontinental flight, Luciano's crow had his head up his ass. Barrie also suspected the Tijuana stop was pure bullshit. Just a way to keep her south of the border until she had to turn right. Wisely, she kept her opinion to herself. "And once we land, I'm free to go?"

"Soon as the car shows for Rollo and Hughes's people take the plane, yeah. My suggestion is you book a slow train to New York. Think about how close you came to havin crabs eat your tits. And if you was plannin to use that dough in Brooklyn to run, forget it. It's been put to better use." He paused, and a grim smile crossed his face. "More important, you don't want me to have to come lookin for you. I don't like doin that for things I own."

The sun was low in the western sky when the ground crew pulled the chocks from the DH.88's wheels and gave Barrie the all-clear to wind her engines. While she'd been with Luciano, Rollo had loaded the Comet. Since she needed to know the additional weight to calculate takeoff speed and fuel consumption, she was aware that they were carrying two hundred and twenty pounds beyond their personal belongings, which was a significant amount for a small plane. She'd made a mental note to avoid overcorrecting any yawing and to not let the tail drop too fast when landing, but she hadn't been allowed to inspect the hold, so she could only hope Rollo had followed her instructions and tied the cargo down tightly.

As she made a final visual sweep of the area, she saw a Panama hat hurrying across the tarmac. J.C. Stinson was carrying two white food boxes tied with string. Using the plane's outside step he handed one up to Rollo and extended the other to Barrie. She looked at him questioningly.

"Courtesy of Mr. Hughes and myself. In case you get hungry."

"Thanks, but I just sip water," Barrie said. "Eating up there makes me sleepy."

"Take it. Just in case." He pushed the box against her shoulder a little harder than he needed to. She was about to refuse again, but something in the lawyer's eyes made her change her mind. Without comment, she accepted the offering.

The narrow space alongside her seat was occupied by her parachute, but she managed to wedge the white box into a tiny recess behind her left leg. She was pretty sure it would get crushed long before she got to eat it.

As Stinson stepped away, Rollo said, "Hey, you forgot the beer." Barrie hit the starter on the port engine, drowning him out. She watched while it gained RPMs, then repeated the process on the starboard side. As she began to taxi, she reached up and lowered the canopy.

CHAPTER FOURTEEN

Pork Sandwiches and Rattlesnakes

MARCH 12-13, 1935
SOMEWHERE OVER THE MEXICAN CARIBBEAN

Barrie had flown many aircraft over the years but nothing like the de Havilland. It was instantly responsive, aerodynamically balanced and breathtakingly powerful. If she had to be forced to fly, this plane was anything but punishment.

Ordinarily, she would have waited until morning, but that would have meant another night on the same island as Luciano, and she'd have rather died at sea. The skies were clear, so she set a course for Cancún, three hundred miles west, where she and Rollo would get a good night's sleep and an early start. At least that's what she told Luciano.

They'd been in the air an hour when she heard snoring behind her. Almost as soon as she'd retracted the landing gear, Rollo had gotten into Stinson's box lunch, which, combined with the earlier beers, put him out. Her sunrise swim seemed a thousand years ago as she watched the water of the Caribbean now turn black. Very slowly and very smoothly, Barrie pushed the Beverly Hills *to a new compass heading. Come midnight, they would land in Matamoros, twelve hours ahead of schedule and long before anyone in Havana would know she had gone rogue.*

Luciano might swing the biggest dick on the ground, but up here, Barrie was boss. From this point forward, she would determine their schedule—and their itinerary. She only hoped the airport had lighted runways.

Juan Nepomuceno Guerra had begun bootlegging for Lansky and Luciano while still in his teens, using extreme violence to compensate for his youth. Matamoros, Mexico was far removed from the consciousness of most Americans, unpronounceable and foreign. Yet, through this remote outpost, Prohibition-skirting rivers of South American, Caribbean and Mexican booze had flowed northward to the nightclubs and grand homes of the Midwest, and cowboys packing six-guns had sat down to dinner with shiny-suited gangsters wearing shoulder holsters. The bodies of the stupid were left to the buzzards.

The repeal of the Eighteenth Amendment had dealt a devastating financial blow to Guerra. Stolen vehicles and rustled livestock still headed south, while nominal amounts of marijuana and cocaine went north. Migrant workers and Mexican prostitutes had always been taxed when they crossed the Rio Grande, but in a search to replace lost revenues, Juan began demanding stiffer payments for transportation and protection.

It amounted to little more than a drop in the bucket, and Guerra's associates began to peel away and set up their own operations. At the same time, the legions of politicians and police who had grown fat from alcohol payoffs now had little incentive to overlook Juan's illegal activities. Some months, he struggled to simply stay out of jail.

Then one day, fate again smiled on him. A yacht sailed into the Port of Matamoros carrying Lucky Luciano and two suitcases of Middle Eastern heroin. American usage was accelerating, but Mexico was out of the loop. The thick brown goo from local manufacturers couldn't compete with Far Eastern white. Part of the problem was the chemicals necessary to refine paste into morphine, and subsequently heroin, were not readily available. But the biggest impediment to the establishment of a south-of-the-border heroin culture was that campesinos abhorred injections of any kind, even vaccines, so there was no local market.

Guerra had made overtures to the Chinese drug lords, trying to convince them that routing product through him was less risky than smuggling it into American harbors. But the Asian networks remained impenetrable to outsiders because of the hammerlock of fear they could impose on families their own kind.

Luciano's genius wasn't in finding an unlimited supply of opium in Turkey and Persia. Everybody knew it was there. His brilliance was in cutting a deal in Marseilles to refine it in their pharmaceutical labs—right alongside legal drugs—then using his control of maritime unions to move it across the Atlantic and into distributors' hands. Overnight, Luciano's "Mediterranean White" became the standard by which all heroin was measured, and the rush to sell it became a torrent.

Guerra's organization was still evolving, but already profits were staggering. His major problem was getting enough product, and he and Luciano had had harsh words and made mutual threats during their last meeting. So it now fell to Rollo Tripoli to resolve the short-term problem while Luciano looked elsewhere for a permanent solution that wouldn't depend on Guerra. Barrie, of course, knew none of this.

The night was so clear that Barrie saw the Matamoros tower light long before she crossed the coastline. Homing in on it, she radioed her speed and altitude. She did not say who she was or request clearance to land.

The replying voice was heavily accented and irritated, but at least it was in English. "Who are you?"

The exchange awakened her sleeping passenger. She could hear him turning to look out one side then the other. "This ain't Cancún."

"Remarkable power of observation. Maybe you really are a pilot."

Static broke into their conversation. "Matamoros tower calling unidentified approaching aircraft. Identify yourself. Repeat, identify yourself immediately."

"This is the Beverly Hills owned by Howard Hughes. I'm carrying a guy named Rollo Tripoli with a delivery for Juan Guerra. Somebody wake him up and tell him we're here."

Rollo sounded like he'd been swatted. "Are you nuts? Don't say that shit over the air!"

Barrie ignored him and went back to the radio. "I want to be refueled and back in the air in an hour."

She could feel Rollo's fury. "What the fuck for? My butt's screamin for a bed!"

The runway was dead ahead. Barrie switched on the Comet's nose light and lined up its beam with the white center line. "Sit back and shut up. Maybe you'll learn something."

Juan Guerra didn't look particularly dangerous. Slightly-built, bespectacled and soft-spoken, he was the anti-Luciano. Add in a white Stetson, string tie and fancy boots, and he could have been a CPA looking for a dude ranch. He was also extremely young. Not more than early twenties, Barrie guessed.

He and his entourage had driven directly onto the tarmac near a remote hangar where the tower had directed her. Guerra smiled, took her hand gently and bowed like an Old World gentleman, his English as perfect as his manners. "Matamoros is a very quiet place, Señorita. You created quite a bit of excitement."

"And she'll pay for it," said Rollo.

Guerra turned to Tripoli and said something in rapid Spanish, his smile intact but his tone razor-edged. Even in the near-darkness, Barrie could see Rollo's eyes change. Despite Guerra's youth, he commanded men, and Rollo was only a soldier.

"I understand you wish to leave quickly," Guerra said to Barrie.

"As soon as possible," she answered. "I want to get over the Sierra Madres while it's still dark. The daytime thermals in those mountains can be treacherous."

"Wise, but it will take the airport time to get a refueling crew out here. In the meantime, Rollo and my men have some things to unload, so why don't you and I get a cup of Matamoros' famous coffee. Very strong, but very good."

"Caffeine sounds perfect. I've got some food I'd like to tear into. And brush my teeth. I'll get my bag."

As she started toward the Beverly Hills, Rollo grabbed her arm menacingly. "Maybe you forgot. Luciano told you stay away from the cargo."

She shook him loose. "The only jerkoff standing here now is named Tripoli." Guerra laughed along with several of his men. The English-speakers, Barrie guessed.

She climbed into the back cockpit and pulled Rollo's seat forward. Her flight bag was wedged between two of four large packages wrapped in canvas and tied with rope. As she tugged, something underneath flashed in the moonlight—something gold. When she leaned forward to get a better look, her blood ran cold.

Benedict Crown's attaché.

Juan Guerra and Barrie sat at an outdoor table in the shadow of the terminal. A cleaning crew was busy inside, their work lights sending slivers of luminescence across the patio. One of Guerra's men had conjured up two demitasse cups of viscous, steamy liquid. Barrie gave it a try and decided it had to be famous for something besides drinking.

Hughes and Stinson hadn't scrimped: silverware rolled in a heavy cloth napkin lay atop a container of sliced tomatoes and onions alongside two fresh plantains and a hunk of tres leches cake. The centerpiece was a thick sandwich wrapped in white butcher paper.

As Barrie opened it, the aroma of spiced pork wafted up, and she suddenly realized she was ravenous. At that moment, one of the cleaners moved a light, and Barrie saw her name penciled inside the butcher paper. Unobtrusively, she folded over a corner of the wrapper to hide the writing and began to eat.

Just before she finished, one of Guerra's men came up and spoke a few words in guttural Spanish. Guerra excused himself and followed the man into the blackness. Barrie slid out the note.

Miss Fontaine-

Mr. Hughes feels terrible that you were dragged into this. When he refused to let Rollo fly the de Havilland, he thought that would be the end of it. He had no idea you were in Cuba.

You are carrying 100 kilos of heroin that will be exchanged in

Matamoros for $1 million. The money is going to Miss Todd in LA.

Mr. Luciano has guaranteed Mr. Hughes that no harm will come to

you, but that, as you know, means nothing. I believe you are safe until the exchange, maybe longer. Rollo is a dreadful pilot.

However, if the plane is fully fueled when you leave Matamoros, there

is no reason to stop before California. Tijuana was never part of the arrangement with Mr. Hughes. If you go there, I believe you will not leave.

Perhaps the "extras" on the "Beverly Hills" will be of some use to avoid that.

I know it's not much, but good luck.

JCS

PS Mr. Hughes has asked me to apologize for the incident in New York. He wanted to do it himself, but could not. He hopes you can forgive him.

Barrie felt her face flush, but remarkably, her thoughts were clear. As much as she would have liked to have blamed Hughes, she alone was the architect of this mess. Somewhere between her husband's infidelity and the terror of losing everything, she had lost something more precious. She had lost herself.

Then she'd pretended that working for a piece of shit like Luciano didn't make her a piece of shit too. But even that wasn't enough. She'd become a criminal as well—one with enough hubris to think she was smarter than a guy who invented a new crime every morning over breakfast. Jesus Christ, what a fool she'd been—right up to thinking she'd be able to walk away from this animal.

She wondered what Luciano had on Hughes. Men that rich didn't put themselves in the hands of mobsters—unless there was something terrible hidden somewhere, maybe even a body. Hughes could look out for himself. She was the one on the clock now.

Barrie took the note to the bathroom, and tore it in two, intending to keep tearing and flush it down the toilet. Something made her stop. She held the pieces together and reread Stinson's warning. If she hadn't known it before, she did now. She was in a race for her life, and who knew what might end up being valuable?

Every pilot carried a zippered, waterproof wallet where he kept his flying license, passport, manifest, money, matches and whatever else he deemed necessary. Barrie took hers out of the snapped thigh pocket of her flight suit and placed the note inside. As incriminating as it would be in the wrong hands, they could only kill her once.

She made an effort to brush her teeth but couldn't get past the brown, smelly liquid coming out of the tap, so she scrubbed her face with a dry handkerchief then went back outside.

Guerra was waiting. "My business is finished, and your plane is ready. Is there anything else I can do for you, Señorita?"

Barrie walked several steps to a terminal doorway and stopped. Guerra followed, looking puzzled. She lowered her voice. "I need a gun. Something that will fit in my pocket."

Guerra took her measure. "May I ask why?"

"In case I have to land unexpectedly. I understand certain kinds of snakes can be very dangerous."

Guerra glanced across the tarmac. Rollo was climbing into the de Havilland, kicking and cursing at one of his men who was trying to help. Guerra removed a snubnose revolver from under his jacket. "This looks like an ordinary Smith & Wesson .38, but the steel has been hardened to fire a new kind of ammunition—something called a magnum round. It was developed for the police to be able to shoot through car doors. But you know how it is... car doors can be a problem not just for the police."

Barrie took the weapon, surprised how heavy it was.

"I had the barrel shortened to keep the weight down. It also makes it easier to clear a holster... or a pocket. Take it with my compliments."

Once Barrie had zippered it inside of her flight suit, the bulge was barely noticeable. "Thanks."

"My pleasure. But remember, snakes can be difficult to kill. Even with a magnum. Keep firing until you're absolutely sure."

"I'll remember."

Corpus Christi was less than an hour north. Barrie left Matamoros heading west, but as soon as she was out of sight of the tower, she turned toward Texas. Rollo wasn't asleep this time and got loud. "You're crossin the goddamn border!"

"Here's the way it is, Rollo, Luciano can make all the pronouncements he wants, but he doesn't have to sleep and pee in some one-donkey town in Mexico.

A little while from now, I'm going to be taking a shower in water that's cleaner than I am and drinking coffee that doesn't eat the spoon. Besides, I thought you were the one whose butt was screaming for a bed."

Rollo backed off a little but not completely. "What about the thermals? I don't like bouncin around up here either."

"I'm not crossing back into Mexico until we're past the Sierra Madres. We'll miss the rollercoaster ride and be in Tijuana ahead of schedule."

The mention of Tijuana seemed to ease his concern. "You had this planned from the start, didn't you?"

"Think what you like." What Barrie didn't say was that as much as she wanted a shower, she needed an American telephone connection more. She'd considered running—maybe grabbing the attaché on her way out—but that would only forestall the issue. It was better to handle it while she had the upper hand. Then, with a little luck, it might stay handled.

Rollo was easing into the new arrangement. "We got no tail number, and there's stuff in the back I can't let nobody see."

"Anybody asks, we're delivering the de Havilland to the army. Top secret. All you have to do is act like a prick. Think you can pull it off?"

"Fuck you." But his tone said they were now playing hooky together.

"You've never landed in a small town with a good-looking girl at the controls. Nobody's going to pay any attention to you. Assuming they're even awake."

She was right. Matamoros had been half-asleep, but Corpus was down for the count. She had to circle the city twice to find the unlighted airport next to a pair of tin hangars on the western edge of town.

A lone mechanic in greasy overalls helped tie down the Beverly Hills *then suggested the Nueces Hotel. "Make 'em give you a corner room facin the water," he drawled. "That'll get you a breeze."*

In a cab, on the way into town, Barrie prayed Danny Dades was still in Laguna Beach.

CHAPTER FIFTEEN

Abalone and Clout

In the beginning, there was BRadshaw. BRadshaw was the telephone prefix for Beverly Hills. Like BUtterfield for the Upper East Side of Manhattan, it marked you as someone special. Everybody moved a little quicker and smiled a little wider when you gave them a BU or BR number.

Today's BRadshaw is the 310 area code, which, in addition to Beverly Hills, includes Bel Air, Brentwood, Westwood, Santa Monica, Pacific Palisades and Malibu. The biggest stars in movies, television and music likely have a 310 number, as do most of the industry's power brokers, a few dozen billionaires, assorted royalty and at least one arms dealer. If you have a 310 prefix, you're one of the chosen few, and if you don't, your star is a little dimmer in a town where symbols matter as much as money.

That number is also where everything started to come apart for Teddy Chessman. *Blood Fog Over the 310* was a spec script about a serial killer in the world's glamour capital, and every big name in town wanted to produce it, direct it, star in it or have their mansion featured. Never one to tiptoe into a room, Teddy mortgaged his home—also in the 310—made a preemptive bid, gave an A-lister his prized Picasso against his $20 million fee and stampeded the studio into three times that number to shoot it.

Then Teddy committed the most unpardonable of producer sins—he trusted his director. When the budget hit $77 million and only half the picture was in the can, the studio fired him. Naturally, they kept the director, because that's what studios do.

Last I heard, *Blood Fog* had grossed $840 million, spawned an announcement for three sequels and Teddy's name was nowhere on it—or on any of the checks from what was supposed to be a first-dollar deal. His share had been grabbed for the Veyron's paint job, the talent agency's ceiling, several emotional distress lawsuits and fines for everything but not having his dog on a leash. Jake Praxis didn't come cheap either. Teddy got to keep the mortgage on his house, but somehow the actor forgot to return the Picasso once he cashed his salary check. Moral obligation? Tell it to the warden.

Teddy looked better than when I'd last seen him, which was on visiting day a few months into his stretch. He'd been glad for the company but told me not to come back. Now, even though his skin had turned the pale gray of the sunless incarcerated, his hair was still jet black, and he had all his teeth, which was no small accomplishment. He was also lean and hard. A little sleep, a few walks on the beach, half-dozen steaks at Morton's, and he'd look better than he had in years. Maybe throw in a randy actress or two, just to make sure.

We hit Carmel-by-the-Sea around seven. The traffic through San Fran had been a bear, and unlike LA, there aren't many alternates. We'd left the rain and hail behind, but not the gloom, so what should have been a welcome-back-to-the-land-of-the-living sunset for my passenger was just a dim glow in the southwestern sky. Teddy said he didn't care where or what we ate, just as long it was hot and soon, so I picked a spot I'd been introduced to recently, *Maison Margo*.

Unfortunately, the lady who'd done the introducing—a vice president at one of the better-known Napa wineries—had banged down three of the house specialty Big Sur Fizzes before the head on my beer settled, then got confrontational about my rumored intimacy with the mutual friend who'd brought us together. I have a longstanding rule that I never discuss one woman with another, and we hadn't even ordered appetizers when she shouted something about silence being the legal equivalent of an admission, tossed her fourth fizz on my shirt and stomped out.

We'd arrived in separate cars, so since the abalone was supposed to be world-class, I dabbed the worst off my Ralph Lauren, switched to an icy

Sauvignon Blanc and ordered dinner. The owner, Margo, a sharp-looking twenty-something who'd apprenticed under one of the *Cordon Bleu* heavyweights, showed off her shellfish skills then joined me for Sumatran coffee and Martell. Later, she washed and ironed my shirt then came back to bed.

When Teddy and I walked in, Margo was putting the finishing touches on some serious ass-kissing of a white-haired four-top with Pebble Beach stamped in their foreheads. As soon as she saw me, she clopped across the Portuguese *azulejo* in her lavender clogs and Frenched me like I'd just sailed into Nantucket with a bowhead lashed to my square-rigger. Aware that we'd become the floor show, I broke her lip-lock as gently as I could, but she stayed entwined around the rest of me. As tall as I am, she probably looked like she was climbing a tree.

"My God, Rail, have I ever missed you. I'm cooking, and you're staying the night. And that's final."

Several of the diners applauded, and when I saw her face coming at me again, I said, "Abalone first."

She gave me a peck and whispered, "Laced with anticipation."

I introduced Teddy, and while they were exchanging pleasantries, I noticed a large diamond on her left hand. "I take it Margo's is about become a partnership."

She held it up. "Partnership, hell. That's six carats. *Maison Margo* is going global." I decided not to ask where the obviously deeply-revered fiancé was spending *his* night.

Margo lowered her voice. "Love the tux, hate the smell. Why don't you run over to my place and shower away the goat while I make your friend comfortable."

I keep a couple of changes of clothes in my car, and fresh jeans, a long-sleeved linen shirt and deck shoes felt almost as good as the soap and water. Margo had us at a table near the fireplace, and Teddy was a martini ahead of me. Before I had a napkin on my lap, Margo reappeared with two glasses of something red. "My own blend," she said. "And since you never want to piss off the chef before dinner, drink it and smile."

I eyed Teddy. "You want to switch to something non-firewater?"

"I was a jerk not an addict."

That kind of logic is what keeps rehab joints buying primetime spots, but I didn't think a guy who a day ago could have lost his life over a Cup-O-Noodles need the lecture.

Teddy lifted his glass to Margo. "I look forward to someday being greeted like my friend here."

"The evening's young," Margo winked then went back to her kitchen. We sipped the grape and pronounced it excellent.

"So who's it going to be?" I asked. "HarperCollins or Random House?"

"Jake tell you that?"

"He just said there was a bidding war available, and you're costing him money."

"I'm not interested in the self-flagellation tour. I never met an abuser who didn't know exactly what he was doing during his most spectacular crash—even enjoyed it."

"Hard to have a *Today Show* moment after you tell them that."

"That's what the publishers said. Right after they pulled their offers. Jake said he wished I'd been killed in prison."

"Nothing takes the romance out of law like a disappearing five percent. Then I presume this little get-together is about Plan B."

"It is. How's my credit?"

"You're good for a hundred million."

"No, I mean really."

"That's really."

"Don't you even want to know what it's for?"

"You'll tell me when you're ready—or you won't. I'm good either way."

Teddy looked at me with a mixture of uncertainty and amusement. "You didn't even hesitate."

"It's been my experience that when someone wants to talk to you in person, it's about money, so I'd already decided. When a guy is trying to get back on his feet, he's a lot less effective if he's always chasing a check."

"What if it's more than a hundred?"

"Then you've got that too."

"Jesus Christ, Rail, you don't even know me that well."

"You helped me help a friend once, remember? Without asking why or reminding me later what you'd done. That puts you in a very short book, so you want, you got."

"Makes me wonder who else is out there waiting for me to ask."

We clicked glasses to his finding out. "Another drink?"

"If I don't, I might have trouble holding my fork."

I made a circular motion, and the waiter dashed over to refill our glasses. "Jake will transfer what you need."

His voice got a little husky. "I'll swing by his office and sign the note."

"No note, no terms. Truck hits you, what am I going to take? Your fuckin Picasso's already gone."

We laughed, but Teddy quickly turned serious again. "Don't take this the wrong way, but I really need this to be business."

I understood. It's why I trusted him. "Tell you what. I'll have Jake work it out so the money comes from Black Group. That way, if my managing director thinks you've gone Cimino, he can shut you off. Otherwise, no questions."

Teddy lifted his glass. "To freedom," he said. "And guys you can count on."

"Especially that last part."

After we both took a good swallow, Teddy borrowed my phone. While he was dialing, a drop-dead gorgeous, white lace-clad bride and her equally good-looking white-tuxedoed groom came in and went into the bar. A moment later, a loud pack of ushers and bridesmaids followed. Several were feeling no pain, and one had her heels hanging from a strand of ribbon around her neck.

Every wedding I've been to, once the dancing was over, the happy couple retired to the main event—alone. But there was a time I wouldn't have been able to imagine the bride's bare back inked with a shoulder-to-shoulder red and green Venus flytrap either.

Teddy's end of the telephone conversation brought me back to our table. "Like I said, make the deal. The price is fine." After a pause. "He's right here."

I took the phone and heard the familiar voice of our mutual ambulance chaser. "Teddy's a lot of things, but he's not a liar. Did you just loan him a hundred mil?"

"Nice to talk to you, too. Did you get my message about Holly Subinski?"

"Already handled. That wasn't the question."

"Actually, he can have whatever he needs. And if he doesn't lie, why ask?"

"Oh, I don't know. Maybe professional responsibility. Or maybe I just wanted to see if you needed a ride home before somebody asks for a kidney."

"Last time I checked, they were still my kidneys to do with what I wish."

"First Wind Fortune, now a felon producer. Next thing I know you'll have a script and be trying to get a meeting with Tarantino."

"You should write that stuff down, Jake, it's gold. Now, if you don't mind, I've had a long day."

"Somebody took out Morrie Solo. How do you feel about letting him walk now?"

After what Nate Dovidio had said, I wasn't surprised. I just thought it might take longer. "How'd it happen?"

"The way it usually does. Two to the back of the head. Three in Consuela. Too bad, I really wanted to fuck her."

"Maybe you can cover that in the eulogy. Where'd it go down?"

"Parking lot at Union Station. They had tickets all the way to Managua."

Morrie must have figured the airports were covered, which they probably were. "Somebody obviously cared enough to send the very best."

"And according to the *Times*, nobody saw nothin."

"If you're finished, my stomach's empty, and I'm dead tired."

"Just one more. Are you done for the night, or do I need to put on an extra shift?"

I rarely presume my ethic on others, but sometimes, Jake is like an actor who doesn't know how to get off the stage. "What are you going to do with your clout when you're dead?" I asked.

"My clout?"

"Influence, power, whatever you want to call it."

"I know what clout is, asshole."

"Your estate's going to that stepdaughter of yours who won't return your calls, but as greedy as you are, you don't really care that much about money. The only reason you get up in the morning is to make people bend to your will—sometimes just because it amuses you. But your imperium and pulse have the same 'sell by' date, and you're two bypasses closer to hitting the carpet on your face than you were a few years ago."

"I thought you were in a hurry to eat."

I ignored him. "Have you ever had a client who fell on hard times through no fault of his own? Maybe got really sick or just had a bad run of luck?"

"Where are you going with this?" He sounded irritated, which was good.

"And when you saw it happening did you say to yourself: 'I'm the most powerful lawyer in Hollywood. Powerful enough to make the sun stop if I want to. So I'm going to give this guy back his life. Part of it will be because it'll make me feel good, but if that's not enough, it'll be because I fuckin can.'"

There was silence on the other end. The kind of silence that gets thicker the longer you let it sit. I gave him a minute then said, "My guess is the day that guy stops earning, he comes off the Christmas card list."

"I'm a Jew, I don't send Christmas cards."

"You're also Catholic when it's convenient."

"Look, once people get on their feet, I usually take them back."

"I hope you're kidding because I'm reevaluating my life, and that line may have just put you on the list of things I need to change. Think about it." I clicked off.

"Not pleased, I take it," said Teddy.

"In the big book of things I worry about, Jake's happiness comes right after Taliban tooth decay."

"I'd like to tell you what I'm doing," Teddy said. "Who knows, you might find it interesting."

"I assume you're making a movie. Probably a big one."

"I am, but it's a lot more than that."

"If you've found a way to bring back McQueen, count me in. Otherwise, I leave show biz to the deranged."

"Hear me out anyway. We've got a meal coming, and I'm a little short of stories these days about the herds of hot women chasing me."

"Okay, as soon as Margo gets an appetizer out here, the floor is yours."

Just then, there was yelling in the bar, followed by several thunks of shot glasses on hardwood. Tequila shooters for the wedding party was my guess. The prelude to the bride or the groom saying something the other would never forget… or forgive. I gave the marriage a year.

As it turned out, I was off by 364½ days.

CHAPTER SIXTEEN

White Lace Doesn't Stay for Breakfast

Teddy and I had moved to Margo's back patio and were enjoying the afterglow of an extraordinary dinner over a couple of 21-year-old Dalmores. I'd gotten a box of English Ovals from the Rolls, and, along with our single malts, we were taking in a stream of nicotine just this side of lethal.

It's probably against the law to even spell cigarette in Carmel, but despite California's ever-vigilant pleasure police, I've managed to avoid tobacco gallows so far. I don't smoke often, but when I do, I'm the wrong guy to start speechifying in the direction of. More than one sour-faced, misery toad has gone away sputtering or bruised—depending on how much spit I endured during his rant.

The fog had dissipated enough to see lights on the beach a half a mile down the hill. While I enjoyed the view, Teddy explained that he was using my money to buy control of Colosseum Pictures, the most successful mini-major in Hollywood.

"A profligate producer with his own studio," I said. "Lucky me."

Teddy laughed, and it was good to hear. "Shit, Rail, I don't run companies, I make pictures. That's why I hired Ross Dare. The kid's family owns theatres in Chicago, and he was short-counting distributors at twelve and cutting union deals with the Outfit at fifteen. While the Ivy League clowns at the studios are giving blowjobs at Comic-Con, he's dreaming up new ways to monetize assets most people don't even know are assets. Colosseum will be a major one of these days—or we'll take one over."

"If you can overcome your shyness, you've got a helluva future.

Seriously, Teddy, I wish you nothing but success. If there's anybody who knows how to make a commercial picture, it's you."

"Don't kid yourself. Nobody *makes* a commercial picture. They come from great material. The trick is knowing when to stay out of the way of a good story—a concept that gives most directors the dry heaves. But to make a business out of it you have to put people like Dare in charge—not egotistical bullies like me. I can't believe it took me two years of solitary to figure that out."

I remembered my speech to the court about hiring exceptional people. I was looking forward to meeting this Ross Dare. "So how much did Colosseum cost us?"

"Eighty-five mil down and another five hundred over ten years. Six months ago, they wouldn't have talked to anybody for twice that. They're sitting on a 350-picture library, two network series headed into syndication, and they own that primo building on Sunset. Even their music operation is profitable. It's only the feature side that needs attention, and there, you're one picture away from being an industry darling. The Italian financial authorities ordering Banca Passavanti to get out of show business makes this the discount of the decade."

My father had known the Passavantis. I remembered meeting them in Venice when I was very young. "They're one of the oldest aristocratic families in Italy. *Papabile.* Capable of electing popes. They go back to the Medici."

"Seven centuries of piling it up, and it only took Hollywood five years to shake them to their foundation. I figure they're out at least a bil and a half."

"Still a long way to go to catch Credit Lyonnais."

"It's hard not to be nostalgic for the eighties," mused Teddy. "Cannon, Carolco, Hemdale, Dino. It was like they were printing money in the basement."

We drank to basements. "What about working capital and production funds?"

"Short term, the other $15 mil from you. But the Passavantis want to recoup, so they'll come in for half of any new picture through the family trust, providing there's a deep-pocketed partner to cover the rest."

"And you're hoping that's me."

"Well, there's not much point making the first bet if you're not prepared to call the raise. Besides, now that I know you and the Passavantis are friends, you don't want to leave them hanging, do you?"

I laughed, but he was right. "I don't even want to know the amount. Deal with Jake. Now all you need is some of that great material you were talking about."

His smile broadened. "As luck would have it…"

"Why am I not surprised? Anything I might know?"

He shook his head. "Something completely under the radar. But it's *People* magazine cover stuff. Just to make sure, I've got the most bankable star in the world attached… Valentine Jones."

He couldn't have taken me more off-guard, and I burst out laughing. Teddy's eyes narrowed, and I got a look at the face prison teaches you if you intend to survive. "I miss something?"

"Strictly a personal amusement. I'll fill you in later. Didn't I read she recently signed a long-term deal with one of the majors?"

Teddy relaxed and lit another smoke. "Here's the best part. There was a carve-out for anything produced by her family, which the studio didn't think mattered. After all, who the fuck are the Joneses, right?"

"How surprised are they going to be?"

"After what you just said, I figured you'd know."

"I have no clue what you're talking about."

He flashed a kidlike grin. "Her bio says her parents were Walter and Gina Jones from Vegas, but those are a dead aunt and uncle. Miss Jones is actually Valentina Bianca Scarpuzzi—and her grandmother is Duchessa Alegreza Passavanti—who, since the duca's death, rules the family empire with an iron fist."

The studio was going to be surprised all right. As surprised as I was. I had no idea there was a granddaughter. "I hope you know what you're doing. I'm investing in a company, not a lawsuit."

"Oh, the lawyers will huff and puff, but before paper flies, we'll cut a deal. No studio wants a pissing contest with a superstar and her internationally powerful family. Especially when seventy percent of her boxoffice comes from overseas. They've got their own Valentine Jones pictures to protect."

"The Teddy Chessman I know is smart enough to let them eat at the trough between his sequels."

His smile got wider. "Every now and then you let the other guy see you have the winning hand then throw it away. But there won't be any sequel to ours. It's like *Titanic*. You can only tell it once. But if I'm half as good as I used to be, Valentine will want to keep making pictures with me, and we'll figure out a way to make money for everybody."

I believed him. Studios write checks every day to people they hate—and the people who hate them back cash them. "If memory serves me, the Passavantis' only son and his wife were killed in a plane crash years ago. Who's running the bank day-to-day? Certainly not the duchessa."

Teddy shook his head. "Her grandsons Eligio, Loris and Battista. They were raised by the duca and duchessa."

"But Valentine's not their sister?"

"No, the duca and duchessa also had a daughter. Graciella. A wild child. Fancied herself an actress. No talent, but big tits and an easy lay."

"So your actress is Graciella's kid. Probably without benefit of marriage."

"A dangerous Sicilian, Michelangelo Scarpuzzi, was the flavor that month. Graciella liked her men in quantity but not in perpetuity—older and violent got you extra points. Scarpuzzi was twice her age and had a reputation for liking sex with a gun in his partner's mouth."

"I swore off that," I said. "Ups compliance, but muffles the screaming of obscenities in my ear." Another glass of wine, and I'd be ready to open for Chris Rock.

"Remember the Pizza Connection? Marseilles heroin to New York courtesy of the Palermo mob?"

I did.

"Scarpuzzi was the money man. His nickname is *Il Cassiere*."

"The Cashier."

"Scarpuzzi's thugs tabulated every transaction, all the way down to checking register tapes at the pizzerias. Come up short and your replacement had to scrape you out of the oven before he baked his first pie. Not surprisingly, the family wanted Graciella's baby out of reach of both her parents. Gina was a cousin of the duca's, like fourteen times removed, and married to Walter Jones, a Sin City casino lawyer who could make Valentine's past disappear. Welcome to America—through the golden handshake door."

"Where's the happy couple now?"

"Scarpuzzi, no idea. If he's alive, probably tending his tomatoes in Sicily. Guy would be in his seventies—late seventies, maybe. Graciella disappeared without a trace. The whole thing makes the duchessa's skin crawl."

"One of the oldest and most esteemed families in Italy sharing a bastard granddaughter with somebody nicknamed 'The Cashier' who probably killed their child? I can't imagine why. But, hey, what's a little embarrassment with a billion and a half bucks on the line, and Teddy Chessman with a get-out-of-jail movie."

He shifted in his seat—never a good sign. "Actually, Valentine owns the material. My ticket was my two Academy Awards."

My eyes narrowed. "You want to run that down for me?"

Teddy started to perspire, and it wasn't hot. "She came up to San Quentin and asked me to produce it. You could say begged me."

People sometimes equate modest expectations with modest intelligence. I hadn't expected that treatment from Teddy, but like he said, I didn't know him that well. Above-the-title actresses—even desperate ones—don't put their careers in the hands of guys without a pot to piss in. Prison is optional. "Try again," I said. "And this time, give me my hundred million's worth of bullshit."

His pause was longer than a camera reveal of Col. Kurtz. "Look, I'm sorry, I..."

I stopped him and leaned close so he wouldn't have to exert himself to hear me. "If I get up and walk out, you've still got the money. But when I hit the door you're as dead to me as that slab of abalone you just put down. So have another drink, take a leak then maybe a walk around the parking lot, but don't say another word until you're prepared to treat me with the respect I've shown you."

This time, he didn't need to think about it. "You're right, Rail. No excuses. Sometimes I see a stage, I start dancing before I look at the audience. I should have told you about Valentine."

"Keep talking, I'll let you know when I start to believe you."

Gone was the boldness I was familiar with. In its place was something I also knew well—fear. "I was hungry, Rail. Hungrier than I'd ever been. I'm a great fuckin producer, but once I dried out, I realized the town might never let me make another picture. Not the way I do it. With big budgets and big stars. I'd done worse than fuck with a movie and some studio cocksucker's car, I fucked with the system. Pissed on it. Dishonored it.

"Civilians think everybody in Hollywood is an asshole. They're probably right. But the ones who get to the top and stay there love every fuckin rivet in every fuckin camera and get up every morning with one thing on their minds: to have that gate guard wave them through so they can get another whiff of a sound stage. It's a career, but it's also a disease. The greatest fuckin disease in the world, and you can't ever get cured."

"So you were lying around feeling sorry for yourself…"

"Worse, I was timing cell checks and knotting sheets. I kept putting it off because I didn't know how long it takes to strangle, and I didn't want to end up playing with Tinker Toys and relearning my colors.

"Then one day, a guard opens my cell and says Valentine Jones is there to see me. At first, they weren't going to let her in. She wasn't on my visitor list, and the commotion she caused just showing up like that brought the place to a standstill. Guys on their day off were racing back just to get a glimpse. Finally, somebody called the warden. He came down and announced she was his favorite star, and off I went.

"They take me to the day room, and, Jesus Christ, did she look good. I mean really good, Rail. Then she tells me a story that's so fuckin unbelievable I'm shooting the picture in my head. All of a sudden, I felt like I used to. I've done every drug I could pound up my nose, down my gut and into a vein. But not one of them ever made me feel like I did that day, sitting there in a puke green room that smelled like a hundred years of dirty ass. Most of the guys in that place don't belong anywhere. But I did. Really belonged."

"You've got me in the palm of your hand. Seriously."

"I do tell it pretty fuckin good, don't I?"

We laughed, but Teddy's eyes were wet. "So why buy the cow, if you've already got the milk?" I asked.

"Imagine trying to tell a star that big what to do if it's her bat and ball and you're only there because Academy voters thought you had a couple of good years and your competition didn't."

He was right. I hadn't been able to control her, and I'd been trying to save her life. "So instead of coming in to help her raise a few bucks to make her picture, you buy the company from grandma. But how did you know this deep, dark secret about who she was?"

He looked uncomfortable, but got his footing. "She started out bad and got worse. When she was in high school, she was turning tricks in her uncle's hotels. After he shut that off, she began stealing. Not trinkets, but serious bling from the big suites. The hotels picked up the losses, but she had to go. College was out of the question, so they rented her an apartment and shipped her to LA. I met her at an open call. Her acting was raw, but damn, when the camera found her, nobody else in the scene mattered."

"I can guess the rest. Like mother, like daughter."

"Minus the gun in the mouth. If it matters, I waited until she was eighteen. Her birthday, actually. We had a good thing for a couple of years, but as it usually does, stardom got in the way."

"No wonder Jake's upset about the book deal. This is talk show cocaine. Valentine can't be happy about the end run."

"Furious, twice. She intended to direct it, which is now out the window too."

"My money thanks you. I'm not sure the new director will. Who do you want?"

"Joe Cargo owes Ross a favor."

Even I knew Joe Cargo. A marine combat veteran who shoots fast and once tossed an A-lister out of a moving pickup for grabbing a script girl's breasts. Show up without knowing your lines, and Cargo kills the scene. Valentine would be panting trying to keep up. "Good luck with that conversation."

"She knows this is the role of a lifetime, so she'll scream a couple of times a day then get right with God. If I'm half as good as I think I am, and Cargo doesn't kill her, she'll have her Oscar and be begging to do it all again."

What if I hadn't come through with the money?"

"Valentine had been planning to auction the script. Bidders had to agree to co-finance the picture before being allowed to read it. But there was a small legal issue that needed to be resolved first, so I had her put the auction idea on hold, and as soon as you said you'd pick me up, I knew I was covered. Ex-con or not, I've still got two gold statuettes—not to mention the one I should have won—and if you're going to make movies, that's the way you bet."

I didn't like that. "I bet on men not hardware."

"I know, Rail, I'm being glib so I don't end up thanking you until I embarrass both of us."

I understood. Guys who used to be on top, then suddenly aren't, have a tough time asking for help—and a tougher time knowing how to accept it. That's why they're good risks. They never want to travel the hat-in-hand road again. "And the duchessa has the familial juice to keep Valentine in line."

"Nothing holds a young girl's attention like a rich grandmother with a last will and testament."

I held up my glass. "To your missing Oscar."

Teddy raised his. "Stolen. Fuck the winner."

"When do you get the keys to the studio?"

"The vote's Friday, but thanks to you, my money's on the table. Valentine will come by at the end to do the dago schmooze with her uncles and get her picture taken with the board. A couple of hours later, she, Ross and I will hold a press conference. Helluva fuckin business, ain't it." he grinned. "And my rack's still warm at the Q."

"Plus Jake and Marvin Oxford wrestling over who'll get the bigger fee. Maybe there'll be a gunfight. By the way, Cortez said you asked him to write the screenplay."

"Never tell a writer anything you want kept quiet. I wonder who else that pet molester's been blabbing to?"

"Probably nobody. It's a personal thing."

"There's already a script. I just wanted Cortez to fix a few things and do some research to bring the third act together. But the material's so unusual, I won't let copies out of my control. I told him he'd have to work in the office, and he told me to go fuck myself."

"If you need help turning him around…"

"You've done enough. Cortez is almost as impossible as Valentine, on top of being expensive. I'll piss your money away on somebody who'll be grateful."

"You find that guy in Hollywood, give me a call. But don't drop Cortez on emotion. Ask Ross Dare first."

"You're right, Rail. Glad you're aboard."

We lit a couple more Ovals, and midway through, the wedding party stumbled onto the patio with all the grace of Raiders fans after last call. The area wasn't much more than a small porch anyway, and by the time the drunks had bumped into us a dozen times pushing the remaining three tables together and rounding up chairs, I was ready to make my apologies to Margo, find a hotel and call it a night.

Then I saw the bride turn in her chair and lock eyes with Teddy. She hiked her lace up over her thighs, opened her legs and gave us an eyeful of what the well-waxed lady is sporting this season. Just in case Teddy was a thirty-third degree moron, she accentuated her what-are-you-waiting-for smile with a voluptuous tongue doing slow circles around her lips. I put my plans for escape on hold. This probably wasn't going to end in rock, paper, scissors.

Teddy didn't hesitate. Two years of steel walls with a handful of toilet paper had worked their magic. He put a smile on Miss Flytrap that was just shy of a porn poster. The head tuxedo was pretty far gone, but not that far. When he noticed his wife giving her new infatuation a beaver call, he backhanded her over her chair.

Teddy got to him almost before the bride hit the ground, grabbed one handful of throat and the other of nuts and lifted him clean out of his seat. He ran the guy backwards across the bricks and slammed him into *Maison Margo's* privacy wall. I heard the groom's wind go and saw him sag, but when you're used to protecting yourself in the joint, you make sure. Teddy delivered a blow to his solar plexus that was so hard I thought his fist was going to come out the other side.

A stream of booze, food and last week's laundry erupted out of the guy's mouth, nose and maybe even his eyes. Teddy had seen this act before and stepped out of the line of fire.

One of the ushers decided he was going to help, but when I stood up, he eyed my size and rethought his gallantry. Ordinarily, this is when the girl charges her man's attacker, screaming to leave him alone. Miss Flytrap was working from a different manual. She walked casually up to Teddy, took his hand and put it between her legs. "Where's your car?" she asked, and I didn't detect any slurring.

"Bad boys always get the girls," I said as I tossed him the keys to the Rolls. "There's a nice place down on the sand. The Sundowner Bungalows. You got cash?"

"Two years at forty cents an hour, I'm flush." As they departed, the bride was already unhooking her dress. I went looking for Margo, suddenly feeling a lot less tired.

———————

I awakened to something very warm and very soft addressing just the right place. Shortly, I felt something wetter and softer twirling around its head.

As one who believes alarm clocks kill more people than guns, this is definitely a way to cut down on unnecessary deaths. Margo seemed to be enjoying herself, and I didn't want to interrupt her good time, so I lay back and awaited the inevitable. She almost made it last too long. Well, maybe not.

After a jointly enjoyed shower, we wandered back next door to the restaurant, and I mixed a pitcher of aggressive Bloody Marys while she scrambled a half-dozen eggs with Serrano ham sliced so thin it was almost transparent. Putting fire to Spanish cured meat is the kind of sacrilege that makes a Michelin inspector grab his heart—or worse, take your restaurant off his consideration list. So while we sat on the patio and shoveled down this delight with thick hunks of baguette brushed with garlic butter and browned under the broiler, I kept an eye on the Pacific for French periscopes.

We had just finished a post-breakfast fling with her seated in my lap, when I heard the Rolls' horn. "I figured he might show up around lunch," Margo said as she slipped off me and back into her clogs.

"He's a producer," I responded. "They always find their way to free food."

"I wonder if he brought the bride." I looked at her, and she gave it about two seconds of thought before she laughed.

As expected, Teddy was hungry, so Margo made more of her famous eggs, which he got down in prison time. We said good-bye, carrying a pair of go-cups of Sumatran. On our way out, I saw Teddy pocket one of *Maison Margo's* business cards. Carmel was a long drive to take a CAA agent to lunch, so he must have wanted to come back to photograph the view.

Teddy drove while I sipped my coffee. He seemed pleased to be behind a wheel again. He didn't offer what had happened with Miss Flytrap, and I didn't ask. The same went the other way. My kind of conversation about a "night before." None.

"If you don't mind, I'm going to head over to the 5," he said. "I don't like that drive down the guardrail side of the PCH. Don't forget, you owe me the story about how you know Valentine."

My eyelids suddenly felt very heavy, and I yawned. The sunrise double with Margo had taken it out of me. The Bloody Marys probably hadn't helped. "Let me catch fifteen minutes of shuteye first. But before I nod off, what's this script that's so magnificent it's going to save Colosseum, win Valentine Jones an Academy Award and restore seven hundred years of Passavanti fortune?"

"The best kind of magnificent. A story nobody's ever heard. About a heist so big, a chase so wild and a mystery so enduring that, just to make you happy, McQueen's trying to get back to do a cameo. That'd make a helluva poster, wouldn't it?"

"Throw in Harvey Keitel, and I'll be running it every Saturday night until they lay me away." I closed my eyes for a little late morning siesta. "There a title to go with all that?"

"Beverly Hills is Burning."

CHAPTER SEVENTEEN

Cash and Cactuses

MARCH 13, 1935
SOMEWHERE WEST OF THE ROCKIES

The other plane came out of the southwest about sundown. It was a black and red Wedell-Williams 44, a racer Barrie had read about but never seen. Built solely for speed, the W-W was little more than a one-man cockpit behind twelve-hundred pounds of Pratt & Whitney. Despite the single engine, if tuned properly, it could out-sprint the twinned de Havilland. Its major weakness was non-retractable landing gear, which increased drag, cut maneuverability and made it susceptible to wind variations. It also had a tendency to overheat. The W-W was a straight-line, short-distance runner, period.

Barrie was cruising off oxygen at a little under twelve thousand feet. She'd given Rollo the controls after leaving Corpus Christi, but he'd soon handed them back and gotten no fight from Barrie. The Greek was probably a helluva pilot picking up women at a bar, but an arm's length from God, he was shaky at best.

The approaching plane was slightly above, its wing lights blinking in the gathering dusk. Even though there was plenty of cushion, Barrie pushed the nose of the Beverly Hills *down to increase the margin of safety.*

She lost sight of the W-W as it passed then saw it reappear on her starboard side. But instead of continuing on, it banked sharply and disappeared to her rear. A couple of minutes later, it reappeared alongside. There wasn't enough light left to get a good look at the pilot, but it wasn't unusual for fliers to eyeball other aircraft—especially interesting ones. Barrie had done it herself, and there weren't any de Havillands in this part of the world. She waggled her wings and waited for him to do the same. When he didn't, she wrote it off to ignorance.

"What the fuck's that guy doin?" Rollo asked.

"Nosy would be my guess."

"Lose him."

"Why waste the fuel? Nobody knows where we are. Even if somebody had our flight plan, that isn't the plane you'd send up to wander around looking for us. He'll move on in a minute."

Just then, the W-W accelerated ahead then darted in front of the de Havilland, its slipstream buffeting them roughly. Instinctively, Barrie throttled back and jammed the stick forward, dropping several hundred feet and pushing their stomachs against their lungs. Barrie heard Rollo suck in his breath, but before he could say anything, she leveled off and commanded, "Get your mask on!"

As they went on full oxygen, the W-W disappeared into a dive. He was gone so long Barrie thought maybe he'd had his fun and called it a night. No such luck. This time, when he came up next to them, he switched on his cockpit lights. She could see him now, but she still didn't have any idea who he was. He was, however, also on oxygen, and he gestured for her to follow him down.

"Yeah, right," she muttered. She flicked her radio button and tried to contact him on several frequencies but came up empty.

Rollo was back in form. "Put this fuckin tub on the ground, and I'll blow a hole in the cocksucker before he gets unstrapped!"

Barrie didn't think that was much of a plan. On the ground, they were at the mercy of a host of unknowns. Up here, the odds were with them. "The cash Guerra gave you. How was it packed?"

"What cash?"

"We're trying to stay alive here, Rollo. Pretend you're smart. The million bucks for the heroin. How's it packed?"

Rollo hesitated. "Two suitcases."

Barrie hadn't bothered to ask for the weight before takeoff, figuring that money—even that much—was going to weigh less than the two hundred and twenty pounds they were leaving behind. "Did you take it out and count it?"

"What the fuck do you care? No, I looked at it."

"So if something was underneath, you wouldn't know."

Rollo was quiet again, then finally, "What're you talkin about?"

"A radio transmitter. Any reasonably intelligent electronics guy could take the guts out of a Zenith, add a couple of tubes and hook it up to enough flashlight batteries to push out a signal for a week. It would probably be a tone, pulsing intermittently over an easy-to-monitor frequency."

"Somebody could follow that in a plane?"

"As long as they stayed within range."

"Who?"

My guess would be your buddy, Juan. He probably had a tag team on us until he decided to make his move." She looked over at the W-W and got the 'Follow me and land' sign again. "The heroin, his million bucks, plus the Comet. Quite a take for the price of a little gas."

Rollo wasn't sure. "He could have just whacked us in Matamoros."

"Think about it. You know how many planes take off and are never heard from again? I don't think Luciano would call out the National Guard, do you?"

"The motherfucker would figure I stole the money and ran."

"Or the two of us did."

"If we get out of this, some scores are gonna get settled."

"Let's focus on the first part. You strapped tight?"

"Yeah."

"Then let's eyeball the opposition." Barrie turned on her cockpit lights and raised her hand to indicate to the other pilot that she'd follow him down. "If he's a pro, he'll overfly the strip to show us where it is. Then he'll wait for us to go around and land."

Barrie followed the W-W due south and after forty minutes, she was certain they had passed back into Mexican airspace. The darkness was total now, the rising moon blocked by the mountains to the north.

Their escort flashed his cockpit lights and started descending. At five hundred feet, Barrie began looking for a landing strip but saw nothing. Then suddenly, where, a moment before, there had been only blackness, two irregular rows of flickering lights appeared, running off a half-mile into the distance. The W-W lined himself up between them, dropped to an altitude of fifty feet and slowed almost to a crawl.

Rollo had his face pressed against the glass, gun in hand. "Jesus Christ," he breathed, "look at that."

Barrie'd never seen anything like it either. At least a hundred men on horseback, spaced along both sides of a smooth patch of dirt, each holding a glowing red flare. At the slow speed she was traveling, Barrie could make out every detail, from their sombreros and chaps to their silver-encrusted bridles and Mexican saddles. And rifles. Lots of rifles.

The reception was taking place alongside an old railroad station, complete with an abandoned platform and a thirty-foot water tower. As she swept by, she could read the faded black lettering on the huge, round tank: **Tres Cactos**.

Barrie waggled her wings to let the horsemen know she was coming in then pulled up and went into a wide left turn. After completing the go-around, she came level again and began her approach.

Rollo didn't like what was happening. "I thought we were just gonna look."

Barrie ignored him. On her orientation flight, Hughes had shown her the "extras" he and his engineers had designed into the Beverly Hills. One was being able to shut off the backseater's controls. So far, she hadn't used it, but now she reached forward and hit the switch. The last thing she needed was Rollo trying to help.

The second extra was the ability to lay down movie smoke from chemical tanks built into the wings. Barrie didn't know anything about making movies, but she'd told Hughes how fake that always looked. "No offense, Howard, but smoke from a real fire isn't anything like that prissy, white crap Hollywood uses. It's black and scary as hell."

Hughes had laughed. "You're talking to a guy who's seen his share of plane crashes and oil field fires. The stuff that'll come out of these tanks looks like it was sucked out of a locomotive. It isn't toxic, but it irritates breathing passages and scares the hell out of livestock. Should be interesting the first time some stuntman gets lazy on his horse."

Hoping she remembered the right sequence, she twisted one lever then the second, allowing the chemicals to mix. Immediately, a red light on the instrument panel began flashing, indicating she had ten seconds before the pressure buildup automatically released the smoke. As she dropped the Beverly Hills' landing gear, she turned on the headlight and put the plane's nose *squarely in the center of the flares. Then she began counting down, "5-4-3…"*

Busy as she was, she still had time to wonder where the other plane was.

Barrie had given fleeting thought to the possibility that the smoke might panic the men into shooting, but fortunately, that didn't happen. As her wheels touched, they kicked up dust from the desert floor, adding to the plume.

Moments later, over the Comet's engine noise, she could hear horses screaming. It was a chilling sound, and she could only imagine what was happening behind her. She jammed the throttles forward and gave the de Havilland maximum power. It responded instantly, and seconds later, she felt the wheels come back up.

Barrie pulled hard on the stick, and the nose came to a seventy-five degree angle, cutting hard into the night. She turned off all lights, but instead of continuing the climb, she dropped the nose almost straight down. The sudden plunge was breathtaking, and Barrie heard Rollo instinctively grab the rear stick, only to find it non-responsive.

Guessing where the ground was, Barrie jerked the Beverly Hills *hard right and came back past the chaos below, near enough that a wild-eyed, riderless stallion momentarily filled her windshield then disappeared just as quickly. All of a sudden, a black and red shape exploded out of the gloom, and the W-W blew by so close that Barrie thought she heard the tick of metal on metal. The concussion rocked the de Havilland, and Rollo yelled something unintelligible.*

Barrie switched her lights back on, and Rollo erupted. "What the fuck are you doin? Turn those off and get out of here!"

"We're still broadcasting, so we can run, but we can't hide. And I'm not willing to chance somebody ordering him to ram us."

"So what are you going to do?"

"What he thinks he wants."

Momentarily, Barrie saw the W-W off to her left and headed up again. When she was sure he was behind her, she dropped down to where she thought the railroad tracks were. The other pilot did exactly what she expected. He got above her and tried to force her into the ground.

The W-W's fixed wheels were inches above the de Havilland's clear canopy—so close that in even in the dark, Barrie could see bits of gravel stuck in the treads. With her landing gear retracted, she was able to lower the Beverly

Hills *almost against the rusty steel rails, which is where she was when the two planes entered the inky smoke that had now rolled across the tracks.*

Barrie concentrated on the only thing she could see: the twin rails streaking under her at such velocity it felt like she was riding them. An instant later, she caught a glimpse of the water tower spout hanging over the tracks. Then she was under it.

The pilot of the Wedell-Williams saw nothing. He hit **Tres Cactos** *head on.*

CHAPTER EIGHTEEN

Riverbeds and Thunderstorms

MARCH 14, 1935
THE CALIFORNIA DESERT

The sound of rain on the Beverly Hills' *wings awakened Barrie. It was still dark, and she was as exhausted as if she hadn't slept at all. She checked her watch. She and Rollo had been asleep for two hours. They were lying under the de Havilland, wrapped in their extra clothes against the desert cold. Now, however, tiny rivulets of water were seeking them out, soaking whatever they touched.*

Rollo hadn't argued when Barrie told him Tijuana was out. Only a fool would have crossed into Mexico again. With the moon finally up, reading the night landscape had posed no problem, and they'd flown deep into the Mojave before putting down on what, in dinosaur times, had been a vast inland sea. Now it was a miles-wide stretch of hard-packed sand that turned out to be smoother than most runways.

The transmitter in the suitcase had been smaller and more sophisticated than Barrie'd expected. She'd wanted to disable it and take it with her, but Rollo had pushed her away and emptied his gun into the tangle of wires and tubes, proclaiming that he was going do the same to Juan Guerra. Afterward, lathered up from gunfire and threats, he'd grabbed her by the hair and dragged her down, pawing between her legs and ripping at her flight suit. "What you and that wiseass attitude need is a hard fuck," he grunted.

Barrie had been working around Luciano's crew long enough to know that nothing threw cold water on a Latin libido faster than announcing it was her time of the month. She hoped it worked for Greeks too. What it got her was a choke and a punch in the jaw, but it ended the courting. To sooth his savage beast, Rollo broke out a bottle of Tequila and an envelope of heroin and, after consuming both, blacked out. Gentleman that he was, Rollo had offered to share his needle. Barrie passed.

Now she rolled away from the pooling rain and felt the magnum press against her chest. She took it out, tested its weight then knelt over Rollo. He was still clutching the empty tequila bottle, and she had a difficult time imagining he had once been some mother's pride and joy.

Resting the barrel against his temple, she watched the revolver rise and fall with his snoring and imagined his brains splattered across the grit. In a couple of weeks, the scavengers would pick him down to bones; in a month, what was left would be scattered for miles. But as much as she wanted to rid herself of this man who would murder her without blinking, she took a deep breath and slid the gun back inside her suit. She was her own kind of criminal, but not his kind.

Barrie walked out into the desert and confirmed what she feared. The ground was turning to paste. Another fifteen minutes and the de Havilland would be there until summer. She got her gear in the plane, climbed aboard and wound the engines. She told herself that if Rollo awakened, she might wait. Fortunately she didn't have to make that decision, and when she had enough RPMs to taxi, she closed the canopy.

As she turned to the west, the rain started coming in sheets, and forward visibility became nonexistent. The takeoff roll seemed like forever, and she had to feed the twin Gipsy Sixes twice the normal power just to get to speed. At one point, she thought she saw a figure running toward her in the dark, but she couldn't be sure.

When she finally felt the wheels release, she let out a breath she didn't realize she'd been holding and pointed the Beverly Hills *into the murk.*

San Bernardino was down there somewhere. Barrie just couldn't be sure where. Each time she tried to get through the storm, the wind tossed the plane around so violently, she was afraid she'd lose it.

Barrie keyed her mike. "San Bernardino tower. This is the Beverly Hills. *Do you read me?"*

There were several long moments of crackle and screeching, then a voice came on so clear it sounded like the man was standing next to her. "Beverly Hills, *this is SB tower, I read you. You're Mr. Hughes's de Havilland, right? All the way from Havana."*

"I am. Can't see much of your town right now, though."

"I heard you go by a couple of minutes ago, so you're right where you're supposed to be. Only problem is that mess between us. Who am I speaking to?"

"Barrie Fontaine. Out of Floyd Bennett in Brooklyn."

"Gus Fox, on this end. You got yourself quite a reception committee down here, Miss Fontaine. The Hughes team came in last night—four engineers and a pilot. I guess they're going to give your crate the once-over before taking it to Mr. Hughes's place over in Glendale. Then this morning, two more fellas showed up looking for a Mr. Tripoli. They seemed to be under the impression he'd be flying the de Havilland."

Suspicions confirmed. It was time for the first lie. "Rollo's here. Fighting a serious case of Matamoros Mambo, so I'm helping out."

"Roger that. I see Mexico on a map, I gotta get close to porcelain."

"What's it like down there?"

"Dark as my ex-wife's heart. And more coming. Ceiling two hundred, visibility not even that, wind gusting to sixty. You don't want to hear this, but you're better off where you are."

Wasn't California supposed to be sunny? Rain or no rain, though, it beat being dead. Suddenly, there was an enormous burst of thunder below that rocked the Beverly Hills *hard.*

The tower voice was anxious now. "Whoa! Lightning just took out one of our generators. You might want to find someplace else to roost, ma'am. We're tying down even the big stuff. How are you on fuel?"

"Good for another hour, but I've been getting some conflicting readings on my starboard engine. Can't tell if it's overheating, or the gauge is bad."

"The storm's coming out of the north, but it's just inching along. I were you, I'd hightail it down toward Corona. You know it?"

"I landed there once. Not much more than a flyspeck."

"That's being generous, but I talked to them a little while ago, and the birds were singing."

"Then, flyspeck, here I come. Wish me luck, Gus."

"Let me know when you get in, and I'll send everybody your direction. Give my best to Mr. Tripoli… when he can handle it."

Barrie was in a band of relatively stable, clear air, sandwiched between two layers of the darkest clouds she could remember. Lightning flashed above and below. She was tense, but she was also more excited than she had ever been. If she managed to pull this off, as far as the world was concerned, she would be dead. If she didn't, what the world thought wouldn't matter.

Suddenly, Barrie felt goose bumps all over her body. Every hair was vibrating, down to the tiniest. She had heard about this but never experienced it. An electrostatic charge was building outside. Inevitably, an opposing charge would cross through it, and the result would be lightning.

If it happened sooner, there would be a jolt, and because her brain had its own electrical field, she would have a stunner of a headache afterward. She had also heard of women experiencing orgasms so intense that sex was never the same again.

However, if the charge continued to build, eventually, there would be a blinding flash, and it would be the last thing she ever saw. Her heart would stop, and so would the electrical system of the de Havilland. They would fall from the sky together.

It was now or never.

In Cuba, Hughes had shown her one final "extra." Concealed inside the de Havilland's engine cowlings were two bladders of flash gas connected to a manifold of tiny aluminum tubes, each no thicker than a pencil point. Knobs on the plane's instrument panel opened them, sending a fine mist of gas into the hot exhaust of the twin Gipsy Sixes.

Shutting down and restarting each engine, would create the flame necessary to ignite the flash gas, which burns hot and loud but is consumed in a split-second. Wind rushing over the wings would add oxygen and extend the fire's tail tenfold. Movie audiences do the rest, sucking in their breath and grabbing armrests while onscreen airliners shake and passengers scream.

Ignoring the electrostatic buildup, Barrie opened the port bladder's valve all the way. She then shut down and restarted that engine. The resulting whoosh shook the entire plane, and a flame appeared that extended almost to the tail. Seeing it, she thought about dialing back the starboard valve halfway, then said, "Fuck it."

This time, when she restarted, the blast turned her almost sideways, and she had to fight the Comet back to level. The fire trail was even longer. Keying the mike, she elevated the anxiety in her voice, though she realized most of it wasn't acting. "Mayday! Mayday! I'm on fire! Repeat, Fire! BEVERLY HILLS IS BURNING! BEVERLY HILLS IS BURNING!"

*Almost immediately, Gus was back on the air. "*Beverly Hills*, this is SB tower. Please advise extent of problem."*

Barrie didn't answer. The electrostatic charge in the cockpit was so strong now her gauges were gyrating wildly and simply moving an arm felt like swimming through mud. She jammed the stick forward and, at the same time, jerked it hard right. The de Havilland's nose fell to almost perpendicular, and the left wing rose above her, chasing the right.

What had been a lazy downward corkscrew soon accelerated, and as she entered the storm, the world went dark. The engine fires against the angry sky were almost beautiful, until colliding winds began whipping the plane from one axis to another. Metal shrieked, propellers moaned, and it sounded like someone was hurling gravel against the canopy as hail tried to bang its way through the glass.

A minute passed, then two, and suddenly, without warning, Barrie broke free of the clouds. Her gravity-leaden muscles pulled hard on the stick, but it fought back. For a long second, she thought she was going nose first into the ground. Then the spinning started to slow, and she felt the de Havilland come horizontal. The Beverly Hills *was inverted when the airport tower filled her field of vision. She gave the plane a burst of power as she slid past the window, close enough to see the upside down expressions on the faces of the men inside.*

Gus's taut voice filled the cockpit. "Holy Mother of God! Beverly Hills, *can you hear me? Acknowledge, please!* Beverly Hills, *acknowledge!"*

Barrie righted the plane and pulled back into the clouds. The buffeting winds and pelting hail were still there, but she had set the stage. It was a helluva lot more show than she'd planned, but she'd pulled it off. When the weather cleared, they'd search and they'd wonder, but eventually they'd figure the wreckage would turn up one of these days and all go home. And that would be that. All she had to do now was get as far from there as fast as possible.

Then it happened. Somewhere high above, the estranged electrical charges found each other, and the air around the de Havilland exploded. The flash of lightning was so intense, Barrie thought her corneas might be burned out. The jagged bolt racing to the ground, missed the de Havilland, but it was impossible to escape the horrific, following thunder.

It was like being hit by a train, crushing Barrie against her seat, mashing her lungs against her spine and forcing blood out of her ears. In the wings, the concussive boom flattened the flash gas bladders, spraying the remainder of their contents into the exhaust. Simultaneous explosions ripped through each engine's cowling, twisting metal, shredding rivets and hurling chunks of English craftsmanship into the storm.

Some pieces hit the fuselage and tail, lacerating it and peeling more parts loose. A blade from the starboard propeller tore through the canopy, shooting shards of tempered glass into Barrie's face and body. The sudden eruption of air tore her oxygen mask loose and sent it earthward. Finally, one of the suitcases broke open, and hundred dollar bills were sucked like so much confetti into oblivion.

From the San Bernardino tower, the conflagration had been only an expanding ball of red and orange flame inside the black clouds, but there was no question in anyone's mind that the Beverly Hills was gone.

Gus Fox summed up everyone's thoughts. "Those poor sonsabitches."

CHAPTER NINETEEN

Long Barrels and Laser Pointers

Matty Aspirins stopped the DTS in front of a just-this-side-of-seedy hotel a block off Fountain. In the teeth of West Hollywood, most of these places were gay-only, but the Tambourine Inn wasn't so in-your-face. The owner, Phil Kosmedes, was a former Brooklyn plasterers' union official who got tired of New York winters right around the same time his wife's family and the D.A. started asking why Mrs. Kosmedes hadn't been seen in seven months.

In return for the grand jury appearance of a barely literate Greek chef who testified he'd recently had an affair in Athens with the missing 200-lb. housewife and who had produced some extremely grainy photos to back it up, Phil now made no-charge rooms available for guys from back East who needed to lay low for a while. You still had to listen to some weird shit through the walls, but it was a small price to pay for no record you were ever there.

The Kansas City Tata brothers came out without Matty's having to honk. He'd worked with them on other jobs, and they didn't drink or do drugs. The only problem was sometimes they got carried away and didn't stop shooting, which could be a problem if you were on a tight clock. They also had a habit of opening fire when they didn't have to, which could be a problem for a lot of other reasons.

Timo, the oldest, got in front, and Matty waited until Pontos was situated in back, then he turned sideways so he could look at both of them. The Tatas had always had long hair, but it was in ponytails now—and greasy. Jesus, thought Matty, where the fuck had grooming gone?

"Look, we been over your crazy-ass shooting a dozen times," he said, "but I don't want any fuckups. Once the bodyguards are out of commission, you guys are just there to scare the civilians while I take care of business. I'm gonna whack four guys, but I don't want no panic where things could get outta hand. So I'm gonna walk them out first. Nobody else gets hurt. Not even a scratch. Understand?"

"That about it?" asked Timo like he'd heard this too many times already.

"No, asshole, it's not. You gotta blast something for effect, that's what ceilings are for. And listen to me real good, I yell stop, you stop, got it? No extra casualties."

"No problem," said Timo, and his brother nodded.

"Just so we're clear, here's the fuckin deal. Either of you fires one extra round, I hold back half your fee. *Katavow*?"

"Don't tell me, tell my brother," said Pontos. "Motherfucker's always ridin my ass I mighta left a witness."

Matty wasn't interested in this shit. "You heard what I said. Half." He swiveled back around and put the Caddie in gear. The traffic on Sunset was heavy, but they only had to go a few blocks. When Matty got to Colosseum Pictures, he turned up the hill away from the building and wound around the neighborhoods for a while.

He'd checked the news before leaving, and nothing had caught his attention, but you never knew when some show biz asshole was gonna beat his fuckin girlfriend, and half the cops in LA would show up to get their faces on camera. This morning, though, it was quiet except for a rent-a-cop backed into the overgrown driveway of a foreclosure, catching some Zs.

"You see that shit?" said Timo. He rolled down his window and yelled, "Hey, wake the fuck up! Insurance companies are dependin on you!" The guard came out of his slumber long enough to flip them off, and Pontos laughed. Matty just shook his head.

The neighborhood south of the boulevard was equally quiet. Matty checked his watch. 10:59. Everybody should be there. "Showtime," he said and eased off Sunset into the Taylor Street spur and around the corner.

The garage entrance to Colosseum was usually manned by a security guard, but the desk was empty, like it was supposed to be. Once inside, straight ahead was the gate to the lower levels. To the right was valet guest parking, only this morning, that area was jammed so tight with limos packed in among the usual Ferraris and BMWs that there wasn't room for a Moped.

Matty stopped while Timo got out to double-check the valet stand, which was around a blind corner. As he waited, there was the sudden blast of a horn behind him. Echoing inside the concrete garage, it sounded like a train.

Matty glanced in his mirror and saw the familiar grille of an old right-hand drive Rolls, a gray-uniformed chauffer at the wheel. He sat tight, and the horn came again, this time longer.

"You want me to do something about that?" asked Pontos.

"I want you to stay right where you are."

Momentarily, Timo came back into view, shaking his head that the valet was gone too. Seeing him, the chauffer gave everybody another wakeup call. Matty knew what was coming and was powerless to stop it. Timo changed direction, jerked open the Rolls' door, pulled the chauffer out, threw him against a fender and kicked him a dozen times in the nuts.

The passenger got partway out of the left rear suicide door then thought better of it. Matty glanced in the mirror. The guy was sixty, minimum, and wearing a powder blue suit over a salmon-colored Calypso shirt open to his waist. Capping the disco look was an orange toupee that looked like it had been harvested from an orangutan's ass. Fuckin Hollywood, thought Matty.

When the chauffer crumpled to the ground, Timo spit on him for good measure and got back in the Caddie. He didn't say anything and neither did Matty, who put the car in gear and proceeded past the rolling gate into the bowels of the garage.

Two levels down, Matty backed the Caddie into a row of empty spaces marked

RESERVED FOR COLOSSEUM
TELEVISION EXECUTIVES

Matty left room between the car and wall and popped the trunk. The men got out quickly, went to the back and opened the dive bags. A few moments later, wearing surgical gloves and Velcroed into black bulletproof vests and leggings, they threaded suppressors onto three AR-15s and slammed home 30-round banana magazines. Pocketing three more mags each, they donned black, SEAL-team balaclavas, closed the trunk and headed toward the elevator corridor.

On the first level, Pontos held the elevator while Matty and Timo moved out quickly, rifles leveled. The lobby was empty. Timo threw the floor and ceiling deadbolts on the revolving door to the street while Matty slipped behind the vacant security station. An abandoned Marlboro burned in the ashtray. Whoever Big Bush Busalacchi had told to clear the area had been on the ball, no fuckin around.

In the old days, you'd know where the security tapes were and take them with you. Now, with everything digital, things might be being recorded two or three places, maybe none of them onsite. Matty allowed himself a drag on the cigarette, then stubbed it out and entered a code on the keyboard. The nine monitoring screens went immediately dark. He tapped again, and text came up

DELETE VIDEO FILES FROM _____ TO _____

Matty looked at his watch and filled in the first blank with the day's date and a time beginning thirty minutes earlier. In the second blank, he typed the time thirty minutes from now. When he pressed ENTER, a progress bar appeared, and a timer began counting down. Matty knew something would still be recoverable. It always was. But that would get handled. If it didn't, he'd be making another trip.

Removing a pair of keys from his pocket, Matty used one to open the elevator control panel and inserted the second into the EMERGENCY

OVERRIDE slot inside. He closed all but one of the circuit breakers, left that key in place, relocked the panel and joined Timo back at the lift. Pontos pushed ROOF ACCESS, and they went up.

The elevator opened silently into a concrete utility area. Old office equipment, cleaning supplies and movie promotional materials were stacked wherever there was space. Around the corner, and up a short stairway, a gray steel door led to the roof. It was propped open a few inches with a concrete block.

Pontos climbed the stairs, flattened himself against the wall and pushed gently on the fire bar. The door swung all the way open, letting sunlight splash into the room. "*Yo, frocio,*" he called out and eased back down the steps, concealing himself alongside.

After a moment, they heard footsteps approaching, and a hulking shadow carrying an Uzi filled the doorway. "*Che casso?*" the man spit out.

Pontos leaned forward and fired once. The man jerked then pitched forward, his dead weight hitting the stairs face first, breaking teeth and bone before sliding the rest of the way down. Matty was already up the stairs and running toward the awning. The TV was on, but the area was empty. Two walkie-talkies and two cell phones sat on the desk. The other bodyguard had his Uzi but no communication.

Matty swept the roof carefully with his eyes. There weren't many places to hide. The guy had to be behind one of the air conditioning units. But which one? Matty laid down on his stomach and looked across the hot surface. The sun was starting to generate heat waves along it. Toward one corner of the farthest unit, he saw the waves rolling instead of rising straight up. He raised his AR-15 and shot through the metal, head-high. There was a scream, and the second bodyguard stumbled around the machinery his cheek gone, but firing wildly.

Matty dropped him with a second shot then dragged and rolled the body under the awning. The guy was big, and by the time Matty finished, he was sweating heavily and out of breath. All he could hope was that somebody up in the hills—or on another roof—hadn't been watching.

The sixth floor corridor was softly lit and carpeted in gray plush. To the left was a set of large double doors. Above them, a red-lighted panel read

BOARD MEETING IN SESSION

PLEASE PLACE ALL ELECTRONIC DEVICES ON TABLE BEFORE ENTERING

A long, narrow table next to the doors held a collection of phones. Forty feet to the right of the elevator bank, a young blonde sat at a reception desk, her back to the men. She was holding a light blue, rectangular-shaped book and talking animatedly on the phone. Matty was pissed. There wasn't supposed to be a receptionist. Somebody would get his ass reamed, but right now, he needed to put her out of commission.

He guessed the other two security men would be around the corner in the reception area, probably one on each side. He locked off the car and motioned for Timo to pay attention to the right and Pontos to the left.

Matty was out front. When he came to the corner, he didn't look either direction, just crossed to the girl and jammed the butt of his rifle into the back of her skull. She crumpled without uttering a sound, the book still grasped in her hand. Simultaneously, Matty heard the two AR-15s spit. When he turned he saw another pair of black-clad men, one on the floor, his lifeless hand frozen to a Sig 9mm. A second sprawled on a couch, blood from his head running onto the butterscotch leather.

Pontos checked the rest of the area, and Timo severed the cable to the phone. The three men crossed back to the main conference room doors and stopped. A long corridor ran off to the left. Halfway down, also on the left, were a pair of restrooms with a drinking fountain between them, and at the far end, on the right, another set of doors into the conference room. Matty directed Pontos and Timo to the second entrance, and when they were in position, he nodded, and they all went in—fast.

The room was darkened by blackout drapes covering a wall of windows. A slideshow was being projected onto a pull-down screen at Matty's end. Standing next to it, a heavyset older man in suspenders was using a laser pointer to highlight his presentation. A dozen men and women scattered around the aircraft carrier-sized conference table followed along from binders lighted by tiny directional spots in the ceiling and emblazoned with the Colosseum Pictures logo.

When the man with the laser saw Matty, he instantly went from zero to incensed. "Can't you read, asshole? This is a private meeting!"

A tall man seated near the head of the table stood up. In the dark, it was difficult to make out his face, but when he spoke, his voice was calm, very much in control. "Take it easy, Eli," he said to the man in suspenders. He turned to Matty. "I'm Teddy Chessman. I just bought this place. There's no money here, but if you want my wallet…"

"You the guy with the Academy Awards?" Matty shot back.

Teddy looked confused. "Yes, they're in my office, but they're not worth anything except to me."

Matty cut him off. "Then, shut the fuck up, and you'll be back to polishing them in a few minutes." He looked around the table. Three young men in suits sat together about halfway down-room. Even in the dim light, he knew who they were. "You… the three guineas…," he commanded, "get up and walk toward me. And keep your hands where I can see them."

"Fuck you," one of them said in a light Italian accent.

From the other end of the room, Pontos and Timo started toward the men, indicating with their rifles for them to do as they were told. Matty turned to Teddy. "You seem like a smart guy, so stay that way. I'm takin one more. Have somebody turn on the lights, so I get the right…"

But before he could finish, the man with the laser pointer aimed it at Matty's face and flicked it on. Suddenly, the vision in the Greek's left eye went blazing white then exploded in red. It felt like somebody had shoved a hot poker through his skull, and he staggered back.

"Grab his gun!" the man in suspenders yelled.

Teddy wheeled on his employee. "Eli, what the fuck…?"

But it was too late. Matty let go with a burst that tore both men to pieces. It was all the Tata brothers needed. They opened fire at the other end of the room, laying waste to flesh, furniture and fixtures. In a blind fury, Matty closed his now useless eye, pivoted and raked the table at his end. Screams, muzzle flashes and gunsmoke became inseparable.

Some board members died where they sat, others dove to the floor, where their backs presented wide, stationary targets for Timo and Pontos. A heavyset man in a black jogging suit clawed his way past the drapes and hammered at one of the heavy-tempered windows with his fists. When Matty shot him in the head, pieces of bone ejected upward, and neural viscera spattered the glass.

A middle-aged woman in a business suit ran directly at Matty, her mouth open in a harrowing scream. He put a burst into her chest, but she kept coming, still screaming. Pontos slammed rounds into her back, but they just propelled her faster, and her outstretched hands were almost touching Matty when he blew her face off.

The antique Rolls owner in the light blue suit tried to flee into the kitchen. Matty and Pontos both got him, and the combined concussive whiplash flung the man's bad rug across the room.

In less than a minute, it was over, and the Tatas were walking down opposite sides of the table, finishing off anybody who was still moving.

Matty stood over Eli, the still glowing laser lying next to the man's outstretched hand. "Crazy, stupid motherfucker!" he shouted, shoved another magazine in the AR and blasted what was left of Eli's head to pulp.

When he finished, Timo Tata was next to him. "Just remember, you're the one who went batshit, not us. So no deductions, *katavow*?"

CHAPTER TWENTY

Snubnoses and Yorkies

The hallway was as quiet as they'd left it. Timo and Pontos started toward the elevators, but Matty shook his head. "Check the restrooms." The Tata brothers moved quickly back down the long corridor next to the conference room. Matty stopped halfway and waited while Pontos entered one restroom, Timo the other.

The twin stalls in the men's room were empty, but Pontos pushed the doors open completely to be sure. Then, he stopped at one of the urinals to take a piss.

In the women's room, there were three stalls on the right side. The doors on the first two were ajar, the third, closed. Timo bent and saw a pair of black high heels under the locked door. He stayed against the sinks as he inched his way into position for a head-on volley into the soft metal.

Suddenly, an explosion ripped through the tiled room, so loud it seemed to move the building. A fist-sized hole ruptured the stall door, jagged shrapnel chasing a huge slug across the room and into Timo's jaw. The shot blew out the back of the Greek's skull along with most of its contents. A mist of blood rainbowed upward then fell slowly as Timo pitched forward, dead before what was left of his face crashed against the tile.

Matty went into the restroom, low and fast. Pontos, still working his zipper, was behind him. Seeing Timo on the floor, Matty raked all three stalls. Blue smoke swirled from his muzzle, and metal fragments ricocheted in all directions. Pontos charged into the middle stall, stepped on the toilet,

133

reached over the top and fired a burst into the locked stall without looking.

Another stupendous explosion rocked the room, and a second heavy bullet came through the stall's side panel. It caught Pontos in the shoulder, missing his vest and nearly ripping off his arm. He screamed and fell backwards into a corner.

With his ears ringing from concussion, Matty made his second major mistake of the last few minutes. He stood up.

Instantly, a third shot ripped out of the stall and hit the wall-length mirror inches from Matty's face. Thousands of razor-sharp shards sprayed outward, bombarding him from hairline to waistline.

Through his one good eye, the world went red again, then midnight black, and a hot, deep pain rushed through his brain, pushing aside what the laser had done. Matty's AR clattered to the floor as he clutched his face with both hands, blood pouring between his fingers. As a fourth and final blast shattered one of the porcelain sinks, Pontos stumbled out of the middle stall and used his good arm to guide Matty into the hallway and toward the elevators.

Behind them, in the women's room, the lock on the stall clicked, and the door swung open. Valentine Jones stepped out, a snubnose .357 Magnum hanging at her side.

Inside the DTS, it was chaos. Pontos drove, but his shredded left arm ran with blood, and stabs of pain caused him to lose focus and occasionally scream. Matty was still clutching his face and moaning.

"Where the fuck we goin?" yelled Pontos.

"Turn right, down the hill," Matty managed to get out.

Pontos exited the garage and executed the turn one-handed, but not without hitting a parked Camry across the street.

"Right at the first street, one block, then right again. Green building on the left. The Gardenia. Garage opener's on the dash."

The last thing Pontos expected when the elevator opened onto the second floor was some old broad carrying a Yorkshire Terrier. When she saw the bloody men, she screamed, and the terrier jumped at Pontos's face and sank its teeth into his cheek. With his good arm, he backhanded the little fucker down the hall then clocked the woman with a hard right to the jaw.

The dog came tearing back in a frenzy, yipping and nipping at his legs. He kicked at it but missed, and the mutt continued circling and attacking as Pontos stepped over the unconscious woman and led his blinded companion to Apartment 203.

"What's going on?" grunted Matty.

"Shut the fuck up, and give me the key."

Inside, Matty felt for a wall and guided himself across the living room to the sofa. Pontos went back for the woman. Her head had hit the tile floor, and there was a wet puddle gathering around her gray hair. Her tongue lolled out of the side of her mouth, her breathing coming in gasps.

Ignoring the crazed Yorkie, Pontos dragged her to the apartment and dumped her on the kitchen floor. He went back to deal with the dog, but it sensed danger and retreated out of reach. He opened the door to the emergency stairwell and chased it in. When the steel door slammed shut, the barking was muted to down to almost nothing.

The men had dripped a trail of red all the way from the car. They couldn't leave it that way. Pontos found the bathroom and wrapped an oversize towel around his dead arm then examined his cheek. The bite was already turning purple, but it wasn't bleeding excessively. He put his head sideways under the spigot and let cold water run over the wound until it went numb.

When he returned to the living room, Matty took his hands away from his face. "How do I look?"

Pontos wanted to say like a pound of fuckin hamburger but went with, "You ain't gonna die."

"You?"

"Cold as shit."

"Blood loss."

Like that was news, thought Pontos. "There a bucket in this joint?"

"What for?"

"I gotta clean up the mess we made comin in. The hallway's tile, but the cement in the garage is gonna take some work."

"Can you move the car over it?"

Pontos wasn't in the mood for second-guessing from a guy who couldn't help. "I'm a little tired of you right now, motherfucker, so shut the fuck up and let me handle it."

This was the second time Pontos Tata had asserted himself, and Matty didn't like it. You let things like that go unanswered, you ended up with problems. For the moment, though, he needed eyes. And he was right about the blood. It might be a while before they could get out of there. "Look under the kitchen sink, but before you leave, bring me the phone. There's a landline on the bar."

Matty carried a cell phone, but he didn't like using it. It took a lot of time and paperwork and some serious dancing in front of a judge to tap a landline. Then it was one line, one tap and go through the whole process again if the target changed locations. A cell phone was like stapling a homing beacon to your ass. It only took some cop with a laptop five minutes to find out what transponders it was bouncing off of and the numbers you were calling. They might not be on the line with you, but it was like handing a jury a roadmap.

Pontos had to push the woman out of the way to get to the bucket, and he noticed her breathing had fallen off to a whisper. Fuck her and her dog. There were a couple of sponges in the cabinet too, and while he let the bucket fill in the sink, he got the sponges wet and went back out.

The elevator was still open, and he went inside and wiped the tile floor and a couple of places on the wall where he'd bumped into it. Then he did the same down the hall to the apartment.

"I told you to bring me the phone," Matty snarled.

Pontos ignored him, turned off the water and rinsed the sponges. He noticed the blood was coming through the towel around his arm. It would have to wait. He crossed the living room, took the phone off the bar and dropped it in Matty's lap. The hitman winced but didn't say anything.

As soon as Pontos left with the bucket, Matty felt his way through the dial pad. It rang a long time on the other end before a young man's voice came on, "Papazian's."

"Put the Cypriot on."

It was just after three in the afternoon, and Matty was flying. Whatever the Cypriot had given him for the pain had hit that part of his brain reserved for the good stuff. He hadn't felt like this since that time in Philly when they'd given him straight pharma morphine after he'd been stabbed in the belly.

Matty was in the backseat of an SUV. That much he knew from having to step up into it. He also knew the time, because one of the guys with the Cypriot had told him. He hadn't heard any shots, but he knew Pontos and the woman were dead, probably in the trunk of the DTS. That had been part of his instructions.

The other part was that the Cypriot should bring somebody to clean the apartment who knew how to keep his mouth shut. The Cypriot was upstairs handling that now. A few minutes went by, and Matty heard the elevator then footsteps. Somebody got in the passenger seat—somebody heavy. The SUV started, and the sound of the garage gate going up was unmistakable.

"I don't know what went wrong," said Matty.

"You got old fast. Happens."

"Gotta figure it out. Can't fuck up again," Matty said, feeling his words slur.

"Shit," laughed the Cypriot, "you sound like you're talkin underwater. You're gonna be out of it for a few hours, so just lay back and enjoy the ride."

"Somebody took my eyes. They took my fuckin eyes."

"Lay back, my man. Think about that Mediterranean sun. The Cypriot's here now, and everything's under control."

CHAPTER TWENTY-ONE

London in Laguna

MARCH 14, 1935
LAGUNA BEACH, CALIFORNIA

The storm was Barrie's worst enemy and best friend. Fighting what was left of the de Havilland through the slamming winds, she had to use every ounce of strength just to keep from spiraling out of control. Most of the time she couldn't even see the plane's nose through the curtains of rain. But that also meant she was out of sight from the ground, and the almost continuous thunder obscured the stuttering, uneven struggle of her remaining engine.

She turned off what was left of the radio and touched the edge of her parachute. Barrie never wore one in flight. Besides being uncomfortable, she didn't think it sent much of a message to passengers if they thought the pilot had an out. She doubted she could even get the chute on with the plane being tossed around like it was, but it was reassuring knowing it was there. Then, just when she thought the sky couldn't get any darker, it did.

The newest squall didn't last very long, but a series of updrafts pushed her a thousand feet higher where the thunderhead roared so loud it made her ears hurt.

Twice before, Barrie had felt raw terror in a plane. Once, when clear air turbulence almost upended the Trimotor and a second time when a passenger threw a lighted cigarette in the restroom trash and the tail section nearly burned off. This was different, less immediately intense but seemingly never-ending.

She reached into the webbing under her seat, hoping to find the small flask commonly carried by American pilots. Not only was there one, it was full-size. Apparently, the Brits sometimes needed a little nerve juice too.

The stuff was strong—and bad. Cheap gin. On her empty stomach, the burn quickly gave way to a dull, queasy glow that pushed past the adrenaline and let her take stock of the plane and herself. The blood on her flight suit had washed away, and she felt no further pain. Her compass said she was headed southwest, and though the buffeting was swinging her from side to side, she was able to hold a course close to true.

Once she adjusted to the rhythm of the swaying, she decided to gamble. Tucking the flask back under the seat and clutching the stick with her knees, she unhooked her harness, leaned forward and swung the bulky parachute over her shoulders. Only then did she realize that one of its straps was jammed into the hatch release, and there was no chance of freeing it in her current position.

There wasn't much left of the canopy anyway, so she grabbed the lever with both hands and jerked hard. Ripped free by the wind, the six-foot long section of glass and steel barely missed her head as it tumbled away. One arm still in her chute, she grabbed onto the stick to keep from being sucked out in the initial blast. After it subsided, she fought the remaining parachute strap over her shoulder, snapped the clasps home and refastened her harness.

The coast was ahead somewhere, and she had to be careful not to overshoot it. About thirty minutes later, a pair of pelicans appeared alongside, riding the gusts as they unhurriedly made their way toward some eating destination. Seagulls travel hundreds of miles inland, but pelicans stay close to water, so Barrie tilted the nose of the Comet down.

Whitecaps came visible at a hundred feet. Barrie turned south and shortly came upon a long string of jagged rocks jutting upward from the water. The clouds began to thin, and eventually, the rocks merged with a wide beach bracketed on the landward side by high, dirt cliffs. On the road above, a milk truck plodded along, its wiper blades pushing the rain off the windshield. The peaceful normalcy of the scene seemed surreal.

Until Barrie met Danny Dades, she had never heard of Laguna Beach. From a tiny patch of turn-of-the-century, hillside-hugging homesteaders dispensing gasoline and sandwiches to Angelenos heading to the playgrounds of San Diego and Tijuana, by the early 1920s, Laguna had become a destination *itself. Tiny motor courts, rooming houses and places to pull trailers directly onto the sand attracted weekenders who slogged out livings in the oilfields to the north and the farms to the east. Here, barefoot men in work overalls watched their children play in the waves while their wives cooked on open fires. At night, groups of families sat together, roasting marshmallows, telling stories and singing songs under constellations close enough to touch.*

Not long after, Hollywood stars, millionaire businessmen and land-rich ranchers began building their own homes in Laguna to while away the hot summer months. A decade later, many were living there permanently. Where money settles, artists follow, and painters, sculptors, woodworkers and assorted bohemian hangers-on pitched tents among the oceanfront rocks and up the canyons, gradually fabricating shacks from driftwood, scavenged glass and corrugated tin. They worked by day, and nights were filled with music, drink, Mexican reefer and free-spirited sexual encounters in various combinations.

Now Barrie searched for the navy and white awnings of the landmark Deep Blue Inn. Danny's house on the hill was amazing, but she preferred hearing the waves outside her window. So at least one night each trip, she and Danny stayed in the gorgeous, whitewashed hotel terraced down to the sea. They ate room service steaks, drank white wine and made love on the balcony. The thought of doing that tonight had kept her going.

Then, suddenly, directly below, Barrie saw a man in a suit standing on the edge of the surf. He had a gun in his hand, and he was taking careful aim at something out in the water. When he heard the de Havilland, it broke his concentration, and he lifted his head toward her.

Barrie looked out the other side. Twenty yards offshore, a woman in a green satin evening gown was running as fast as she could through knee-deep swells, the terror on her face evident. Without hesitating, Barrie threw what was left of the Comet into a steep bank. The plane groaned and creaked, and the remaining engine coughed and began to lose power. She coaxed it past its stall point and came level again.

By the time she returned to the spot where she had seen the man, he was running up a path cut into the cliff-face, still carrying the gun. A long, red Packard convertible sat parked above, top down, both front doors open. But when Barrie looked back toward the water, the woman in the green dress was gone.

Then all hell broke loose. Barrie never saw any smoke, but one moment she was beginning her turn to the south again and, the next, a blast of flame shot out from under the instrument panel and swept around her, fed by the unimpeded outside air. Fire seared her boots, and she smelled the smoldering wool of her flight suit.

Instinctively, she jerked the stick all the way back, pointing the de Havilland's nose almost straight up, simultaneously feeding the remaining Gipsy Six as much fuel as it would take. At the apex of her climb, when she could stand the heat no longer, she unbuckled her harness and rolled the plane all the way over.

As Barrie fell free, the flame-engulfed Comet continued gaining altitude then began to follow its natural trajectory and returned in her direction. After all she had been through, she thought, wouldn't it be an ironic ending, if she were mown down by her own ride. She pulled the chute's cord, and it snapped her skyward with such force that she lost consciousness.

The wet sand felt good on her face, better still on her legs. Whoever was bathing them was her favorite person in the world. Barrie heard the surf, and it sounded very close. She remembered swimming in the ocean in the recent past, but she couldn't remember where. New York, maybe. No, that wasn't it. Finally, it came to her. Havana.

She fought one eye open, but it was too much effort to focus. Then she heard a voice. "Miss, can you hear me? Miss? Miss?"

Barrie opened both eyes this time. She was on her right side, and foamy seawater swirled under her chin then receded. She waited, and it happened again. Barrie realized the lower half of her body was in the water, and a dark shape was looming over her. She tilted her head to see what it was.

Kneeling beside her was the woman in the green dress, her hair hanging in soggy tangles. "Well, thank God for that," she said. "After dragging you up here, I'd have been real bitchy if you'd been dead."

Barrie lightly grasped the woman's wrist. "How about you?"

She laughed. "Are you kidding? The only thing that can kill a screenwriter is a bad director."

Barrie wasn't sure what to make of that answer. "I need to stand."

"Let's get that damned parachute off first. It nearly pulled us both under, and the color doesn't do anything for your eyes."

The woman unhooked it and worked the straps off Barrie's shoulders. With some effort, Barrie rose, first to a knee, then all the way. Other than a banger of a headache, everything seemed to be working. No bones were broken, but her boots had been burned down to the fleece lining, and the woolen legs of her flight suit were charred. She bent and pulled at the fabric near the knee. It crumbled in her hand. Underneath, her skin was red but undamaged. She pinched it, and it hurt, but only superficially.

Barrie took a few tentative steps. Sand chafed the insides of her thighs, but it was a small irritation, considering. For the first time, she looked closely at her rescuer. Barrie guessed her age at roughly ten years older than herself. Late thirties, no more. But still exquisite, even soaked to the skin. Dark-haired and considerably taller, she was delicate-boned and perfectly proportioned, and her dress was clearly couture. Barrie had seen similar ones at the Hotel Nacional, but only on the wealthiest guests. Her diamond necklace and bracelet were, at a minimum, Tiffany, and on her left ankle, she wore a tiny, silver flying bird on a matching silver chain.

The woman saw Barrie staring and raised her bare foot slightly to show it off. "Like it?" she asked.

"I do. Very much."

"My own design. I call it Wings of Submission. See, rather than fly free, my little bird has chosen to adorn me."

Barrie thought that was about the oddest thing she'd ever heard, so she just nodded. "A thank you doesn't seem enough for what you did."

"It's probably not, but until we find a bar…" She laughed as she extended her hand. "Lakeland London. Just Lake to my friends."

Barrie took the hand. "Barrie Fontaine."

"What a fabulous name. A movie star name. And you're quite the hot little fly-girl—even wet—if you don't mind my saying so."

Barrie didn't know what to say to that either. But the woman's voice and that she held their handshake well beyond what would have been considered cordial made her feel strange inside. Maybe she was just traumatized from hitting the water.

"But you're not from around here, are you? I hear New York in that voice."

Lake London may have saved her life and flattered her drowned rat appearance, but Barrie wasn't looking for a confidante. "You wouldn't happen to know where the Deep Blue Inn is, would you?"

Lake pointed down the beach. "About two miles thataway."

"You up for a hike?" Barrie asked.

"I've got a better idea." Lake put her hand inside the low-cut neckline of her dress, fished around and came out with a key dangling from another of her silver birds. "Let's drive. Not only is Conrad a lousy lay AND a lousy shot, now he has to hoof it home."

"Aren't you afraid he might be nearby, waiting?"

Lake looked at her like she'd just heard the dumbest thing anybody'd ever said. "He's an actor, dear. Once he sobers up, he'll get busy looking at himself in the mirror and forget what day it is."

Barrie burst out laughing "You're really something."

"Everybody in movies is really something, honey; that's the problem. By the way, the tide's coming in. You want to leave a mark on the cliff so you can find that later?" She pointed toward the ocean.

Barrie turned and saw the blue tail section of the de Havilland protruding from the water, not more than fifty yards out. "You up for another swim?" she asked.

Lake held her arms outstretched so the full impact of her barefoot wetness was evident. "How could I say no?" She laughed with abandon. "While we're out there, maybe we'll find whatever's wearing my goddamn heels."

When she and Lake got to the Comet, the cockpit was already full of water, and each time the surf retreated, the plane slipped a little further under. "The locals say there's a steep drop-off out here somewhere," Lake offered, but Barrie ignored her.

She leveraged herself into the back seat and felt around in the hold with her foot. She then ducked her head under, unhooked her flight bag and handed it over the transom to Lake. As she did, she saw the older woman staring at dozens of hundred dollar bills floating on the surface.

"You rob a bank?" Lake asked, only half-joking.

"Unless you're Pan Am, refueling is a cash business. My money box must have broken open."

Barrie didn't know if the woman believed her or not, but Lake began gathering up the bills she could reach. While she was occupied, Barrie went back underwater. It was murky, and the cargo had shifted. The suitcase that had burst open in the storm was gone, probably having floated away. For several, long, anxious moments, she couldn't locate the Benedict Crown attaché, and her heart began to sink. Then, just as her oxygen was about to fail, her finger caught one of the case's straps. She dragged it out, got it open and slipped the necklace down the top of her flight suit, surprised at how heavy it was.

After surfacing for another breath, she managed to pull the remaining suitcase of cash out of the deep recesses of the hold. Enough air remained inside to give it some buoyancy, and she was able to get it up and out of the plane, letting its considerable weight take her with it.

As the two women headed back to shore, they heard a crack followed by a groan, like a great dying beast. They turned and watched Howard Hughes's formerly new toy slip into a watery grave.

CHAPTER TWENTY-TWO

Day Managers and Far, Far Away

THE DEEP BLUE INN
LAGUNA BEACH

After what Barrie'd been through, entering the lush lobby of the Inn made her lightheaded. It was hard to believe that only a few days earlier, she'd been going about her business in Cuba, blithely unaware of how close she was to a slit throat and a shark-food burial. Now, she was safe, and her old life was gone forever, but at this moment, she was too tired to rejoice.

The imperious, young desk clerk wasn't pleased to see two drenched women, lugging a dripping suitcase and soggy flight bag across his Spanish tile, and he made no attempt to disguise his disdain. Before either could speak, he held up his palm. "You ladies will be much more comfortable at the trailer park on the beach. I'll have the bellman give you directions. Do run along now."

Barrie was too exhausted to argue. Lake was another story. Ignoring the brass sign on the counter that read, SCOTTY, she locked eyes with him. "What's your fuckin name, Junior?"

Flustered, the clerk managed a weak, "Excuse me?"

"Excuse you is right, you rude little fruit. I asked you a question."

"Scotty," he said, pointing to the sign, his demeanor now less certain. "I'm the day manager."

"Well, Scotty, do you know who the fuck I am?"

Scotty wasn't doing too well in his new role as supplicant. "I'm... I'm sorry, ma'am," he stuttered, "I'm new here. I..."

"Where's Julius?"

Scotty lost most of his color. "Mr. Burke?"

"No, Julius Fucking Caesar, asshole," she sneered. "Of course Burke."

"He's at our Newport Beach property."

"Well, you better find him—fast. And when you do, you tell him that if the broad who financed this joint doesn't get an apology from SCOTTY, THE DAY FUCKIN MANAGER in the next sixty seconds, I'm gonna call the loan then get on the horn with that wide-ass wife of his and run down the hit parade of cooze he brings to my place to bang."

And presto, Barrie was swept to a four-room oceanfront suite with a fireplace already burning. Five minutes later, chilled Dom Perignon and two tins of caviar followed, carried by a waiter who bowed so low, his chin almost scraped carpet. Barrie imagined Scotty throwing up in the cash register.

Lake had gone home, which she said was a few miles down the coast, but she promised to be back at seven to take Barrie to the *"best damn French dinner in California."*

Barrie was supposed to call Danny Dades as soon as she arrived. At least, that's what they'd discussed from Corpus Christi. But she'd been cautious even then. She hadn't told him when or where she was going to ditch Rollo. First, because she hadn't figured it out yet, and second, because all she really knew about Danny was that he was handsome, lived in a fancy house and the sex was good—or as good as she was used to.

Now, however, as she stood looking at the phone, she reminded herself that Danny was a craps dealer. He could have called Cuba as soon as they'd hung up. After all, who did he need more, Luciano or a broad on the run? She decided to get a good night's sleep then decide.

When Barrie opened the thigh pocket of her flight suit, the charred wool again fell apart in her fingers. Miraculously, the waterproof wallet was only singed, and the two halves of the Stinson note, along with her flying license and passport had survived. She put the wallet and the .357 in the nightstand drawer. The remnants of her suit and the rest of what she was wearing went into a brown paper bag she found in the closet, which she set it in the hall to be taken away.

The waiter who'd brought the champagne sent up a valet to retrieve her wet things. He gave her a terrycloth bathrobe with *Deep Blue Inn* stitched over the breast pocket and promised to have her clothes back by seven, cleaned and pressed. However, when he'd tried to set her suitcase on a stand to open it, Barrie wrestled it out of his hand with far more force than necessary. To apologize, she tipped him one of the wet C-notes Lake had rescued, and he went away smiling.

After a long, hot shower, her hair wrapped in a towel, Barrie appreciated her nakedness in the bathroom's full-length mirror. She had taken the time to shave her pussy—twice—and she let her fingers linger over her its smoothness, finally feeling civilized again.

Crossing to the table where she'd left the Star of Havana, she stared at it for a long time. Then, on impulse, she clasped it around her neck and walked from room to room, admiring herself in every mirror she could find. Barrie had always thought her eyes were too far apart, her cheekbones too prominent, but men and women alike called her exotic, mysterious.

At the same time, she was proud of her exceptionally long, dark brown nipples, pleased that wherever they had come from, they were a gift she would not trade for narrower eyes and a more conventional look. Now, she rolled the sensitive protrusions between her fingers, bringing them to their full extension, and thought they—and her face—set off the blue diamonds perfectly.

She poured herself a flute of champagne, dragged the suitcase onto the white bearskin rug in front of the fireplace and opened it. Barrie was no stranger to suitcases of cash; she'd certainly flown enough of them. But this one was different. It was hers, and it took a while before she could bring herself to touch what was inside.

When she did, she discovered that the bills on the top and bottom were soaked, but the three-inch stacks had been banded together so tightly that only the edges of the interior ones had gotten wet. She removed each packet and built several tall piles, laying them two-across in alternating directions like Lincoln Logs. Then sitting back with her champagne and an open tin of caviar, she licked a tongue full of roe and chased it with French bubbly.

She was a long way from home, and it felt fine. Just fine.

Barrie awakened in the dark to a pair of warm hands on her breasts, pinching her nipples though fingers curled into tight fists. Barrie drew in her breath as her head spun, and her vision blurred. Lake London's perfume was subtle, citrusy and intoxicating. The lips that lingered on Barrie's neck were the softest she had ever known, and the tongue that traced around each diamond in her necklace, electric.

Through the exquisite pain in her nipples, she became aware again of Lake's long handshake and the confusion she had felt. Something was happening inside her that she had never experienced before. This wasn't like the seductions of her blackmail targets. That had been going to a job. To be sure, she had participated in the sex with enthusiasm, reached climaxes and even engaged in pillow talk. But it had always been business.

At this moment, however, Barrie was completely defenseless. Lake could do almost anything to her, and she wouldn't stop her. No, that was wrong. Not almost. She wouldn't stop her even if she were about to kill her. She would beg her to make it last as long as possible. It was that kind of surrender.

"Your nipples are extraordinary," Lake said huskily. "I thought you might want me to hurt them. Was I right?"

Barrie tried to say yes, but managed only a nod and a whimper.

"I'm so glad," Lake purred as she balled her fists tighter, and Barrie groaned, clasping her own hands over Lake's fists and pinching the tips that protruded through the other woman's fingers. She fought for breath as she bucked through an orgasm. "Yes! Yes! Hurt me!"

"Don't worry, my darling, I won't stop. Come again. Go ahead, I'm right here." Lake put her tongue in Barrie's mouth and swirled it around her lips as Barrie came once more, every muscle in her body shaking.

When she started to ease down, Lake whispered in her ear, "Have you ever had your pussy loved, sweet one? I mean really loved. By someone who wants it more than life itself?"

Barrie was helpless to answer. In the light of the last flickering embers of the fire, she saw Lake pulling off her own dress as she went down on her, Lake's long, lean body as taut and sensual as her younger partner's.

"Oh, how wonderful, you're shaved," Lake breathed into her skin. Then the tip of her warm tongue flicked Barrie's clitoris, and something cold and hard

and slippery slid ever so slowly into her rear. "Do you like that, my love?"

"God, oh God, yes, what is it?" Barrie gasped as she pressed her hips down, making it go deeper.

"Your gun. And it's cocked. I think sex is always better when it's dangerous, don't you?"

Barrie moaned from deep in her soul, and she began to work her own nipples. She lay all the way back and went someplace far away. The best place she had ever been.

CHAPTER TWENTY-THREE

Area Commanders and Do-Gooders

I got the news about Teddy Chessman the long way around: Venice to London to Santa Monica. Sir Gregory Bone, Black Group's managing director, received a call from a Banca Passavanti executive informing him that three Passavanti family members, their bodyguards and several other people had been killed at the Colosseum Pictures offices. The executive had no further details, only that the duchessa was aware of my investment on behalf of Mr. Chessman and wished to convey her concern for my safety. She had gone into seclusion.

Bone immediately placed calls to all my numbers and, when he was unable to locate me, phoned the dockmaster at the yacht club. Hearing that the *Sanrevelle* was buttoned up tight in her slip, Bone next tried the operations manager at Santa Monica Airport.

When the call came in, I was five thousand feet above the tower, while my two pilots, Jody Miller and Eddie Buffalo, were being recertified by the FAA. The inspector performing the checkride, a florid-faced Irishman named McMannis, was pleasant enough but more interested in how much my Boeing cost than the competence of the men up front.

That was okay with me. Jody and Eddie are as good as it gets, and the BBJ is a remarkable plane. "If it ain't Boeing, I ain't going," isn't just a clever saying. Ask any professional. Scarebus doesn't belong in the same sentence. Things are better in the private aircraft world, but only the BBJ has the dimensions someone my size needs not to feel claustrophobic. You pay for the privilege, but the range, speed and quiet more than compensate.

Still, I never look at the maintenance bills. Some things are better left to the accountants.

Jody and Eddie were performing the last of their required touch-and-goes while McMannis and I were belted into a pair of oversized, red and black leather seats in the main cabin. We were just climbing out of the final touchdown when Eddie came over the intercom. "Boss, the tower says you have an important call, but you'll have to land. It's against FAA regs to patch it through during a checkride."

There weren't any cell phones onboard either for the same reason. I picked up the handset next to my seat, "Whoever it is will have to wait. I don't want to sit three months for a reschedule." I looked at our guest of honor. "What's the verdict, Chief?"

The inspector had one eye on my well-stocked bar and another on his watch. "You're good to go, and I'm off-duty, so why don't we break open that bottle of Bushmills."

"There's probably some Jerry's Deli in the fridge too," I said.

"Make mine a corned beef, and if your arm gets tired pouring, switch hands."

I went back to the receiver, "Tell the tower we're swinging around Catalina to do a little whale-watching."

Jody didn't get it. "Say what, boss?"

"Give us an hour." I looked at McMannis to see if that was enough time, and he gave me a nod and smile as wide as the whiskey I was about to hand him.

By the time Sir Gregory and I finally spoke, he'd been called by Area Commander K.O. Rampulla of the LA Sheriff's Department. "When you find Mr. Black, tell him I want his ass at the West Hollywood station—*now*. And that means ten minutes ago, or I'll send a couple of deputies to round him up. Is that clear?"

My backing of Teddy's buyout hadn't been publicized, so the commander could only have known about me from Jake. Thanks, counselor. I wasn't too surprised about the attitude, though. My reputation among the local constabulary is spotty. On their better days, a lot of them consider me a jerk.

Sir Gregory wasn't much impressed with K.O.'s tone, so he gave him a little upper class British fuck you, "I was just going to ring the sheriff about this Colosseum unpleasantness. We entertained him and his wife on his recent trip to London, you know. I'm certain he'll be pleased to hear you're treating Mr. Black like a suspect. May I please get the correct spelling of your name?"

There had been silence, then a gruff, "Please have Mr. Black get in touch with me… at his—and the sheriff's—convenience, of course."

I have enormous respect for most law enforcement, but when the fire is the hottest, their hearing disappears. If they were this anxious to talk to *me*, it was like announcing they were flying blind. I had nothing meaningful to tell them; the problem was that the sooner I went to the station, the longer it would take them to figure it out. Sir Gregory had bought me some time without having to be asked. It's why he was head of Black Group.

The radio in my Ram was blaring breathless reports on what was being called the Sunset Blvd. Massacre. Anyone who thought Colosseum Pictures might be included in the label didn't live in LA. Paramount or Columbia, absolutely. A mini-major like Colosseum? No marquee value. But SoCal headline writers know that if you throw in one of our signature locations, you're the lead story from Melrose to Madagascar. The movie was probably already in development at five studios.

The published body count was nineteen. The victims' identities were being officially withheld in the kind of twenty-first century fool's errand only the most simpleminded public information officer could be handed. The Internet ghouls had ferreted out a list of fourteen names, addresses and bios within the first hour. The newsreader was throwing up solemn disclaimers but repeating every detail. You could almost hear the guy's erection.

In addition to Teddy Chessman and Eli Zodsky who had been Colosseum's CFO, all twelve board members were dead. Though some of the names were familiar, I didn't know any of them personally. Nine were local, and the three Passavanti brothers were being trumpeted as Italian royalty. Five victims remained unidentified, which could mean anything, but I had confidence the nerds hacking into databases would let us know shortly. Black Group's reporters would be on it too.

The last time a crime in LA reached this level of shrill, O.J. was about to get away with a double murder. The time prior, the Menendez brothers weren't. But both of those were before 24-hour news. Now, I could picture sweat-drenched reporters around the world running for planes. It wouldn't be long before one of them found out about my investment, then my picture would be running alongside those of the victims.

"Rich Man's Curse," my father called it. No matter how tangential, if you had money and could be connected to something unsavory, you became the story. There was a certain irony to it this time, inasmuch as Black Group owned more media properties than almost anyone, meaning many of those overheated word-hustlers winging their way toward LAX were on my payroll. I made a mental note get my own spin out before I ended up on defense.

I thought about calling Mallory and warning him to get himself and Wind out of the house, but after the Paulie Stuben publicity, they were probably better off where they were. I stopped at a Shell station on Bundy, and while the pump ran, I went inside for a pack of Turkish Golds. The cashier, a dirty-looking guy named Dudi, handed back my change in a haphazard clump of coins and bills, making it inevitable some was going to hit the floor.

Change counted correctly into your palm, accompanied by a smile and thank you, disappeared when electronic cash registers took math—and civilization—out of retail. A world-class pain in the ass I know, Benny Joe Willis, purposely drops everything behind the counter at least once so the clerk has to chase it around. However, the Waffen SS tat on Dudi's chin and his double-studded, split tongue argued against that message penetrating, so I juggled my money back to the Ram.

My phone was ringing when I got there. Jake. "I assume you've heard?"

"What, that my overpaid attorney has a hotline to the sheriff's department? Commander Rampulla sends his regards."

"Here's some news, ass breath, the cops have computers. Anybody with a parking pass is in the system, and I told Teddy to put us both on the Colosseum list. So how long do you think it took some rookie deputy to run down the hall screaming, 'Holy shit, that dimwit Black is mixed up in this.'"

So now the G even knew where I parked? Thanks, Osama. "Put the insult in a drawer, you'll earn it back. What do you want?"

"There are two dozen pieces of shit calling themselves reporters clogging up my lobby. They can't find you, and they're looking for some kind of comment. Fuck comments, that's PR work. I make statements."

"Get to the point, Counselor."

"We have a ninety-day due diligence window on the Colosseum deal. My housekeeper could draft paper to get you out of it. What say we save a hundred million? You still feel generous, you can cover what Teddy owed me."

I ignored him. "Tell me about Ross Dare."

It took a while, but he finally answered. "Dare's as smart as they come but an asshole."

That meant he'd beaten Jake in a deal, something that doesn't happen often. I liked him already. "Look in the mirror, I collect smart assholes. So why did this one leave the fast track to work for an ex-con?"

"Two words: Star Cock. He doesn't have one."

"Use language I understand."

"His schwantz doesn't bang the underside of his desk when some thirty-mil-a-picture douchebag walks through the door. He'll overpay for material, but when it comes to actors, you work at his price, or he casts down."

"Even I can figure this one out. The agents killed him."

"If there's one thing an A-lister can't stand, it's watching a dream role go to the second string. But they get over it quicker than their reps do. Aspen lodges and Tuscan wineries are maintained by packaging fees.

Ratchet down too many budgets, and the next thing you know, you're skiing Vail and drinking Californian."

"So Ross moves someplace he can call the shots."

"The guy's a brand machine. He turns half-ass song titles into five picture franchises. A decade from now, he won't be working for a studio, he'll own one."

That sounded familiar, and it sounded even better coming from Jake. "I want to meet him."

"If that means you're keeping Colosseum, take back dimwit and insert dumb fuck."

"Where's that on the scale of banging a judge's wife? Take out a pen, here's what you're going to do."

"Fuck your scale and your pen. You don't know enough words I can't remember them."

"I need to be able to operate without finding the media camped on my doorstep, so call Sir Gregory in London and tell him Black Group is to proceed with the Colosseum deal, but he's to do it in the dark. Use a cutout, and run the transaction through a country where I don't have any holdings. It also might be a good idea to walk the money around a few time zones first, just to remove any remaining fingerprints. Bone will know how.

"Then get in touch with the managing director of Banca Passavanti and tell him that no matter what he hears, reads or somebody whispers in the john, nothing's changed, and he's to assure the duchessa that I'm in this with her—all the way. More, if necessary."

"I think you're..."

I cut him off in a voice I rarely use. "Jake, I don't give a fat fuck what you think. If you say one more word, Marvin Oxford is my new lawyer."

Being very rich has its moments. After the previous conversation we'd had about helping others, he was treading gingerly. The one more word didn't come, so I continued. "Then powder your face, zip up your fly, march downstairs and issue this *statement*: 'Mr. Black extends his deepest condolences to the families of the victims of the Colosseum Pictures tragedy. He had contemplated buying a stake in the company, but under current circumstances that will not be taking place. All discussions, preliminary though they were, have been terminated.'"

"There'll be hell to pay when the press finds out we lied to them."

"And what's *that* penalty? They won't eat as many shrimp at our next premier?"

"You'll sing a different tune when awards season rolls around. Anything else?"

"Yes, I want to know everything there is to know about Teddy Chessman's private life. But you've got time on that. Right now, text me Ross Dare's number and tell him I'll be in touch. And Jake..."

"What?"

"You're probably right about everything, but the Passavantis and Blacks have a history."

"Blessed be the do-gooders, for they shall insert the dildo into the rest of us."

CHAPTER TWENTY-FOUR

Doctors and Writers

My house and Jake's were out of the question. So was a hotel. All were in the sequence of places an intrepid investigator would check. When you want to be invisible in LA, hang with a writer. In this case, a writer who used to be a veterinarian. Maybe one who is also a passable poker player.

Cortez Detroit lives in the penthouse of one of the Wilshire Corridor high-rises. In a city not known for stacked living, the one-mile stretch between Beverly Hills and Westwood is our version of Sutton Place. Billy Wilder used to live in the same building, and his eye for art made him far wealthier than his movies did. Cortez's assemblage of vintage detective novels doesn't have the same wow factor, but auctioneers who know about it are chasing him for the day he goes to the big Dewey Decimal System in the sky.

The first thing you encounter when you enter his 6000-sq. ft. duplex is a life-size black and white photo of a cigarette-smoking Dashiell Hammett standing back-to-back with Raymond Chandler, pipe clenched between his teeth. It's an engineered picture, but I've told Cortez all he has to do is name his price. So far, silence.

There have been at least three Mrs. Detroits, and I have no idea what happened to any of them. Cortez doesn't have a backyard, so I assume they left. But as much as I like him, I'm always edgy when I visit. Eighteen glass stories up only a few miles from the San Andreas Fault is something I can't put out of my mind. Especially since earthquakes seem to follow me. I rode the Northridge one halfway across my bedroom, and that's only on the second floor. From Cortez's place, a good shaker might get me to the Palisades. He says I could read *The Maltese Falcon* again on the way. Amusing chaps, millionaire writers.

Just as I pulled into the high-rise's circular drive, the guy on the radio began panting. "I've just been handed something incredible! There are two *survivors* of the massacre! One's a receptionist! We don't know about the other! Stay tuned, we're on it!"

Despite the extra chrome on my Ram, the valet looked at it like I'd come to a state dinner with a turd on my shoe. Then he took in my height and the bill in my hand and found his Ben Franklin smile. "I'll keep it close, sir."

"Close is fine, but out of sight. In case my wife drives by."

He winked at our newfound bond. "Absolutely, sir."

As I started in, my cell rang again. It was a blocked number, so I almost didn't answer, then decided it probably wasn't the cops. It wasn't. It was Wind, and her voice sounded on the edge of hysteria.

"Uncle Rail, Uncle Mallory says I have to ask you if I can use one of the cars."

There had to be more to the call than that. Mallory has free run of everything, including my cars. He normally drives the red Navigator, which is what Wind had been using too, but there are a couple of dozen vehicles in the underground garage, including some rare ones, and they're all available. If you can't drive them, what's the point?

"Take a breath, Wind."

I waited while she composed herself. "Okay, I'm better now."

"Where are you headed?"

"To the hospital." She paused. "I think one of my friends is there."

"Anybody I know?"

"I don't think so. Glenda Van Allen. She used to be my personal assistant. When her mother was diagnosed with dementia, she didn't want to be on the road anymore, so I got her a job as a receptionist at Colosseum. Mallory and I have been watching all the stuff on TV, and they just said…"

"I heard it too. Do you know which hospital?"

"I called her roommate. She's trying to find out."

The only thing that could make the press even more berserk was being able to add Wind Fortune to the story. "Find out what you can, then stay put. I'll call you back."

"But Uncle Rail, I've got to do something."

"Wind, please don't argue. I'll call soon, I promise. Let me speak with Mallory."

Momentarily, the Brit's voice returned, "I assume you scotched the idea."

"For the moment. How's she doing?"

"The medication has eased some of the worst of the mood swings, but she still complains about being desperately lonely. The doctor said that would happen, but if it gets worse, we're supposed to call."

I understood. Unrelenting loneliness is a well-trod road to suicide. "She needs to be busier, but not making movies. I'll be back in touch in a little while."

In war, you see, hear and smell things you would otherwise never notice. It's the brain's way of helping you stay alive. Trained properly, it also shuts out distractions. Pilots can see their buddies blown out of the sky but continue flying into heavy flack. It's why the conventional military drills you until your eyes cross, then drills you some more.

Delta Force is different. Special operations training is designed to find a man's breaking point then exceed it. Not because of some macho bonding ritual. The cowboys and loners have been weeded out long before their first sleep-deprived, ice cold, nighttime, underwater infiltration exercise. But because first you have to experience your limit—which is often much closer than a man thinks it is—then you have to learn to work on the other side as effectively as when your belly's full and you just got laid.

Sooner or later, every Delta operator is going to find himself beyond hunger, fatigue, pain, isolation and sensory intake. His equipment will have failed, and his last drop of adrenaline will have been spent. He will know he's never going home, but he will also know that the only thing standing between completion of the mission and the oblivion of failure is him. Delta isn't about getting out alive—it's about getting the job done. If you survive, it's a bonus, but don't expect it to become a habit.

I didn't like what I felt right now. Nothing. Not anger, not sadness, not even curiosity. The familiar cloak of inevitability had descended over me, bringing with it the simple vacancy of the professional. I'd been here far too often. Being several years older made me wilier, but a recently-noticed leadenness in my legs wasn't a plus. Then there was the stupidity of my recent plunge into the Pacific.

There were a lot of reasons to walk away from this mess, which couldn't do anything but get worse. Watch from the sidelines. Let the cops do their job. Something about it bothered me, though. Not the deaths, as violent as they had been. I barely knew Teddy, and the others were just names. And certainly not because I had an agenda with Colosseum. Jake could get me out without losing a cent. Hell, he'd probably figure out a way to make something on the deal.

Area Commander Rampulla's bad attitude wasn't it either. He was under pressure to show he was on the job. Besides, when did my skin get so thin? No, this was something else. I just hoped it wasn't what I thought.

The desk attendant eyed me suspiciously as sometimes happens because of my size. Usually by a short guy with issues. "Yeah?" he asked with something less than a smile.

"Dr. Detroit, please."

He called upstairs, got an okay then made me show my ID and sign a visitor's log. When he came around the desk, I was right. Five-two, max. At the elevator, he looked me up and down once more then leaned in, swiped a key card over the panel and stepped back out, frowning.

The lift rose swiftly, and deposited me in the penthouse foyer. From a security standpoint, one-to-a-floor condos seem like a good idea, but any big-city cop will tell you there's no such thing as random high-rise crime. A few are committed by invited guests of residents; most are an employee whose background check was ignored.

Cortez was waiting at the door. We shook hands. "That kind of shit happen to white guys?" He lifted his eyes toward the ceiling. I glanced at the twin security cameras. One was aimed properly at the elevator, but the second, supposedly covering the rest of the foyer, was pointed straight up. "Chick hit it with a laptop," he said, shaking his head in disbelief.

"You bullshit a woman who throws things, she doesn't check your skin color during her windup."

Just inside the door sat a pair of Tumi suitcases with a garment bag draped over them. "Going somewhere?"

"Haven't unpacked from Buenos Aires. Even with my genius, the picture's still gonna be a piece of shit. So what brings you to high country in the middle of earthquake season?"

"Thanks for mentioning it."

"I love seeing Mr. Delta twitch when the floor creaks. By the way, that was something with Morrie, wasn't it? You ever see that Nicaraguan trim he was banging? Fuckin shame to waste her too."

"You and Jake should maybe vacation together. You been watching the news?"

"If you mean Colosseum, pretty hard to miss. I liked Teddy's balls, but there was a crazy gene wandering around in there too. I'm not the only one who's thinking it was just a matter of time before he fucked with the wrong guy."

I didn't like what I was hearing. "You really think somebody killed all those people because a movie producer was a prick? Where the fuck's your head, Cortez?"

He looked like I'd punched him, which was my intent. "Damn it, Rail, I've been sitting here thinking how if I'd taken that writing gig he offered, I could have been one of them. I'm trying not to show how shook up I am."

"For yourself. You disappoint me."

"I disappoint myself. Ever since I got off the sauce..."

"That wasn't off-the-sauce talk. That was jerk talk. But don't worry, you're going to get right with me and Teddy."

"I don't understand."

"Colosseum is mine now. You're going to hear it reported differently, but I own it. And you're going to fix that script and help Teddy Chessman make his comeback... posthumously."

"*Beverly Hills is Burning?*"

"That would be the one. Teddy said it was one of the best stories he'd ever heard, so I'm going to double your fee to make sure we both get your best."

"As long as it's not embargoed. I'm not writing on a secure computer in your office or anybody else's. Especially after the shit that went down there. You want a trained chimp, call Joe Gillis."

Cute, but I wasn't in the mood for cute. Apparently, this was my day to be the rich prick. "Cortez, I'm going to take you back a few years. To a time when a drunken vet stuck the wrong needle into a Preakness contender, and half the racing community wanted him sent to prison. The other half wouldn't have been satisfied with anything less than a firing squad."

He looked away. "Goddamn it, Rail, that's not fair. I thanked you for stepping in. More than once."

I do favors because I want to, not to accumulate markers. But every now and then, a man needs to be reminded that decency begins at home. If Cortez had had another writing commitment, I would have wished him well, but I don't do bullshit. "My friend, what I was hoping to hear was that if I wanted you to write in crayon in the trunk of my car, all you'd need were the keys. But I understand a man's got to have standards. Sorry to have gotten in the way of yours."

There were tears in his eyes. People react differently to being made to look at themselves. He'd lashed out, but it was over. He was a very good man, he'd just wandered off the path like we all do. "You know, if you've got those keys, I'll put my crayons in there now."

I took my foot off the gas. "Thanks, you're a good friend, and I need you."

"I'm with you all the way, Rail. All the way."

"It's over. I'm going to leave the final decision up to Ross Dare. He's running Colosseum now. But I'll tell him that, as far as I'm concerned, you can write wherever you're comfortable. First, though, I want you to explain to me why anybody would embargo a script."

Cortez nodded. "In the old days, you leaked a storyline, you could turn in your table at Spago and go back to covering city council meetings. Now, these social media motherfuckers got janitors downloading iPhones. Then there's the fuckin Chinese hacking every server on the planet. I know a director who was in Beijing. He stops in a theatre to kill a couple of hours and sees his next picture already on the screen shot with local actors. I don't blame the studios for having the yips, I just don't work that way. Too much like a real job."

"Understood. Can you put me up for a few days while this all gets sorted out?"

"You intend to do the sorting?"

"It could come down to that. First thing I need is to find out what hospital the injured Colosseum receptionist is in without setting off alarms in Detectiveland."

"Let Dr. Detroit make a couple of calls. In the meantime, I'll show you to the Presidential Suite. I should warn you, though, two of the walls are glass."

As I followed Cortez down the hall, I made a mental note to ask Ross Dare for a copy of the script.

CHAPTER TWENTY-FIVE

Flying Birds and Harsh Mistresses

CHEZ YVAIN
LAGUNA BEACH

Chez Yvain, the elegant, French dining room just off the lobby of the Inn, was busy, and everyone, patrons and staff alike, seemed to know Lake. Amid much fawning, Yvain himself led the two women to the farthest corner of the restaurant where a white-tableclothed, semicircular booth along the oceanfront windows provided both privacy and a magnificent view.

Yvain bowed as they slid into their seats. "As you prefer, Mademoiselle London, I have instructed the staff not to approach unless you summon them. Will there be any special instructions this evening?"

"I'm expecting a call. On your private number. Tell the person to come to the bar and wait. I trust that won't be an inconvenience."

"Consider it done, Mademoiselle. Will that be all?"

"No, I expect to be here quite late. Please have someone available to provide for us. Someone discrete."

"I will see to it, Mademoiselle. Everyone at Chez Yvain is always at your service."

Barrie had been walking gingerly and wobbling a little. Now, she sat slowly on the burgundy leather, aching from lovemaking that had threatened to leave her unable to move. There was something else as well. At some point during the last hours, Lake had produced three tiny, silver flying birds, like the ones Barrie had seen on her anklet and keychain. "Do you remember?" Lake asked.

Barrie nodded, but as she quickly learned, these were not ordinary jewelry but a pair of nipple clamps and a clitoris clamp, all of which could be adjusted to increase or reduce the tension of their grip. Barrie had shrieked in sweet agony when they were first applied, but as she became able to tolerate them, Lake had removed them and tightened them further.

She didn't think she could come any more, but each time Lake replaced the newly-tightened clamps, a deeper orgasm exploded through her. Lake was doing things to her Barrie hadn't known existed.

Eventually, tears flowed from her eyes and sobs lodged in her throat, but after Lake had taken the clamps off and given her time to collect herself, Barrie begged for them to be put back. "Please, Lake, please. I can't bear the pain, but I can't bear being without it either."

"Men have hurt you deeply, haven't they, my love? Not like my birds but in ways only another woman can understand."

Barrie's tears came in torrents now, and she shook uncontrollably as she wept into Lake's neck when the clamps returned. "I've been searching for you all my life. I had such emptiness inside. Sometimes, I didn't even know I was alive. Does that make any sense?" Barrie thought her flesh could extend no further, and her sobs gradually became moans.

"In Hollywood, there are many accomplished women who find comfort and pleasure in one another. A soothing protection in a world where ruthless men use us then toss us aside. We call our little groups 'sewing circles.' It's a bit of verbal burlesque that reminds us how far we've come from being some dick-swinger's domestic hostage and breeding animal."

While she continued teasing Barrie's nipples, Lake pushed her knee against her lower bird, causing Barrie to whimper. Lake licked the tears and tongued them into Barrie's eager mouth. "I'm very selective about my circle, but your anguish moves me—and your beauty overpowers me."

"Would I belong only to you? I don't think I could stand being touched by anyone else, ever again."

"I will be there, but we will not always be alone. I have responsibilities to others and needs no one woman can fulfill. Not even one as irresistible as you."

The thought of sharing Lake was almost more than Barrie could accept, but not having her at all was beyond comprehension. "Oh, God, Lake, please. Do with me what you will. Just don't leave me."

"Be certain, my sweet, because you are about to cross a line from which there is no return. I caution you, I am a harsh mistress."

"Anything, please, anything. I don't ever want to be without you again. I can't be."

"I'm so glad. You will be too."

Later, after both had climaxed in a raging flood of writhing screams, Barrie lay in Lake's arms. "Why don't you tell me about J.C. Stinson," Lake said.

Barrie tried to regain her composure; to be sure she had heard her correctly. "Stinson?" she repeated."

"I found his note with your gun—torn in half for some reason. He only signed his initials, but I'd recognize that cocksucker's handwriting anywhere."

"I... I'd really rather not."

Without warning, Lake twisted her clitoris clamp sharply. The unexpected pain caused Barrie cry out. "Never tell me what you would rather do. Ever."

"I'm sorry," Barrie choked out. "He... I met him twice. Once, in New York when he came to pay for a dress Mr. Hughes... mussed. And once in Havana. At the airport. Both times, we only talked for a few seconds. That's all, I swear."

Lake bent and licked around the clamp, soothing her tormented clitoris. "I believe you. Not completely, but enough for now."

"Do you know...?" Barrie caught herself. "Is it all right to ask you a question?"

"Good girl. Yes, it's permissible."

"Do you know him? Mr. Stinson?"

"The worms should eat the fucker twice. We were married for a minute and a half, most of which I spent on my back, hoping he'd only want to do it once. Jesus, what a fuckin libido that Irish sonofabitch has. A week after I filed for divorce, the rabbit died. I was on my way to have an abortion when a couple of his private dicks grabbed me and took me to a sanitarium."

"A sanitarium? For wanting an abortion?"

"In this state, all it takes is a friendly judge and a greedy doctor. A husband with wife trouble can put her away for 'observation' anytime he wishes. It's completely up to the doctor how long she needs to be 'observed.' A friend of mine spent a year in a straitjacket because her old man got tired of her bitching about *his drinking. My sentence lasted until I had the baby. The day after, I was standing at the curb, waiting for a cab."*

"My God."

"That's how Stinson plays. Five steps ahead, and for keeps. I was in restraints with gauze taped over my eyes when I delivered, so I couldn't even see if it was a boy or girl. He sent the kid to Europe to live with some fuckin relative I could never find. Not that I looked that hard. I didn't want it anyway, but I wanted to make him pay for what he put me through, and a baby always makes an impression on a judge. When I tried to take him to court, though, my lawyers heard the name Stinson, shit their pants and ran the other way."

"How could anybody do something so heartless?"

"When you're flying the Howard Hughes name, there isn't anything you CAN'T do. I'll never forgive that prick for locking me up with those drooling loonies."

"I'm so sorry, Lake."

"Don't be. But let me make up for hurting you. Would you like that?"

Barrie couldn't find her voice to answer, so she nodded.

Lake had brought Barrie a stunning black dress and a pair of silver high heels. "Just in case yours didn't dry," she smiled."

"These are spectacular," Barrie gasped. She clutched the dress against her with one hand and the shoes with the other and waltzed around the suite, looking at herself in the mirrors.

Lake brought out her own dress, a dramatic crimson and black Garbo-type with a neckline cut to her navel. "I've never seen anything so elegant... or so sexy," Barrie exclaimed. "Not even in Havana, and all the Paris designers have shops there. These must have cost a fortune."

"One could argue that they cost some people everything and others nothing. They're from Hollywood, my love, and not even the Aga Khan could buy one."

Barrie considered that for a moment. "They're from a studio?"

"I won't tell you who yours was made for, because she isn't nearly as gorgeous, but tonight, my angel, I want you to make an entrance like a leading lady."

"I don't know what to say."

"How better to flaunt such a jaw-dropping pair of delightfully well-fucked tarts?" And they laughed until they collapsed on the bed.

Barrie had never even tried on something so finely tailored, and she immediately understood that even if others can't tell quality, the wearer can. The dress fit her perfectly—as did the shoes—and she loved that it was shorter than current fashion dictated, the heels higher. She was proud of her legs, and she couldn't wait to show them off. She hoped the restaurant would be crowded.

"From now on, you will always keep your legs apart. Always. And you will never again wear panties. I want to be able to touch you—or have you show yourself—whenever the spirit moves me."

Barrie nodded. "Yes, Lake."

"That will also be the last time you use my name. You are to address me only as ma'am. I'm not in the habit of repeating myself, so if you can't follow my rules, I will abandon you. Forever. Do you understand?"

Barrie felt panic start to well up. "I said, do you understand?" Lake repeated, an edge in her voice.

"Yes, ma'am. A thousand times yes."

"So very, very sweet you are. I am so lucky." Lake knelt and opened her hand to show Barrie a silver bird anklet identical to her own. She hooked it around Barrie's left ankle. "Do you like it?"

Barrie was fighting not to collapse. "Yes, ma'am. Very, very much."

"Do you remember what it's called?"

"Wings of Submission. It makes me feel so special. Thank you, ma'am."

"You are special. And isn't it ironic that it should grace a woman who flies? From now on, there will never be a question who loves you—or who you belong to." She then lovingly kissed Barrie's ankle and returned to her feet.

A starched waiter placed a pair of very dry martinis in front of them. Earlier, Lake had instructed Barrie to place the now-dry cash inside two pillowcases, which she had hidden behind the headboard. But when Barrie had taken off the necklace and started to put it into one of the pillowcases, Lake had stopped her.

"But, ma'am, I can't wear it. It's…"

Lake had taken her by the shoulders and kissed her deeply. "Honey, I've been to Havana. I know what it is. Put it in your purse. I want to talk about it."

"My purse? But…"

"Barrie…"

"Yes, ma'am. Certainly, ma'am."

Before coffee, Lake excused herself to take the phone call she was expecting. While she was gone, a waiter came by with a plate containing a pack of Gitanes and a box of matches. "Miss London invites you to smoke if you wish," he said.

Barrie was extremely grateful. She smoked only rarely but found herself wanting a cigarette very badly right now. The waiter opened them and shook one loose. After he lit it for her, she thanked him and dragged deeply while staring at the dark ocean. Barrie had never had women friends, so she didn't know how many others walked the bewildering backroads of sexual vacancy. But if she died right now, she would never again have to wonder what she was capable of. This was the most incredible night of her life, and she fought to gather herself so she could experience every remaining second.

When Lake returned, she said nothing about the call, and Barrie knew better than to ask. Lake ordered an absinthe for each of them with their coffee. Barrie had never been much of a drinker, and the martini followed by wine with dinner had left her lightheaded. The absinthe was strong, but she sipped it without complaining.

Lake sat next to her, her arm around Barrie's shoulders, fingers stroking her hair. Twice, she leaned over and kissed her, and Barrie was grateful in a way she couldn't explain. Finally, Lake told her to place the necklace on the table. Barrie hesitated, and before she knew what was happening, Lake grabbed her face and turned it roughly toward her. "Didn't I warn you about disobeying me?" she hissed.

Barrie was at once terrified and sick to her stomach. "I'm so sorry, ma'am." She fumbled the necklace out of her purse and arranged it on the white cloth. Confused and wanting Lake to love her again, she apologized once more. "If you want it, ma'am, please take it. The money too. Just don't leave me. Please, ma'am… PLEASE."

Lake did what Barrie least expected. She laughed. Then she kissed Barrie long and deep. "Oh, my delicious one, you are so naïve. So very, very wonderfully naïve. Daddy owns half the oil in Los Angeles and is trying to steal the other half. I don't want your money… or your necklace. I want your STORY."

At first, Barrie didn't understand. "My story, ma'am?"

"Yes, I want to know how you got the plane, the money, AND the diamonds. That necklace has never been for sale. I know because half of Hollywood has tried to buy it. At any price Benedict cared to name. I've been writing screenplays for fifteen years, and I can smell this blockbuster before I hear it."

Barrie's head was swimming. "You want to write it? Like for a movie?"

"As much as you want more of this." Lake put her hand under Barrie's dress and touched her until Barrie buried her face in the older woman's neck.

When Barrie could catch her breath, she was trembling, "If you write it, I'll be killed. You will be too, ma'am."

Lake patted her. "Let me worry about that for both of us. If it's that good, putting it on paper is the best protection anyone can have.

CHAPTER TWENTY-SIX

Ice Cream Blondes and a Desperate D.A.

CHEZ YVAIN

There was never any question Barrie wouldn't tell Lake. After a childhood of filthy orphanages and crushing loneliness, a husband who devastated her, her own dreadful crimes and the stark terror of Lansky and Luciano, she had finally found a good place. A place where the rules were clear, and if she followed them, love would follow.

She didn't know how Lake had understood she needed pain to feel wanted. She hadn't known herself until now. But at this moment, she realized that all her life she had been looking for someone to hurt her in such a special way and make her obey. She remembered reading somewhere that finding your place in the universe was like "going home." She now knew that was true. And having finally found home, she would do anything to never, ever lose it.

So, for the next hour, Barrie told Lake about her life. All of it. Often through tears. When she finished, Lake didn't speak for a long time, just held her in her arms and kissed her forehead. Then she looked at Barrie with a pair of eyes that seemed to melt on her, "Barrie Fontaine, you are the most fantastic woman I have ever met. No, the most fantastic person. So brave, so brilliant, so coolheaded. I cherish you."

Brave? Brilliant? Coolheaded? Barrie certainly didn't feel like any of those things. She felt more like a little girl, holding onto the mother she never had. A mother who would love her and make her mind and punish her when she didn't. She cried softly for a while. A gentle comforting cry, because she was finally, completely at peace.

When she calmed, Lake looked at her in a new way. "Barrie, I'm giving you permission to call me Lake. Your courage makes me feel almost unworthy of you."

Barrie shook her head. "Ma'am, I don't want to change anything. Please. I've never had anyone like you in my life. I want to let go of the past and all the bad things. I NEED to let go. With you instructing and protecting me, I can finally let that happen."

Lake stroked her hair. "I will protect you. And if I hurt you—sometimes more than you think you can stand—it is because that is what is best for you."

"I know, ma'am. And I'm ready."

Lake looked out at the ocean. She was one of those people who was used to good fortune, but this was more than even she could have anticipated. All wrapped up in a most delightful package of beauty, sexuality and subservience. She tilted Barrie's chin so she could look into her eyes. "Benedict Crown, Meyer Lansky, Lucky Luciano, Juan Guerra, Howard Hughes, J.C. Stinson—and Thelma Todd, a cheap, drunken has-been if there ever was one. Barrie, you have no idea what you're carrying around."

No, Barrie didn't, and she hadn't had time to even think about it. "Thelma Todd, the movie star? Is that who Mr. Stinson meant in his note?"

"The ship's sailed on 'star.' Anybody calling her 'Hot Toddy' these days hasn't seen her in a bathing suit. But Thelma's got something more valuable than her worn out pussy. A roadhouse in the Palisades right smack on the PCH. Thelma's Sidewalk Café. With an upstairs nightclub and a huge apartment above that. All on a fabulous piece of hillside overlooking the ocean. Luciano wants the place as his entrée to the limitless money of Hollywood, and he's pushing hard to get his hands on it. He even had one of his guys, Pat DiCicco, marry the cow."

"I flew Mr. DiCicco from Havana to Miami once. He was so handsome. I thought he was an actor until somebody told me he worked for Mr. Luciano."

"I'll give you handsome, though when he kills you, you're just as dead. But marriage or no marriage, Luciano still can't get even a gin game going at Thelma's."

"If she's managed to keep thugs out, you have to admire her, don't you?"

"Are you kidding? Thelma'd roll over in a heartbeat. She's broke and

sinking fast. But LA's not like New York. You don't have silent partners out here—especially when it comes to servicing movie people. Everybody knows everything, and the First Commandment is to protect each other. On the beach across from Thelma's joint, million-dollar stars, studio chiefs and their bankers are putting up mansions. I call it Minsk on the Pacific."

Barrie understood. If a rich guy found himself sitting next to Luciano at the Stork Club, it was exciting. But he didn't want to exchange waves when he stepped out his front door in a bathrobe to pick up the morning paper.

"You're a smart girl. Power's the same everywhere. Imagine all those ass-licking famous faces suddenly unavailable for charades because they're across the street throwing dice, banging hookers and slamming heroin."

Barrie thought of the things she'd seen in New York and Havana. Lake didn't know the half of what Luciano was capable of. She wondered if there were any donkeys in the Palisades. "So the Hollywood people are leaning on Thelma."

"Oh, it's a lot more than a lean, sister. First, some WASP law firm representing a group calling itself Californians for a Natural Coast tried to buy her out. What a laugh. The only Californians who supposedly care about a 'natural coast' are pouring concrete on the fucking sand. But the cheap schmucks lowballed her, not grasping that if she didn't have enough cash to run forever, she was dead.

"Next came the D.A., and the cops sitting outside her café 24/7, fucking with people just going in for a cup of Joe. And for good measure, hauling Thelma and DiCicco in front of a grand jury once a month to keep their lawyer meter running... and more importantly, Luciano's attention."

"Sounds like she's boxed in."

"That would be true until a few months ago, when the D.A. got himself indicted for taking a bribe from a big-time developer to drop a statutory rape case. The girl was sixteen and hand-delivered by a local madam. Magically, the cops showed up at the guy's hotel in the middle of the action. Guess which developer owns the land north, south and up the hill from Thelma's? And which D.A. has an election coming up?"

Barrie had seen this movie before. It was vintage Luciano. Whoever the madam worked for reported to Lucky. "It makes my skin crawl, but I used to fly the bagmen—the girls too, some a lot younger than sixteen."

Lake grinned. "This is going to get ugly—real ugly. Or a lot of people are going to go into a room, and when they come out, it'll all be gone. Either way, I'm betting on the Bank of Luciano to be the one left standing."

"Set 'em up, knock 'em down, rescue the useful—who quickly become the sniveling grateful. That accounts for the million dollars. But why the necklace?"

"It drew crowds in Cuba, didn't it?"

"Enormous. Wives insisted on traveling with their husbands just to see it. So many that the casino started giving discount cards to the stores in Havana to get them out of their husbands' hair."

"Care to bet that Luciano and Lansky were getting a slice of those sales? Well, compared to LA, Havana is Poughkeepsie. And because of you, tonight there are some very unhappy people across this great hemisphere. Very, very unhappy."

Barrie was quiet for a while. "I know you don't think much of Miss Todd, but Luciano doesn't do the kind of business you're talking about with women. The moment he takes over, she's in real danger."

"Barrie, honey, if Luciano doesn't kill her, Thelma will find somebody who will."

Suddenly, there was shouting at the front of the restaurant, followed by scuffling. A voice called out, "He's crazy! Call the police!"

The French accent of Yvain intervened. "Non. No police. Throw him out."

Barrie heard the unmistakable sound of fist on flesh, then glass breaking, and a large, well-built man in his thirties burst into the dining room. He was expensively-dressed, but disheveled, and had a wild look in his eyes. Several waiters were in pursuit, but nobody seemed anxious to catch him. Yvain brought up the rear, holding a bloody handkerchief to his mouth.

The man headed directly toward Lake and Barrie. Lake put her hand on Barrie's leg as if to reassure her. "Stay calm, my love. This is nothing."

When the man reached them, he drove his fist into their table with such force that the silverware jumped a foot. "I knew you'd be here, you miserable cunt! Where is she?"

Lake raised her hand at the waiters, and they stopped, watching warily from several feet away. She leveled her gaze at the intruder. Barrie recognized him now. *It was the same man who had been shooting at Lake on the beach. What had she called him? Conrad.*

"Go home," Lake said. "Before you do something you won't be able to recover from."

He seemed to notice Barrie for the first time. "Who's this, another of the London Muff Club? If you're smart, baby, you'll pack your needle and thread and get as far from this piece of shit as fast as you can." He turned back to Lake, "I asked you a fucking question! Where is she?"

"Somewhere you can't get to her. And never will again."

Barrie thought the man might leap over the table, but all of a sudden, he did a curious thing. He began to sob. "You set me up," he wailed. "You wanted her to find us in bed together!" He sank to his knees and put his face in his hands. "Oh, God, I love her! I love her so much!"

"No," Lake said, "you love what she means to your career. Wake up, Conrad, it's over. Now run along before I decide to tell some enterprising rag reporter the real story of your life, and you'll never make another picture."

The threat hung there like a cleaver, and after a few seconds, "I'm sorry, Lake. I just..."

"Go." She nodded at Yvain, and the waiters got him to his feet and half-escorted, half-dragged him away. "Yvain?" Lake called to the owner.

"Oui, Mademoiselle London?"

"Send a bottle of your very best champagne to every table in the place. Tell them I apologize for the disturbance."

Yvain dabbed at his bleeding mouth, but he was smiling now. "Right away, Mademoiselle, right away."

A few minutes later, as waiters fanned out across the restaurant and began popping corks, one diner began to clap, and soon everyone joined in. Lake raised her absinthe in acknowledgement, and Barrie was quick to do the same.

CHAPTER TWENTY-SEVEN

Autographs and Black Rage

After I got Cortez's eyes back in his head when he saw Wind Fortune, I drove his H2, and he sat shotgun. Wind hunched down in back, her face hidden under an Indiana Jones hat, which wouldn't have fooled a cloistered monk. We dropped Cortez outside Cedars-Sinai's emergency entrance then drove the perimeter.

It was business as usual except for a row of satellite trucks parked along San Vicente. The hair-sprayed aristocrats of the airwaves, accompanied by their disheveled camera crews, were vying for talking-head shots with the hospital in the background. They might as well have been reporting from Schenectady. The LAPD has some things they could improve, but stiff-arming the media away from the best sightlines of the go-to place for the sick and dying of show business isn't one of them.

Back on Beverly Blvd., I killed a few minutes idling at a meter. Pretty soon, Cortez was dodging traffic crossing to us, a stethoscope dancing against his Brioni pinstripe. He looked doctor-sharp in French cuffs and hand-tied bow tie and, as expected, nobody had challenged him.

"A cute little thing at reception said Miss Van Allen's chart is open, which means she still in ICU. But she's only scheduled for tests, not surgery, so it's probably just a concussion."

"Thank God," Wind sighed.

"She can't have visitors until she's cleared by the chief of neurology, which won't be till tomorrow. There's only one cop hanging around. A uniform, not a detective, and he's busy trying to get laid by a buck-toothed X-ray tech."

"You up for a visit?"

"You kidding? I haven't had a chance to trot out any black rage yet."

I pulled into a parking structure off George Burns Road, which was as distant from the ER as we could get and still be on hospital property. In case we had to beat a hasty retreat, I wanted lots of corridors to lose any foot posse. I drove around the first level until I found a space near an exit with a large, yellow sign commanding me to HEAD IN ONLY. I backed into it.

Even sans makeup, I didn't know how we were going to get Wind past anyone, but Dr. Detective Novel rummaged around the back of his Hummer and came out with an old trench coat and a walking stick with a chromed, flying stork handle that looked like it had come straight off an early thirties Hispano-Suiza. "If you've got the car that goes under that, I'll pay retail."

He shook his head. "Wife Number 2. Grabbed this as she was trying to run me down. Hope they went off a cliff together."

Once Wind was belted into the coat with the collar turned up, I showed her how to use the cane to affect a limp. Not pronounced, which causes people to stare, but a subtle rolling gait like she'd been born with one leg shorter than the other. In test after test, the only thing people remember about a person with a limp is the limp. Sometimes they can't even tell you if it was a man or a woman.

Actress that Wind was, after a few tries, not even a cop would have noticed she was faking it—especially in a hospital. We threaded our way through the labyrinth of buildings with one of paparazzidom's biggest "gets" limping between us and no one paying the slightest attention.

The ER waiting room was a third full and quiet. Cortez stopped in the hallway and gestured for us to do the same.

"What are we doing?" asked Wind.

"Back in vet school, when we needed a little entertainment, we'd take a couple of six-packs and a deck of cards over to Cook County and watch the paramedics bring in the wounded. You never knew what was gonna happen, and it beat the shit out of the movies."

"This is Cedars," I said, "not the West Side of Chicago."

"Humor me."

A couple of hospital staff in blue scrubs passed us, noticed Cortez's stethoscope and nodded. Trotting out the traditional doctorly response, he ignored them. A few minutes later, the automatic doors across the waiting room opened, and ten, maybe twelve, heavyset Hispanic men and women burst in. The women were crying, the men arguing. On their way to the nurses' station, one of the women collapsed onto the hard terrazzo in a dead faint. A man knelt over her, but this just set the others into another frenzy of yelling, and he immediately forgot about her, jumped up and rejoined the fray.

I speak several languages, including Spanish, and the chaos was over an Uncle Diego who'd had a heart attack. They were blaming each other for causing it, but the real issue seemed to be that Diego had a new will that wasn't signed yet, and somebody they were calling *Calaca* was currently the only heir. Since *calaca* means skeleton, and that didn't apply to anybody in this group, I guessed the lucky guy was back at the house, going through drawers.

Suddenly, one man cold-cocked another, and the victim threw a roundhouse back, missed his intended target, and caught a woman on the nose. Nurses, attendants and security descended on them, but that only intensified the melee. As Cortez led us toward ICU, no one even glanced in our direction.

"Cook County, Cedars, Chattanooga General," he said. "Families. All the same."

Glenda Van Allen looked like she was napping. No breathing tubes or monitors, just a saline IV and a series of tiny adhesive dots along her hairline. She was propped on her right side, sandwiched between two, long, rolled pillows, her knees pulled up slightly. Her arms were crossed in front of her chin, infant-like, her hands in loose fists. I looked at Cortez and he shook his head. I agreed. This was not the position one wants to see a patient in after a head wound. Glenda wasn't simply unconscious, she was in a coma.

Wind went to her side, took one of her hands and held it for a moment. When she let go, the arm and hand returned to their previous pose. "Is that normal?" she asked.

"I'm sorry, I'm just a vet."

Wind was young, but she wasn't a fool. "But I thought you said…"

"I was repeating what I was told."

"No EEG?" I asked.

"Those dots are microsensors transmitting to a monitoring station."

"Think you can go out there and get a look?"

"No, he may not." The voice was strong, female and thickly-accented African. We turned to face a tall, slender young woman with skin so black it was iridescent. She was more regal than pretty, but there was no mistaking her command. Her nametag read Ndidi Ba, ICU Supervising RN. "Who are you?"

Cortez, the actor, instantly became Cortez, the player, flashing his best your-place-or-mine smile. "Dr. Cortez Detroit. Let me guess… Tanzanian, right? You really are an eyeful, Supervisor."

She didn't even blink. "Put your underwear back on, and dig out some ID besides that thing around your neck."

If this was what Cortez meant by black rage, it was wearing a skirt. He made quite a show of going through his pockets and came up with a Clippers ticket, a roll of Tums, two broken Lucky Strikes and an empty condom foil.

Nurse Ba eyed the treasure, lingering on the Trojan wrapper. "Must be a lot of desperation out there. Now, would you folks like to leave the way you came or in a squad car?"

Wind took off her hat and shook her hair loose. "Nurse, I'm Wind Fortune."

"Why hello, Miss Fortune. I didn't recognize you. You usually arrive in an ambulance."

Wind handled it exactly the way I would have told her to; she let it pass.

"Glenda used to work for me. I'd really appreciate it if you'd let me stay a while."

There are tiny moments upon which lives can change. Nurse Ba looked at the young actress for a long time. "If you went to all this trouble, there must be something worthwhile in you. Shame it's taken a tragedy for the rest of us to see it. You've got half an hour, but these two go with me." As she herded us out, she turned to Cortez, "I'm Sudanese, which makes me smart enough to stay clear of the Clippers. Nice tie, though."

Cortez grinned at me and winked.

An hour later, in the H2, Wind handed a blue-covered book between the seats. I took it and saw *Glenda's Autographs* in gold script on the cover. Cortez was driving now, and he glanced over. "Where'd you get that?"

"She was clutching it when they brought her in. Ndidi said she's seen people with head wounds still holding a phone to their ear. The EMS guys don't move anything they don't have to."

I opened the book and fanned through a few pages. Some of the names were familiar, most weren't.

"When I told Ndidi that Glenda's mother doesn't know up from down, she let me take it. Her purse too, which EMS used to ID her. Turn to the last page."

I did and saw a large, feminine script written diagonally across the entire space in bright pink ink. This name I didn't need help with. Valentine Jones, with the "i" dotted with a heart. Under it was today's date. "A receptionist hustling autographs? Seems unprofessional."

"It's an automatic termination anywhere in the business, so I called Carla again—Glenda's roommate. She said Teddy Chessman gave her the okay to ask for it when they were in the car together."

"You lost me."

"Anywhere Valentine Jones goes, there's a feeding frenzy—even worse than me. Glenda told Carla that there was going to be a big announcement after the board meeting, and Teddy wanted to spring Valentine on the press himself. He didn't even trust the limo service to keep quiet."

"So he sent a *receptionist* to pick up a $30 million star?"

"My God, Uncle Rail, if you're that dense you might want to think about retirement."

"Wake up, my man" said Cortez, "the conversation happened on a pillow. If that's still not clear enough, Teddy was banging Glenda. He probably sent her in his car."

Why was I even remotely surprised? This was the same guy who jumped a bride on his way home from prison. Sleeping with an attractive receptionist wasn't exactly stop-the-presses material.

Cortez said what I was thinking. "None of the news reports mentioned Miss Jones. Do you suppose she was there when…?"

I did. And she wasn't one of the dead. Nothing could have kept a lid on that.

Wind was upset. "Why wouldn't she say something? She could help the police."

Cortez reached back and took her hand. "You've been scared, haven't you, Wind? I mean like really scared."

"Oh, God, yes."

"Just think how Valentine must have felt." And he continued holding her hand… a lot longer than I thought he needed to.

The sun was long gone by the time Cortez pulled into his drive. My stomach had been growling for the last hour, and I was looking forward to something hot, greasy and large, followed by an early turn-in.

Wind announced she was going to meet some friends at *Trellis* before heading home to Mallory. *Trellis* is one of the must-be-seen-at restaurants for the Hollywood set, and the paparazzi and rubberneckers sometimes get so thick that traffic on the boulevard out front comes to a standstill. I didn't think that was a good idea and said so. Her voice hardened. "Uncle Rail, I appreciate your looking out for me, but I can't hide in the hills forever. If Dr. Detroit doesn't mind letting me hang onto his coat and walking stick, I might try out my Bogart on the paps."

The problem with actresses is they pretend they don't want to be noticed until they aren't. My bet was the cane, coat and hat would never get out of the car. If I was still awake, I'd be able to watch it on the news.

A sheriff's department black and white with both front doors open sat at the curb in front of Cortez's building. A ramrod-straight deputy was talking to the doorman. A second deputy was pointing toward the garage. It was the same doorman who'd taken my truck earlier, only now he was sporting the body language of a guy who'd just been caught with a trunk full of hot TVs. It didn't take a Mensa candidate to realize the three of them weren't discussing soybean futures.

"When the cops get bored, they cruise the parking structures," Cortez said. "Use that goddamn scanner to see how many millionaires haven't paid their tickets."

"Spoken like a guy who's seen a boot or two."

"Fuck the asshole who invented that thing. But it's usually LAPD. Never seen the sheriff here before. That commander you mentioned must be getting impatient waiting for your call." Cortez headed directly for the garage, and the doorman never looked up.

Inside, another squad car, lights out, was sitting next to the valet parking area, the outlines of two deputies visible inside. Rampulla's troops had definitely hit the Rail Black jackpot: my Ram and Wind's Navigator. Cortez turned onto the ramp that wound down into the bowels of the building. On the second level, he and Wind got out, and I took over the wheel.

"I'll buy you some time," Wind said. "Cops like talking to me."

My guess was she'd get an escort to the restaurant.

"You better have left me the Rolls," Cortez said. I decided to let him be surprised, dropped the H2 into gear and headed out the back entrance.

I fished out my cell phone and broke thirty laws dialing it. "Verizon four-one-one-connect. City and state, please." The voice on the other end sounded like it had been put through two scalded roosters and a paint shaker. Was breaking up AT&T really necessary?

When the West Hollywood Sheriff's Station answered, I asked for Rampulla, intentionally skipping the commander part.

"I'm sorry, he's not here. May I...?"

"No, you may not. Put me through to his home."

Cops—even ones manning phones on the night shift—don't like being given order by a civilian. This one was no exception. "That's not gonna happen. Who's this?"

"Rail Black."

I waited through several long seconds of silence before I got, "Hold the line."

I was going to ask for a please but didn't get the chance. Roughly a minute later, I heard a rasp that sounded as pleasant as I felt.

"Where the fuck are you?"

Is there a cop on the planet with a different opening line? "The only thing that matters is where I'm going to be when I'm ready to talk. The minute that happens, you're welcome to bring as many people as you like, and I'll answer questions until you beg me to stop. Right now, I want room to breathe, or I'll lawyer up, and you'll get nothing."

I could hear the wheels turning. "You been on the phone with your good friend, the sheriff?" Standard operating procedure, worry about your career first.

"Why? Is he looking for me too?" He wasn't expecting that, but he wasn't going to thank me. I changed gears. "A crime this big means a task force. They going to let you head it?"

"Look, motherfucker, I'm the cop, and you're somebody I want to talk to. Until that happens, that's the only relationship we got."

So he'd already been passed over. That wasn't going to improve his mood. "Call your buddies at LAPD and get some protection on Valentine Jones."

"What the fuck for?"

That confirmed he didn't know she'd been on the scene. There was a risk she'd admit to being there when she saw the cops, but I'd seen her in action around uniforms and didn't think so. "Because Miss Jones is doing a picture for Colosseum, and until my lawyer tells me I'm not going to be sued for walking away from buying the place, she's an asset and needs to be kept safe."

"You want fries with that?"

"Is this where we measure our dicks, or are we still cooperating?"

"Anything else?" he grunted.

"When we meet, bring Marvin Oxford."

He came off the rails. "Marvin Oxford? I wouldn't let that schmuck wipe my ass. He's sure as hell not calling a press conference on my nickel."

"Bring him." I hung up. I had confidence he'd figure it out.

I couldn't be sure Rampulla would call off the dogs, and I really didn't want to sleep in Cortez's glass coffin. I found some Sinatra on the radio, and while Old Blue Eyes eased into "Summer Wind," I pointed the Hummer toward the beach.

CHAPTER TWENTY-EIGHT

Tigers and Heroes

CHEZ YVAIN

Yvain brought fresh drinks, and Lake put two cigarettes between her lips, lit both and gave one to Barrie. "You were very brave, ma'am," Barrie said.

Lake exhaled a long stream of smoke. "Actors are always acting, even when they think they're not. Enough of Conrad, let's get back to your story."

"If all this is about some silly nightclub, what's in it for somebody like Hughes? My God, Luciano's a murderer."

"I know a director who keeps a Bengal tiger in his backyard. In Beverly Hills. He likes to walk out in the morning with his coffee and feel the rush that this could be the day the tiger has had enough. Howard lives his life on the edge. If you've got all the money you're ever going to need, what's left? There are only so many planes a man can fly. So when he gets bored, he fucks around. But even being a half-step from a fiery death or financial catastrophe gets old. Luciano is Howard's tiger—only more unpredictable and deadlier.

"Howard and Thelma also used to be an item. Their getting together doesn't raise any red flags with the D.A. or the studio heads—and there are some interesting stories about Hughes's bedroom proclivities."

"Howard is letting Luciano use him?"

"Where else can he play with that kind of dynamite? But Howard has a real bad habit of stepping in shit, which he doesn't like at all, so he keeps the highest-priced lawyer in Creation around to anticipate problems and fix them before they become bigger problems."

"J.C. Stinson. But why would he warn me? I'm not important."

"Well, not because he has a conscience. I can attest he doesn't. The worst case scenario is always a corpse—or somebody who knows where one is that can be tied to Howard. Bodies wake people up."

Barrie thought about Woody Yates. And how close she'd come to joining him.

"Stinson's seen Hughes on a witness stand, and it's not pretty. That, and Howard's big news in Antarctica. For all J.C. knew, you left a diary, or had a long, lost relative you called before you took off. He weighed the options, which were all bad, and went with the one that gave you the best chance to live—and return the favor by keeping your mouth shut. Then he sat back and crossed his fingers."

"Well, whatever the reason, I'm grateful—very."

"You should be, but not for the reason you think. Dead, you were only a potential headache. Alive, you're Hughes's worst nightmare. A pair of living, breathing eyeballs that can put him in a room with Lucky Luciano—in Havana, yet. Then you deliver a load of heroin to one of the biggest criminals in Mexico—aboard one of Howard's planes. Got knows what other secrets you've got in that beautiful head of yours.

"Even if I wanted to—and I sure as hell don't—I couldn't fictionalize this enough to even slow down the cocksuckers in Washington who despise Hughes. It'll be hard to come up with a price he WON'T pay to keep this story out of circulation. And Stinson will force him to do it."

Barrie was confused. "I don't understand. You're going to use a screenplay to blackmail him?"

"No, I'm going to use Hughes to set the price. I wouldn't miss the chance to see this picture on the screen for any amount. I can think of five studios right now who'd empty their vaults to stick it to Howard. I can't wait until that Irish sleazeball of his oozes down here to try to make a deal. When I'm through with him, we'll be on our way to the Oscars, and Mr. J.C. Douchebag will be looking for a new client. Maybe he'll even have to move off that fucking hill of his down to where the common folk live."

"But won't I be in trouble? For the drugs and the necklace… and my own blackmail?"

"Who's going to testify? Luciano? Hughes? Guerra? And do you think any of the women you clipped are going to run to the cops in Rio or Buenos Aires because they heard there's going to be a movie? Why? To make sure we spell their names right?

"Barrie, the first lesson of Hollywood is that there's real life, then there's the movies. Everybody watches what we do, but nobody believes us—even when we're telling the truth. If you're a prosecutor, are you going to bet your mortgage chasing a movie plot or a nice safe homicide with a stiff in the morgue? My darling, you're about to become the biggest celebrity in the country, and you don't even have to leave home to do it."

"I don't want to be a celebrity. I want to be with you."

"You'll be both. And I'll get my pound of Stinson flesh. It won't be as sweet as watching him wheeled into electroshock, but it'll do."

Barrie was suddenly uneasy. Why did everything always have to get complicated? Why couldn't she just love somebody and be loved back? She'd had her own share of heartache—a big share—but she didn't want a pound of anybody's flesh. And she sure didn't want Mr. Stinson to get hurt. Maybe he was a bad husband, but without him, she'd be dead in ditch in Tijuana. She'd have to figure this out, but her head wasn't clear enough right now.

"And don't even think about contacting Danny Dades," Lake said. "I've known that waste of time since he built his fuck palace up on the hill. It's only a matter of time before some angry husband cuts his pecker off. Tonight, you move in with me. I'll have Julius bury your paperwork here, and you'll no longer exist. Time is now your friend, like it's always been mine. Tomorrow, we'll be watching the ocean and writing the Barrie Fontaine story."

"I hope you won't think I'm foolish, but until today, ma'am, I didn't even know women wrote movies."

Lake laughed. "There are a lot of us. Most are studio chattel, begging for work then living and dying by what some fat schmuck in thousand-dollar silk pajamas thinks while he's taking a shit with their script. I have what they so delicately refer to as, 'fuck you money,' so I don't have to suck cock or work for an egg salad sandwich and a boozy lay. I also do something none of the rest do. Not even the butchest."

"What's that?"

"I write like a man. It just looks like words on a page to me, but every studio putz who reads it thinks a guy wrote it. Part of it's my name. When I was starting out in silents, they just assumed anybody called Lakeland London had to have a dick. Then I moved way the hell down here and won't take studio meetings or work behind their gates. I write what I want and sell to the highest bidder.

"The rumor is I stay inaccessible because I have my stuff ghosted by men, which is laughing-out-loud funny because if I were paying some ball-scratcher who was this good, why wouldn't he just do it for himself? The truth is, though, the imbeciles in LA don't give a shit if I'm pulling it out of a duck's ass. Just as long as I keep the pages coming."

"I've never even seen a screenplay, but I've watched a lot of movies. What's so different about yours?"

"I don't write my women weak. You want pouty, prissy and dumb, call Loos or Fitzgerald. The cliché about Hollywood is the men aren't quite men, and the women aren't quite women. Well, the women I write are heroes—first, last and always. How about it, Barrie? You ready to be a movie hero as well as a real one?"

"I'm not sure, ma'am, but whatever you want is just fine with me."

Lake leaned over and kissed her sweetly.

"May I please use the restroom, ma'am? Those drinks ran right through me."

"No," said Lake, "stay where you are. Yvain just signaled that that certain someone I want you to meet is waiting at the bar."

"I must look a fright, ma'am, and I couldn't help it, but I'm soaking wet, if you know what I mean."

"You look like an angel, and the scent of you is something I want our guest to experience. Knowing you're sitting here in your juices makes me want to come myself. Trust me, you'll thank me later."

Barrie looked down and saw her nipples pushing against her dress. They felt like they might burn through the material. She took a deep breath. "I trust you, ma'am."

CHAPTER TWENTY-NINE

Platinum and Convertibles

The sculptured, platinum blonde who strode across the dining room was so dazzling that everyone remaining in Yvain's stopped what they were doing and stared. Barrie recognized her immediately. Madalynne St. Timothy. The twenty-two-year-old ingénue who was rumored to be engaged to MGM's most dashing leading man and whose last picture had broken boxoffice records at Radio City and Grauman's.

Wearing silver and blue sequins against skin so pale she seemed ethereal, her overly high heels appeared to be made of blue-tinted glass, and she walked with a demure sexiness that froze men and women alike. Barrie realized Madalynne was what the word star was invented for.

But Barrie was more struck by how tiny and delicate she was. Small breasts, no hips and with ankles so thin Barrie thought she could probably put her fingers around them, Madalynne looked as if she might break. Barrie remembered reading that Mary Pickford and Jean Harlow were barely five feet tall, but when you saw them onscreen, you never thought about it. It was the same with Madalynne St. Timothy. One thing Madalynne did have that Pickford and Harlow did not was a long, perfectly proportioned neck that was accentuated by being devoid of jewelry.

Instinctively, Barrie reached for the necklace to return it to her purse. "Leave it," Lake commanded, and Barrie pulled back her hand.

When the actress arrived at their table, Lake smiled but did not rise. "Nice of you to join us, Madalynne. Conrad came by earlier."

Barrie saw Madalynne's face flush. "I'm so sorry. I..."

Lake cut her off sharply. "It's over, but I'm tired of cleaning up your messes. Steal them from their wives and sleep with them if you must, but stop pretending you love them. Men think you mean it."

"I won't do it again, ma'am. I promise." Madalynne's lip was trembling, and Barrie thought she might collapse where she stood."

"I know you won't. And save the tears for the screen." The threat made, Lake's tone changed. "Madalynne, meet Barrie Fontaine, the woman you'll be portraying."

Portraying? Barrie's head was spinning. She rose slightly in her seat to be polite, but Lake grabbed her thigh. "Stay where you are." To the actress, she said, "Sit down, Madalynne."

Madalynne's eye caught the necklace, and she froze. "Oh, Jesus, that's it, isn't it?. The Star of Havana."

Barrie turned to Lake for guidance, and her new love answered for her. "Stunning isn't it, Madalynne? And the way I'm going to write this picture, you'll steal it from a very dangerous man in an incredibly daring caper, then escape in a plane you'll pilot yourself. I think that befits a star of your magnitude, don't you? Now, don't make me tell you again. Sit down. All the way in, please."

Madalynne slid into the burgundy booth on the other side of Barrie, scrunching in until she was against her. She seemed even more petite than when she had been standing. Almost immediately, a waiter arrived with three absinthes. Madalynne took half of hers down in one gulp, still staring at the necklace. Barrie felt the actress shiver. She thought it was from the drink—but maybe it was the diamonds too.

Lake looked at Barrie. "Show Madalynne your pussy, dear. And leave it available."

Barrie flushed all the way to her toes, but she knew better than to hesitate. "Yes, ma'am." She lifted herself slightly until she could fold her dress above her waist. The leather was cold on her bare rear but also sensual. She kept her legs apart, but just to be sure, she opened them a little further. She tried not to think of the juices under her.

Barrie heard Madalynne began to breathe heavily, and she turned to see the young actress staring at her lap as perspiration formed on her neck.

"Do you like it, Madalynne?" Lake asked.

The young woman could only nod.

"I thought you would. Now, Madalynne, show Barrie yours."

The actress managed to say, "Yes, ma'am," then she too folded up her dress. She also opened her legs as far as she could, and Barrie felt her warm skin against hers, her incredibly slender thigh almost certainly now feeling the dampness of Barrie.

Barrie looked down and saw a little silver bird at the top of Madalynne's porcelain pale, shaved vagina. The bird quavered and trembled like it was alive, and there was a drop of moisture beneath it. She stole a glance at Madalynne's left ankle, and the tiny bird on her matching anklet was shaking too. She was right on the edge.

"Would you like to touch her, Barrie?"

The roaring in Barrie's ears was so loud she was afraid she might pass out. "Oh, God, yes, ma'am."

"Madalynne?" The actress seemed lost in a trance, staring at Barrie's soft womanhood, the tip of her tongue playing against her lips. "Madalynne, I'm speaking to you," Lake said sharply.

Madalynne jumped like she'd been slapped. "I'm so sorry, ma'am. I can barely think. I want with all my heart to touch her. Oh, God, so, so much."

"You may kiss. One time. Chastely. Nothing else. I have something special planned. To celebrate our new partnership."

"Yes, ma'am," they said, almost in unison.

Lake lit a Gitane and sipped absinthe while Barrie and Madalynne stared at each other, the dew of desire forming on their foreheads. Finally, Barrie leaned forward and Madalynne's lips met hers with a softness she would never have imagined possible. Lake smiled as her charges trembled from their hairlines to their toes.

While Lake supervised Barrie's things being packed into the red convertible and her name expunged from the hotel register, she gave the two young women permission to walk down to the beach for some fresh air. Two drinks had made

Madalynne unsteady, and Barrie had had a lot more than two.

Disobeying Lake' instruction about touching, they strolled hand in hand, flushed from the absinthe—and each other. The downhill was steep, and both were having trouble in their heels, giggling like schoolgirls as they stumbled. By the time they reached the beach, they were barefoot and began kicking their way through Laguna's deep sand, arms around each other's waists.

Barrie, nearly a head taller, felt like she was walking with her kid sister, only there was nothing sister-like about her emotions. Or about the way, Madalynne had briefly run her fingers over Barrie's mound when Lake turned to order more drinks.

The night was unusually warm, and a balmy, onshore breeze carried the distant tropics inland. A line of freighters, steamed north, their flickering lights competing with the stars. Even though it was after midnight, several couples were out walking plus one man standing in the surf, staring out to sea. No one seemed to care that two beautiful women were sharing affection, and no one seemed to recognize Madalynne—or if they did, they were too caught up in their own lives to be interested.

They had gone maybe a hundred yards, when a man they had passed a few seconds earlier came running back and stopped in front of Barrie. He smelled strongly of beer and was unsteady on his feet. He squinted at her and slurred, "I know you."

Barrie had no idea who he was, but this wasn't good. "I don't think so," she answered pleasantly and tried walking on. But he moved in front of her again.

"Sure I do. I'm Price Galloway, and I met you last year at Danny's. You're that pilot broad he was screwin. Helluva dancer too, but I'm havin trouble grabbin onto your name. It's Mary or Terry or somethin like that, right?"

"Sorry, my name's Gertrude, and I don't know anybody named Danny. Don't dance either. Bad knees."

Madalynne thought that was funny, "C'mon Gertie, let's get on with our walk. I'll massage those knees later." And she burst into a fit of giggles.

But Mr. Galloway wasn't that easy to shake. He grabbed Barrie's arm and twisted it up in front of him. "Nobody makes a fool of me. Especially one of Danny's twats. I remember now. You're Barrie. Barrie Fontaine. You work for Lucky Luciano."

"Get your hands off her," Madalynne shouted. Price looked at the actress for the first time. The girls' arms around each other seemed to register through his haze. "Aren't you two a sight. Jesus Christ, wait'll I tell Danny his old punch is a tongue and groove gal. How about we head to my place, and between rounds, I can watch you two?"

Barrie tried to pull away, but his grip was too strong. Madalynne let go of Barrie and jumped on his back. She was so slight that when he shook her off, she flew ten feet. Barrie lost her mind. She kneed Price Galloway squarely in the nuts, causing him to release her arm. She then grabbed a handful of sand and threw it in his eyes.

He bellowed like a crazed mule and swung blindly with a sweeping right. Barrie stepped under the fist and kicked him in the groin again. This time, he clutched his crotch and fell to his knees, groaning in agony.

Suddenly, a shape came from the left and something thunked off Price Galloway's temple. He keeled over like he'd been shot, and blood began running out of his right eye onto the sand. He was breathing, but he wasn't getting up for a while... a long while.

Lake stood over him, holding a leather sap. Even in the dark, the look on her face was savage, and she hit him again for good measure. It made a helluva sound, and his mouth flew open, spewing vomit like a fountain.

Lake turned to Barrie who was helping Madalynne to her feet. "Are you two all right?"

"I'm fine, ma'am," Barrie said.

"Yes, ma'am," said Madalynne.

"You shouldn't have talked to him. Either of you," she snapped.

Barrie was taken aback. "But, ma'am, I didn't..."

Lake started to say something else then got herself under control. "I'm just afraid for you."

Lake looked up and down the beach. No one was in sight. Barrie remembered passing a blanket somebody had left behind.

"Get it," Lake ordered.

After Lake kicked sand over the blood and covered him with the blanket, Price Galloway looked like any other drunk who'd decided to sleep it off on the beach, his vomit adding to the effect. Then, just as they were leaving, he turned *onto his side, pulled the blanket over his head and began to snore. In Laguna, he wouldn't merit a second look, not even from a cop.*

Lake's red Packard, a '35 Dietrich four-door, sat under the Inn's portico. Barrie's clothes were in the front passenger seat, the pillowcases of cash on the floor. Barrie and Madalynne slipped into the hotel ladies room where they washed the sand off their feet, put their shoes back on and fixed their faces.

When they returned, Lake had driven the Packard a hundred feet down the road and parked on the shoulder. She flashed the lights, and the girls ran toward her, high heels clacking on the asphalt.

The convertible top was now down, and Lake was standing next to the right rear door, which was open. "It's time for your surprise," she said. "Take off your dresses and give them to me, along with your purses."

Barrie looked at Madalynne, but the actress was already pulling hers over her head. Barrie did the same, and the two stood naked in their heels and anklets, each unable to take her eyes off the other.

Madalynne was every bit as slight as Barrie had expected, but delicately feminine too, and Barrie felt herself beginning her journey to the precipice. But this time, it was different. She loved Lake and everything she had done to her, but she knew she was in love with Madalynne. Hopelessly, head-over-heels in love.

Madalynne felt it too. She stared into Barrie's eyes, her face more sensuous than any camera could have made it and mouthed, "I love you," and it was all Barrie could do to keep her shaking legs from failing her.

Lake handed Barrie the Star of Havana. "Put this on her."

"Yes, ma'am."

Barrie stood in front of Madalynne and placed the necklace against the actress's throat, but Madalynne's attention was elsewhere. "Your nipples... my God, they're so much more enormous when they're out." she said huskily.

Barrie brushed them against Madalynne's tiny buds and the smaller girl gasped.

"She likes it when you hurt them," Lake smiled. "Use these." She handed Madalynne the flying bird nipple clamps.

While Barrie tried to get the necklace clasped, Madalynne tongued her nipples and affixed a clamp to each. Barrie closed her eyes, lost to the sensation.

Lake finally had to help Barrie with the necklace then stepped back to admire their adornments. A truck roared by, the driver nearly losing control at what he saw before he righted his rig and appreciatively leaned on the horn as he disappeared to the south.

"I think we're missing one more thing," said Lake. She knelt in front of Barrie and Barrie saw the third clamp in her hand. Barrie couldn't take her eyes off it as Lake tested it on her finger. Just the sight of what Lake was doing caused blood to rush into Barrie's clitoris, engorging it, making it more eager. Barrie sucked in her breath.

Without being told to, Barrie used both hands to expose her now-exaggeratedly swollen button. Lake took her time getting the clamp positioned just so, then, as she had earlier, she let it slowly close on Barrie's throbbing flesh.

Barrie bit her lips between her teeth, but then just as suddenly, Lake opened the clamp again. She rubbed it lightly over Barrie's clit several times then let the protrusion find its own way back into the clamp before slowly closing it once more.

This new pain and pleasure were simultaneously explosive. It was too much for Barrie. She put her head back, fighting against the orgasm but feeling it slipping away.

Lake gave her a moment then said, "Get in the car, my two beautiful girls. No rules, this time. I just want to be able to see your faces in my mirror. That's my treat."

Madalynne climbed into the backseat and was waiting for Barrie with her arms open. Barrie couldn't keep her mouth from Madalynne's miniature breasts which were sweeter than any flesh she had ever kissed. She cried out into them as she felt Madalynne's small fingers twist the clamps on her already-aching nipples and press her own silver bird against hers.

They were lost in each other when Lake finally pulled onto the PCH, lots of hair blowing and dreamy moans riding on the wind.

CHAPTER THIRTY

Mac and Red Ass

Mac Timken gets a lot of stares. Partly, it's LA where people expect to see famous faces. The other part is when you're an exquisite, 6-3, sun-streaked blonde with five percent body fat, you're going to draw eyes on Galapagos. Mac doesn't make movies, but her micro-bikini tan is the wallpaper of choice on several million desktops. Such is the price of beach volleyball stardom.

Mac is actually Charlotte, but her father had a John D. MacDonald jones, so she was Mac from the day she hit the bassinet. It didn't hurt her athletic career either. Lots of Charlottes, not so many Macs. Even if there had been, it wasn't much of a contest.

Mac and I have an arrangement. When one of us wants sex without complications, we call. The answer is usually yes, but if it isn't, nobody gets their nose out of joint. Sometimes we spend an hour together; sometimes a week, and once, we departed Newport Beach for an overnight cruise to nowhere and ended up in Bermuda.

I've never had anything less than an interesting conversation with Mac. I've also never heard her mention any politician. The two are probably related. On our Bermuda trip, we put in wherever it suited us and stocked up on local delicacies, just enough clothes to remain civilized and loads of books, which we read out loud to each other then passionately argued our positions over excellent meals and even better wine. The jury met in my stateroom. Sometimes we had to go into extra session.

I don't remember how long we were gone, but one day, without saying a word, Mac kissed me gently, took a cab to the airport and flew home. Rare is the woman who knows that another minute would be too much— and rarer still, the man, especially when the lovemaking is superb. I meandered back through the Panama Canal alone, enjoying the solitude.

Sex with Mac isn't an athletic event or a study in insecurity. You want, you ask, you get. Often, it's just slow, gentle and lingering. Lately, I've found myself calling her more frequently. Or has it been the other way around? Time seems to get away from me when we're together, and a couple of times, Mallory has threatened to send a deprogrammer.

I awakened to a seagull sitting in one of the open second-floor windows, taking in our nakedness. A short walk down the hill, the surf was hitting Manhattan Beach. On the breeze was something south of the border and spicy coming from Pancho's, a baseball throw the other direction.

The night had gone by without dinner, and I suddenly realized how desperately hungry I was. Then Mac moved her behind against my manhood, and I decided to slide it somewhere it wouldn't catch cold. I thought about sending the seagull for chimichangas, but I couldn't reach my wallet. Then I had other things to deal with.

Half an hour later, we were getting out of the shower when my phone light went on.

Kevin Costner and Venus Williams' hometown of Lynwood is fourteen miles due south of Staples Center, but you would be hard-pressed to find many Angelenos who could point to it on a map. For the authenticity-obsessed foodie, however, there are a couple of restaurants—*Guelaguetza* and *La Huasteca*—worth the trek.

The city is bisected by the 105 Freeway, which a thousand pilots a day follow into LAX. The result is a steady overhead droning and an occasional mist of jet fuel on your windshield. At least, one hopes it's jet fuel. Lynwood is also the location of the Century Regional Detention Facility— more commonly known as the LA Women's Jail—successor to the crumbling stinkhole of Sybil Brand, where the nation watched decades of bad girls, most famously, Manson's, be paraded to court in polyester blues.

At the guard booth, Sheriff's Deputy Hernandez ran my driver's license through two scanners. One I knew was for wants and warrants; the second I hadn't seen before.

"Feds," Hernandez said. "Terrorist Watch List and some other stuff—or so they tell me."

"If it's hooked up to the IRS, better step back. Could overheat."

Hernandez grinned with a set of perfect teeth over a well-groomed goatee. "Guy who installs these things swings by every now and then to ask how it's doin. I got no idea. Still waitin for my first underwear bomber. He drives himself an S-Class, though, so I'm workin him for a job."

Upward mobility. It makes the world go round. "Good luck."

"Thanks, who you here to see?"

"Wind Fortune."

He looked at me again, studying my face. "The night shift deputy said so many camera trucks were followin her black and white, he thought maybe Al Cowlings was drivin. You ain't the bondsman; I know all them. So you must be the lawyer."

"Just a friend."

"They're not gonna let you see her unless you're family."

"I'll take my chances."

He shrugged and handed me my license. "Parking Lot H. Leave your phone in the car. You got a weapon? Legal or otherwise?"

"Just my smile."

"You can leave that in the car too. Rosie Fanning's workin Visitation. Woman's got no feelin for people."

As I parked, I noticed dark clouds rolling in and taking away what, moments earlier, had been a sunny afternoon. When weather moves that fast in LA, it's not good news. Walking toward the administration building, I saw three flashes of lightning in the west. Another bad sign. We don't do lightning.

Deputy Hernandez had been charitable. Sgt. Fanning was a female Charles Barkley. Add in the bulletproof vest and thirty pounds of upside-your-head gear, and she was one of the most imposing cops I'd ever seen, man or woman. Her charm you could have stored in a thimble and had room left over for an investment banker's sincerity.

She barely glanced at the paperwork it had taken me the better part of half an hour to fill out, and on which I had carefully detailed my connection to Wind. "Not related, go home."

She was looking past me for her next victim when I stepped into her line of sight. "All I'm asking is that you check with Miss Fortune or, if you prefer, the sheriff. I'm as close to family as she has left, and this is a very fragile young lady."

Sgt. Fanning rose to her full height, surprising me that there was more of her, and narrowed her eyes. "Mister, we don't do star treatment. Miss Fortune is being detained under the same rules as everybody else. And if there's one way to frost my butt, it's to hand me a call-the-sheriff speech. So before I take my next breath, you better be heading out the way you came in, or I'm gonna have a couple of deputies toss you and your Beverly Hills sass in a sober-up cell that needs a good hosing."

When I didn't move, she put one hand on her Taser and reached for the "come whip some ass" button I knew was under the counter. Before she activated the twitch muscles in her finger, I said very quietly, "It's your stage, Sergeant, but take a good look at me and ask yourself if I seem like your standard-issue jerk. Beverly Hills sass, notwithstanding."

When she hesitated, I knew we were going to be friends. "So before we end up with enough brass humping down to Lynwood that you'll have to send out for extra salutes, how about we find a way to make each other's day? You familiar with Cdr. Rampulla in West Hollywood?"

The sergeant eyed me suspiciously. "Red-Ass Rampulla? Yeah, I know him, but he's got nothing to do with what goes on down here."

So I wasn't the only one who found the commander enchanting. "Well, give him a call, and mention you're sitting on Rail Black."

"You a pain to him too?"

"He's got half the department out looking for me on the Colosseum Pictures mess. I don't know anything, but he's got to cover his bases."

I felt the thaw. "My momma's in from St. Louis, and she loves her some Indian casinos. I'm thinking if you're really that important to him, it should be worth a couple of extra personal days." Her smile could have lit the Morongo marquee.

"Minimum. And tell Red-Ass not to forget Oxford. Then step back from the phone."

Wind looked better than I expected. Somebody who liked to screw with celebrities had given her a jumpsuit three times larger than necessary, and even with the cuffs rolled up, she had to ball the waist in her fist to keep from tripping. They had us in a tiny lawyer consultation room where the table and two cheap plastic chairs were bolted to the floor. The door was closed, but I could still hear a chorus of female voices in the cellbock chanting, "Movie star pussy gonna be mine!"

Wind hugged me, trembling, until the guard watching through a window knocked on the glass with his can of pepper spray for us to stop. She smelled of institutional soap and nightmares. "Uncle Rail, I'm so sorry."

I stroked her hair then sat her down. "Relax, honey, Jake's on it. You'll be out in a couple of hours. Tell me what happened."

"I went to *Trellis*, like I told you. Just me and a bunch of girls. There were these three guys at another table. One of them was in one of my pictures. Renaldo, I think his name is. Not much of an actor, just eye candy, but he was always real nice. We used to talk between takes."

How do you tell a naïve star that some wannabe hanging on by his fingernails wasn't looking for radiant conversation.

"Anyway, they kept sending frozen Bellinis over to us. I tried to wave them off because I can't drink, but the other girls were having such a good time I finally let it go and just gave mine to somebody else. When I got ready to leave, I looked around for Renaldo to thank him, but he was gone.

"There hadn't been any paps out front when I got there, but all of a sudden, the sidewalk was so crowded, people couldn't walk by. I never saw so many cameras. Some of the guys were shouting really ugly things, trying to make me angry so they could get a crazy picture. I just wanted to get out of there.

"The valet stopped my car in the street so I wouldn't have to deal with pulling into traffic, and a couple of waiters helped get me through the crush. I was just about to close my door when, out of nowhere, Renaldo comes flying past everybody and grabs my arm really hard. I tried to push him away, but he got a handful of my hair, and I just lost it." She started to whimper. "Uncle Rail, I was so scared. I just remember screaming and screaming and screaming."

She jumped up again, and I ignored the guard's tapping and held her until she regained her composure.

"Somehow, I got the Navigator in gear and floored it. Renaldo hung on for a second, then let go. I didn't feel anything, but I guess his foot got smushed under my wheel. Next thing I knew, I was clear up on Sunset, and there were cops everywhere. Then I was on the ground, and somebody was putting handcuffs on me." She was sobbing now.

"And you didn't have anything to drink?"

She shook her head strenuously. "Nothing, Uncle Rail, honest. Just club soda. One of the girls knocked over a Bellini, and some of it spilled on my jacket, but I didn't drink a drop. You can check with the police. I gave them permission to take blood when I got here." She pulled up her sleeve and showed me a Band-Aid in the crook of her elbow.

I didn't know who I was angrier with. "What's Renaldo's last name?"

"If I remember right, it's Zamora. Soon as I get out of here, I'm going to find him and beg him to forgive me. I feel terrible about his foot."

She wouldn't have to worry about the apology. I'd be handling that. First, though, I'd practice my delivery. I wanted it to come out just right. "Listen to me, Wind, the bondsman is Jake's cousin. He'll take you home. Do you want Mallory to have a doctor come to the house?"

"No, I'm fine now that you're here. Uncle Rail, I miss my parents, but I don't know what I'd do without you and Uncle Mallory."

As they led her away, I could already hear the actor's lawsuit being dropped on some judge's desk. I wondered what sound they made when they were withdrawn.

CHAPTER THIRTY-ONE

A Task Force and a Plum

The theory behind a task force is that a team of focused professionals will get to the bottom of a high-profile case, fast. The reality is that, unless you're trying to take down the Gambinos, a pair of no-bullshit detectives is usually the smarter play. Mostly, task forces end up being PR instruments for politicians and resume-builders for prosecutors. Straight-ahead detectives make that crowd nervous.

Nineteen dead people at a movie company meant that anyone lucky enough to be on this task force would be guaranteed book deals, movie contracts and talk show appearances for the next half-decade. It went without saying that every high-ranking badge and bar card in LA would be calling in markers.

I wasn't surprised to find that Rampulla had commandeered the detention center's cafeteria and even arranged a show of spit and polish deputies to guard the doors. However, eleven somber, decked out members of law enforcement and two court reporters sitting around the employee lunch table seemed excessive—until I realized how critical it was to their future talking points to be able to say they were in the room when Rail Black was interviewed. I just hoped they wouldn't each feel the need to ask questions.

Cdr. Rampulla wasn't what I expected. No bulldog face or belt-stretching gut. He was a slender guy in his forties with neatly-combed black hair and a pencil-thin moustache. His uniform looked tailored too, the brass glittering like a marine. His one affectation was a large USC ring on his middle finger that he rapped loudly on the table whenever he made a point. In his favor was that he smoked unfiltered Pall Malls and didn't care where he lit up.

He sat at the head of the table. To his left was his homicide chief, Capt. Al Bricklin, a husky Mickey Spillane-type in a wrinkled suit and a stained tie searching for a neck. On the commander's right was Deputy District Attorney Wendy Plum, a pinch-faced thirtysomething whose frizzed hair and lack of makeup screamed Berkeley—and manless. Ms. Plum introduced herself as the Acting Director of the Sunset Strip Massacre Task Force. So they'd already dropped "Blvd." and added "Strip." Punchier, I thought. Producers would like that.

The rest was an assortment of standard-issue gun-carriers and bureaucrats, including, for some reason, an LAFD arson investigator. Sizing up the crowd, my money was on Bricklin. He'd probably solved more murders than Wendy'd eaten granola bars.

Pink and powdered Marvin Oxford sat next to Bricklin, looking as out of place as five figures of cashmere, silk and gold—not counting his watch—could look. He crossed his Kiton-clad legs and stared at me. "Black, unless you're paying my hourly rate, you've got five minutes."

As good an actor as his class of attorney was, I didn't think he was posturing. He still didn't know his Number One client had been at the scene of a multiple murder. "You can leave anytime you like, Marvin. If something comes up that affects Miss Jones, you can read about it."

"What's she got to do with anything?"

"Try listening for a change."

He harrumphed but stayed put.

They'd left me a chair between the two court reporters. "If there are any FBI here, I prefer they sit where I can keep an eye on them." I said as I took my seat. "Last time they interviewed me, I got a rifle butt to the back of the head."

Rampulla allowed himself a smile. "You're okay. They're still waiting for Washington to give them permission to gas up the car."

Ms. Plum gave the commander a hard look and in a voice shrill enough to crack teeth shot back, "I'm liaising until they can free up one of their O.C. experts."

Liaising? Definitely Berkeley. I guess she hadn't taken the class about what Feds do to local prosecutors, especially if they sniff organized crime.

She turned her attention to me. "Before we get started, Mr. Black, I want to know why you've been evading law enforcement? And let me warn you that, depending on your answer, I may ask Capt. Bricklin to Mirandize you."

I looked at Rampulla whose return stare said, you're on your own. Bricklin had apparently already had his fill of Ms. Plum. "You can show us the hair under your arms later, Wendy. Right now I'm only interested in who killed a shithouse full of rich people. Mr. Black, why don't you give us your thoughts."

I ran through what had happened since I'd picked up Teddy at San Quentin, leaving out Wind, Cortez Detroit and our trip to Cedars. The reporters typed, the task force took notes, Rampulla smoked, and Bricklin watched me like a poker pro looking for a tell. When I finished, the detective asked if I thought the shooters might have been after me.

"Most people who want me dead would like it to take longer."

Everybody seemed to like that except Ms. Plum. "I'm sure a man of your breeding finds this all very *de classé*, but I'd like an answer to that too."

"From what I can tell, the operation was blueprinted down to the second. That kind of planning takes time. I didn't decide to invest in the company until the week before, and only Teddy and my attorney knew about it. But if there's something I haven't put together, the quickest way to bring it into focus is for you guys to share the unpublished details. Otherwise, you've wasted enough of my time already."

Wendy closed her notebook. "I believe we're finished here. Mr. Black, don't leave town. I'll be sending people over to run through the last ten years of your life. You might want to have your accountant available too."

I'd been wondering when the commander was going to show the flag. "What do you want to know?" he asked.

It was a good thing Wendy wasn't strapped. "Commander, don't even think about…"

Rampulla cut her off. "Thanks for your input. Exception noted." Turning back to me, "Please continue, Mr. Black."

"The news said there were two survivors."

"We've got a receptionist that's close to flatlining, but that's it."

Wendy nearly levitated out of her seat. "If you get into this with a civilian, I'll have you off this task force so fast…"

Rampulla lit another Pall Mall, blew smoke in her direction and continued. "One of the shooters got whacked. Timo Tata. He usually works with his brother, Pontos, so he was probably there too."

"Timo and Pontos. Greeks."

"From that snappy little island called Kansas City. They're in the O.C. database—with a star."

"Star?"

"If you hire the Tatas, you're finished talking about your problem. They've also got a reputation for never using one bullet when fifty will do. We think they chased somebody into the ladies room—most likely a bodyguard because he had a gun too. It's a fuckin mess in there, and we've got blood splatters from at least two more people, but only Timo's body."

"Why the ladies room?"

"You been in that building?"

"No, I know the conference room is on the top floor, that's all."

"It runs the width of the place with double doors at each end—east and west. The restrooms are across a long hall alongside—ladies to the east, men to the west. We think the guy ran out the east doors, down the hall and into the first place he came to."

I nodded. "Only Timo and Pontos are right behind. The bodyguard kills Timo and wounds his brother, but they nail him too."

"Yes."

"So where's the bodyguard?'

Wendy decided to get back in. "We don't know. We think maybe he became disoriented and ran. He could be unconscious someplace—or dead. We've got units going up and down the streets in the neighborhood."

A glance at Bricklin and Rampulla confirmed they thought that was as ridiculous as I did. "Wouldn't an employee headcount tell you who's missing?"

Bricklin shook his head. "The Passavantis brought their own security with them from Italy. Two were clipped on the roof and two more in the reception area. We got the IDs the dead ones were carrying, so we know. But the aircraft manifest lists six plus the three brothers, with no names for anybody."

"So you're missing two, not one."

"At least. We're still not sure who else might have been in the building. Seems the camera system was tampered with."

"Who do the Tatas work for?"

"They're independent contractors, but the list of people they've been associated with runs five pages, single-spaced. Unfortunately, a lot are just aliases and nicknames. We're working up the probables, but it's slow-going."

I tried to think of a way to get a description of the restroom crime scene out of Bricklin, but underestimating his antenna wasn't smart. "What's your best guess on motive?" I asked Bricklin.

"Money, what else? Not pocket change, but serious jack for whoever sent them. But I'm also betting at least one of the victims was walking around with a bigger story than anyone knew."

One of the live ones too, I thought. Yep, Bricklin was the one to be careful with. Ninety-nine percent of the time, professional murder is about money. Politics, revenge or a message might be spliced in, but man is an acquisitive beast. A messy, daylight slaughter on one of the busiest streets in the world could only be about a lot of money. Maybe other things too, but money first.

"If you don't mind my asking, what do you intend to do with Colosseum?" asked Rampulla. "I know your lawyer told the press you're out of the deal, but the LAPD sent me their file on you, and next to being a major pain in the butt to the badge class, you're the patron saint of backing up friends. I figure even with Teddy Chessman dead, it doesn't much matter. It didn't with Chuck and Lucille Brando."

I hadn't expected to hear those names, and even though it was going on three years, I felt a wave of sadness rush over me. My respect for the commander went up another notch. "I'm going to make the picture we were scheduled to make. That's why I wanted Mr. Oxford here. He needs to know Miss Jones is going to be safe before he'll let her work. Colosseum can provide security, but only you guys have intelligence capabilities, and I want to be in that loop."

Wendy hadn't liked this from the beginning. Now the wheels came off. She glared at the court reporters. "Stop recording," she commanded. As soon as their fingers were off the keys, she got down to business. "With all due respect to your goddamn movie, Black, that's your problem, not law enforcement's. We don't do protection nets for half-ass actresses. And we don't share confidential information with outsiders—even rich ones. So in language I'm sure you'll understand, go fuck yourself."

Marvin had just been planning a bank deposit, and now Wendy was jerking away the pen. "Wait a minute. My client's at risk here."

She was on a roll. "Mr. Oxford, fuck you and your overdressed, under-mannered, publicity-seeking, no-talent client."

Marvin might have agreed with all that, but if I weren't canceling the picture, it was music to the ears of his first love—Marvin. He fixed his stare on Ms. Plum. "How about I call the DA and remind him of Miss Jones's participation in his wife's fashion gala? Better yet, why don't I just call his wife? She's my client too."

Wendy started to say something else, but Marvin had a howitzer. He removed his silk pocket square and pulled something small and wafer-thin out of his breast pocket. He placed it on the table. "That's a new model Sony's testing. I may have inadvertently left it in record mode. Shall we check?"

Recording without consent in California is a felony, but by the time anybody got around to prosecuting this, Wendy would be manning a cookie kiosk at a mall. She stared at the little gizmo like it might explode, and after a moment, bit her lip and sat back. Jake would have approved.

"Miss Jones lives in Holmby," said Rampulla. "The old Judy Garland place. It's LAPD territory, and we've already worked out a rotation. But intel's a two-way street. If we're going to help each other, I don't want any more bullshit. I call, you pick up before it rings. Got it?"

We were making progress, but like cops always do, he'd reverted to grabbing his nuts and giving them a public shake. "Let's both avoid disappointment. I suggest the captain act as middleman."

If he could have reached me, Bricklin would have torn my throat out. "No fuckin way. I'll find some deputy who wishes he'd gone to film school."

Rampulla banged his ring on the table. "No, he's right, it has to be a pro. Welcome to show business, Al."

"With all due respect, Commander, fuck you."

Wendy regained her footing. "I insist everything go through my office—everything, understand?"

Rampulla was really good. "I wouldn't have it any other way."

As I headed back to my car, I barely noticed what had become a steady rain. The fear I'd had yesterday had come to pass. These murders were beyond the pay grade of civil servants. Way beyond. But even with all the eyeballs on it, no one had yet figured out Valentine Jones was a Passavanti.

I dialed the number Jake had left me, and a deep, Chicago-accented voice answered. "Dare here."

"Rail Black."

"Nice to finally meet you, Mr. Black. Hope you don't mind, but I'm making decisions. In this town, you can't afford to sit still."

He was already my kind of executive. "I'm sure Teddy would approve. And call me Rail."

"He was a good man. Going to miss him."

"I want to read *Beverly Hills is Burning*."

"No problem."

"I'll be home in a couple of hours. You know where I live?"

"Dove Way, and your houseman's name is Mallory. It'll be waiting."

"Question. Anything in it rise to the level of murder?"

There was a long pause. "If you believe the story, all of it."

CHAPTER THIRTY-TWO

Razor Strops and Confessions

MID-JUNE, 1935
LAGUNA BEACH

The weeks had flown by. Early on, Barrie slept so much she thought she might be sick, but Lake assured her it just was her body regenerating itself after prolonged stress. Often, they spent most of the day in bed with Lake making love to her then plying her with detailed questions. Barrie did her best to remember names and events before falling asleep again.

Sometimes, Lake would so relentlessly probe a point that Barrie would pretend to doze off to make her stop. But that only delayed the process because Lake always came back to the question she wanted answered. Eventually, Barrie realized that this exhaustive attention to detail was probably what made her such a good writer.

When Barrie started to feel like herself again, they moved their sessions to the stone courtyard just a few steps up from the waves. Lake wrote in red journals in a small, oddly constructed script that Barrie sometimes tried to read over her shoulder but couldn't decipher. The journals themselves had three L's on their covers, and one of Lake's trademark silver birds embedded under the initials. But when Barrie asked what the middle L stood for, she got a look that reminded her not to be so inquisitive.

Lake lived on a stretch of Laguna Beach that was rocky and deserted. There were no other houses in sight, so if weather permitted, they wore only sunglasses while they worked. Sometimes, Barrie would drift into a nap and awaken to

Lake's licking her. Other times, Lake made her wear the flying birds on her nipples and clitoris while she talked. Those times, Lake would say, "I want all of your emotion on the page," and words would tumble out, frequently resulting in Barrie's crying in the older woman's arms.

In the evenings, Lake retired to her study to type while Barrie remained by herself, playing music and reading or listening to the radio. Madalynne came every weekend, and Barrie waited breathlessly for her arrival. They would rush into each other's arms, and Lake would lead them to the bedroom where she would sit in an armchair and watch as they made love. Lake rarely participated, but afterward, she would have them kneel between her legs together and bring her to climax.

In the living room, there was a large wall safe behind a hinged, plein air mural of Laguna's Main Beach. Lake kept her journals and finished pages there, along with Barrie's necklace, money and gun. Once, as Lake was locking her work away for the night, Barrie asked if she could read what she had written. Lake hadn't answered. Instead, she had instructed Barrie to bare her bottom and bend over the arm of the sofa. Lake had then whipped her buttocks with a thick, razor strop until Barrie was sobbing. "Never ask to read my work. Ever."

"Yes, ma'am. I'm sorry, ma'am," Barrie finally choked out. The episode was not spoken of again.

There had been another incident with the strop that Barrie wished she could forget as well, but for a different reason. Barrie had been tied down, and Madalynne had hesitated doing something to her that Lake had demanded. Barrie didn't want it done either, but she remained silent. For her disobedience, Lake put the restraints on Madalynne then handed the strop to Barrie and ordered her to lash the actress's smooth pussy. "Just once, but hard, or I will do it myself. And what I will do to you for your disobedience will be worse."

"It's okay," Madalynne had said. "Do what ma'am says. I deserve it."

Barrie had seen the silky flesh between Madalynne's legs quiver and her nipples swell and become hard. When she brought the strop down on the helpless girl, it cracked like a whip. Madalynne screamed, and with no warning, an orgasm as intense as Barrie had ever experienced enveloped her so totally she began to shake uncontrollably and had to fight to find breath. She was horrified *at her reaction to inflicting pain, but more horrified at the pleasure she saw on Lake's face.*

She spent the rest of the evening cuddling Madalynne and trying to sooth the young girl with her tongue, but she couldn't erase the picture of Lake's satisfied smile—as if she had somehow graduated into a new reality.

Later, when Lake went to her study to work, Barrie kissed Madalynne deeply and whispered, "She's completely crazy. We have to run."

Madalynne jerked away like she'd been hit again. "Leave ma'am? Have you lost your mind?"

Barrie reeled. "But, I thought…"

"What, that because I love you, I'd throw my life away? I get a thousand fan letters a week along with fifty marriage proposals. People throw themselves at my car. I'm somebody. A star. And when ma'am finishes her script, I'll be an even bigger one. With an Academy Award. Why would you ever think I'd give that up? Because she told you to whip my pussy? I almost wish you'd refused, because ma'am would have hit it harder."

Then Madalynne came back into Barrie's arms and said, "Now make love to me. But gently. I'm still sore."

Suddenly everything was different. If Lake could order pain, how was she different than Luciano? And if Barrie had become so twisted that she could climax by hurting the woman she supposedly loved, what was she? How far was left to descend?

Something inside her died.

Lake had begun letting Barrie take the Packard into downtown. Sometimes it was only to walk around, but occasionally Lake would give her a list of things they needed. Soon Barrie knew most of the shopkeepers, and after the second strop incident, she casually begin asking if anyone knew Danny Dades.

Most did, but no one had seen him for a long time. So on her way home, she began turning into the road leading to Danny's house, parking behind some trees so she couldn't be seen from the highway and sitting there as long as she dared. She never saw any cars going up or coming down.

Lake had a fancy, brass telescope that stood in the window, facing the ocean. When she saw large yachts or ships out to sea, she liked to dial them in and watch the people aboard who never suspected they were being spied upon. Barrie would look when Lake told her to, but it made her feel creepy.

What she did like was taking the telescope into the courtyard and looking at the moon and stars. One night, while Lake was inside, she swung it toward the ridgeline and eventually found Danny's house. But it was totally dark.

A few weeks later, "Daddy" London sent his limousine to fetch his daughter for lunch in Long Beach. Lake was spending a lot of time up there lately. Sometimes overnight. Barrie was forbidden to leave the house without permission and never when Lake was away. She was aware that Lake would somehow know if she took the car, but she had already made her decision. First, however, she sat down at Lake's desk and took out a piece of LLL stationary.

The Santa Ana winds were blowing hot and hard, making the steep winding road up to Danny's more treacherous than ever. Drifts of sand littered the blacktop like tan snow, and Barrie saw no tire tracks through them. High above the surrounding hills, the ground leveled onto a narrow plateau. The house itself loomed another seventy-five feet above, set atop its own narrow promontory like the final layer of a wedding cake.

Scrub undergrowth had migrated onto the road's surface, and a large palm had blown down, blocking Barrie from getting all the way to level ground. She set the parking brake and got out, struggling to keep her balance on the incline. Walking the rest of the way to the plateau, she stood for a long time, catching her breath then listening, but she heard nothing except the distant sound of surf and the wind buffeting the Packard.

From where she stood, it was evident that Danny Dades' house had been deserted for some time. The windows were caked with dust, and tumbleweed blew along the retaining wall that framed one side of the upwardly tilted driveway. Several of the neon tubes set into the concrete spelling HIGHROLLER HILL had been broken—likely from a rock dislodged by the wind. Miraculously, the tubes in the shape of a pair of giant dice had been spared.

Barrie shielded her eyes and lowered her head into the gusts as she made her way to the closed gate. She had kidded Danny about the ugly steel barrier that greeted visitors to his fabulous home, and she saw that the bougainvillea she had planted to camouflage it had climbed almost to the top and sent tendrils laterally along its length. "Another ten years," she said out loud, "and this unsightly steel will be completely hidden by pretty pink flowers."

Barrie had to search for the hollow rock where Danny always left a spare key, but when she found it, there was nothing inside. She folded her note and forced it into the empty slot then returned the rock to its place.

The beating for leaving the house was bad, but Barrie didn't care anymore. Rather than wait for Lake to discover her indiscretion, she "confessed." She said she'd gotten lonely for Madalynne and started to Los Angeles, then guilt had overcome her, and she'd turned back. Barrie couldn't tell if Lake believed her or not, but it didn't matter.

She didn't cry this time, though involuntary tears did jump from her eyes when the strop fell the first time. The worst part was that Lake made her remain over the arm of the sofa for a long time afterward, legs spread, wearing only high heels. Each time she moved, she got another lash. It was well into the night when she was finally allowed to stand upright, then her legs wouldn't hold her. She crawled to bed.

CHAPTER THIRTY-THREE

Beverly Hills and Mythical Islands

JUNE 27, 1935

Barrie boarded the train from the white stucco, mission-style station at San Juan Capistrano. It was a blisteringly hot day, and she took a seat next to an open window, willing to risk the occasional blast of soot from the big Santa Fe locomotive in order to have wind in her face. As she rode north, even the Pacific was languid, as if making waves was too much effort.

Lake and Madalynne were in Chicago for the premier of Madalynne's newest picture—a screwball comedy about a ditzy department store clerk who unwittingly precipitates a strike when her breaks aren't long enough to get to the ladies room and back. Lake had screened "Run Daisy Run" at the house, and Barrie had laughed until she almost peed herself. She was amazed at Madalynne onscreen. So different than she really was. So talented at being someone else.

Lake had a second agenda in the Windy City: meeting the owner of the Biograph Theatre and the FBI agent who'd shot John Dillinger. Even though the story was a year old, it had lost none of its public fascination, and Lake wanted to write it for Madalynne to play the Lady in Red.

As the train lurched forward, Barrie couldn't help but think about the strop that surely awaited her when Lake returned, but like with the car, she didn't care. In fact, she enjoyed thinking about Lake in a hotel two thousand miles away, getting no answer when she called and seething. Perhaps even taking it out on Madalynne.

At the elegant La Grande Station in downtown Los Angeles, Barrie was surprised to see that the fabled Moorish dome was gone. A sign on a barricade said it had been removed because of earthquake damage but would be rebuilt. Barrie hoped so. It had leant character to an otherwise uninteresting city.

She caught a streetcar, rode north a few blocks then transferred to the Santa Monica line. It was even hotter in LA than Laguna, and at the first stop, she leaned out the window and bought a lemonade from a kid with a pushcart. Forty minutes later, she stepped onto Roxbury Drive in Beverly Hills and approached the first taxi in line. "I'm looking for Dove Way."

"That would be the Stinson place," the driver said. "He's the only one up there. Climb in." When she was settled, the cabbie gave her an admiring glance in the mirror. "You some kinda actress, Miss?"

"Not even the bad kind," she smiled. "Mr. Stinson entertain a lot of them?"

"No, but a friend of his does."

Barrie didn't need to ask who that was. She'd found the street name in Lake's address book, but no house number, and an operator told her they had no listing for a Stinson anywhere in the area. A letter probably would have gotten to him, but she owed him more than that.

The ride up the hill was like entering another world. Interlocking jacaranda trees formed a canopy of fragrant violet over the street, framing the grand homes as if in a painting. Japanese gardeners knelt on lawns too perfect to be real, and expensive cars adorned the wide driveways. But in this wonderland, there was no evidence anyone actually lived there. Barrie didn't see a single resident strolling a sidewalk or even sitting on a porch.

The driver seemed to read her mind. "I owned one a these joints, I'd be standin out front with a big arrow over my head, so everybody knowed it was me."

Barrie laughed and agreed. They crossed Sunset, and the upward grade suddenly increased, lowering the temperature appreciably the higher they went. By the time the cab reached J.C. Stinson's gate, the air was comfortable.

"Somebody expectin you, Miss?" the driver asked as she paid him.

"Not exactly."

"Mr. Stinson's gone a lot. You want me to wait? It's supposed to be double meter, but I won't pull the stick."

"I'll be fine."

"Suit yourself. When you need a ride back, tell the dispatcher you want Slim."

"I will, Slim, thanks."

A square, gold plate was affixed to the stone column anchoring the gate. It contained two words engraved in script and highlighted in black enamel.

Mag Mell

She didn't know what it meant, but Barrie had seen names like Oheka, Falaise, and Inisfada on houses in New York and understood that the rich aren't just different, they delight in being obtuse. It took her a moment to locate the ringer, which she finally found inside the steel bars. She pressed it several times, but the gates remained firmly in place. No sound reached her except rustling leaves and the screech of a blue jay, apparently irritated at the intrusion.

There were no neighbors to ask about Mr. Stinson or to use their phone to call Slim, and she suddenly felt foolish for letting him go. She couldn't even find a pen in her purse to leave a note. After a few more rings, she reluctantly turned and started back down the steep road.

She had gone about a quarter-mile when she heard a motor coming at high RPMs. She stepped into the drainage ditch to give it room. Barrie wasn't an expert on cars, but she knew a Rolls-Royce when she saw one. This was a silver, teardrop-shaped convertible that was almost as long as her coach on the Santa Fe. It blew by so quickly, she didn't get a look at the driver, but he was wearing a white Panama hat. Then suddenly, the brake lights came on, and the Rolls began backing up.

Barrie had never seen such a home. The mansions on Long Island were larger, but none were as striking. In the East, big money erected dark-beamed castles and white marble palaces, set amid intricately manicured geometric gardens that exuded the formality of Old Europe.

Mag Mell's rambling grounds could have been lifted straight out of Babylon. Thousands of colors from hundreds of exotic plants playing hide-and-seek with a house that combined the best of architectural Spain with the lazy ambiance of the Caribbean. A casual sumptuousness that once experienced was impossible to forget.

J.C. Stinson's art was a little too flamenco and bullfight for Barrie's taste, but the extensive interior woodwork and pastel murals were as sophisticated as any Vanderbilt commission—and without a gargoyle to be had.

"I'm speechless," she said.

"Most of the time, so am I," J.C. replied. "So I get up every morning and pretend South Philly's right outside. It keeps me from getting too full of myself."

Barrie really liked this man. This was her third interaction with him, and he was nothing like Lake described. "Do you mind my asking about the name?"

Stinson twisted a new cigarette into his holder and lit it. "Mag Mell is the Irish version of heaven. A mythical island where the generous, the just and the innocent spend eternity. I'm pretty sure that doesn't include lawyers, so I'm grabbing my slice now."

"You're absolutely charming."

"There's a word a man never wants to hear from a beautiful woman. So much for my dreams."

Barrie laughed. "I'll take it back for a glass of water."

"Somewhere amid all this fluff is a staff. Let's both have something while you regale me with stories of your grand adventure."

"I don't think anyone's here. I rang the bell for quite a while."

"If I'm not home, they ignore it. I don't encourage drop-ins. Present company excluded, of course."

"And Mr. Hughes," Barrie ventured.

"That's precisely why they don't answer."

They sat in wrought iron chairs looking across the hills toward the ocean. Mrs. Thompson, the housekeeper, had served them iced tea and a plate of chocolate chip cookies that Barrie was trying to keep her hands out of. She had told Stinson everything—but without mentioning Lake London.

"Howard's flown over every inch of real estate between San Berdoo and San Diego, looking for that de Havilland."

"I'm sorry, but unfortunately there's a lot of water on top of it."

"Put it out of your mind. I presume you're staying with Danny Dades."

The remark caught Barrie off-guard. "You know Danny?"

"Never met him, but as soon as I heard you were missing, I had a friend in the state department pull the names of people out here with multiple Cuban visas. Once I eliminated the Hollywood crowd and a few others, there were two left: a horse breeder at Santa Anita and a craps dealer in Laguna Beach. I skipped the guy who's seventy and called the one who's thirty-four."

Panic welled up in Barrie's throat. "You talked to him? What did he say?"

"That the two of you used to have a thing, but he hadn't heard from you in a year. Then he asked if I'd seen you."

"But you didn't believe him."

"I'm a lawyer. I don't believe much. But if you were just an old fling, why ask the second question? It suggested you were alive, though, and that's all I cared about."

"I appreciate your concern."

"And I appreciate your coming all the way to Beverly Hills."

"Are you going to tell Mr. Hughes what happened to his plane?"

"Good God, no. Howard doesn't care about that piece of metal anymore. It's the challenge of finding it. If he knew it was a thousand feet down, he'd start writing checks to bring it up because nobody's ever done that before. I prefer having him fly search grids. His bankers do too."

"I don't know how to thank you."

"Not necessary, but I'm going to give you a little heads-up. My ex-wife lives in Laguna, and it's a small town. You run into her, sprint the other direction."

Barrie turned her head so Stinson wouldn't see her face flush. "Divorce is always unfortunate."

"Not from Cyanide Sue. I'm not aware she's actually killed anyone, but she's batting a thousand for poisoned relationships."

Barrie was confused. "Sue? As Susan?"

"Lakeland LaSuzette London. How's that for a pretentious mouthful? She hated it when I called her Sue, but she hated it when I said good morning too.

The only person worse is her old man. Daddy. Together, they're capable of anything, so I keep tabs on both."

Barrie was relieved. At least she wasn't going to have to come clean to warn him about Lake. "I'll be on the lookout. Thanks."

Stinson fished around in his pocket and came out with a pencil stub and some business cards in a rubber band. He slid a card out, wrote a number on the back and handed it to Barrie. "You need anything, leave a message on this line. I'll get back to you as soon as possible. If it's an emergency, forget the card and call the police. Don't take any chances. You never know who's out there."

Barrie glanced at the card and noticed that the number was different than anything she'd seen before. She was about to ask about it when she saw he was staring at her. It made her uncomfortable. Did he already know about her and Lake? Then she realized he seemed nervous. No, not nervous, emotional. He stood up. "I want to show you something."

Barrie followed him across the wide expanse of lawn past a swimming pool and a separate building with a movie screen inside. Fifty feet beyond, near the edge of a precipice that fell away to a heart-stopping view of the Great Basin of Los Angeles, they approached the backside of a free-standing, eyebrow-shaped marble wall set into a matching apron. Six feet high and ten feet across, the wall gleamed in the sunlight like some ancient Roman monolith.

Stinson led her around to the concave side where a marble bench had been placed opposite the structure. Barrie could now see that the wall was a memorial, and a narrow niche had been cut into its center where a polished silver, cremation urn sat in quiet repose. Above the urn, the wall was engraved

JILLEEN CAIT STINSON
BELOVED DAUGHTER OF J.C. STINSON
FEBRUARY 1, 1933

THOUGH SHE ONLY GRACED THE WORLD FOR AN HOUR, IT WAS THE MOST MAGNIFICENT HOUR OF ALL.

"What a beautiful, beautiful name," Barrie said.

"After a beautiful woman. My grandmother. Everybody in the family has

been a J.C., but Jilleen's where it stops, I'm afraid. End of the Stinson line. Howard saw this and said I was making too much of a non-event."

"How utterly cruel."

"You have to reach Howard on his own level, so I suggested we stop paying storage on all those crashed planes we're warehousing. You'd have thought I'd stuck a knife in him. We had a shouting match right here, but somewhere in the middle, the parallel dawned on him, and he apologized. He's the end of his line too. He pretends it doesn't bother him, but it does. That's why occasionally, he needs to be reminded he's human."

Barrie didn't know how anybody could work for such a person.

"He did make one observation I hadn't considered. The next owner isn't going to be particularly sensitive to my loss. This will be gone within twenty-four hours. He's right, of course. I'm just not ready to contemplate moving her yet."

Barrie saw tears well up in her host's eyes and decided there was nothing she could offer. "Come, let me introduce you to my daughter," Stinson said, and he slipped off his shoes and socks and stepped barefoot onto the slab. Barrie realized it was a sign of respect and did the same. Even in the heat of the day, the marble was cool to her skin.

"I thought Jilleen would like the view from here," he said. "It's as close to the real Mag Mell as I can give her."

CHAPTER THIRTY-FOUR

Bathrobes, Irish Whiskey and Junior Walker

Matty Aspirins couldn't sleep. The pain wasn't as sharp as it had been earlier, but the bandage over his eyes felt too tight. He slid a finger under the gauze at his temple and stretched it slightly. It seemed to help. The bottom half of his face was covered by a burn mask with a small opening for his mouth, and the skin beneath it felt hot from the antiseptic. He tried not to imagine what he looked like.

He got out of bed and slipped into the bathrobe the Cypriot had brought him. A pack of cigarettes and lighter were in the pocket. He felt his way into the galley, found a row of bottles and grabbed one at random. Picking his way through the main salon, he opened the sliding glass door and stepped into the night. The teak deck was cool under his bare feet, the breeze touched with fish and diesel. He shuffled along until he ran into one of the large wicker chairs near the stern and sat down heavily. He propped the bottle on his lap and lit a smoke, enjoying the hit of nicotine.

The creaking of ancient wooden pilings and foam bumpers rubbing against the pier was overhung by the low rumble of a large boat heading in from open water. In the distance, the bell on the channel buoy clanged intermittently. Matty uncapped his bottle and took a swig. Whiskey, Irish. Not his favorite, but better than another trip to the galley.

The Cypriot said the houseboat was moored in a commercial area of San Pedro Harbor. There were no pleasure craft nearby, and fishermen kept to themselves, so no one was likely to wander over and start shooting the shit. If somebody did, his cover was that he was recuperating from reconstructive surgery. Period, end of conversation.

Using the contents of several heavy suitcases they'd lugged aboard, Dr. Nick and two assistants had worked almost five hours plucking pieces of mirror from his face and eyes. Matty had counted seven trips to and from their cars for more equipment. He didn't know Dr. Nick's full name, and nobody had introduced the assistants, but all three had spoken mostly Greek during the procedure. The Cypriot had made it clear they could be trusted.

Most of Matty's vision had returned. Dr. Nick said the blindness had been trauma-induced, nothing to worry about. While he worked through a large magnifier, Matty was sedated but not completely under so he could be periodically instructed to move his eyes to a different position. There hadn't been any actual pain, but the specula that held his lids open and stretched the sockets were uncomfortable.

At first, being able to see the needle and forceps as they approached made him queasy. Then would come a push on his eyeball followed by a tug, and a tiny shard of glass would be lifted and dropped into a metal cup somewhere to his left. After an hour or so, Matty was able to ignore what was happening and just do as he was told.

The eye that had been hit by the laser still felt twice its normal size, even though it wasn't. The doc said the jury was out on how long that would last, but he'd be back the day after tomorrow to remove the bandages, and he'd check it again. He left one of the suitcases for when he did.

Once Dr. Nick was finished, the Cypriot helped move Matty from the portable operating table to the bed. "I talked to New York," he said.

"Stay outta my fuckin business."

"They called *me*, asshole. Lot of unhappy people back there."

"And I'm havin the time of my life."

"Look, my friend, I wish you'd never come to the shop, but now I'm involved too. They want you out of LA—in a hurry."

In their place, Matty would have felt the same way. The Venetians were dead, but he'd fucked up. It didn't matter how it happened. He was the guy responsible. When a job went bad, you didn't play catch-up, you went home and somebody else got handed the problem.

"You're supposed to stay away from the East Coast and anybody who knows you."

"How long?"

"A year, maybe longer. The good news is your name hasn't surfaced, so you can still travel. But with Timo's body in the hands of the cops, it's only a matter of time before somebody connects the right dots, so you gotta go now."

A fuckin year! Jesus Christ! "My whole fuckin life is in New York."

"So you'll get a new life. People do it all the time. Soon as Dr. Nick says you're good to go, we'll get you out of here. Before you know it, you'll be on the ferry from Athens to Cyprus and thinking about a blowjob. The guy who manages my building will make sure you're left alone."

Matty didn't want to go to Cyprus. "I was thinking Miami."

The Cypriot blew. "Why the fuck not? It's consistent with the other stupid decisions you been making. Look, not even my wife knows I own the place over there. Just my boys. I got a Cypriot kid on the payroll. Gabriel. He'll meet you at the dock and get you settled. Bring you food and as many broads as you can handle. I'll see you at Christmas. Maybe by then you'll understand what I been trying to tell you."

He didn't think so, but the Cypriot was right. He needed to reorient himself. Get his head straight. "Okay, let's do it."

The Cypriot patted his shoulder. "Hang in there. I'll be back when it's time to move you."

Matty was jolted out of his thoughts by footsteps on the dock. He didn't know what time it was, but it was too late for visitors. Besides, there weren't supposed to be any. He thought about going back inside, but whoever was coming had probably already seen him, so he lit another cigarette and waited.

"You Matty?" The voice was male and nasal.

"Never heard of him"

"Yeah, right."

Matty felt the deck creak slightly as the man stepped aboard. "I thought you were supposed to ask permission to board a boat."

"Here's my permission, asshole: I don't move this fuckin tub right now, come mornin, you're gonna be pickin coast guard outta your teeth."

Matty thought about that. If somebody wanted him, they wouldn't send the military. "How about a little more information."

"Monthly drug sweep. They don't want to find nothin, just keep their teams sharp and work some of that fancy equipment you and me pay for."

"They let people know they're coming?"

The man was already heading forward. "Word gets around," he said over his shoulder. "Gonna move you to the other side of the harbor for a few hours."

"You got a name?'

"No."

Matty took another swig of Irish. As he did, the houseboat engine coughed and caught. Then he heard the man untying and casting off lines. Matty wasn't an experienced sailor, but he'd owned a couple of boats. It wasn't a good idea to be sitting around in a bathrobe if something went wrong.

He banged around the unfamiliar stateroom for a long time getting dressed and was feeling for his shoes when he noticed the water getting choppy. He hadn't heard any other boats go by, so it wasn't a wake, but they were bumping enough that he had to sit on the bed to avoid being tossed into the furniture. Then he heard the channel buoy bell. It was right outside.

The only reason to take this rust bucket into open water was to either sink it or sink something on board. Better yet, both. Matty was willing to bet there was a runabout uptop that the guy intended to use afterward.

He unwound the gauze from his eyes and removed the patches over both. He then carefully lifted the burn mask over his head. Even the low light of the cabin made him wince, but shortly, his eyes began to acclimate. He didn't rush. The man at the wheel would have his hands full maintaining his course and not colliding with another boat.

When he could see well enough to move, he looked around for

something to use as a weapon, but everything heavy was bolted down. He then spotted the suitcase Dr. Nick had left. He pawed through the lenses and lights until he found an instrument slightly longer than a pencil with a tiny scalpel on one end and a needle-sharp four-inch point on the other. Not exactly Rambo, but it would have to do. The blade was too small to do much damage, so to keep from getting cut, he wound adhesive tape around it and far enough up the instrument's length for a grip. He slipped his makeshift pig sticker into his pocket and headed back to the galley.

Just to make sure, he checked the drawers for a knife. As expected, there weren't any. The guy was definitely a pro. Between the sink and refrigerator was a narrow wooden door that opened onto a dark stairway. Below, he could hear the unmistakable rumble of an engine. He found the light switch and went down.

The lone Volvo Penta power plant wasn't designed to push a blunt chunk of fiberglass through anything rougher than a birdbath, let alone ocean chop, and it was laboring mightily. The open driveshaft was spinning harder than it probably ever had, and the acrid stench of hot metal burned his nostrils. Matty located a pair of work gloves and a crowbar and pried the protective cover off the engine's guts. He disconnected a sparkplug, and the Penta began to misfire. After two more, it stopped completely. Immediately, the boat began to pitch and roll.

Across the room was an identical stairway which probably led up to the helm. Just then, the door at the top opened, and Matty moved quickly under the steps and took out his weapon. A pair of feet started down, then stopped. One more, and Matty would be able to reach between the treads, grab an ankle and send him the rest of the way on his face. But the guy didn't take the step. He stood still for a long moment, evaluating the situation. Matty knew he couldn't see the disconnected sparkplugs from that position, so the guy sensed danger. Shortly, he went back up and closed the door, but not before turning out the lights.

The percentages said that Matty should head to the galley. He was familiar with the layout, and he could be waiting when the man came looking for him. But the dimensions of the rear of the vessel indicated there were two-thirds more of her forward. That meant additional room to maneuver. Matty circled around the stairs and climbed. At the top, he listened, heard nothing and slowly opened the door.

The helm was empty, the wheel tied off with two, looped canvas straps. Ahead, behind a protective brass railing, a wall of tempered glass overlooked a small forward deck. The white-capped ocean lay beyond, and waves were beginning to sweep over the bow. Overturned aluminum chairs and an umbrella table rolled back and forth on the deck, occasionally bumping into a raised padlocked hatch. The houseboat was wallowing in a deep trough, then suddenly, her bow reared as she rode the upside of a swell. Just as suddenly, she banged down the other side, and Matty lost his grip on the door. It slammed shut loudly, and he staggered into the wheel. He froze, but no one came.

The interior of the boat was dark, but two long rows of emergency lights set into the floor allowed him to see some sixty feet to the back wall. This deck was a spacious lounge filled with sectional sofas, anchored lamps and large chairs. An oval bar in the center of the room was bracketed by a statue of Venus and a Yamaha baby grand piano. A safety chain allowed the piano to roll a few feet, catch, then roll back when the deck shifted. This, along with the overmatched Volvo below, confirmed the vessel's party boat status. She had to be wondering what the hell had happened to her quiet life in the marina.

Out of nowhere, a whip of water hit the glass front. At first Matty thought it was spray, then lightning flashed close-by. Seconds later thunder rolled over him, and rain pounded the deck above. A perfect night to put a blind Greek in the drink. The Cypriot wouldn't have knowingly set him up. He'd been used. Just to be sure, though, Matty would ask him in a way he'd get the truth. But first he had to deal with the asshole who was there to kill him.

Matty moved through the dark, staying between the windows and the furniture in case he needed cover. The glass was opaque from rain, so he couldn't tell how far they'd drifted from land. Then the floor shuddered slightly, and from deep in the boat's bowels, the engine started again. He waited for lights, but none came on.

Near the rear wall was an elaborate DJ console sunk five feet into the floor. Since there was no railing, Matty presumed the equipment elevated when being used but hadn't been fully retracted. Now that they had power again, why not give himself a little audio cover.

Matty eased into the pit. Tiny green lights on the electronics glowed eerily in the gloom. The rack of CDs was mostly old R&B, and Matty grinned as he made his selection and loaded it as quietly as he could. Suddenly, a pair of legs and an arm carrying a semiautomatic pistol went past his face. Matty was dead if the man saw him, but the guy apparently had other things on his mind—probably getting clear of the channel before he attracted the harbor patrol.

Matty dialed up the sound knob as far as it would go and hit PLAY. He hadn't anticipated speakers imbedded in so many places, so when the opening 12-guage blast on Junior Walker and the All Stars' "Shotgun" exploded through the room, the entire boat shook.

Rocked by the audio gunshot, the man, pivoted, dropped to a knee and fired two rounds into the ceiling, one through a window and took out a lamp with a fourth. Over the music, it was difficult to tell, but Matty thought the gun sounded like a .40-cal. Instinctively, he'd counted the rounds expended, but he knew it was pointless. He would have at least one backup mag.

As Junior's hit continued at ear-splitting volume, the man got his bearings, stayed in a low crouch and ran toward the helm. Matty moved at the same time, dropping behind the bar. The chain restraining the piano was run through a pair of thick, eye screws, one embedded in the floor, the other in the leg of the instrument. The links were held together by a simple safety hook. Matty unclipped it and waited.

Shortly, the boat wallowed again, and the bow pitched up. As it began its descent, Matty stood and added his two hundred pounds to the force of gravity. The piano shot forward, picking up speed on the downhill until it slammed into the brass railing protecting the forward wall of glass. The railing didn't give, but the lid of the piano opened like a giant yawning clam and shattered the window. Rain and spray cascaded in, and Matty rushed the helm, Dr. Nick's taped instrument in his hand.

He hit the man in a low, rolling tackle, and they ended up on the forward deck amid the broken glass and lurching furniture. Matty jammed the pointed end of the scalpel into the guy's ribs over and over as the shooter tried to get his gun pointed in the right direction. A sudden gust of wind blew the umbrella table into them. The man was knocked sideways, and Matty lost his weapon.

Matty grabbed a long, triangular shard of glass and felt it cut his hand. He ignored the pain and thrust the point toward the guy's face. It caught his nostril, laying it open, then slid up into his right eye, puncturing the orb and releasing the vitreous gel. But before Matty could jam the shard in for the kill, the blood and water made him lose his grip. He kicked hard, and the man fell away. Two more shots rang out, but they went wild.

The man scrambled to his feet and lurched down the engine room stairway. Matty was right behind, hitting the light switch on the way. The man reached the bottom and turned to fire. Matty launched himself at him. The top of Matty's head hit his attacker in the face, and the bullet went into the ceiling.

As they rolled amid the machinery, the man tried to disengage, but Matty held on, continuing to slam his forehead into his face. Pretty soon, there was so much of the guy's blood in his eyes, he thought he might have gone blind again.

Matty smelled rather than saw the driveshaft. The stink of overheated metal permeated the small area. Then the steady clatter turned to a shrill whine, and Matty knew it was going to come apart—and soon. He shook his head violently, trying to clear his vision. When he did, he saw that the rotating steel was only an arm's length away.

He leveraged one foot against a cooling unit, put his knee in the man's nuts and heaved him up and over. His head came down on the spinning shaft, and his hair immediately caught in the forward U-joint. The immense torque ripped the man's scalp completely off, and the rest of him became entangled in the high revolution assembly. Pieces of unrecognizable flesh flew in all directions, and moments later, the entire driveshaft blew. Matty was protected by being low, but that didn't keep him safe from the odor of cooking viscera.

Matty shut down the smoking machinery and staggered back to the galley. He cleaned himself up as best he could, tying a dishtowel around his sliced hand. Other than that and a major headache, he was in one piece, but the painkillers for his face had worn off, and it felt like it was on fire. He found the bottle in the stateroom and slammed down a handful then gathered anything that could be remotely connected him, including the bathrobe, jammed it into Dr. Nick's suitcase and threw it overboard.

Whatever escape the hitman had planned had to be on the upper deck. It was. Sitting in the driving rain was a green and white Kawasaki jet ski, tethered by a single rubber strap. Without power, the deck pitched violently, and the jet ski danced. Matty knew it could be tossed overboard at any second, but he couldn't gamble that the boat would capsize and go down on its own. He went back below.

Fifteen minutes later, the houseboat's seacocks and portals wide open, Matty Aspirins straddled the idling Kawasaki fifty yards off starboard and watched it roll then completely invert before disappearing. He kicked the Kawasaki into gear and sped toward shore, the Cypriot more on his mind than pain or weather.

CHAPTER THIRTY-FIVE

Big Macs and Dead Chickens

When I got to Dove Way, it was pitch dark. The rain had been pounding for several hours, knocking out the streetlights north of Sunset—a frequent indignity, home prices notwithstanding. The gutters were slick with mud, and emergency crews were pulling a Range Rover out of my neighbor's wall. I rubbernecked a little too long and had to swerve to avoid a dim bulb teenager, skateboarding down the middle of the street.

At least there were no paparazzi. They feel about rain the way Ned Beatty feels about canoeing. Add some broken bones and a tour of the LA court system for one of their fellow maggots, and the Black estate had moved a lot lower on the pap stakeout list.

I was dead tired, but my stomach was finally full, and I'd dealt with the Zamora matter, which hadn't gone exactly as planned. By the time I'd left the jail, I'd added another twenty-four hours to my hunger streak, and if somebody had looked at me cross-eyed, I'd have shoved Cortez's Hummer down his throat. The list of things that chaps my ass keeps getting longer. Near the top is the push by the grim and the brainwashed to label McDonald's a baby butcher every time some tofu-gargler farts in the direction of a Happy Meal. If I had my way, you'd have to show a Big Mac wrapper to vote. But I could just be an American.

So every now and then, I cruise into the Golden Arches and pay the manager to start cooking and not stop. Then I hand twenties to a bunch of local kids and tell them to let the neighborhood know Mickey D's is free until they run out of cholesterol. A couple of times, the cops had to be called. We feed them too.

Tonight, because of the weather, I had to lower my sights and just pick up the tab for the people in line, which I extended to a couple of homeless guys pawing through a trash barrel. Two Macs, two large fries and a pair of chocolate shakes later, my disposition was restored, and the entire restaurant, including the trash diggers, was singing, "You Deserve a Break Today." Fuck the food meddlers.

At Cortez's place, I switched back to my Ram and told him he was being denied the pleasure of my company.

"Remind Mallory he owes me fifty bucks," he said. "We play this word game on our phones, and he sucks. I thought his people invented the fuckin language."

"Good luck, I live in the same house, and I'm still trying to collect on Tyson-Holyfield."

As we shook hands, he held my grip. "I'd like your blessing to call Wind."

I wasn't born yesterday. "That means the two of you have already made plans,"

Cortez is never reticent, but he seemed to be having trouble forming words. Finally, he found some. "She told me her life's a little fucked up right now, then I caught last night's news. Man, she's got some scary shit goin on."

"What happened to the Ndidi Ba Project?"

"Nurses work a lot of nights."

"Cortez, slip into a bottle of Opus One and get a good night's sleep. Wind is twenty years your junior."

"Twenty-seven. But we connected, Rail. Like really connected."

"Cortez…"

"Rail, I'm a *doctor*."

"I have no idea what that even means. You *used* to be a *vet*. Now you're the worst thing an actress can get mixed up with—a goddamned writer. A couple of weeks from now she'll be curled around you in her underwear while you write her a part."

"I hadn't thought about that. I like it, though—except for the underwear."

"Look, I'm not her dad. She wants to go out with a guy who can't remember the last time he wasn't thinking about pussy, she's an adult. But I'm going to tell her about you myself."

His grin couldn't have been any broader. "That'll save me a lot of time."

Renaldo Zamora and two roommates shared a tiny bungalow on Norma Place, just east of Doheny and a few doors down from where Dorothy Parker once skewered the industry that overpaid her. He wasn't hard to find. My new best friend, Capt. Bricklin, popped his address in fifteen seconds, not counting the grumbling.

A guy with a gym-ripped upper body and wearing only a pair of tight jeans, cracked the door against the chain. I could see the hospital boot on his right foot as he managed a, "Yeah?"

"If you're Mr. Zamora, I'd like to talk to you."

He flicked on the porch light and spent a long few seconds staring at my face. "You're that Delta guy who watches out for Wind Fortune, aren't you?" It looked like Snive's courtroom theatrics were the gift that kept on giving.

I stuck out my hand. "Rail Black. Mind if I come in? It's a little wet out here." He ignored the hand, so I added. "I'm not looking for trouble. Just conversation."

The door closed, and when it didn't immediately reopen, I thought the moment had passed. Then, it swung inward, and I saw he'd stuck a Beretta in his waistband.

"You plan to use that?" I asked.

"Only if I have to." Renaldo's accent was High Spanish. He'd probably been educated in Spain, but unless I was very wrong, he was South American.

I believed him and stepped slowly into the small foyer. In better light, the guy wasn't young—at least not struggling-actor young. I guessed late thirties, maybe older. His roommates, also Hispanic and also without an ounce of fat on them, sat in a pair of upholstered chairs in a living room immediately to my right. They were fully dressed, but not fashionably. They didn't seem like Hollywood types, and Renaldo didn't introduce them. They took in my size and said nothing. Everybody was way too cool with a gun visible.

Renaldo motioned to a straight-backed chair facing away from the fireplace. I sat, and he eased down on the sofa. "Okay, you're in."

"You're a little long in the tooth to be an ingénue," I said.

He smiled easily. "You testing my macho or just being a jerk?"

He seemed genuine, and he didn't have the shifty nervousness of a creep being confronted for preying on young girls. "Wind's concerned about your foot."

"My fault all the way. Once you've slept with them, you gotta watch out for the fangs—or in my case, Michelins."

That backed me up a step. I didn't think he was kidding, and he couldn't know what Wind had told me. So much for her not being sure of his last name. "I take it the parting wasn't mutual."

"I'm good for a couple of weeks, then I get bored. Sometimes with actresses, it doesn't go the full two. The problem seems to be that I'm a very good lover."

One of the other men made a crude remark in Spanish, which I pretended not to understand. It got a laugh from all three. I noticed the speaker had the guttural inflection of the Southern Andes, probably Argentina. America is a melting pot; the rest of the world isn't. Unless I was very wrong, Renaldo was the boss and not just because he was better-looking.

"I hope you're not here to play cupid. That ship sailed."

"None of my business," I said. "I just wanted to know if you needed anything. Maybe cover your doctor bills."

He took a minute. "You're serious, aren't you?"

"Why am I getting the feeling I missed a chapter."

"You missed the whole book, man. I don't need your money. But you can do me a favor. Tell that blonde *concha* if she leaves another dead fuckin chicken on my doorstep, I'm gonna take out a restraining order. And while you're at it, maybe explain that just because a dude trills his r's doesn't mean he knows shit about Santeria. The first couple of times I just thought KFC had fucked up."

This time, I laughed along with them. Now I knew why Wind had walked off her New York picture. I was actually glad it was something ordinary, like a crush. Renaldo Zamora, though, intrigued me.

"This house is wrong," I said. "It doesn't fit you—or your accent. Who're you hiding from?"

That stopped the merriment. Renaldo's hand went casually to the butt of his Beretta, and two men across from him reached down between the cushions of their chairs.

"What happened to our budding friendship?" I asked.

He relaxed, but not all the way. He'd misread me and was trying to get back on equal footing. "It's a dangerous town."

"But not as dangerous as Buenos Aires."

Gone were the smile lines. "The *Times* said you're Brazilian."

"My mother was."

"Then you know in that part of the world half the army doesn't go to sleep until the other half is snoring. And officers with time on their hands start to see enemies in their *cortados*."

"Who forgot the rules?"

"My father."

"I'm sorry."

He shrugged. "Price of being a political general."

"And you?"

"I was a major in *Las Buzos Tacticos*."

The Argentine version of the SEALs. I cross-trained with them. "Good unit," I said, but it wasn't difficult to figure out. "Your father's sins derailed your career."

"Now there's a price on my head, and I'm just another Hollywood asshole."

"If you're trying to keep a low profile, why take bit parts in movies?"

234

"Wind tell you that too?"

I immediately felt foolish. "Another missed book it would seem."

He smiled and shook his head. "What a girl. Beautiful but dangerously damaged. I went to boarding school with the director of that picture. Billy Nunn. For a teenage kid from Argentina, Miami Beach in those days was the pussy machine that never ran dry. Billy and I fucked our way up one side of Collins Avenue and down the other. When he found out I was living here, he called and invited me to the set. Turned out, he was having trouble with his star."

"Since you're probably not the go-to guy for acting advice, I take it the problem was personal."

"Billy was trying to break up with her, and she was threatening to walk off the picture."

"Cue the Collins cavalry."

"So now, who do *I* call?"

I smiled. "This, I can probably handle. It's actually helpful to know."

"Glad to be of service." He held up his booted foot. "I think."

"If you don't mind, what *did* happen tonight?"

"A great girl I know just got a part in the new James Bond flick, and I put together a little surprise dinner for her. You know, a few friends, a few laughs. Just as the food shows up, here comes Wind and four of her crew. I knew right away she was looking to make a scene because she had the maitre d' move the people at the table next to us so she could sit there.

"I'm trying to keep things peaceful, so I send over a round of Bellinis. Wind promptly makes a production of tossing hers on the floor, and some of it hits her outfit. That sets her off, and while the waiters are scrambling to get her cleaned up, she starts in on my actress-friend calling her Double-O-Snatch and Bondocunt."

I didn't know whether to laugh or be sick.

"Well, this chick is from Compton, and she goes after Wind like she's on a fuckin mission. By the time we get everybody separated, there's a hundred paparazzi out front, long-lensing us, and Wind's screaming that she's going out and tell them I'm hiding from an execution squad.

"The valet hadn't put her car away, so while a couple of waiters clear a path, I'm trying to get her calmed down. Meanwhile, I've got my hand over my face like a fuckin criminal, thinking how this is going to play in Buenos Aires. When we get to the car, she turns to me with a big smile, like nothing's happened, puts her arms around my neck and says, 'Now that I've got you all to myself, let's go someplace and fuck.'

"I want to smack her, but I do something I know will sting more. I tell her I'm not interested because she's starting to look old. And she goes batshit, swinging, kicking and swearing at the top of her lungs. Then she jumps in her car and does this crazy U-turn."

"And naturally, your foot is where it's not supposed to be."

"My foot and the rest of me should have been home watching Netflix."

As I stood, I said, "Let me know if I can do anything for you, Major. I'm just up the street."

"Thanks, but probably not."

Waiting for the gates of my home to open, I reprimanded myself. As much as I professed to care about Wind, I'd done nothing but give lip service to her real needs. Even a cursory look would have revealed what was likely an endless parade of men. Freshman psych. Promiscuity replacing parental love. Aunt Maggie's influence hadn't helped, but she didn't care about anyone but herself. I didn't have that excuse.

Instead of going into my underground garage, I parked in the entry oval and, as usual, found the front door ajar. No matter how many times I lecture Mallory, he refuses to lock anything. It almost got him killed by a pair of nasty Corsicans, and recently there was Paulie Steuben. But he just looks at me and says, "I'm in and out of this house fifteen times a day, and I'll be damned if I'm going to look around for a key when I have to yell at the gardeners."

I don't expect any such thing, and he knows it, but there's no point in arguing with a man who always does exactly what he wants. So we sit, waiting for the next Night Stalker.

There was a thick manila envelope on the foyer table with a messenger's ticket and the initials RD in the upper left corner. I took it with me. I didn't hear Mallory or Wind, but something Italian and herby in the air got me thinking about food again. I found the two of them in the kitchen, Mallory hovering while Wind worked on two tubes of the best-looking manicotti I'd seen since the last time he'd made it.

"Welcome home, sir, and if I may say so, you look like you slept in those clothes. If I thought she knew how to plug one in, I'd buy Miss Timken an iron."

I skipped responding. Mallory and Mac didn't get along from the moment they met, and I've learned it's better to let these things seek their own level. "You have any more of that manicotti?"

"It's awesome, Uncle Rail," said Wind.

I looked down at her. "Soon as you're finished, you and I need to talk."

She stopped mid-bite. "What about?"

"Dead chickens and Double-O-Snatch."

She got off an, "Oh, my God!" before she fled toward her room, crying hysterically.

Mallory turned from the stove. "Dare I ask?"

"What's the name of that therapist you see for your claustrophobia?"

"Irene Landau. And I see her for insomnia. For claustrophobia, I don't lock myself in closets."

"Don't quit your day job, Shecky. Call her tomorrow and make an appointment. Then call Jake and give him the address. He's going to bitch and moan, but tell him to turn off the meter and be there. We're going to be a foursome."

"If that means Wind's staying longer, we're going to have to build more shoe racks. Anything else, Your Excellency?"

"Now that you mention it, yes. Send an email to your game buddy, Cortez. Tell him if he goes near Wind, I'll break him in half then help myself to his Hammett and Chandler photograph."

CHAPTER THIRTY-SIX

Indian Chief Reunion

A week after Lake returned from Chicago, she still hadn't said anything to Barrie about leaving the house without permission. When she'd first come back, Barrie had toyed with the idea of just stripping and assuming the position, then decided to let it play out the way Lake wanted it to. She was afraid, but she was trying to find something of the old Barrie inside her too.

One morning, Lake told Barrie she was going to Beverly Hills to meet with her agent. "Be dressed at six. I'll be bringing Madalynne, and we're all going to dinner."

"What would you like me to wear?" she asked, deliberately omitting the ma'am, something she'd been doing a lot lately. Lake hadn't said anything about that either.

"Your studio dress. I want you to look rapturous. It's a big night."

Barrie didn't know what to think.

She was sitting in a chaise in the courtyard watching a pair of dolphins play when she heard the engine. She looked down the beach and saw an Indian Chief motorcycle coming toward her. Danny! She ran down to the sand before she realized she wasn't wearing anything. When he dismounted, she jumped into his arms, weeping tears of joy and relief. She'd practice being strong again later.

"Oh, Danny, thank God."

"Your note said to come when Lake wasn't here. I tried calling, but no one picked up, so I didn't know if you were gone too."

"I heard it, but I'm not allowed to answer the phone. Sometimes she calls to test me."

"How in the world did you end up with that piece of shit?"

"I'll tell you everything, just take me away from here. Right now. Please."

After a few desperate kisses, he tried to disengage, but she wouldn't let him. As he held her close, his hand drifted over the still-swollen ridges on her thighs and buttocks. He turned her around. "Jesus Christ, did that sick cunt do this to you?"

"I was so scared and so mixed up, but I'm not anymore. Oh, Danny, when you didn't come, I thought you were finished with me. I wouldn't blame you if you were."

"I've been away. Lansky's opening a joint in New Orleans, and I'm pulling together a crew. I'm a manager now."

When she heard the name Lansky, Barrie got a sick feeling in her stomach. This was like flying toward the sun. "Are they looking for me?"

"They think you're dead. I thought so too. The report was your plane blew up. Then, out of the blue, some lawyer called and asked if I'd seen you. And just before I left, I bumped into an old friend who said he'd run into you on the beach holding hands with some blonde girl. But he's a drunk, so I wrote it off."

"Price Galloway."

"So he wasn't hallucinating. Was he right about the blonde too?"

"I promise, I'll tell you about her. But, please, let's go. Anywhere." Barrie was trying to pull him toward the bike.

"All right, but we need to get you dressed first."

"Don't make me go back in that house again. Take me like I am. I'm begging you."

"I'll be right there. Nobody will hurt you."

Barrie dressed rapidly, found her flight bag and put the remainder of her things inside. When she came into the living room, Danny had swung back the mural and was staring at Lake's safe."

"How did you know that was there?" Barrie asked.

"I've known Lake London a long time."

Barrie didn't ask how.

"Is Luciano's money inside?"

Barrie nodded. "What's left of it. And the necklace."

"What necklace?"

"The Star of Havana."

Danny looked at her like he was seeing her for the first time. "The Star of Havana? How is that possible?"

"It's complicated. But I don't care about it or the money. Please, let's go." She was frenziedly tugging on him now.

Danny didn't move. "But the Star's still in Havana. Right where it always is. I saw it a couple of weeks ago."

"Then you saw a copy."

Danny seemed to be thinking something over. "Benedict Crown's dead."

"Dead?"

"The story is he went back to New York, but he didn't. There aren't any secrets on an island. Crown didn't have any living relatives besides that setup wife of his, which means the necklace belongs to Luciano—except you're telling me he doesn't have it."

"Yes, but what difference does it make?"

He nodded toward the safe. "I've got a guy who can open this cheap piece of shit in fifteen minutes. Maybe less."

"Danny, I can't."

"Yes, you can."

"I…"

"I think you've earned it, don't you?"

CHAPTER THIRTY-SEVEN

Flying Birds and a Bug-a-Lug

Barrie was elegant in her black dress and silver heels, as was Madalynne in white chiffon and matching shoes. Neither wore jewelry except their anklets. Lake glowed equally, wrapped in a turquoise gown that had been a gift from Daddy. Before they left, Lake had put the little silver birds on Barrie's nipples, but tonight, she barely felt them.

As they rolled away from the sunset in the big Packard, the two girls held hands in the backseat. Occasionally, Madalynne would lean over and kiss Barrie and nuzzle her neck. Barrie feigned return tenderness, but it was all she could do not to throw herself out the door. The pavement at sixty miles an hour seemed more inviting.

Barrie had tried her best to find out where they were going. She thought maybe she could leave a note for Danny. But assuming he'd even look for one, there was a better chance Lake would see her doing it. All she could get out of her was that their dinner destination was someplace new and exciting. Where they could celebrate.

Celebrate what, Barrie didn't know. She contemplated the long evening ahead with dread. All she wanted was to get back to Laguna, make an excuse to go for a walk and meet Danny on the beach. She could already feel the hard metal of the motorcycle between her legs.

They had been driving for more than two hours when the "Welcome to Palm Springs" sign loomed out of the dark. Illuminated by a single spotlight, against the blackness of the desert, it shone as brightly as the moon. Barrie had heard of the "Springs," but all she knew was that movie people went there. She didn't think she'd ever seen a picture of it.

As they traveled, the air had gradually become warmer, and she could feel its increasing dryness. Now, Lake lowered her window, and a sweet fragrance enveloped the car. "It rained here last week, and the desert bloomed," Lake said. "Don't you just love it?"

Barrie had to admit that it was like nothing she had ever smelled. She rolled her window down too and wished she could see what it looked like.

"Madalynne, with all this perfume in the air, I feel like watching Barrie come. It'll be fun having my girls' hair mussed at dinner. Put her other clamp on too." She reached over the seat to hand it to her.

"Yes, ma'am. I'd like that too, ma'am." The actress slid to the floor on her knees and raised Barrie's dress, her small hands fingering the clamp destined for Barrie's clitoris.

But Barrie had had enough. She grabbed the clamp and roughly pushed Madalynne's head away. Then she removed the ones from her breasts and ripped off her anklet, tossing all four pieces out the window. "Oh, what a pity," she said, "the birdies can't fly. All that submission really takes a toll on a gal, doesn't it?"

She waited for the explosion, but none came. Lake stared straight ahead as she drove toward the city lights. Madalynne got back up, a look of sheer terror on her face.

The El Mirador and the Desert Inn had long been destinations for studio heads and other wealthy men associated with the movie business. Deals could be cut around tennis courts and swimming pools out of sight of boards and stockholders, and extramarital affairs were immune from the long lenses of private investigators.

The Racquet Club catered to a more visible and extravagant clientele. Charlie Farrell, a leading man at Fox and his tennis-playing best friend and fellow skirt-chaser, actor Ralph Bellamy, had built it for people like themselves—the "fun crowd" as it were—and the place immediately attracted a Who's Who of actors, directors and writers.

Gangsters also found the desert to their liking, particularly the show business company they could rub elbows with. Cleveland's Mayfield Road Mob and the Detroit Purple Gang became regulars at the Racquet Club too, while Mickey Cohen preferred the El Mirador. And before taking up residence in an oceanfront suite at Alcatraz, Al Capone had held court at Two Bunch Palms, which he'd built.

Making Palm Springs even more attractive, law enforcement centered its efforts around making sure no one bothered the celebrities—regardless of stripe.

The Sirocco had begun as a supper club. A small place with gourmet food and fine wine where power brokers could escape for a quiet dinner, a high-stakes poker game or a solitary drinking session. Eventually, a low-rise hotel and twenty secluded bungalows were added along with tennis courts, spa, health club and two pools—one for mixed company, one for men only. Children were forbidden to enter the grounds, and the hotel's habitués ran the gamut of famous faces from both coasts and Europe.

The centerpiece of the Sirocco was the Pharaoh's Rotunda, an open-air dining room and dance floor dramatically accented by thousands of tiny lights arched overhead. And when the desert evenings turned cool, valves could be opened so that water from a natural hot springs flowed over strategically positioned waterfalls, warming the entire area. The Rotunda's under-the-stars Christmas and New Year's parties were booked ten years out.

No one knew who actually owned the place, but suspects ran from the Aga Khan (the name), Joseph Kennedy (the life-sized portrait of Gloria Swanson that greeted guests) and "Yellow Kid" Weil, who often spent months in residence between running big cons. There was also a persistent rumor about Harry Bridges and his West Coast Longshoreman's Union, but if true, nobody wanted to know. Better foreigners, stock manipulators and confidence men than Communists.

A white-shirted valet took the Packard, and the Sirocco's longtime manager, Randolph Pennyman, hurried out and bowed low. "Miss London and Miss St. Timothy, how wonderful to have you with us. Mr. Gable and Mr. Grant are at the bar with the studio crowd… and that wonderful Russian prince who won't let anyone pick up a check. Shall I take you in?"

Lake shook her head. "Thank you, Randolph, but Miss St. Timothy would prefer to keep her distance from certain individuals, if you catch my drift. Perhaps Clark, Cary and the prince can join us for a cocktail in the dining room."

Randolph was as discrete as he was obsequious, "Absolutely, Miss London, I'll make sure they know you're here. Let me show you to your table."

As he started to turn, Barrie spoke up, "I'm sorry, but our host seems to have forgotten to introduce us. Perhaps some feathers got caught in her throat. I'm Barrie Fontaine."

Lake's lips tightened, but Randolph didn't miss a beat. "The fault is all mine, I should have asked. He took Barrie's offered hand. "Randolph Pennyman, Miss Fontaine. Welcome to the Sirocco. Are you by any chance related to Joan and Olivia?"

"I'm not, but please give Mr. Gable my regards. I flew him to Havana last year."

Randolph brightened even further. "My goodness, a pilot, and a lovely one too. I'll pass along your respects immediately." Turning to Lake, "You always have the most fascinating friends, Miss London."

"I certainly do," she answered, staring at Barrie.

As they passed the Scorpion Bar, Barrie saw a handful of famous faces inside, including a pair of well-known dancers, showing off some steps. The Pharaoh's Rotunda in turn was magical. She didn't think she'd ever seen anything so beautiful. It was like being inside and outside at the same time. The orchestra area was empty, and the women's heels clicked loudly as they crossed the hard surface of the dance floor. Lake waved at some people, and they waved back. Madalynne looked neither right nor left.

Randolph ushered them to a round table with six chairs, situated between one of the waterfalls and an open space where they could look out on a lighted courtyard. Beyond, two couples in evening wear strolled across a perfectly manicured lawn.

Once Randolph had taken their drink orders—during which Barrie had overridden Lake's choice for her—Lake smiled, her voice theatrically sweet but *with an unmistakable edge. "I like a little moxie in my girls every now and then, but don't make the mistake of overplaying it."*

"And don't YOU make the mistake of taking me for one of your GIRLS anymore, you sadistic bitch."

Madalynne gasped. Lake calmly lit a cigarette and blew smoke upward. She reached inside her clutch and laid J.C. Stinson's business card on the white tablecloth. "If you're counting on this, you might want to think again. Lawyer Asshole is in Hong Kong, watching over his meal ticket. But if you don't believe me, feel free to check for yourself."

Barrie looked at the card then pushed it back. "Lake, he's as irrelevant to me as you are." The older woman's smugness disappeared for a split second, but she quickly recovered.

Their drinks arrived—a bottle of champagne for Lake and Madalynne and a Johnnie Walker, neat, for Barrie. After the sommelier went through a precise ceremony of opening and pouring the Taittinger, Lake ran her finger around the rim of her glass and looked at her companions. "The reason I wanted tonight to be special is because I've written enough of the script to let my agents read it."

At this, Madalynne became animated. "Oh, ma'am, what did they say?"

"No one's ever paid a million dollars for a screenplay. The agency thinks I might get twice that."

"Oh, ma'am," Madalynne gushed, "how absolutely wonderful. Have you put a title on it yet?"

Lake patted Madalynne's delicate hand. "I have, little one, I have. I'm calling it Beverly Hills is Burning. *"*

"God, I love it, ma'am. I mean, LOVE, LOVE, LOVE it! Barrie, you're going to be rich!"

Madalynne raised her champagne glass, and clicked it against Lake's. "To Lake London, the most fabulous writer in Hollywood," she said exuberantly. "The most fabulous writer anywhere!" They waited for Barrie.

When she didn't move, Lake said, "Since one of us seems to be on a different track, perhaps she should offer the toast."

"I thought you'd never ask." Barrie held up her glass. "To your baby. It was a girl, by the way. Jilleen Cait Stinson. And she was born dead. I think she's

better off. Don't you, SUE?" Barrie threw back her whiskey, smiling all the way.

Lake looked stricken. Madalynne looked worse. "My God, Barrie, how could you?" Madalynne said in near agony. She turned to Lake. "Ma'am, please don't listen to her. She doesn't know anything; she's just trying to hurt you."

But Lake saw the look on Barrie's face and knew she wasn't lying. Only twice in her life had she not been in control, and J.C. Stinson was responsible for both. Somehow she would murder that cocksucker. Very, very slowly. She got her champagne to her lips, hoping her hand wasn't shaking, but the liquid tasted bitter.

Barrie continued smiling. She had already decided she wasn't going back to Laguna Beach. Not tonight, not ever. She didn't need Danny Dades or J.C. Stinson, or anybody else. No one was looking for her—not actively, anyway. With a new name and a new story, she could build a new life. Fuck Beverly Hills is Burning. *Fuck everybody.*

She'd go to Canada, or maybe Europe. Get certified under a new identity and fly again. When she'd been a little girl and found herself afraid of something, she called herself Tess. Tess Power. She'd read it in a book somewhere, and it was the kind of name that made her feel brave just saying it. When she'd been Tess, she could face anything. That was how she would run her life from now on. Not on anyone else's power, but on Tess-power. She couldn't wait. But first, she'd have one more meal on Lake London, then excuse herself and disappear into the night.

"Daddy!" Lake's voice brought Barrie back to the present. The man standing at the table was handsome in a businessman sort of way. Tailored, sixtyish, slightly overweight and with a cigarette in the corner of his mouth. He was like the men Barrie had flown for Luciano. Aware of their position and comfortable with it.

Next to him stood a tall, skinny girl no more than twenty, expensively dressed and draped on Daddy to the point he was wearing her. "This is Ramona," Daddy said, not offering a last name and apparently not intending to.

Lake had collected herself enough to appear normal. "Daddy, please sit down. Meet Madalynne and Barrie. Ladies, this is Beck London, my daddy."

The arm decoration recognized Madalynne and squealed so loudly Barrie thought she was going to get out her autograph book. In a voice the tonal quality of a bad Shirley Temple impression, she said, "Madalynne St. Timothy! It's you, isn't it? Really, really you! Oh, God, I'm your biggest fan!"

This was familiar territory for Madalynne, and she went instantly from kittenish sex toy to hardened actress. "Glad to meet you, Ramona. I've seen all your pictures." That seemed to stump Ramona, and while she worked on it, Madalynne turned away as if she had evaporated. She extended her hand to Daddy. "Mr. London, it's a pleasure."

Barrie had no grievance with this guy or his squeeze, so she was polite. After the newcomers settled into a drink, Daddy said, "Lake, darling, I'm so glad you invited me. I don't know that much about what you do, but I like to see my little girl happy."

Barrie thought maybe she'd enlighten him a little then decided another whiskey was a better idea. As she looked around for a waiter, Ramona decided to let the room know she was as refined as she looked. "Daddy, that last martini at Melvyn's ran right through me. I have to tinkle real bad."

Barrie thought there was probably a phone book full of psychiatrists who would have walked over from LA to comment on her calling him Daddy too, but, hey, Ma'am London wasn't exactly a by-the-book kind of gal. What could you expect from Daddy?

Lake pointed toward the front. "You passed the loo on your way in."

Ramona grabbed Madalynne's arm, a little too tightly. "Would you come with me, Miss St. Timothy. I'd LOVE to get some makeup tips from the most beautiful woman on Earth."

Madalynne shook off the hand, and her indifference could have filled an auditorium. "I'd rather not, thanks."

Barrie hadn't eaten yet, but she decided now was as good a time as any to take her leave from this pack of sick fucks. Forever. When they'd arrived, there'd been a cab sitting out front. Maybe it was still there. Besides, she had to pee too. "I'll go with you," she said. Then she caught herself. It was a Hollywood crowd, why not go out with a little show biz flair. "Providing, of course, it's okay with MA'AM."

Lake gave her a big smile, not seeming to notice the sarcasm, and patted her wrist. *"Well, well look who's returned. Yes, you may, darling. Just hurry back. I miss you already."*

Barrie shuddered. She couldn't wait to smell those desert flowers again. Alone.

The bar had picked up steam since they'd come in, and a white dinner-jacketed orchestra passed them, headed toward the Rotunda. The black female vocalist saw Barrie, and her face broadened into a smile. Barrie remembered her from Havana, but she was unable to put a name with the face. She smiled back and gave her a small wave.

"You know her?" asked Ramona, excitedly.

"Not really," Barrie answered.

"I just love the way they sing, don't you? Negroes, I mean. Daddy says they got so much sex in them, it just comes out natural when they hear music."

Barrie thought sitting around talking to Daddy and Ramona must really be something special. She told Ramona to wait a moment and went out the front door to check on the cab. It was still there. Randolph saw her and hurried over. "Something I can do for you, Miss Fontaine?"

Barrie took a twenty out of her clutch and handed it to him. "Yes, Randolph, I'm not feeling all that well, and I may want to leave early. Could you please ask that cabbie to wait, just in case?"

"Certainly, Miss Fontaine, but this isn't necessary." He started to hand the bill back, but Barrie put her hand over his and gently pushed it toward him. "Then give it to the driver, would you please? And I'd appreciate your not mentioning anything to Miss London. This is a big night for her, and I don't want to spoil it by having her worrying about me."

"Of course, Miss Fontaine. I hope you feel better."

Barrie was on her way back inside when Ramona came out too, rummaging around in her purse. "Everything okay?" Barrie asked.

"Damn it, I had my compact out on the way over, and I must have left it in the car. Walk with me, will you. I'm a teensy afraid of the dark."

"Just send the valet."

"Good heavens, Daddy won't let one of those people near his Bug-a-Lug. He always parks it himself."

"Bug-a-Lug?"

"Oh, that's just what I call it. It's some kinda Eye-talian sports car. Looks like one a them space planes you see in the funny papers. And, sister, let me tell you, as low as it sits, it sure beats up a girl's ass."

"Do you mean a Bugatti?"

"That's it. Jesus, when he told me how much he paid for it, I just about...," she was already walking toward the lot, and Barrie missed the last part of what she was certain was an insightful observation. She was tempted to let her go, just use the facilities and take off, but she wanted to send Ramona back to the table with a cover story that would buy her some extra time. She hurried to catch up.*

The evening was beginning to cool, and from the Rotunda, the soft lyrics of "Smoke Gets in Your Eyes" drifted across the grounds. Barrie remembered the vocalist's name now. Shirley Boston. She had one of those throaty voices that made people stop and listen.

There were a couple of floodlights at the far end of the lot, but most of it was engulfed in the shroud of the desert night. Ramona stopped next to a low-slung, dark blue sports car and opened the passenger door. A tiny yellow floor light came on, and Barrie saw her reach into the seat.

Then a deep voice behind her said, "Hello, Barrie." She wheeled around so quickly she nearly fell. The figure was almost against her. She didn't need light. Rollo!

Another man came from her right and clapped his hand over her mouth. Then there were more. Big men in dark suits who smelled like Aqua Velva and sweat. They had her by the arms and hair, and when she tried to kick, somebody drove a fist into her solar plexus and bent her arm so painfully she dropped to her knees, weeping without wanting to.

A large woman had appeared next to Rollo. She looked familiar, but Barrie couldn't place her. She recognized the instrument in her hand, though. A hypodermic. While one of the men held Barrie's left arm, the woman squeezed her bicep in a viselike grip. Someone struck a match so she could find a vein, and Barrie felt the sharp stick of a needle in her forearm. As the heroin flowed in, she remembered where she had seen the woman. Benedict Crown had introduced them. Her name was Novi. Novi Montez.

Seconds later, the men released her, and she tried to move, but everything was receding, and very soon it was too far away to touch. Then she was stumbling in the gravel, or was she being dragged?

Barrie didn't know what kind of car she was in, but there were a lot of people in the backseat with her. Or maybe it was just two. She couldn't be sure. What she could be sure of was that as they sped past the front entrance, Randolph and a valet were holding open the doors of the red Packard for Lake and Madalynne.

But before Lake got behind the wheel, she turned to Ramona and kissed her on the mouth, hard and deep, her right hand cupping Ramona's pussy through her dress. Daddy smiled, stepped forward and draped an arm around each woman's shoulders. Lake leaned into him and put her free hand between his legs.

Shirley Boston was finishing her song. Then Barrie couldn't hear her anymore.

CHAPTER THIRTY-EIGHT

Old Movies and Thunderstorms

My appetite had disappeared, so I tucked the envelope containing the script under my shirt and braved the rain in a sprint across the backyard to my pool house, which doubles as a screening room and office. From old photographs I found in the attic, I discovered that Stinson's original décor had been Nebuchadnezzar Throne Room, so in the main house, I brought it into the current millennium. In my private lair, I went all the way to boringly comfortable Beverly Hills contemporary, including a ten-foot sofa where a lot of Zs get chased down and caught.

The legend is that Howard Hughes used to lie out there in the nude for days on end, watching old movies. The nude part's only happened once on my watch, and I was a little too busy to remember the picture. Unlike Howard, I wasn't alone.

I took a long shower, changed clothes and threw Lancaster and Frankenheimer's classic, *The Train*, up on the big screen. If the first scene doesn't grab you, you have no soul, and while Scofield strutted and scowled to his inner SS colonel, I opened a bottle of 2001 Back Bay Cuvée from the Newport Beach Winery. It's a blend and pricey, but for those who don't think SoCal knows anything about wine, hold that thought. It leaves more Cuvée for me.

Settling into my seat, I reached for my laptop and Googled a map of the neighborhood around the Colosseum building, which coincidentally included Renaldo Zamora's place. West Hollywood is exceptionally dense. As large as LA is, there are only a few places the young, the pretty, the soon-to-be-famous and the involuntarily anonymous want to live. In New York, there's no shame in working on Wall Street and bedding down in a microscopic, Upper East Side studio. The show business equivalent is a miniature, West Hollywood bungalow, shared with three roommates and an equal number of dogs.

I didn't know exactly what I was looking for, but this was what the lead shooter would have done, and I wanted to try to get inside his head. Delta spends a lot of time sharpening your body, but they spend an equal amount teaching you to think. Sometimes, it's not enough to out-train, out-plan, out-arm and outnumber your enemy. Special ops missions usually rely on surprise, and you better know how your quarry will react, or you'll be the one surprised.

My memory's not photographic, but combined with living nearby and going over the grid a few times, by the time Burt took control of the French train, I knew most of the street names. The Tata brothers' reputation for wild shooting wouldn't have put them in a position to run things. They had almost certainly been there solely for numbers and additional firepower.

But if the operation had been intended as the mass assassination that ensued, any reasonable planner would have brought five shooters, maybe more. This smelled like three guys coming to do one thing and running into something else. Teddy could have reverted back to his San Quentin manners and gotten everybody killed, but I thought it more likely that if he'd done anything, it would have been because he was trying to protect others—or my investment. I truly hoped it wasn't the latter.

The cops might or might not find the other Tata. I was betting he was dead, either from his wounds or because he was a liability. Greeks aren't on anybody's short list of being easy to manage either, so my gut told me their boss—and the guy I wanted—was Greek too. You hire your own.

On another night, I might have dozed while I thought, but I wasn't even slightly sleepy. I used the control panel next to me to lower the picture's sound, turned on an overhead reading spot and picked up the envelope containing the script.

An hour later, I reached the last page.

INT. SAN BERNARDINO AIRPORT TOWER - DAY

A clear, California day. Through the glass, we see small aircraft taking off and landing. TWO CONTROLLERS wearing headphones manage the operation. One is balding, chain-smoking GUS FOX. He watches the runways as he talks to a tall, mustached MAN in a dark suit. It is HOWARD HUGHES.

                    GUS FOX
     Hell, yes, Mr. Hughes, I saw the goddamn
     plane blow. Right out there. (pointing)
     That Fontaine woman almost took us out.

                  HOWARD HUGHES
     And nobody could have survived?

                     FOX
     Look, I wrote this all down for the
     investigators.

                    HUGHES
                 (ignoring him)
     You're absolutely sure nobody could have
     gotten out?

                     FOX
     A few more pieces, I coulda built my own
     de Havilland. No, sir, nobody got outta
     that. Sooner or later, some farmer's
     gonna run across the rest. Not gonna be
     pretty, except for maybe the money.

Fox turns his attention to a crop duster on the runway, and we see it rev its engine, preparing to take off.

> FOX (CONT'D)
> Tower to Boogie Four, you're…

Hughes reaches over, jerks the headphones off Fox and fires them across the room. Fox turns, shocked. Hughes stares at him so intently Fox starts to twitch.

> HUGHES
> Your report says you might have heard an engine AFTER the explosion.

> FOX
> Jesus, Mr. Hughes, we were in the middle of the worst storm anybody's ever seen. I'm not sure what I heard.

Hughes doesn't move. After a moment, Fox looks off in the direction where he last saw the *Beverly Hills*. Finally...

> FOX (CONT'D)
> (pointing)
> The fire was there, but the last time I heard an engine was there.

> HUGHES
> Southwest.

> FOX
> Yes, sir. Southwest.

It's a strange feeling finding yourself connected to a past you knew nothing about. The Benedict Crown necklace had traveled thousands of miles and nearly nine decades to end up in my pocket on a warm night off Newport Beach. I don't imbue inanimate objects with mystical meaning, only history, but it was difficult not to be reflective.

Here were some of the great and nefarious characters of the twentieth century, set against New York, Cuba and Mexico, laced together by the most unlikely of unknowns, a young woman pilot named Barrie Fontaine. It almost didn't matter if it was true or not, but I had little doubt it was.

But if Barrie had survived, where had she gone? And how, after all these years, had Valentine Jones come into possession of her story? And? And? And? My questions kept multiplying.

From the page count, what I'd read was at least two and a half hours of screen time, but there wasn't an ending. Teddy had said he wanted Cortez to do some research for the third act, but there wasn't even a starting place. I looked carefully at the brads affixing the cover. It didn't appear anything had been torn out. I also checked the title page again. I hadn't made a mistake. There was no screenwriter or agency name. Not even the usual copyright declaration, just the title. I hadn't read that many screenplays, but in an ego-crazed business, those were unusual omissions. It was likely the current title page had been substituted for the original. I picked up the phone and dialed.

This time it took a dozen rings to get Ross Dare, and he sounded like he was out of breath. I didn't ask why. "I just finished the script. Where's the rest?"

"That's all we have—all anyone's ever had. When Valentine's agency was going to auction it, they told buyers we could read a hundred and fifty-one pages at their offices beginning at nine on a Friday. Bids were due by five."

"I assume that was to keep it from being ripped off by some direct-to-DVD hustler."

"And to protect the publishing deal. Not the first time a screenplay has been used as a book proposal. Publishers hear the word movie, they start going down on their checkbooks."

"They won't be able to run the presses fast enough or long enough on this one."

"The short reading window really ginned up the studios. This is an emotional town, and everybody was panting to overpay. Some of us had our own publishing houses too, so the agents could insert it twice."

"Then Valentine flies to San Quentin, makes a deal with Teddy Chessman, and it comes off the market."

"Twenty-four hours before the read. Buyers started booking time at the shooting range. Not only did they hate the idea of Teddy's getting back in the game, but some had already submitted seven figure bids—blind. Imagine the exec who signed Valentine for millions then had to tell his boss they didn't have a shot at her next picture. I was right there with them, studio cash burning a hole in my pocket. In my heart of hearts, I was glad when it went south. I didn't believe anything could live up to the expectation."

"What do you think now?"

"You're the man with the money; I'd be more interested in your opinion."

"I don't know anything about the movie business, but I'd make this picture with my last buck."

"Helluva fuckin story, isn't it?"

He didn't know the half of it. "You believe in coincidences?"

"Where I come from, those are called alibis."

No question. He was from Chicago. "I live in J.C. Stinson's former house. And I'm talking to you from the screening room where Howard Hughes hid out from process servers." I didn't mention Valentine or the necklace.

He was quiet for a moment. "I'm going to need a little time to process that."

"If you come up with something besides a *Twilight Zone* episode, let me know. So who wrote this masterpiece?"

"Don't know. The literary fingerprints of the usual suspects aren't there.

I can tell the guy's a pro, but that's all."

"And, of course, the agents have all been sworn to silence."

"You should be in the business. What intrigues me most is that the writer uses a couple of conventions from the Stone Age. Today, if you can get by with three words, make it one. If you can get by with one, make it none. Nobody reads, and nobody wastes film on subordinate characters. *The Godfather* had sixty-nine scripted parts. There are three fuckin scenes with Luca Brasi, for God's sake.

"If a producer tried that now, they'd haul him outside to watch his name being painted off his parking space. At best, you'd meet Luca on his way to the garroting. More likely, he'd never be cast. The dead fish would show up at the Don's house, and the murder would be implied."

"And motion picture history would have lost one of its great characters."

"Not to mention the culture. *Beverly Hills is Burning* is literary. Lots of description. Lots of career-defining parts. You stay with it all the way— even a guy like me who's known for being three pages and out."

I would never have thought about it, but he was right. Tentpoles have become hardware shows or thinly-cast dramas. Every few minutes, insert an effect or have a couple of high-priced actors talk you through what you're not going to see. The scene between Howard Hughes and Gus Fox could have been conveyed a hundred different ways without shooting a frame of film. Instead, the writer took us back to the airport so we could watch Hughes intimidate him.

"What else?" I asked

"The guy uses the term 'INTERTITLE.' Those are the cards that pop up in silent films with description or dialog. For the last eighty years, they've simply been called 'titles,' sometimes 'legends.' Ninety-nine percent of the time, they're over a visual. Every one of these is separate from onscreen action."

"Are you telling me this guy wrote silent pictures?"

"I don't know. In the transition to sound, some writers didn't totally acclimate. But he'd be too old now, likely dead, so it could just be a red herring to further disguise his identity."

"Teddy wanted Cortez Detroit to do the polish."

"Cortez is the right guy. Just terse-up the dialog, though. Don't screw with the continuity. I want the director to have all that description. Without it, the picture will end up feeling like a YouTube kid playing with big boy toys."

"By director, I assume you mean Joe Cargo."

"To get this much story onscreen, we need a no-bullshit shooter—not some guy in tight jeans channeling David Lean who can't stand the sight of unexposed film. Think about it. We've got a period piece; challenging locations; vintage cars, boats, airplanes and trains; horses; deep water and more roles than any picture in forty years. Build in wiggle room for the ending we haven't figured out yet, and we're looking at $200 million. That's if everything goes right. But God has also blessed us with Valentine Jones, who goes over budget taking a shit, so what are the odds?"

"Teddy thought Valentine would lose her mind about Cargo then settle down."

"Teddy was an optimist. Eventually, she'll behave, but we have to let nature run its course."

"If nature drags its feet, Miss Jones will be on the unemployment line."

"That could happen too."

"I think it's time we meet with her."

"I was just waiting for the word."

"Let's make it an event. Dinner tomorrow at *Tacitus*. Eight-thirty. Tell her to bring a date. Maybe it'll sweeten her up. You bring one too."

"Sounds good. My wife loves the food there. I'm a little iffy on the owner, so I don't take her as often as she'd like."

"Mr. Gambelli is an acquired taste. If he's talking to me this week, I'll make sure you don't have to deal with the horseshit again. And, Ross, if our actress gives you any trouble, drag her."

"There won't be anything but a smile. Her lawyer already called looking for an advance on her fee."

I had to hand it to Marvin. "What's your wife's name?"

"Candida. She's the best international marketing and distribution exec in the business."

"Why isn't she working for us?"

"It's a conversation I was going to have with you."

"We just had it. You're the CEO, not me. Candida? She Hispanic?"

"After a fashion. Carioca."

"Then you're fired if you don't hire her. And Ross, one more thing…"

"What's that?"

"Bring Joe Cargo. I hate easing into things."

"Well, that'll pretty much guarantee we won't."

I checked the clock. It was heading toward eleven, and the storm was picking up. I wanted to get a look at that restroom at Colosseum, but maybe the rain would let up if I gave it an hour or so. I turned off the overhead and laid my head back. I'd just rest my eyes.

I came awake to a monsoon hammering the windows and roof harder than I could ever remember. Intermittent lightning flashed silhouettes on the walls, and thunder boomed through the hills much like the Caribbean storms I had grown up with. The movie was over, and the room was dark except for the screensaver on my laptop. I closed the lid, and a few seconds later, it went out.

My screening room is furnished with three rows of four oversized leather chairs with ottomans. As tall as I am, I can get lost in one. Each row is stepped six inches higher as you move back, and I sit in the middle of the last row next to the control console, where I can raise or lower lights and speak to the projectionist through an intercom if we're running a 35mm print. Tonight it was just me, a Blu-Ray and the storm. I listened as the downpour accelerated.

One wall is French doors, and when the weather's cooperating, I can open them onto a large patio next to the pool. Tonight, even with the blackout curtains retracted, I could barely see the outline of my house through the gloom. There was sudden flash of lightning, and I waited for the thunder, counting like you do when you're a kid. When the concussion came, it rolled across the room, rattling my empty wine glass and a pair of paintings on the back wall, and I thought of Barrie in her tiny plane.

Then I saw the man. He was standing on the other side of the nearest

French door. Staring in at me. I thought I might have drifted back to sleep, but when I shook my head, he was still there. I became enraged. Once again, one of Mallory's unlocked doors had brought danger into our home. Well, this would be the last time. He'd been with me my entire life, but enough was enough.

Suddenly, without warning, I felt something I've only felt twice before. A deep, core-consuming chill. The chill that had awakened me at the very moment my father had been killed and come again, years later, as I searched futilely for the wife I knew was at the bottom of the sea. Then it was gone, and a calm stillness washed over me.

The man outside was diminutive, but with a solid thickness to him. He was dressed in all white, topped by a Panama hat, and his feet were as bare as Mallory always described them. Despite the rain, the tip of the cigarette in its long, black holder glowed.

His mouth didn't move, and even if it had, there was a thick pane of glass between us. But I could hear him just as clearly as if he were standing beside me. A soft voice with a hint of Irish wistfulness. A voice that had guided the richest man in America past enemy dragons and self-constructed serpents. "She's been waiting for you, Rail. We both have."

"Who?" I stammered. "Who's waiting?"

There was no answer. I bolted from my seat toward the door. The man remained where he was, his words coming again. "Go to her. Go to her now. She needs you."

I shoved the door open and burst outside. But there was no one there. Only the gale. I charged into the rain, whipped by the wind and soaked to the skin before I had gone more than a few steps. But there was no sign of any living being. I stood for a long time, staring into wet nothingness.

Suddenly, a tree limb broke loose and blew past me, nearly taking off my head. I made my way back to shelter. As I stood inside looking out, a lazy blue veil of cigarette smoke drifted around me, filled my nostrils, then was gone in a gust.

CHAPTER THIRTY-NINE

Headlamps and Ballet Flats

As I rode down the hill toward Sunset, I was shaken. I don't believe in ghosts and goblins and things that go bump in the night. I remain open on UFOs, but I've been to the darkest corners of this planet, and there are no spectres or vampires. No Bigfoot or Chupacabra or Nessie. All that's really out there are terrible people doing terrible things, and they all die when you put a bullet in their heads. It just doesn't happen often enough.

My father had been the most important man in my life. My connection to him was to be expected. And I would have had to have been dead myself not to have felt the last whisper of life leaving my pregnant wife.

Though I had never seen the man in white, I knew him, of course. J.C. Stinson, the attorney who had built my home. But who was "she?" And what could I do for her? His, "It's time," line made no sense either. I was here because I bought a house, period, and I was on nobody's time but my own. Fuck him and his bare feet. But brave as my words were, they didn't make me feel any more comfortable.

The rain had lessened, but the streets were littered with debris. My pickup would have been a better choice, but I needed the Rolls for what I was about to do. At 4:30 in the morning, with the traffic lights dark from the storm, it was just me and a few other lunatics, blasting through intersections, each headed for his own, pressing business.

The Colosseum Pictures building loomed over the surrounding shops, all of which were shuttered except for the Arcade Bookstore next door where half a dozen umbrella-carrying insomniacs huddled under its awning, pawing through the international newspaper racks. I turned into the wide drive. The building gate was open, but a sheriff's car sat sideways just inside, blocking entry.

The deputy at the wheel looked up like he'd been awakened from a siesta. He lowered his window and made a turn-around-and-get-out-of-here gesture. If he'd bothered to get out of his car, I might have tried honey. Instead, I skipped to asshole and high-beamed him.

There are headlights, then there are Rolls-Royce *headlamps*. They say you can light up a chipmunk at a thousand yards, and the next time you see him, he'll be using a white cane. The deputy got out of his black and white like he'd been hit with a power line. His first couple of steps his feet didn't touch ground. By the time he got to me, he had his chrome flashlight out, and spit was collecting at the corners of his mouth. I could almost hear the adrenaline. I left the glass up and stared straight ahead.

He lifted the flashlight to clock my window when suddenly, somewhere, deep in the pension district of his brain, a neon sign went on, ROLLS-ROYCE! ROLLS-FUCKING-ROYCE! His flashlight hand was shaking, but he Dr. Strangeloved it down.

I lowered my window. "I'm Mr. Black. I own this place."

He stared in at me, trying to get himself under control. He'd almost certainly heard the media reports that I hadn't made the Colosseum deal, but then why else would I be there? A moment earlier, he'd been catching some warm snores, now he was on sensory overload. "I'm sorry, Mr. Black, this is a crime scene."

I glanced at his nametag. "No shit, Kirkpatrick. It's costing me a million a day while you guys jerk off in there."

"Sir, I…"

I was really getting into my part. Maybe I should read more scripts. "Deputy, a few hours ago, Cdr. Rampulla, Capt. Bricklin and a tight-ass DDA named Plum asked for my help. Okay, it's heading on five in the morning, and I feel like hell, but I'm willing to do my part. So call anybody you have to, but get that goddamn squad car out of my way. I'm going inside."

I felt sorry for him—almost. The investigators were finished by now. The place was just sitting here for detectives to walk through a few more times. If he made the call, everyone in his chain of command would have to okay kicking it up to Rampulla. And no matter what happened, Deputy Kirkpatrick would be the moron who couldn't handle a simple situation without getting his superiors in the middle of a pre-dawn wakeup of Red-Ass. On the other hand, if he happened to be in another part of the building when some rich schmuck slipped past him…

He put his flashlight back in his belt. "I gotta check out a couple of cars in the alley. Had to run off some souvenir hunters earlier. Elevator Three is open. Stay outside the tape."

Right.

The conference room smelled like stale gunpowder and violence. They say you can train yourself to "feel" death. It's a lesson I never needed. There's a metallic residue to savagely spilled blood that never quite goes away. It clings to you like tiny strands of invisible spider silk, resilient to everything but time—and sometimes, not even that.

The room-long conference table had been dismantled and propped against the wall, covering some of the red-circled bullet holes in the plaster. Hundreds of forensic markers coded by different colors and shapes alongside notated index cards formed a hodgepodge mosaic over the carpet, glass, walls, drapes and even the ceiling. I stood over the card marked "T. Chessman," lying next to a wide brown stain. I tried to imagine the man I had shared dinner and a brawl with less than a week ago, but his face wouldn't come.

I'd ignored the crime scene tape blocking the conference room doorway, but as I returned to the hall, I stayed on the narrow path along the right wall the cops had roped off for investigators. Anyone leaving the killing field would have had to walk through a sea of blood, and on the other side of the yellow plastic ribbon, three sets of footprints were clearly visible heading toward the restrooms. None, however, were running, which put the lie to someone trying to escape.

Two sets had the same distinct treads, which probably belonged to the

Tatas, the third was different and larger and on top of the Tatas, meaning he was *behind* the boys from Kansas City. All, however, were overlaid and smeared in places by the blood trail coming back up the hall.

I had to stare for a long time before the Jackson Pollack cleared to a Vermeer, but after a while I was certain. Three people had gone down the hall but only two had returned, one leaning on or, at least, leading the other. Bricklin, who had made a career out of this kind of thing would have known it too, which left the captain's story at the jail one bodyguard short of a full load of bullshit. But with cops, lying to civilians is genetic, and if I got upset every time it happened, I'd be one bend in the road away from burning my Frank Bullitt shoulder holster.

Standing opposite the two restrooms, I saw a small, brown smudge on the metal kick-panel of the men's room door. It wasn't yellow-taped off. I crouched, touched my finger to my tongue and rubbed the smudge. With enzyme dampness, the brown turned red. Blood. It was possible it had been put there accidentally by one of the scores of officials visiting the scene. Possible, but not likely. They would have been wearing paper booties which absorb liquid, not transfer it. No, one of the shooters had taken a piss after the board room shootings and before the second ones.

Inside, the men's room looked like Sunday sunrise in a college bar. I've been in cleaner sewers. The cops had apparently come to the conclusion that nothing significant had happened there and designated it for use rather than making CSI trek downstairs. After the first few occupants, the stain on the kick-panel would have been meaningless.

The ladies room door was propped open a few inches with a hunk of crime tape wadded up and stuffed under it. It had probably been all the way open at one point so forensics could lug in their equipment then had slid almost closed. I went in.

Again, evidence markers were everywhere. I couldn't walk without crunching shards of mirror, much of it swimming in coagulated blood. With no carpet to absorb it, as the oxidized surface was disturbed, the liquid underneath ran further into the grout around the tiny squares of tile. Small pieces of viscera, some still retaining the look of fresh flesh, stuck to the walls, and a man's whole, dirty fingernail clung to the corner of the broken mirror. The smell was of stale sweat and rotting garbage.

Someone had bled profusely into two of the three sinks then onto the floor between them. But he didn't appear to have gone down. A copper-colored smudge the size of a hand on one indicated he had used it to support himself after being wounded.

A few feet away, a note card reading "T. Tata" lay on the floor. Timo had clawed his way in the direction of the door, leaving a snail-like trail before he stopped for good. The imprint of his ear was visible on the white glaze.

I pushed open the door to the first stall and, except for some glass on the floor, it was spotless. The middle one, however, looked like someone had opened a can of red-brown paint and thrown it against the green metal partition separating it from the first stall. A significant piece of gristle and black fabric was embedded in the roll of toilet paper. It was too prominent for the cops to have missed, so my guess was they had reached the saturation point and just quit. It happens, even at murder scenes. I bent for a closer look at the fabric. It was from assault gear—military grade. Pros, no question.

The third stall explained everything. The splayed bullet holes in the door looked like very good movie effects. The thin steel had offered little resistance to the heavy slugs passing through it. Magnum rounds. Possibly .44, but more likely .357. And they were outgoing, not incoming.

I closed the door, latched it and sat down on the toilet. Through the slit next to the latch, by moving my head, I could see a five-foot wedge of room. So three killers had come in, one had died on the spot, and two others had been grievously wounded. With no evidence of blood here, the occupant of the stall had simply walked away.

She might not have been able to hold her liquor or untangle a parachute, but Miss Valentine Jones certainly knew how to shoot. And without a car downstairs, there was no way to connect her to anything. She probably left on foot. With the security system disabled, no one would ever know. Well, almost no one. Just her swimming partner.

I went out to the reception area where Glenda Van Allen had fallen. The investigators had moved the desk several feet to the left and emptied its drawers. The usual array of office supplies was piled on the desktop, but not what I was looking for. I got down on my hands and knees and checked under the furniture and along the row of bay windows. Still nothing. I sat in one of the chairs and thought for a moment.

I took out my cell phone and dialed Mallory. The man rarely sleeps, and even when he does, he's on a hair-trigger. He picked up midway into the first ring. "I heard you leave," he said.

"I need to speak to Wind. Right now."

"So you're sending me into the lion's den."

"I don't think she'll pick up if she sees my number."

I waited a long time. Finally, I heard a sniffle and the vocal hangover from a long crying jag. "Uncle Rail, I can't bear the thought of disappointing you."

"Later. Right now, I need to know about your pen."

"My pen?"

"The pink one you were using in court. Is there some significance to it?"

"It's my own personal color. One of my cosmetics licensees created it. *French Me by Wind Fortune.* There's lip gloss, nail polish, everything."

I suddenly felt completely disconnected from modern culture. "Would Glenda have had one?"

"Of my pens? Sure, they're everywhere I am. I encourage people to take them. It's good for business."

"So if she wasn't working for you any longer, it would be a keepsake. Something special."

She hesitated. "I guess. Actually, I think Valentine Jones's autograph was done with one."

"It was, but the pen wasn't in her book, so where would Glenda have kept it?"

"In her purse, probably."

"You have that. Was it in there?"

"No, just her wallet and makeup." She thought for a moment. "You know, Uncle Rail, Glenda had a habit of taking her shoes off at work.

Sometimes, people would have to move them to keep from tripping, and there'd be money and keys inside. She said if anybody ever walked off with her purse, at least she'd be able to get home."

"I'll call you back." I surveyed the reception area again with the same result. The retracted floor-to-ceiling drapes in each bay window were too long, resulting in their gathering in clumps against the carpet. I went to the window behind where the reception desk would have been and pulled back the material. A pair of gold ballet flats sat there, previously concealed from view. The pink felt tip pen was plainly visible in the right one. It was possible the cops had simply checked them and moved on.

I set the time and date to appear on my phone's screen and photographed the shoes from several angles, making sure the pen was always in frame. Then I knelt and used my index finger on the sole to tip up the toe of the left shoe. A set of keys and a pair of twenties, folded into tiny squares, slid into view. Cops don't leave two twenties. They'd missed the shoes.

The CSI people had left a box of Ziplocs in the conference room. I retrieved one, and, using my handkerchief, carefully placed the pen inside and photographed it again. It remained to be seen if it mattered, but Valentine's fingerprints were almost certainly on the pen. Lennie Briscoe wouldn't have been impressed, but it might come in handy for what I needed.

I called Wind back. "Found it," I said. "Thanks, now get some sleep."

"Uncle Rail…"

"Sleep first, talk later. You've been a great help. Please put Mallory back on."

The British accent returned. "I'm glad you called, sir. It really settled her down."

"Mallory, I want you to tell me the truth about something."

"I might be out of practice."

"How many times have you seen J.C. Stinson?"

I could have knitted a sweater in the time it took him to reply. "You're out of your mind if you think I'm going to answer that."

"Why?"

"Because this is the same Rail Black who told me—and let me get this exactly right—'Keep your bullshit zombie sightings to yourself.'"

"You know what I think about supernatural crap. I was trying to be funny."

"It might interest you to know that your sainted Scottish grandmother talked to spirits, and she'd have told you *Yer bum's oot a windae.* In case your Gaelic's rusty, that's 'The bare ass of a fool flaps in a breeze.'"

"My grandmother lived by herself in an 80-room castle and drank a fifth of Scotch a day. My heart goes out to the ghosts."

"Spirits."

"Stop dodging the question. How many times?"

"Maybe once a year." He hesitated, "But for the past couple of weeks… every day."

"Every day! Why didn't you ever mention something?"

"I'm hanging up now."

"What did he say to you?"

"Everybody knows zombies can't talk."

"Goddamn it, Mallory. All right, *spirits* not zombies. Now answer me… please."

"Not until you tell me why."

Now I was the one who was slow on the draw. When I didn't answer, Mallory did it for me. "You finally saw him, didn't you?"

I still wasn't ready to give it up.

"When?" he asked.

"Tonight, outside the pool house."

"He said he was going to do that."

"So he does talk."

"Not like you'd expect. But you can hear him. He told you there's something you have to do, didn't he?"

"Yes, but it didn't make any sense, so I'm leaning toward its being a dream."

"And naturally, I would know you were about to have that dream and how to interpret it. Good night, Mr. Black."

The phone went dead.

CHAPTER FORTY

Tess

The airstrip was carved out of the middle of nowhere but carefully graded and paved. Blue landing lights set into the tarmac ran off into the distance. Somewhere, a generator rumbled. The plane was a large one: four engines mounted on an immense wing above the fuselage, each propeller blade taller than a man. A long row of empty cabin windows glowed softly, and two pilots sat in the cockpit, going over a map.

The heroin had leveled off, and Barrie no longer felt like she was watching the world run away from her. She knew what was happening, but she couldn't do anything about it. Her arms and legs were where they were supposed to be, but she couldn't lift them. Even her head was too heavy for her neck, lolling lifelessly on her shoulders. She wasn't fighting any longer, but she needed the men on either side of her to keep her upright.

When she was pulled from the car, she saw three vehicles in the procession. Two long, black sedans and a familiar, red convertible that she put her brain to work trying to recall. Rollo Tripoli said something to Novi, and the Cuban woman took the place of one of the men on her arms. Barrie wanted to tell Novi something with "fuck you" in it, but even though the words were in her head, they were all scrambled up, and her lips couldn't grab onto them.

Lake London and Madalynne St. Timothy crossed from the Packard—Lake purposefully, Madalynne numbly, seemingly propelled by only the power of the

269

older woman's domination. Lake stopped a few feet in front of Barrie, and though she was smiling, there was no warmth in it. "All the way to Palm Springs I kept asking myself, should I, or shouldn't I? I could just turn around and go home. A little discipline, and you'd have come right back. Then you made the decision for both of us."

Even through her haze, Barrie knew that was bullshit. Madalynne was crying now, and she was glad. The actress stumbled toward her, arms outstretched, makeup smeared. "Barrie…" But Lake stopped her and led her a few yards away. "Why, why?" Madalynne wept. "We were so happy."

Lake pushed the mussed hair off the actress's face and smoothed it soothingly. She held Madalynne's cheeks between her palms and spoke softly. "Sometimes, sweet one, we have to do things we wish we didn't. But there's a silver lining. The biggest movie of your life—and mine—didn't have an ending worthy of the story. Now it does."

Madalynne let out a couple of spasmed sobs, and Lake left her and walked back to Barrie. Barrie gathered what strength she had and forced her head up. She stared at Lake with dead opiate eyes mixed with a brutal smile of contempt. This time, she found words. "Your lipstick's smeared, ma'am. That from Ramona… or Daddy?"

Lake slapped Barrie—hard—and Barrie laughed. Lake lost complete control and attacked her with both hands, trying to claw out her eyes. "You fuckin ungrateful cunt! You ran to that miserable prick ex-husband of mine! After all I did for you!"

Rollo grabbed Lake and wrenched her away. He ran her a few feet and pushed her so hard she almost fell face-first in the dirt. "Wait by the car. And shut the fuck up."

Barrie wanted to tell Rollo that it didn't matter. That Barrie Fontaine couldn't feel anything anymore. Because she was gone. Tess Power was here now, and she would be staying.

Suddenly, Barrie saw a figure move into the plane's doorway and stand in framed silhouette. The man who hated flying had come three thousand miles just for her. "Get her in the plane, so we can get the fuck outta here," Luciano snarled.

Barrie felt the blood-rush of raw fear, and rivulets of warm urine trickled down the insides of her legs.

CHAPTER FORTY-ONE

Danny

BEFORE DAWN—JULY 8, 1935
LAGUNA BEACH

Danny stood smoking, one foot resting on the seat of his Indian Chief. The surf was extremely strong. Six-footers banged into the shallows, masking all other sound. He was half a mile down the beach, obscured from Lake's house by a line of rock that ran perpendicular to the ocean.

With a powerful pair of field glasses, he had watched Lake arrive home with a diminutive blonde. A dark-haired man had come in behind them. When Danny dialed down on the man's face, he looked familiar, but it took a minute to put a name on him. Finally, it came to him. Rollo Tripoli. Luciano's drug guy.

After turning on the inside and outside lights, Lake and Madalynne went into the bedroom. Shortly, those lights went off, and Lake came out alone. Rollo followed her into the kitchen, and they emerged with drinks. Rollo waited in the living room while Lake disappeared again, this time into her study.

When she returned, she was wearing black high-heeled slippers and a chemise that left little to the imagination. Rollo unzipped himself and beckoned her over. Lake said something and shook her head no, but Rollo angrily pointed to his crotch and pulled out a gun. This time, Lake did as she was told, dropped to her knees and took out the Greek's cock. It was already fully erect. Rollo wasn't much for foreplay, and he pulled her head onto it with his gun hand while he sipped his drink with the other.

Danny smiled as he watched Lake work. She wasn't particularly fluid, but she was energetic, which probably had something to do with the gun. Before long, Rollo's back was arching. Lake tried to pull away, but that wasn't in Rollo's plan. He dropped his drink and used both hands on her head, slamming into her mouth with enough thrust to make her choke. He seemed to like that more than she did and finished quickly.

Lake collapsed on the floor, gagging for breath.

Rollo zipped up and walked to the mural. He swung back the Main Beach artwork and pointed to the safe. Lake got to her feet and began to work the dial. When she grabbed the handle, it didn't move. Rollo hit her in the back of the head, and Lake's face ricocheted off the mantle, dazing her and bloodying her nose. She covered it with her hand, stumbled to the coffee table, and retrieved a pair of dark-rimmed eyeglasses. She went back to the safe.

She spun the dial to clear the tumblers and started over, her hands trembling. Same result. Danny could see the surprise on her face and allowed himself a small chuckle. With Rollo shouting and waving his gun, Lake disappeared into the study and returned, holding a handkerchief over her nose with one hand and a small scrap paper in the other. She looked back and forth at the paper as she worked the dial once more, this time barely able to make her fingers work. When it didn't open, Rollo hit her with his fist, and Lake flew across the room.

Danny calmly slipped the binoculars into a leather saddlebag, threw a leg over the Indian and kicked its throaty engine to life. The thundering surf cloaked his arrival. He crossed the courtyard and went in through one of the open French doors. Rollo had Lake up again and was pointing the gun at her forehead.

"Problems?" Danny asked.

Rollo jerked around. It took him a second, then he made the connection. "Danny Dades, right? They told me you were the one who called Luciano. You can run along now. I don't need any help."

"From here, it looks like you need all you can get. The safe's not going to open. There's nothing inside anyway."

"What do you mean there's nothin inside?" Rollo spit.

"I'm moving fast here, Rollo. Try to keep up." Danny turned to Lake. "I've

seen better blowjobs, but at least you swallow."

"Fuck you. I would have called Luciano myself."

"Before the movie or after?" Danny asked.

Lake didn't say anything, but her eyes darted to Rollo.

"What the fuck you talkin about? Rollo snarled.

"Didn't you lovebirds discuss careers? Let me help. You see, Rollo, the woman who just so adoringly inhaled your load is a famous screenwriter. Expensive too. She's written a helluva motion picture. I didn't get a chance to finish it, but you're front and center. You kinda look like a schmuck, though, when Barrie leaves you in the desert, so I'm not sure we'll be able to get a big name to play you."

Rollo was having trouble processing. He looked at Lake. "You wrote a fuckin movie? About this shit?"

Lake had turned ghostly white. "It was just an exercise. Something to keep Barrie here until I could get a message to Mr. Luciano."

Rollo was incredulous. "She's been gone THREE FUCKIN MONTHS! You coulda fuckin walked to Cuba and told him in person!"

"Where is the lady in question, anyway?" Danny asked.

"Already gone," snapped Rollo, but his attention was still on Lake. "You wrote a fuckin movie?" he repeated, as if he couldn't get his mind around it.

Danny watched Lake rifle through her mental bag of bullshit, trying to think of something that might mollify Rollo. Finally, Danny said, "Too bad Barrie isn't here. She would have really liked this next part."

Danny turned slightly, and Rollo didn't see him take the .357 out of his waistband. When he turned back, he raised it and pulled the trigger all in one motion. The bullet caught Rollo in the throat and blew out the back of his neck. He was dead before his head crashed into the fireplace. Danny had killed a guy before and found it didn't bother him at all. This time, he liked it.

"Thank God," Lake cried. "Danny, anything you want, I'll…"

He pointed the gun at her. "Shut the fuck up, Lake. "Is Madalynne in the bedroom?"

"You know Madalynne?"

"Like I told Rollo, I'm moving fast. Pay attention."

Lake nodded. "She's sound asleep. Double dose of Nembutal."

"What a good mother. You were probably planning to be all over that comatose pussy half a dozen times before morning, weren't you?"

Lake started to shake. "I'm going to change the names in the script. Take yours out completely. It won't even be set in Cuba anymore." Lake took a step, but her legs wouldn't hold her. She grabbed onto a chair to keep from going down and dropped her handkerchief. Blood began running from her nose down between her breasts.

Danny smiled, "You don't know how happy it makes me to see you like this. Nice tits too."

Lake was desperate now. She lowered her top baring them, blood and all. "You want to fuck me, Danny? I'd sure like to fuck you. Do things to you that…"

"Oh, Jesus Christ, Lake, pull that back up. I wouldn't fuck you with Rollo's dick."

Lake stiffened. "They'll come for you too. Barrie will tell them everything."

"That's my gamble. But I don't think she will."

Lake thought about how Barrie had been on the way to Palm Springs. Then at dinner and the plane. No, she didn't think she would either. "Danny, I can pay you. I'm rich. Daddy's really, really rich. Just name your price. Any price at all."

Danny turned his head slightly and called out. "Princess, it's time."

Madalynne came around the corner, wearing nothing, carrying only her clutch purse. The pink nipples on her small breasts were fully erect, and her lips were trembling. She looked at Rollo's body, but it might as well have been a movie prop. It meant nothing to her.

Lake looked dazed. "The pills…"

"I spit them out," Madalynne said without emotion.

"I don't understand."

"You can't take care of me anymore, ma'am. Sir can. He has the screenplay now too."

"Forget her. Back the Packard up to the front door and open the trunk."

"I'm not getting in any trunk," Lake said flatly.

Danny smiled. "You would if I told you to, but don't worry."

Lake was beginning to feel like things might be turning around. "You know you can't just take MY screenplay."

Danny nodded at his gun. "This says I can. I don't know what you told the girls, but you know you can't even pitch that picture without getting everybody near it killed."

"I try not to clutter what little mind is up there, but that applies to you too."

"Give me more credit than one of your muffs. I'm betting the same way you were. Sooner or later, somebody's going to put a coffin or a cell around Luciano and his buddy, Lansky. When they do, Beverly Hills is Burning *will become the hottest property in town. If Hughes is still alive, once his name is changed, he won't make a peep either. Not with heroin in there."*

Danny used his free hand to sweep across an imaginary theatre marquee. "Danny Dades Presents… A Lake London Screenplay."

Lake grabbed at it. "If that's what you want, you've got it. I know somebody who'll do a budget for us on the QT."

"What's the rush? I'm young." Madalynne came back in the front door and handed the Packard keys to Danny. "My bike's on the beach, princess. Wait for me there."

Madalynne was shivering all over now. "May I please get dressed, sir. I'm so cold."

Danny looked at her admiringly. "I like you the way are. Go, now."

Madalynne started toward the French doors. "Princess," Danny said, "cover your ears."

Without turning, the actress put her hands over her ears. As she reached the courtyard, she broke into a naked run, her hands still clasped to her head, the chain of her clutch dancing against her shoulder.

"I think business will be better if I change the billing slightly. How do you feel about 'Danny Dades Presents… Lake London's LAST Screenplay.'" Lake looked at him uncomprehendingly as Danny raised the magnum and shook his head. "I'm not sure even a good fire can cleanse this place, but we'll give it a try."

Lake was shaking violently now. "Fire?"

"I'd like to say I'm sorry, Lake, but I'm not. Don't worry, though, you won't have to ride in the trunk. Rollo can have it all to himself."

Lake was losing it now. "Daddy… Daddy knows everything!"

"Somehow, I don't think he'll be doing much talking either."

The first shot took off Lake's left arm. The second, the top of her head. The following two were unnecessary, but Danny never left anything to chance. He also enjoyed the kick of the weapon. This gun had balls. That fuckin Barrie. She was the gift that kept on giving. Now, if she just kept her mouth shut.

CHAPTER FORTY-TWO

Caviar and Gulags

I went down one floor to where I figured Teddy's office would be. It wasn't hard to find. It was the only one with two Oscars on the credenza.

I sat at his desk and stared at the statuettes. Twice-failed sentries. Good for an epitaph, not much for protecting their owner from needing one. They were the only things in the room that indicated a movie producer had worked there. The investigators had cleared everything else out. Teddy's computer was gone; his credenza doors open, the shelves empty. It must have been a thin take. He'd been there less than a week, and he didn't strike me as an accumulator.

I opened the desk drawers and found only some health insurance forms and solicitations from hopeful vendors. On a shelf under his phone, a row of scripts had been examined then tossed back with little concern for order. Their titles were handwritten on their spines. No *Beverly Hills is Burning*.

I'd learned all there was to learn here.

If you want to get beneath the skin of a neighborhood, talk to a landlord. Their livelihood depends on knowing unflattering pasts, bad behavior and, most importantly, rumors. In areas with minority clusters, where group loyalties keep outsiders at bay, always talk to the landlord who's the biggest prick.

Outside of New York, West Hollywood is home to the country's largest Russian-speaking population. Brighton Beach without a subway stop. Most are Jews who fled the disintegrating Soviet Union, but there are also ethnic Ukrainians, Georgians and Armenians, some of whom were the border troops and KGB hoodlums who subjugated the very people they now live among. History has a way of laughing at victims.

Buka Pasternak, the uncrowned Queen of Little Odessa West, is a Ukrainian I would have once hunted down for the pleasure of cutting her throat. A man-faced, Olympic weightlifter, engineered to the size of a baby bull during the height of Soviet athletic chemistry, her day job had been as a "wet works" officer in the KGB's Directorate Z, where she terrorized political and artistic dissidents and belched out the final bloodshed of a dying regime.

Today, her massive, square head is topped by a swirl of thinning, bleached platinum hair, spun upward like cotton candy, which nicely sets off a mouthful of yellow teeth too large for even her cavernous jaws. Steroids are wonderful drugs. It's said Buka's clitoris is the length of an infant's finger. My goal is to never see it.

Buka dispenses favors and retribution from a table in front of a tiny caviar shop on Santa Monica Boulevard. You can buy a tin of pretty good legal roe at *Oblast*, but the wealth that built her real estate empire comes from smuggling Caspian Sea beluga, which a lot of Hollywood hypocrites can't get enough of… or pay enough for. Pinned on the bulletin boards of the well-to-do across the city is her card. The phone is unlisted, of course.

BUKA PASTERNAK
Private Orders
OBLAST

Buka and I have had a couple of run-ins over the years, and she was able to use her old contacts to find out what I used to do for a living, along with my authenticator code, Blue Jungle. Now she's just biding time until the day she can have one of her flunkies shoot me in an alley.

My sentiments are identical, only I don't use flunkies.

The rain had stopped, and as I crossed Fairfax, I saw a faint dawn trying to get traction against the remnants of the storm. Maybe better weather would improve my disposition—but not until I was finished with KGB weightlifters.

She was in her usual spot, drinking strong Russian coffee interspersed with shots from a nearby bottle of Horilka. She stood and hugged me without affection while she ran her thick hands over my body, checking for weapons or a wire. To amuse myself, I grabbed her butt cheeks and dry humped her a couple of strokes, which infuriated her.

"Cocksucker," she spit as she pushed me roughly away.

I gave her one of my best smiles. "How's the sturgeon plundering?"

"Apparently not so good as what you do up on Sunset. Shame they no waste your ass too."

Touché. "I could use your help."

"Of course you could. Go fuck yourself."

She was a lockdown, ironclad cunt who could snap a neck with the flick of her wrist, but if she got enough amaretto in her, she sometimes loosened up. "I'd appeal to you as a fellow human being, but not without DNA."

I got what I hoped for, a laugh. "I will dance on your grave, Jungle, but you amuse me in enlisted man sort of way. I don't know who did job."

"There were at least three shooters, none local, so they had to stay somewhere."

"I check couple places, but you didn't come down off hill for that."

"Somebody on the inside had a gun the shooters weren't expecting."

She grinned, and I wanted to suggest Clorox, but didn't. "I hate when that happens, but makes for good story."

"Probably not as good this time. It was a cluster fuck on the way out. Two of the bad guys were hit hard."

I waited while somebody from inside the shop brought Buka another coffee. She did a liberal pour of Horilka threw it back and sipped the coffee. Then she looked past me and said, "There is sideswiped Camry across from your driveway. Owner no have insurance, so no can report. In old Soviet Union, people afraid of secret police. Here, insurance company. Someday Geico get guns, then watch the fuck out." She opened her mouth and laughed again. My skin crawled.

"If that's all you've got, you're closer to a dirt nap than I thought."

She didn't acknowledge the remark. "Next street over. Vantana. Family report woman missing. Hannah Halperin. I make her leave my apartments for being pain in ass. She disappear same day of your fun, so TV no report. Maybe mean something, maybe not."

"Disappeared?"

"These old Jews complain about everything, then they die. But never just vanish. Only thing sure, she no go quietly."

"You got an address?"

"The Gardenia. I assume you can read."

I stood. "Off the subject. What's the Bolshevik position on apparitions?"

She looked at me curiously. "Apparitions? Like *pryvyd?*"

"Okay, *pryvyd*, whatever that is. Ghosts and shit."

"What happen? Big man suddenly afraid of dark?"

"Forget it."

She narrowed her eyes. "You serious." It wasn't a question.

"I said, forget it."

"Ever been to old gulag?"

"Missed the pleasure.

"Go, then come back and ask same question."

I sat in the Rolls and contemplated going home. It was a little early to be making house calls, and I was tired of being "on." Then my stomach growled, and I decided to make the decision after I ate—preferably a flotilla of eggs with as much sausage as they could get on the plate. I swung south. If you're going for breakfast in SoCal, and you're headed anywhere but Norms, you're eating second-best.

Wheeling under the big, red-orange letters, I decided to leave my phone in the car so I could concentrate on raising my cholesterol. As I was tossing it on the passenger seat, it lit up with an international number. Italy.

"*Pronto,*" I answered.

"*Pronto* to you, Rail Black. It's truly wonderful to hear your voice. It reminds me so much of your father's. I miss him with all my heart. He always made me laugh."

What I hadn't told Teddy Chessman was that the Black family relationship with the Passavantis had been more than casual. The Duchessa was one of the many extraordinary women linked with my father throughout the years. She was also the only one he would never answer my questions about.

When I was younger, I thought it unlikely he would carry on an affair with a married woman—and certainly not the wife of a man with whom he had business dealings. But as I've gained wisdom, the attractions and needs of lonely men and women have shaded such absolutes. There was also the large ring my father bought her—an unusual gift under any circumstances.

What I hadn't misled Teddy about was that I had never heard anybody mention a Passavanti daughter named Graciella.

"Duchessa, I hope you will forgive me for not offering my condolences sooner. You shouldn't have had to call to hear them."

"Nonsense, Rail. You had other things on your mind."

"I'll be in Venice for the funerals, of course."

"I appreciate that more than I can tell you, but please don't. I must grieve, and I'm not ready to see anyone. Those boys were as much my sons as they were my grandsons."

"Then perhaps when you're up to it, you'll come visit us. We've got plenty of room."

"That sounds like just the ticket. But I'll stay in my usual bungalow at the Beverly Hills. I rarely sleep anymore, and I pace—sometimes without clothes."

"That could put an end to Mallory's wanderings."

"Wouldn't that be an encounter? How is that crusty old *pasticcione*?"

"Considerably crustier. Can I do anything at all?"

"That's why I'm calling. Your authorities are being difficult about releasing the bodies. They've also impounded our jet and pulled my pilots' passports. I know they have a job to do, but it's very painful."

"Say no more. My attorney will speak with the district attorney, and my plane will be on its way with your grandsons as soon as possible. My pilots' names are Jody Miller and Eddie Buffalo, and they're as reliable as they come. They'll be at your disposal until you release them."

"Thank you so much, Rail. I was dreading having to ask someone here. They're all such frightful gossips—and broke. Which is where I'm headed if you don't make something of this movie business for us."

This was a *woman*. Strong, determined and, even at her advanced age and during the worst kind of tragedy, able to maintain focus and stay aloof from the chattering classes. If my father hadn't had an affair with her, he should have.

"Ross Dare, who's running the company, is up to the task. When you wish, I'll put you on the phone with him."

"Not necessary, your endorsement is all I need." She paused. "I assume that by this time, you also know that Valentina—the actress they call Valentine Jones—is my granddaughter."

"Teddy Chessman filled me in."

"Have you met her?"

"Not professionally."

"Unfortunately, her competence in surrounding herself with quality people is not comparable to her fame. I'm afraid far too much of my daughter bred true."

It looked like the familial embrace of the Passavantis was still over the horizon. "I've made arrangements for her to be protected."

"I do appreciate that. No one can tell her anything, and she can find trouble in an empty room."

I thought about Wind. What is it about actresses?

"Have you read Valentina's movie?" asked the duchessa.

"Yes, I have. It's very good."

"My first and last screenplay. I must say, though, I agree with you. It's quite a story. We're all in your hands now—Valentina too—and I can think of no better place to be. *Ciao*, Rail."

"*Ciao*, Duchessa."

I called Det. Bricklin who was as happy to hear from me as the last time. "I got no time for you, Black. I'm suiting up for your autopsies."

Most homicides aren't that tricky. Cops hang around the morgue because it beats filling out paperwork and makes for good conversation. I've heard, *You shoulda seen the snatch on this chick*, one too many times. "I'm betting gunshots, but maybe it'll turn out to be the clap."

Bricklin didn't like my remark, but it got him off I'm-a-cop-and-you're-not for a moment. "Okay, I'm listening."

"Do me a favor and wrap up the Passavantis first. They're the grandsons of a friend, and I'd like to get their bodies back to Italy."

"You think because you got dough you can make the rules?"

"Look, Al, they got one relative—I didn't think this was the time to bring up Cousin Valentine—and she's in her eighties and the head of a very important family. I'm asking a favor. From you. Not some cheese dick in the federal building. But if you're telling me you need to hear it from Washington, I've got a big Rolodex."

He cooled off. "I'll see what I can do."

"Tell the M.E. my pilots will be there at five with a funeral director who'll prepare them for shipment. I'd like to not keep them waiting."

I didn't hear a good-bye. I called Jody next and told him to get in touch with the Masucci Brothers Mortuary and have them bill me. I wanted him in the air by sundown.

"Will do, Mr. Black. Never been to Italy."

Venice is one of my favorite cities. I would have liked to have ridden along. Instead, I got Norms, which wasn't a bad consolation. But I knew I wasn't going to enjoy my meal.

The duchessa hadn't said a single word about the investigation or asked who could have done such a thing. Instead, she'd pointed me toward Valentine, which wasn't exactly breaking news. Venice appeared to be ahead of Los Angeles in more than just architecture and time zones.

CHAPTER FORTY-THREE

An Off-Limits Girl and Prada

Thirty minutes later and five pounds heavier, I went back up the hill and drove slowly past the sideswiped Camry. I didn't know how I'd missed it before. It wasn't just grazed, the left side was caved in. One corner of the front bumper was hanging against the street, and the white paint from headlight to taillight had deep, silver gouges in it. I made a mental note to have Jake track down the owner and have it fixed. Part was to do a good deed for an innocent neighbor, part was to hear Jake bitch. The silver paint could also tell me what the killers had been driving, but I wasn't in the prosecution business. That, and the getaway car wasn't coming back from wherever it was.

The Gardenia on Vantana was a pale green, five-story apartment house with a row of expensive potted plants out front. A sheriff's department missing person notice was posted on the lobby glass next to a homemade flyer with an older woman's picture headed REWARD! Photocopies of the flyer were also taped to light poles and trees up and down the street.

I rang the manager's buzzer and a young lady's voice came on. "If you're a reporter, please leave us alone. Some of our residents are very elderly, and they're already terrified."

"Not a reporter. I'd just like to talk to you for a minute."

"We don't have any vacancies."

"I promise I'll keep it short."

She hesitated then said, "I'll come down."

Denise Spyrou was slender and dark, maybe thirty. She was also heart-stoppingly beautiful, as the Mediterranean tends to breed them. Before she opened the door, she spent a long time looking me up and down. In most situations, my size is an advantage. This wasn't one of them. I took out my wallet and put my driver's license against the glass.

She read it slowly, probably memorizing the address, then cracked the door. "What can I do for you, Mr. Black?"

With this kind of suspicion, being indirect wasn't going to get me anywhere. "I'm trying to determine if your tenant's disappearance had anything to do with Colosseum Pictures. I'm the owner."

Her eyes got wide. "My God, what a tragedy. But you're in the wrong place. Mrs. Halperin's an old lady. She doesn't even have a car. I can guarantee she doesn't know anybody in the movie business."

"Mind telling me what the police said?"

"I'd be happy to if they'd said anything at all. Her daughters had to call a dozen times just to get them to come out and take a report. They couldn't have been here more than half an hour."

I understood. Who wants to mess around with an AWOL senior citizen when there's a full-blown mass murder up the street. "Would you mind showing me where Mrs. Halperin lives?"

"I can't let you in the apartment, but I can show you the floor."

"That'll be fine."

We rode the elevator to the second floor hallway. It was a nice place. High-end Spanish tile, muraled walls and antiqued sconces. "Very elegant. You own the building?"

"Oh, God, no. My father does. I get free rent for managing it, which is mostly to keep me out of the house." She hesitated then added. "He and I don't speak."

"Mind if I ask?"

"Not at all. I'm a lesbian, and my father's from the old country. Cyprus. He's looking forward to ringing in 1876."

"You just ruined my day too."

She laughed, and it was a good laugh. "I get that a lot. You're pretty good-looking yourself. If you decide to switch jerseys, let me know. You'd be a hit with a guy I work out with."

She had crossed the bridge I needed her to cross. "How many Halperin daughters are there?"

"Two, they take turns looking in on their mom."

"When did they discover she was missing?"

"About six that evening. The one that's a doctor, Pamela, came by on her way home. The apartment was locked, and there was no sign of her or Tuffy."

"Tuffy?"

"Mrs. Halperin's Yorkshire terrier." She held her hands about a foot apart. "Tiny little guy, even for a Yorkie, but with major attitude. She always walks Tuffy first thing in the morning, again around noon, and before she eats at five. After that, she's in for the night."

"The daughter check the neighborhood?"

"Right away. Mrs. Halperin and Tuffy don't go far, just down the block and back. When Pamela didn't find them, she searched the garage and every floor of the building. She found Tuffy in one of the emergency stairwells. He had his leash on, but there was no sign of Mrs. Halperin."

We were standing in front of the elevator. The floor layout was U-shaped, with the elevator and three apartments at the base of the U and three more down each arm. "Which one is Mrs. Halperin's?" I asked.

Denise pointed toward the right. "At the end of that hallway. She originally lived on a higher floor, but she complained that the smell of a neighbor's cooking was making her sick, so we moved her. She's kind of fussy, but we get along most of the time."

"And there's a stairwell over there?"

"Yes, right next to Mrs. Halperin's place. But Tuffy was in the one over there." She pointed to the left.

I walked into that hallway, and she followed me. "Who lives on this side?"

She nodded at the first door. "That's Miss Gruber, she's a Special Ed teacher, but she's been backpacking in Mexico for a couple of weeks. The next one is Mr. Schweitzer and Mr. Fuller. They work at CBS. One's an announcer on a game show, and the other's an assistant to some vice-president."

"A couple."

"Yes. The apartment at the end is corporate. A company in New York, I think, but I don't know the name. The rent goes directly to my father, and ninety percent of the time, there's no one there."

"How about now?"

"I live right above. I heard somebody moving around last week, but nothing since the weekend."

"Man? Woman?"

"Always a man. Different ones."

"Did the investigators go inside all the apartments?"

"Are you kidding? They didn't go anywhere but the stairwells, and they only looked in them. But the daughters talked to everybody on the floor."

"Except these two places."

"Yes, but I opened them with my passkey and walked through. Miss Gruber's apartment is neat as a pin. The corporate one's been cleaned, so I think the guy's gone."

"Would you mind showing me?"

She stared and didn't answer. She was trying to make a decision, so I helped her along. "You can stand at the door and keep it open. I'll even let you hold my wallet."

She grinned, "Sure, why not. If you find a big bag of money, we can split it."

"Deal," I smiled.

Apartment 203 hadn't just been cleaned, it had been professionally sanitized. The smell of disinfectant lay heavy in the air, and the footprints Denise had left on her tour were mashed into the carpet, indicating that it had been wet when she came through. I bent and felt it. Still damp.

There was nothing on the counters of the kitchenette, and it didn't appear that there had ever been so much as a quart of milk in the refrigerator. Same with the smaller of the two bedrooms. Like brand new.

The drawers in the master were empty too, until I came to the television remote, side by side with a pair of Brunton Epoch binoculars. Apparently they'd been overlooked. You don't spend fifteen hundred bucks to watch birds from a low-rise in West Hollywood. Only a professional would own those. But a professional what?

The rest of the apartment was immaculate, even the sinks and shower. As I walked back toward the living room, I passed a linen closet. A quick glance inside revealed neatly folded sheets, pillowcases, white towels and washcloths. I was about to close it, when something caught my eye.

Because the hallway was narrow and the door frame overhung the top shelf, an ordinary-sized person would not have seen anything that high. Being tall, I did. Standing on my toes, I could make out two, thick towels stuffed in the back corner. In an otherwise spit and polish apartment, they were out of place.

I just barely got a two-finger grip on one of the towels, and as I pulled it toward me, something heavy wrapped inside came too. I worked the bundle carefully to the edge then gave it a jerk, and the entire thing dropped into my arms. The towel fell away, and I was holding my Prada satchel from the poker game. Still stuffed.

I was taken by surprise and had to think for a moment. There was no longer any question I was in the right place. Morrie had no connection to Colosseum, so the shooter had almost certainly been a professional sent to do two jobs. I had stumbled into both.

Denise came around the corner and saw me. "What's that?"

"I know this isn't going to sound right, but it's mine."

"Yours?"

She thought I meant I was getting ready to steal it, so she got officious. "Put it back, and get out of here. Right now, mister."

"Back off a minute, Denise."

She was very nervous and inching toward the door. I tossed the bag on the floor in front of her. For some reason, Mallory once ordered some extra-wide, black rubber bands with my initials on them. I think they're pretentious as hell, but I sometimes use them on money I keep at the house. "Open it," I said to Denise. "It's going to be full of cash. At the bottom you'll find some banded stacks. Do you remember my name?"

"Rail Black."

"My middle name is Sheridan. I won't say anything more."

She was still unsure, but her curiosity overcame her reservations. She bent and opened the satchel. The sight of so much money actually rocked her back on her heels. "My God," she whispered. She couldn't get to the bottom without taking out handfuls of hundreds and laying them on the carpet. Eventually, she came up with two RSB-banded stacks. "You're right."

"Remember our deal? We split," I said.

"That was just silly talk. I don't understand what's going on, but if it's yours, take it." She began refilling the bag.

"Actually, the guy who took it from me thought half was his. I didn't agree then, but now that I think about it, maybe he had a point."

"What are you saying?"

"Count out $610,000. That was his end. He won't be needing it." She was shaking all over. "Go ahead. Give yourself a little independence."

"That would be so wonderful. My father never..."

I held up my hand. "Money's no good if you don't share it. Maybe you'll help someone one day."

She found a clean trash bag under the sink, and while she was counting, I noticed a landline phone on the credenza. On a hunch, I crossed to it, picked up the receiver and dialed *69. It rang at least a dozen times on the other end, which I thought was unusual in the era of voicemail. Then, just as I was about to disconnect, someone answered. "Papazian's."

"Mr. Papazian, please," I said politely.

Across the room, I heard Denise gasp. I turned, and she appeared terrified.

"Who's this?" the voice in my ear asked.

"Tell him it's his old friend, Rail Black."

Matty Aspirins hadn't wanted to answer, but the fucker kept ringing. He couldn't take a chance it was somebody on his way to pick up a car. He stood in an empty auto bay at Papazian's, the outside doors closed, the lights off, the houseboat hitman's Ruger .45 tucked into his waistband. The Cypriot's two sons lay dead in the next bay.

The Cypriot was duct-taped to a chair, a chain noose around his neck, the other end secured to the hook on the engine hoist. Matty had the control box in his hand and had just raised the Cypriot a few feet off the ground. The slabs of tape over the fat man's nose and mouth billowed and collapsed rapid-fire as his lungs fought for air.

Matty didn't know if there might still be a Papazian associated with the shop, so he didn't hang up. Instead, he held the phone with his shoulder while he pushed the hoist's down button and brought the Cypriot back to the floor.

I heard the whirring sound but didn't recognize it, then the voice said, "You callin about a car?"

I put my hand over the receiver and looked at Denise. "What's Papazian's?"

She shook her head violently.

"It's either me or the cops," I said none too gently.

She bit her lip, and I saw her hands trembling. "My father's place. A body shop on Pico. My brothers work there with him."

I went back to the phone. "Yeah, about a car."

"Tell me which one, and I'll have Papazian call you back."

I took a breath. "One that got sideswiped. Actually, it was the one doing the swiping. Up on Taylor. Near Sunset. Lotta blood inside too."

The guy didn't hang up. He was either paralyzed or cool. It didn't take long to find out which.

"The next sound you hear will be a fat Cypriot flying." And the whirring came again.

CHAPTER FORTY-FOUR

Dads and Tangerine Chases

I was in a box. I didn't want to report my Papazian's conversation, but there was no way around it with Denise's having heard it. When I hung up, she must have read my eyes. "What's wrong? Is my dad okay?"

She'd gone from "father" to "dad." I walked her into the hallway. "Do you still talk to your mother?"

"Absolutely. She comes over once a week and has lunch with Zoe and me. Zoe's my partner."

"Is your mother home now?"

"I think so."

"What about Zoe?"

"At work. She gets home around five."

"I want you to go back upstairs and leave her a note to meet you at your mother's. Then I want you to go there and stay put."

"Now?"

"Immediately."

She didn't understand. "For how long?"

"You'll know."

"But…"

"Denise, you don't know me, but I'm somebody you can trust. Give me your cell phone."

She took it out of her pocket, and I programmed my number into it. "Call me if you need anything. Day or night."

Back on the street, I opened the trunk of my Rolls, put the satchel inside and took a Glock 17 out of the hidden safe. I untucked my shirt and slipped it against the small of my back. I prefer a .45 for stopping power, but the Glock's magazine capacity is worthy compensation.

When I reached Papazian's, I circled the converted gas station twice, driving slowly through the front lot, around the side and down the alley. If someone was inside, it wasn't evident. I also didn't see any silver cars.

After my second pass, I pulled the Rolls close to the first bay, got out and looked through the row of windows. A faint light from a Pennzoil wall clock illuminated the back workbench but didn't give up anything else. I knocked loudly on the glass. No answer. I tried the four bay doors and the front and back office entrances. Locked.

There was too much traffic on Pico to do anything brazen, but the rear was hidden from the houses across the alley by a high, wooden fence. No alarm was evident, so I took out the Glock and tested the door with my shoulder. The latch was double-locked, and the hardware was top-of-the-line. The other side, though, had considerable give. Even smart people will overspend on a lock but leave cheap hinges in place.

I drew back my foot and gave the hinged side all the kick I had. The wood splintered loudly and the entire door cracked lengthwise. Two of the three hinges broke in half. Another kick, and I was inside. I'd made too much noise to surprise anyone, but I still followed procedure and cleared the office, restroom and storage space before entering the garage.

The dead Spyrou brothers were splayed on the oily floor, both victims of head shots. A sudden stream of water hitting cement caused me to spin around in a crouch, Glock leveled. The heavyset man was seated in a chair high above, swinging slightly from the motor chain around his neck. His bladder had released, and the remnants of his last piss dripped over his shoe and into the puddle below. In the center of it was a small gold crucifix. Greek Orthodox.

I used the hoist control to bring him back to earth. His face was deep purple and twice normal size from strangulation, which meant he'd been alive when he went up. There was a considerable amount of blood on his clothes but no obvious wounds. When I pulled the duct tape off his nose and mouth, I discovered that his tongue had been cut out and his nose nearly severed. There was also a separate, narrow ligature mark in his bloated neck which had probably come from the crucifix before the gold chain reached its breaking point.

There would have been no point to the exercise if the questioner had gotten what he wanted. The fat man had apparently been one tough Cypriot.

I took out my phone and dialed. Bricklin picked up on the second ring.

Sitting behind the wheel of a four-door, tangerine Bentley Mulsanne across six busy lanes of Pico Blvd., Matty Aspirins got a look at Rail Black. The news had said he was a billionaire, but he didn't look like any billionaire Matty'd ever seen. This guy was big and moved easy. He also looked comfortable with a gun. Definitely not some Joe Citizen playing Sam Spade.

He heard a distant siren and started the Mulsanne. The car had been in the third of the body shop's four bays, next to where he'd shot the Cypriot's sons. The time-stamped ticket on the dash showed it had been taken from a downtown hotel last night. That meant he had at least forty-eight hours before it got logged into the stolen car registry. What Matty didn't like were the tarted-up color, which made him look like a pimp, and the Nevada plates, which were cop magnets. He'd switch it out in the long-term lot at LAX as soon as he could.

In the meantime, he'd seen a soul food joint on the next block with a row of windows facing Papazian's. He'd grab some chicken and waffles and watch what happened.

I didn't want to spend any more time with Capt. Bricklin than he wanted to spend with me. He didn't hide his displeasure at not being called until after I'd broken into the shop, but there was no point in locking horns over it. We were inside the LA city limits, so all the usual suspects showed up, including a couple of LAPD homicide guys I'd dealt with before. One liked me, and the other thought my head should be mounted over his mantle, which pretty much summed up my batting average with law enforcement.

There weren't any surveillance cameras at Papazian's, and after Bricklin told me what the Cypriot's real business was, I understood why. You don't record yourself changing VIN numbers. That these three humanitarians were dead wasn't going make much of a tear in the fabric of society.

I'd seen the guy in the Mulsanne as soon as I'd arrived. The first order of business entering a possible hot zone is determining who belongs and who doesn't, and this part of Pico definitely wasn't Bentley country. The car was also blocking an apartment house driveway. Not something you do with three hundred and fifty grand worth of shiny steel—even if it is tangerine. The windows were too heavily tinted to get a good look at the driver when he swung onto Pico, but my gut told me he'd spent a few nights in Apartment 203 at the Gardenia.

I hadn't expected him to turn into a restaurant only a block up the street, so when the detectives asked me to move my Rolls to let the investigators open all the bays, I parked it around back, where it couldn't be seen.

While the cops worked, I made a point of going in and coming out of the building through every door several times. It pissed off the cops that I was there at all, let alone wandering around, but I was careful not to get in anybody's way. What I wanted was for the guy in the Bentley to get used to seeing me disappear then reappear.

After Bricklin asked the same questions enough times to make my eyes roll back in my head, he said I could go. He wasn't happy that I wouldn't tell him how I'd found Denise Spyrou.

I circled through the neighborhood south of Pico and came back up several blocks on the side of *Studd's Soul Kitchen* that faced away from Papazian's. I turned into the lot and parked so close to the Bentley's door that the driver wouldn't be able to get in on that side.

Matty was surprised when he saw the Rolls—and angry at himself. He'd made a mistake underestimating this guy, then another leaving the Ruger in the car. It wouldn't happen again. Mr. Black thought he was cute, but he was a step behind.

Studd's had been a dump, so Matty'd left his car where it was and walked next door to a Chinese joint. Now sitting over a just-arrived plate of fried rice and a cold Tsingtao, he watched Black enter the soul food restaurant. Matty tried to get the waitress's attention for his check, but she ignored him. Finally, he tossed a hundred on the table and got up, just as he saw Black start across the parking lot in his direction.

The kitchen was behind a beaded curtain in the rear, and Matty headed through it. A short Asian man was working an open-flame stove with several steaming woks on top. Suddenly, from out of nowhere, an even smaller Asian woman jumped in front of Matty and began yelling in Chinese and pointing back the way he'd come. He didn't need a translator.

He tried to push by her, but she moved with him and yelled even louder. The cook then started yelling too. What the fuck, though Matty. All I'm trying to do is get out of your goddamn restaurant. Then the woman picked up a spatula and began hitting him in the head.

Furious, Matty grabbed a wok off the stove and threw its contents in the woman's face. As the hot oil struck her, she let out a blood-curdling scream, and the man charged him with a kitchen knife. Matty slammed the wok into the side of the guy's head, and he went down. Only when Matty reached the Bentley did he realize some of the oil had struck his arm, and it burned far more than the wounds on his face.

Pissed at the way the Rolls had him boxed in, he managed to climb in the passenger side and over the console, but fumbled momentarily with the unfamiliar ignition. He saw Black coming just as the engine caught. Another mistake. He should have focused on getting his gun.

I was running toward the Mulsanne, and for some reason, the driver was having trouble getting it started. I pulled open the passenger door and reached in. He was a good-sized guy, maybe 6-2, with thick arms that I didn't think were for show. One of his hands had a heavy bandage wrapped around the palm, and he had a slew of small cuts on a face that could have been carved on Mount Olympus. No surprise. Greek.

I got hold of his arm, but it was slick with some sort of grease. I lost my grip when he punched the Bentley. The open door knocked me down, and I would have become a wet spot on the blacktop if I hadn't managed to roll away from the onrushing wheels. The door slammed shut as he accelerated, and a moment later, he fishtailed up a side street.

You don't buy a Rolls for its chasing ability. The Bentley also had a hundred more cubic inches and fifty more horsepower than my stately V12. I didn't like my chances, but my adrenaline was up, my clothes were torn and my pride was back there on the pavement, along with the skin off my knees.

Fuck this asshole.

CHAPTER FORTY-FIVE

Dry Cleaning and Islands

After careening through several neighborhoods and barely missing a good-looking lady, who for some reason, was pushing a grocery cart up the middle of Spaulding Avenue, I caught the Bentley at San Vicente Boulevard. It was obvious the guy hadn't driven a Mulsanne before.

When you have that much weight on a chassis, no amount of suspension, shocks or tires can stiffen it beyond a certain point, or the whole purpose for the extra poundage—ride—disappears. It also doesn't matter how much engineering you pay for, the laws of physics can't be bought. First among them is inertia.

At 60-mph, three tons is going to try to keep going straight, no matter what you have in mind. If you aren't prepared for it, even a small wiggle is going to feel like you're strapped to a drunken whale, which considering that the Mulsanne is more than eighteen feet, makes it longer than some water-based ones.

There are tricks to dealing with this, but they're counterintuitive. Namely, the faster you're going, the sooner you need to start your turn. But not many people can get their head around aiming at a crowded bus stop when they're trying to hit a lane thirty feet beyond. My racing pal wasn't one of them.

He and the tangerine Bentley fishtailed across all three westbound lanes of San Vicente, managing to use both curbs as bumpers and launching a poorly-parked Vespa through a street-side garage door. My Rolls wasn't any better at cornering, but I was willing to surrender style points for efficiency. I took a helluva divot out of the center island grass and got back on pavement before I eliminated one of the dwindling number of LA's signature coral trees—an offense that would have put me first in line for the gas chamber, just ahead of anybody caught smoking at the beach. What a fuckin state.

I had to give the Greek credit for reflexes though. He missed every car he went by. But if he kept accelerating, catastrophe was inevitable, so I backed off a little, hoping he would do the same. My altruism went unrewarded, and by the time I picked up the tempo again, he had put two blocks between us.

The acre-size, triangular intersection of San Vicente, Olympic and Fairfax has been called a lot of things. Brilliantly-designed isn't one of them. All three thoroughfares are heavily-traveled. However, the two boulevards fly, and on a good day, the slow entry, Fairfax Avenue, is a bad limp. Picture two runways at LAX bisected by a wheelchair lane.

As I approached, the San Vincente traffic lights were out, and a DWP cherry picker sat squarely in the middle of traffic, its business end three-quarters vertical. If that weren't enough, a dry cleaning van had been T-boned by a 1950 Studebaker, strewing dirty laundry and a couple of hundred freshly pressed In-N-Out Burger uniforms across eighteen lanes and two center islands. The white-haired driver of the Studie—easily twenty years older than his car—was walking among his fellow motorists yelling about illegals fucking up the roads. Meanwhile the Asian van driver—a woman—who may or may not have arrived via cargo container, was slumped over her airbag while LAFD paramedics and their accompanying pumper crew used the jaws of life trying to free her.

I got the Rolls' speed down as far as I could as fast as I could, but the Nissan Z in front of me was still going to get steamrolled. I had two options: spend the next five years explaining to ten insurance companies why I was up the Z's ass on a clear day on dry pavement—unless the guy died, then it would take less time but cost more—or run the Rolls back into the San Vicente median, in which case, it would take ten years, twenty insurance companies and half a dozen city departments just to clear the paperwork for plowing their sacred turf.

I decided to let Mr. Z see another sunrise and threw my behemoth over the curb and felt six thousand pounds of British steel begin to spin on city grass.

The Mulsanne never slowed.

Matty Aspirins had watched the Rolls drift further back and used the opportunity to push the Bentley faster. When he saw the flashing lights in the intersection ahead, he was already committed, so he slalomed one way, then the other, sideswiped a Domino's Pizza Taurus, catapulted a stray rack of burger uniforms skyward then felt something hard under his wheels, followed by something much softer.

When he glanced in his side mirror, he thought he caught sight of a halo of white hair cartwheeling across Fairfax. Then it was gone.

The next time he looked, the Rolls was gone too, and he slowed to the speed limit, cut right at an intersection and headed north toward the Beverly Center, several yards of dry cleaning plastic still clinging to his undercarriage.

CHAPTER FORTY-SIX

Electra and Zoe

Matty Aspirins found a dark corner on a high level of the Beverly Center garage, wiped the Bentley clean of prints, put the windows down and left the key fob on the dash. If he got lucky, somebody would steal it. At worst, after a couple of days, it would be towed.

He took the elevator to street level and walked a block north to the Sofitel Hotel. In the gift shop, he bought a prepaid cell phone, a pack of Camel Blues for the price of a Ferrari and a Lakers baseball cap, which he pulled down as far as possible to hide the wounds on his face. He exited though the rear and walked west then circled through a residential neighborhood to a bus stop well east of the hotel.

Matty took a seat on the bench, lit a cigarette and watched for a cab. He wasn't surprised when none came by. LA is not a cruising city. There would have been a line of them at the hotel's main entrance, but that would have put him on the security tapes along with a license number. He was taking no chances. The last few days had been a goat fuck. Time to get back to basics.

Matty dialed his voicemail in New York. There were two messages. "Your LA vacation's canceled," which meant exactly what it said. And, "Let us know when we can get together," which meant exactly the opposite—unless you counted calling hours. The people who'd hired him obviously knew he'd escaped the houseboat hit, and they probably knew the Cypriot was dead too. Now they were hoping he'd make it easy to fix their mistake. Jesus, when was he going to catch a break?

He dialed a number in Brooklyn and asked for Dimitrios.

"Yeah?"

"Recognize the voice?"

"Never thought I'd hear it again. Couple of dagos been comin by."

"What'd you tell them?"

"That you like the color green. They said you should go fuck yourself."

Matty wasn't surprised. Half down, half when the job was done meant that if you fucked up, half down, period. And he'd fucked up. It didn't matter there'd been a shitstorm nobody could have anticipated. Anticipation was supposed to be his middle name. The hit on the bookie that went right? Forget it.

"Cash everything out, keep a hundred grand for yourself, and deposit the rest in an off-shore bank. I don't care which one, long as it's not run by Frogs."

"All of it? That's a lot of dough."

"All of it. And put my passports and ten grand in an envelope. I'll tell you where to drop it."

"Gonna miss you. Anything else?"

Matty thought for a moment. Well, if he was gonna do this, he might as well take it all—providing it was still there. "You got somebody out here I can trust?"

"How much you gotta trust them?"

"On a one to ten, nine-nine."

"You know the joint with the bread in the window?"

"Yeah."

"Ask for Electra."

"A broad?"

"Check the calendar. They can vote now too."

This was the second guy in a week to remind him he was getting old.

Matty caught an eastbound bus and settled into the last row. Gang graffiti and crude representations of female anatomy were scratched into the windows. Cops stop beatin assholes, this is what you get.

LA's Greektown, once one of the country's largest, was long gone, surrendered to the inexorable demographic squeeze on the former European neighborhoods west of downtown. One tiny pocket of Hellenic holdouts remained, anchored by St. Sophia's Cathedral, built sixty+ years ago by one of the Skouras brothers, better-known for putting up lavish movie palaces. Telly Savalas worshiped at St. Sophia's, and when your feet have an overwhelming compulsion to *sirtaki* like Zorba, its festival is a must.

Matty could smell the taverna several blocks away, and it reminded him of his interrupted lunch and how long it had been since he'd had a real Greek meal. He strolled through the front bakery to the dining room in the rear. It was a thin crowd: a middle-aged woman behind the cash register absorbed in a Greek newspaper and four old men drinking Retsina and arguing over a game of Diloti. Nobody looked up.

He took a seat against the back wall, and eventually, the woman put down her paper and brought him a glass of water. "*Kherete,*" she said perfunctorily.

"Is the cook Greek?"

"Of course," the woman said as if she'd been insulted. "Everybody here is Greek."

Matty smiled up at her. "Then bring me a bottle of your best Agiorgitiko, and feed me like family."

It was like he'd opened a faucet. She beamed at him. "You have come to the right place. You smoke?"

"I do."

"I'll bring an ashtray. Fuck the mayor."

Matty took out his Camels and offered her one. She accepted, and he lit both. "Fuck everybody who ain't Greek," he said.

The woman nodded agreement and headed toward the kitchen. Moments later, Matty heard her clapping her hands and shouting instructions. An hour and four courses later, he lit another cigarette, poured the last of his wine and closed his eyes. He felt better than he'd felt since he left New York.

"Baklava?" The voice was a new one, younger.

He opened his eyes and saw a tall, thin woman with waist-length dark hair standing over him with a plate of pastry. She was dressed in black skintight slacks, red heels and a short, red silk shirt unbuttoned far enough to see that she wasn't wearing a bra. She was also flashing a navel ring with a tiny Greek E. "Only if you'll join me."

She raised her hand and gestured to the woman to bring another bottle.

I was on my back patio making love to a tuna salad sandwich and a bag of Doritos when Bricklin called. "We found the other Tata brother."

"Let me guess. He wasn't in a parked car in West Hollywood."

I could hear the head-shake through the phone. "They get a law degree, they figure twenty years on the street is taped to the back. Papazian's. Head-down in a 55-gallon drum of used motor oil."

If they kept looking, they'd probably find an old Jewish woman too. "That must have been pretty."

"Another reason I drink. But there's not much I don't drink about anymore."

"How many holes did he have in him?"

"A few, but the only one that mattered was the one in his eye."

So Mr. Tata had gotten out alive and been executed later. "The other guys were who I thought?"

"Apollo Spyrou and his sons. Turns out Papazian was two owners ago. I talked to him at his nursing home. Never heard the name Spyrou, and the guy he sold the joint to bit the dust in a drive-by. Just to round out the black hole, Apollo's wife and daughter wouldn't even give me their names, which is par for the course with Greeks. I was a few years younger and thirty pounds lighter, though, I'd make a run at the girl."

"Lesbian," I said.

"No shit. Well, I'm okay with that too."

I didn't want to conjure up any images I'd have to forget, so I left it alone. He hadn't said anything about the Gardenia or the missing Mrs.

Halperin, but if he'd gone to the Cypriot's home he wouldn't know there was an apartment house. Unless they volunteered it, and that didn't seem to be their style. "Any other family?"

"A brother-in-law in Fresno, but the last time somebody in the stolen car business had a relative who knew anything, God can't remember. And the last time the relative was a Greek and talked to the cops, God wasn't born yet."

"So what do you think?"

"What do I think, or what am I gonna do?"

"Both."

"I think maybe a couple of people were supposed to get whacked, but something went wrong. Other than the dead Tata, there's nothing in any of the victims' backgrounds that would point to this. Not even Chessman, unless you count talent agents. I got no fingerprints, so much DNA the lab don't know whether to shit or go blind, not a single snitch with anything close to a good story, and my only witness is brain-dead."

"What about the security staff at Colosseum? And the parking attendants?"

"Just before the murders, a couple of LAPD uniforms rounded everybody up and took them to the second floor lunchroom. They were grilling them about stuff missing from cars in the basement when the shit went down. Twenty minutes in, the cops said they had to check on something and left. The staff hung around a while before somebody decided to go looking."

"Gotta admire a well-planned operation."

"We'll probably never know the whole story unless somebody calls Dr. Phil. The only thing I'm sure of is it ain't local—it might not even be American—which means I'm about as likely to make a case as my wife tell me she's not sucking my cock enough."

"What about the Feds?"

"You're kiddin, right?"

I couldn't argue. If it touched on some other case, which big shit always does, it would take longer than Frau Bricklin's fellatio schedule for the G to cough up anything to the locals.

"As for what I'm gonna do, for the time being, I'm gonna let the investigators churn the swamp and see if anything else floats to the top."

"But you don't expect that to happen."

"What do you think?"

"I think you've already put it to bed. You've got two dead Tatas, a professional criminal to hang the planning on and his sons for loose ends. Motive: who the fuck knows? But it's mixed up with movie people, and they're all nuts. I can name ten Hollywood murders that're still open, and you can probably double that. Forensics is a problem. So is who was stretching Spyrou's neck and why, but there's not going to be a trial or even a grand jury, so it doesn't matter."

"You think like a cop."

"More like a homicide captain."

"Careful, I could begin to like you. So once we get to the point where there's nobody left to slap around but space aliens, I'll start easing people onto other cases, and leave this motherfucker for Jimmy Ellroy. He'll figure out a way to make a few mil off it, and I'll try to hustle him out of a steak dinner. Sometimes it's the writers who come up with the stuff we never thought of."

"And if Wendy Plum doesn't like it, she can start knocking on doors herself."

"I'm betting she doesn't."

I couldn't blame him. Major murders get headlines, but somebody up the chain of command gets the credit when they're solved. Guys like Bricklin get paid by the pound. The only way this one could ever get in his win column was by accident or after everybody else had given up. I was surprised, though, to hear him admit that somebody other than a cop might have IQ.

"So since I got five years of unsolveds on my desk, I'd appreciate it if you'd give me a heads up when you run into something."

"When, not if?"

"I said what I meant. I wanted to be sure you remembered we had a deal."

"Since we're talking cooperation, remember that list? Guys the Tatas might have associated with? You know, the five-pager that probably doesn't include the name Spyrou."

The phone went silent while Bricklin decided whether I was a comedian or a threat. Eventually, he picked the one he wanted. "Here's where you have to hand it to the FBI. They gotta get ten okays to wear a pair of brown socks, but show them a pile of paperwork, and they start calling guys back from vacation. Only two intersected. One's been in federal lockup in Houston since last May, and the other doesn't have a name. Leastways not one anybody can agree on. The aliases are dead ends too. No picture, no prints, no record, no nothin. He's probably from New York, but that's only a guess based on other hits that came out of there."

"What's the name on the list?"

"The guys who hire him call him Aspirins. He cures what ails you."

The sun had gone down. Matty Aspirins and Electra Fordas sat in her BMW across the street from the Gardenia. "This shouldn't take long. How are you at bullshit if somebody surprises us?" Matty asked.

"You said the manager's Greek, right?"

"Cypriot, but yeah, Greek. Name's Denise, but I've never met her. Don't know about the girlfriend."

"Doesn't matter. If she lives with a Greek, you'll have a tough time shutting us up."

They crossed Vantana to the front door, and Matty used one of the two master keys he'd taken from the Cypriot's desk. Apartment 203 opened with the other one. While Electra turned on lights in the living room, Matty went to the hall closet. As soon as he looked inside, he noticed the top shelf had been disturbed. He got a dining room chair and stood on it, so he could reach all the way back. The satchel was gone.

Furious, he began a methodical search of the apartment, knowing he wasn't going to find it. In his anger, he knocked over a lamp on a bed stand, which crashed loudly against the wall. Less than a minute later, he heard footsteps coming down the emergency stairwell then somebody knocked on the door. He looked at Electra, but she waved him off, put a big smile on her face and opened it.

Zoe Levy was surprised to see an attractive, young female welcoming her. "Hi," Electra said, "you must be Denise. My husband and I love the place, but we have a few questions."

Caught off-guard, Zoe stepped inside and got a look at Matty. He was still wearing the Lakers cap, and he'd pulled it even further down. "I'm sorry," said Zoe, "but Denise isn't here. There's been a family tragedy, and she's with her mother. I was just about to leave to go over there myself."

"Oh, I'm so sorry," Electra said soothingly. "Please give her our condolences. My goodness, you don't know who we are. I'm Barbara Kontos, and this is my husband, Paul. I've been talking to Denise on the phone about taking this place, and she left a set of keys with my secretary so I could show it to him after work."

Zoe was skeptical. "Denise tells me everything, and I've never heard of you. Besides, this is a corporate apartment that her father handles." Miss Levy was all the way in now and could see down the hallway where the dining room chair was still standing in front of the open closet. She started toward it. "What's going on in here?"

Electra was right behind her. "We were just deciding if it was big enough to hold a body."

Matty remembered thinking, Jesus Fucking Christ, you're supposed to *talk* to her.

Zoe whirled, knowing something wasn't right but not yet able to process it. She had her mouth open to say something when Electra hit her in the throat with an open-handed chop. As the young girl gagged for breath and clawed at her neck, Electra crushed the bridge of her nose with another chop then used the heel of her palm to drive the shattered cartilage upward into the frontal lobe of Zoe's brain.

She staggered back, blood from her nose gushing over her forearms. Matty had his gun out, but he didn't need it. Zoe was already turning purple from lack of oxygen. Seconds later, she was convulsing on the floor, then she was still.

They rolled her under a bed and went room to room, using towels to wipe down anything they might have touched. Matty assumed the Cypriot's cleaners had done a good job the first time, but just in case, he decided to go over every surface again. Then he got a trash bag and stuffed the binoculars and the used towels inside.

On their way out, Matty dialed down the air conditioning as far as it would go and turned out the lights. Somebody would eventually find the blood and Zoe, but at least the corpse wouldn't smell for a while.

As Matty tossed the bag into the backseat of the BMW, he couldn't help thinking he'd been here before. So much for Electra's bullshitting prowess. The only thing separating her from the Tata brothers was a gun.

On the other hand, he'd never had sex with a woman who'd killed somebody. He was looking forward to finding out if it made a difference.

CHAPTER FORTY-SEVEN

Rex, Hooper and Hoop

In every industry, there is a pecking order. At the bottom in Hollywood—beneath the most clueless intern, the lowliest PA, the most junior shit shoveler—are writers. I prefer them to the town's anointed royalty because they see everything and forget nothing. With few exceptions, however, even the greatest screenwriters are as anonymous to the public as best boys. As compensation, their onscreen sting or ennobling clings to its target longer than any journalist's. The downside is they can be as careless, petty and vendetta-driven as the rest of us.

For the past thirty-plus years, a group of the best screenwriters have met irregularly at a sketchy bar in a sketchy neighborhood on the fringes of Hollywood. They call themselves the Rex Magnus Rum and Chowder Society after the most bitingly sarcastic writer who ever told a shallow, preening A-lister to go fuck himself.

The late Mr. Magnus was also at various times, a studio president and a producer, and he snarled with equal venom from those vantage points as well. With the exception of Gable, Wayne and Holden—men who drank hard, knew how to use their fists and were so unaffected by their success they were in the phone book—Magnus's circle of friends were mostly writers. Those he despised covered everybody else.

Rex never let anyone forget the fundamental truth of motion pictures: *Until the writer writes, nobody works.* And contrary to a century of studio heads, producers, directors, actors and talk show hosts pretending brilliant words magically materialize from the ether when you need them, it's still true. Nine out of ten people can tell you Poe immortalized, "Nevermore." The same nine think Eastwood adlibbed, "Go ahead, make my day." (He didn't.) So a word of caution to the unappreciated: Don't seek out a screenwriter for a hug.

Nobody knows whose idea the RMRCS was. It doesn't have a website, logo, bylaws or membership list. If you find somebody who says they belong, they don't. First, you have to be a very, very good writer. Second, you have to have been fucked by a studio; which if you're the first, the second is automatic. Then comes the hard part: you have to be invited in. And since there's no one to ask, you have to hope.

It's the most exclusive club in the movie business, but also the most dangerous. You have to be willing to bet your career, since if you're outed, you won't be able to get a gig writing flash cards.

That's because, every December, the Society stays sober long enough to vote on the most asinine line uttered by a development executive during a pitch meeting. The year's winner and its originator are then entered into the Big Book of Rex—basically a greasy notebook kept under the bar—and a trophy called the Magnus is messengered to the exec. Over the years, the Magnus has evolved into a loving cup-sized, golden figurine of a distinguishedly-dressed gentleman, script tucked under his left arm, right hand extended, flashing the customary Hollywood salute. Originally, the figure mooned the recipient, then someone remembered that execs are conditioned to kiss that.

One particular bright light has won four. Last year's runner-up was a young lady with an Ivy League sheepskin proudly displayed on her office wall who interrupted a million-dollar screenwriter's pitch of a heartrending, WWII love story to ask—drum roll, please—"Why were we mad at the Germans?" And she was only the runner-up.

I sometimes pick up the tab for the Society's on-again, off-again booze and bitterness sessions—writers are always broke and bitter—and occasionally they let me stop by for a mug of loudmouth soup. This time, by prearrangement, I took along several copies of *Beverly Hills is Burning*, which got their pages turned while generous drinks were swilled, chunks of black bread were buttered and gluttonous bowls of ambrosial clam chowder were downed.

We all had a glow on by the time Stick, the group's unofficial leader, closed his script. "I don't know if you're aware of it, my friend, but this is the Lost Dutchman of screenplays. People have been looking for the goddamn thing for decades."

"I'd like to tell you I knew that, but I didn't. It accrued to me in a business deal."

"Colosseum Pictures?"

There wasn't any upside to jerking him around. "Yes."

Stick nodded. "We all respected Teddy Chessman's balls." He turned and gazed at a skinny, pockmarked guy with a lot of miles on him. "Hooper, why don't you tell our friend what he wants to know."

Hooper's grunt was as gravelly as his face, and it didn't sound agreeable, but after a long slug of JW Blue—neat, as opposed to another writer who was mixing it with RC Cola from a bottle under his coat—he started talking. "I first heard about this script from my old man, Hoop Senior. Or just Hoop."

"A writer?"

"One of the best. Died the same year as Kennedy, so this would have been back in the fifties. I was in like third grade but, even then, writing all the time. I already had a spot picked out on my bookshelf for my first Oscar, and I used to wear out our old bulldog with my acceptance speech. Hoop said I should deliver mail instead. Steady money and no roomfuls of buzzword-spewing D-punks who can't write telling you how you should do it. But it was his fault. Once you walk on a movie set and see your words coming to life, what the fuck else you gonna do? Kinda like passing along a crack habit."

A couple of guys laughed, but I wasn't looking for a stroll down memory lane. "I appreciate your sharing that, but I'm interested in the script. Your father'd seen it?"

Hooper stopped, glanced at Stick, calmly took out a pack of Luckies and went through a practiced ritual of selecting just the right one, tapping it down and lighting it. A couple of puffs later, he looked back at me. "You still here?"

It was an uncomfortable moment. Most of the time having money matters. People don't breathe until you say it's okay. Writers have a different ethos. Novelists don't give a shit who you are; screenwriters would prefer you were dead.

"Here's the way this works," he said finally. "I talk, you listen. You don't like the way I do it or think my stories are getting in the way of your fantasizing about your bank balance, thanks for the drinks, and there's the door. You pull on it to get out. Now, I'm gonna hit the head. I come back, and you're still occupying space where I relax with my friends, I'll figure you got the message."

Hooper returned, and I was right where he left me. I was also quiet.

"My old man never said exactly, but he worked on the script. Pages anyway. He was banging the chick who wrote it. Not all the time, but when she wanted a hard ride and dialog help. She had a fuck palace in Long Beach. A mansion owned by her old man, who was in oil or something. She'd send a limo for Hoop when her libido was up and her typewriter cold."

He'd caught me off-guard. "Are you saying a woman wrote this?"

"He didn't mention having to flip her over, so I'm pretty sure."

It took me a moment to process that, and he waited. "Go on," I said.

"It was early-on in talkies. Hoop was one of the new young studs around town. Just in from the Big Apple with a hole in his shoe and a hard-on in his pocket. Silent scenarists were trying to move into sound pictures, but it was spotty going. They were part of the past everybody was running from. Studios were making deals with anybody who could put words in an actor's mouth. Playwrights, advertising guys, newspapermen, even comic strip writers—which considering where the business today is fucking funny. My old man wrote radio adlibs at NBC. Benny Goodman needed to shoot the shit with Gene Krupa between sets, Hoop made them sound like they'd done twenty years of vaudeville together."

He held up a copy of the script. "This broad was like a lot of silent film writers who had a gift for plot but couldn't deliver two good lines of back and forth, because they never had to. Hoop could write ten pages of roll-on-the-floor stuff before lunch. It was the only thing I wanted from him. I got to pay for the funeral instead."

He waved for another drink. "Back then, a talkie screenplay might have a couple dozen writers on it, all working independently of each other. Producers would cut and paste then call in guys like Hoop to write bridges so everything sounded like it belonged together. Men could move around in genre and character, especially if they wrote funny. Women got handed female fluff, and if they wanted to eat, they colored inside the lines.

"Lake London had written some very successful silents, but even though she was only in her thirties, she'd become a dinosaur. She was also difficult—code for she had her own ideas. The good news was she had her own money, so she could tell the studios to stick their bullshit assignments and write her own stuff on spec. And because she had a knack for finding edgy material, she got a pass on having a pussy."

"I've never heard that name."

"It's actually Lakeland London. She's in the books, but she only worked when she wanted to, so her output was thin. She also lived an unusual life."

"As in?"

"If it fucked or sucked, or it could be fucked or sucked, she took it on. But mostly, she did women. Women who would let her hurt them—in every possible way. Back then, she had plenty to choose from because of what she could do for their careers. She probably didn't care about my old man's cocksmanship, but he wasn't looking to cuddle, and she needed that Hoop magic in her scripts. Then she died. Still young. House fire."

"In LA?"

"Laguna Beach. There wasn't a fire department down there back then. By the time somebody reported the blaze, and they got a pumper and some volunteers to the scene, there was nothing left but cinders. Word is they hauled out Lake's body—what was left of it anyway—then leveled the place. They attributed it to careless smoking or a fireplace ember."

"In other words, no investigation."

"Who would have done it? There's about thirty mil worth of house on that lot now. Some asshole who makes stuffed animals. Couple of years ago, I got invited to one of his parties. Turned out he had an idea for a movie. What a fuckin surprise. I told him I'd been waiting for his call. Him, and the guy who did my colonoscopy. It was now official. Everybody had one."

I waited patiently. When he ordered another drink, I decided it was safe to ask another question. I thought I already knew the answer. "Where did this script fit into her bio?"

"Right at the end. The few talkies Lake had done had made money, but this was her ticket all the way back to the top. Madalynne St. Timothy was attached, so it was a lock for a Radio City premiere. I recognize my old man's dialog all over the place. Kinda like opening an old trunk you found in the attic."

Madalynne St. Timothy was a name anyone who followed movies knew. As blazing hot as Harlow for a decade, then gone. Not just out of movies, out of Hollywood. It was a longshot, but maybe she had taken a copy of the script. "Any idea what happened to her?"

"She made only two more pictures after 1935, neither memorable. In 1966, an author writing about vanished stars—who some people think was using the book project as a pretense to find this script—located her in Rochester, living with a woman named Petunia Rentsch. When the guy knocked, Petunia said she was Madalynne's legal guardian, and the actress was too frail to receive visitors.

"He didn't believe her, so he watched the house, and when Petunia left, he called. A woman answered who wouldn't identify herself, but her voice was strong and lucid. She admitted that she had lived in Los Angeles a long time ago and left after a tragedy.

"When he asked if the tragedy had anything to do with Lake London, she gave a fascinating response. 'I don't think Ma'am would like me to talk about that.' 'Who's Ma'am? he asked.' 'Why, Ma'am Petunia, of course.'"

"What's with the Ma'am?" he asked.

"That's what Lake insisted her girls call her. The special ones. The ones she really hurt and who stayed for more. Petunia likes me to call her that now."

I didn't want to think about Barrie's being one of those girls.

Hooper wasn't finished. "Before the woman hung up, the author managed to ask about the script. If she'd ever had a copy. 'Oh, no, Ma'am always kept that locked up. I never even got to read it.'"

"If you had to guess, where do you think the rest of it might be?" I asked.

"Hoop mostly referred to her as 'the cunt,' so I don't think they did much confiding. He also said her father had some dangerous friends and wasn't shy about using them on people who pissed off his little girl."

"Including him?"

"Hoop had a couple of scars he wouldn't answer questions about and a nose that was in a different place depending on when the picture was taken."

"People looking for the script?"

"Consensus is everything burned with her." He nodded toward the script on the table. "But that would seem to argue against it."

It wasn't exactly an answer. "What did your father think?"

He looked at me. "Your old man still alive?"

"He was murdered."

Hooper nodded. "He leave some things unsaid you figured out later?"

"A few I'm still working on."

"I can get with that. But one thing I'm sure of, script or no script, the story survived somewhere—maybe several somewheres. All of it."

I didn't ask him how he'd come to that conclusion because I didn't think he'd tell me... even if he knew. "You can keep that copy if you like. For the dialog."

He stared at the script like a man stares at himself in the mirror when he realizes his youth is gone and the good memories are under too much dust to trot out any more. Then he pushed it back at me. "Thanks just the same."

Writers.

CHAPTER FORTY-EIGHT

Archie and Neon

I despise helicopters. Having two fall out of the sky with my butt strapped to them didn't help. Both happened when I was in Delta. One took an RPG, the other, no one's really sure. I can, however, say with conviction they don't glide.

The tallest building in LA, Library Tower, is a little over a thousand feet. Climb in the elevator at the top and cut the cable. For good measure, make sure it's twisting on the way down. That will give you a rough idea of the feeling. What it won't give you is the possibility of being sliced in half by a rogue rotor blade.

Piloting one of these birds is the gutsiest job in the air. Which may explain why I've never met a chopper jockey who doesn't talk a blue streak while he flies. It's tough to drag a loud yawn out of a fighter jock with an engine on fire. The ball-heavy guys who fly helicopters blast music, tell stories and sometimes sing. They also laugh a lot. I love their attitude, I just don't like visiting them at work.

Unfortunately, every now and then, I have no choice. It's why God invented Valium. Two will usually do it, unless the trip's going to last more than fifteen minutes.

Before having dinner with Valentine Jones, I wanted to speak with her midnight flying partner, Archibald Hatt. I asked my Beverly Hills real estate guru, Jhanya Devereux, to set a meeting—without giving my name. In the event he remembered me, I didn't want Miss Jones muddying the waters.

Jhanya didn't need to look him up. "I have to warn you, Rail, Archie's a very strange man," she said. "Brilliant and one of the top luxury real estate agents on this coast, but emotionally unchecked. I've seen him begin sobbing during a negotiation. I don't think you two are a good match. If you're interested in Laguna Beach properties, I've got classier and more stable people to put you with."

"Duly noted, but it has to be Archie."

Jhanya and I have been working together a long time, and she never asks for more information than she needs. "Consider it done. Anything else?"

"See if you can come up with the address of a Danny Dades. He would have lived down there around 1935. On one of the hilltops."

"Tall order in Laguna."

I knew what she meant. Thanks to America's forfeited requirement that people work to eat, idle fools who have nothing better to do than demonstrate against the clearing of canyon brush and modern runoff techniques have made summer wildfires and winter mudslides regular occurrences in the high terrain of California. Not to mention eight decades of teardowns and rebuilds.

But it was worth an effort. Places, especially private homes, never completely lose the character of their original owner. The references to Danny in the script were few, but he and Barrie had spent passionate time together, and like violent death, that can't be totally erased.

Jhanya struck out with the title companies and property tax rolls. "Nobody's records go back that far, so I tried the Laguna Beach library, figuring maybe they'd have an old city directory or phone book. Apparently, until they built their new facility, the place was a sieve. People walked out with whatever they wanted, and there's nothing left that's relevant."

"Any other recommendations?"

I could hear her grinning. "While I was setting your meeting with Hatt, I took a flyer and asked him. History helps move merchandise, so if there was something to know, maybe he would. Care to guess?"

"And spoil your fun."

"He lives in it."

I let that sink in. "Archie Hatt lives in Danny Dades' house?"

"He bought it on spec a couple of years ago after the previous owner died."

"Which wasn't Dades, I presume."

"No, a bachelor who lived there sixty-seven years. Archie blew a lot of smoke up my skirt about what a fabulous investment he'd made, but reading between the lines, he's having trouble flipping it. The place is unusual and attracts gawkers. Vacant, that translates into vandals, or a Realtor's worst nightmare, squatters. My bet is security's too expensive, so Archie moved in himself. He's probably in a panic to unload it."

"How unusual is unusual?"

"It's not on MLS, so I had him shoot me some pictures. Let's just say, I've never seen anything like it. Dades had quite an aesthetic, and those who came after him seemed to like it just the way it was. Nothing's been touched. It needs work, but for what Archie's got in it and the location, I think it's a steal. You've got a boat down that way, don't you?"

Just what I didn't need. A white elephant in Laguna. "Pass."

"Well, dig out your acting shoes, the meeting is premised on your being a buyer. That's the only way he'd do it. I also had to tell him who you were."

"How'd he react?"

"He didn't seem to have a clue, and I think he was telling the truth. He's not exactly a close-to-the-vest guy."

I remembered the screaming. No, he certainly wasn't.

"He asked for some background, so I told him you'd recently bought Colosseum Pictures then changed your mind after the shootings. I figured when he Googled you, that would be the first thing that popped anyway."

"And?"

"He hung up on me. I thought maybe the call got dropped. Then he did it twice more. Finally, I told him to stop acting like a child. And, Jesus, it was like I set fire to his Mapplethorpe."

"Now I'm confused."

"He wouldn't stop talking, but it was mostly indecipherable. The only thing I remember is, 'I wish that psycho cunt had been killed with the rest of them.' I have no idea who he's referring to, but I assume you do."

"I have a pretty good idea."

"Once you lay on some of the famous Rail Black charm, I'm sure he'll open up."

Charm or otherwise, he would definitely open up. In the meantime, it seemed pretty certain he wouldn't be calling Valentine.

T.T. Barcella is a former army aviation captain who was at the controls of the chopper I rode sideways into a Central American jungle. He was singing opera at the time, and I don't think he missed a note. T.T. and his four brothers run Barcella Charters out of Hawthorne Airport, catering to famous names in sports and show business.

"Hey, big guy. Long time, long time." If I'd been within a mile, I could have heard him without the phone. The *libretto* in the background might have reached two.

"I need a ride to Laguna Beach. As soon as possible."

"What's your pleasure, stun gun or drugs?" he boomed.

"I'll be sufficiently docile. You got anybody with laryngitis?"

"I'll send Dino, he just won a hundred grand in the lottery. You can give him some investment tips."

Dino is T.T.'s youngest brother, and the only thing he needed to do with a hundred grand was catch up on child support. Dino doesn't do opera. His addictions are women and sports talk radio, and he's the king of harebrained opinions on both. I could hardly wait. "Tell him he's going to have to cool his heels for a couple of hours then bring me back," I said.

"If I know my brother, that's enough time to get laid. Maybe twice. Where do you want to be picked up?"

The ride down was par for the course with Dino, and I made it without pharmaceuticals. Word hadn't reached me that as long as you're still sleeping with your ex-wife, child support is optional, but Dino said he'd overheard a couple of guys discussing it in a tit bar. Where else would you go for that kind of information? I didn't ask if the former missus had been clued in on the lottery win.

The Dolphin Bay Yacht Club has an auxiliary parking lot where you can land a chopper if you have advance permission from the club and the Newport Beach Police. We had neither but landed anyway. There was some initial waving of arms and a long stream of profanity, but the manager finally agreed to get on the phone and straighten things out with the cops. The grand I slipped him may or may not have made a difference.

A very hot blonde in a Prius was there to pick up Dino, and I complimented him on being environmentally sound. Archibald Hatt was waiting next to a big, black BMW, his coat, shirt and tie, black also. He was even thinner than I remembered, but his voice was still right on pitch. He gave no indication he recognized me. "Mr. Black, I'm Archibald Hatt, but please call me Archie. Jhanya is one of my dearest friends. I told her I'd do my utmost to make your time here absolutely delicious."

Delicious? Really?

"Do you mind my asking?" he said. "Are you some kind of athlete? I mean, your size... it's really quite... electrifying."

From delicious to electrifying. Lucky me. "A swimmer," I answered truthfully.

He stared at my face, and a light may have gone on, but if it did, he recovered quickly. "Well, Laguna Beach is certainly the place for that."

"I understand you're going to show me your home."

"It's not actually on the market, but Jhanya was sooooo persuasive."

"Archie, you're in real estate. Of course, it's on the market."

That was exactly what he wanted to hear, and his grin indicated greed had kicked our friendship into high gear. He got on the southbound PCH, hauling ass, then inched through downtown Laguna Beach where the lights are synchronized to maximize ticket revenue and fuel consumption. He returned to speed long before it was safe to do so and, after a couple of miles of clenched sphincter, turned inland.

Immediately, the road began to rise, and the further up we went, the sharper the switchbacks became. Off in the distance to the north, I could make out Richard Halliburton's home, regally commanding its ridge, awaiting its architect's return. After a few minutes, we were above even it, and I began to hope we wouldn't meet anything coming the other direction. I doubted even a motorcycle could get by. The Pacific receded vertically, and I felt the familiar thrill of dramatic height.

Eventually, we ran out of pavement on a small plateau. Above, I could see a portion of a house, but I didn't know how we were going to get to it. Left was two thousand feet of oblivion, and right, a dead end into an impenetrable, fifteen-foot high barrier of bougainvillea that ran around a bend, out of sight.

Archie hit a button on the overhead console, and the blazing pink flowers parted, revealing a blacktop drive heading straight up. Just inside the gates, a sloping concrete retaining wall rose on the right. Set into it in Wilt Chamberlain-sized overkill, were a pair of giant, red neon dice and in corresponding blue, an even larger

HIGHROLLER HILL

"Stand too close, you could get a tan," I said.

"You should see it at night. Pilots use it to get their bearings. You fly?"

"I ride."

"I used to have a King Air, but…" He seemed to catch himself. "Everything about this house is a little dated." Then ever the salesman, "But that's part of its charm. By the way, if the neon's not to your taste, I can have it replaced or removed completely. Only take a couple of days."

Actually, I liked it. It was exactly what I would have expected from a craps dealer, and it fit the history. As we hit the driveway, the angle of the BMW's nose tilted upward like a rocket ship. "Sometimes, it'll be sunny down below," said Archie, "and we'll be in parkas up here. Other times, it's reversed."

"We?"

"Hector, my houseboy. I mix the piña coladas, and Hector cooks and keeps the place spotless. He's teaching me Spanish too."

I prefer "houseman" to "houseboy," but Hector sounded like quite a find. "Look forward to meeting him."

"The fishermen arrive back in Dana Point about now, and I sent him down for fresh halibut. I thought maybe you'd stay for dinner and check out the views when the sun goes down."

That wasn't going to happen, but I said, "Depending how our conversation goes, maybe I will."

His voice literally vibrated with excitement. "That would be fabulous."

When we finally hit level ground, we were on an apron next to a hulking, rectangular, three-level monolith of white concrete and dark timber beams, probably mahogany. The walls under them were stained brown from years of exposure, but a good sandblasting would take care of it.

The windows were wide and many, and a narrow, railed deck ran the length of the first and second floors. The views had to be phenomenal. "The third floor is the owner's suite, and there's a sundeck on the roof," Archie said. It's completely open."

"Sounds like an adventure if you've had a few."

"I can't go up there," he admitted. "Vertigo."

I could only see one side, but it took up almost all of its allotted pad. Archie read my mind. "It's a little over four thousand square feet," he said. "Not counting the apartment above the garage."

"How about the lot?"

"Forty-four hundred."

That meant that somewhere, part of Highroller Hill was hanging over the side.

"Dades had them drive pilings, so it's sitting up on supports, not the hill itself."

I couldn't fathom the logistics or cost of such an undertaking—especially in the thirties. "What in the world for?"

"In case he wanted to add more floors. Danny was all about

entertaining, and once you got up here, you weren't going back down that road with a bellyful of hundred proof. There are seven bedrooms in addition to the penthouse, and when Mr. Dades was in town, they were all full. I would have loved to have seen it then."

Frankly, so would I. I like people who live out loud.

We took a cramped, old Otis up to the main level, and my imagination couldn't have matched the reality. The windows had enough height and width so that anywhere you stood or sat you looked out at three hundred and sixty degrees of green hills, distant mountains and blue Pacific. The interior was dated, as advertised, but immaculate, and most of the furniture appeared to have been made specifically for where it sat. I'd been in hundreds of view houses in California, but none like this, not even in Big Sur.

"What are you asking?" I said.

Archie wasn't expecting the question so quickly. I hadn't even been upstairs. "Five million, and it's not an ask. It's firm. To the right buyer, it's worth ten, easy."

He'd been sitting here for two years, dreading going up and down that hill. He couldn't even use the sundeck. "I'll give you three, cash. Tomorrow. If there's ten out there, it's in a bank in Asia. Mine's in Beverly Hills, and I'm standing in front of you."

I thought he was going to faint. "I... I... can't. I owe..."

"How much?"

"Three-nine, all in."

"Which means, three-five, max."

I waited while he swallowed a couple of times. "I could maybe go three-seven."

"Tell you what, Archie, show me the rest of the house and answer a few questions, and I'll give you four-two. And if Hector wants to come to work for me, he goes with the deal."

"Four-two? Are you kidding? You were just at..."

It was interesting he didn't mention Hector and his vanishing Spanish lessons. "Are you going to negotiate against yourself?"

"He stuck out his hand. Four-two and a few questions. Hector too, if you want him, but he can be real bitchy, and he snores."

I ignored his hand. "Answers first. And don't say 'delicious or electrifying,' or I'll deduct another hundred grand."

He didn't even blink, and his voice dropped half an octave. "What do you want to know?"

"What you and Valentine Jones were doing right before I pulled her out of the drink."

CHAPTER FORTY-NINE

Redwood, Teak and Tile

If I thought I was going to have to prod Mr. Hatt, I was wrong. The problem was slowing him down. People in the intelligence business know that torture works, but you get so much information so fast it's difficult to create a timeline, determine which names your subject is spewing are significant and prioritize implications. That's why interrogators interrogate and analysts analyze, and it takes ten times as many analysts as questioners to do an adequate job.

Archie Hatt's waterboard turned out to be Valentine Jones. By simply saying her name, I had opened the tap all the way. Jhanya's mention of Colosseum had lit the fuse, and he'd been looking for a place to explode ever since.

After fifteen minutes of an arm-waving, room-pacing soliloquy that came out in such a torrent I couldn't discern any single train of thought, I stopped him with some difficulty and told him to get us a couple of drinks. He was sweating profusely, and his chest was heaving dangerously. I kept an eye on him so I could catch him if he fainted. Eventually, he got himself under control and made his way to a cocktail lounge-sized bar on the far side of the living room. I followed and sat on one of the leather seats.

"How about a Highroller Hill Special?" he asked. "My own creation."

I opted for a Sam Adams then watched while he constructed something tall, slushy and yellow that included several shots of rum and a few more from an opalescent bottle without a label. When I thought he had enough alcohol his system, I gave him a calm down gesture. "Now, Archie, pretend

I'm a really slow learner and take it from the top."

He nodded. "I'm sorry, this happens sometimes when I get upset. For it to come out right, we need to start upstairs." I didn't ask why, I just followed. I thought it curious, though, that we didn't take the elevator we'd used earlier, especially in light of the steepness and length of the open stairway. But I let him play it his way.

The master suite was enormous and dramatic. Wide panes of glass, Spanish tile and old-growth redwood from a time when California's forests were many, its inhabitants few, and fine artisans could be found on any block. Every available inch of wall and ceiling was planked or inlaid with various gradations of the wood, which, all these years later, still exuded the scent of northern wilderness. The wide windows, which pivoted on a center axis, were also framed in prominently grained redwood that decades of waxing had turned a deep mahogany.

The low, emperor-size platform bed had been built into the center of the room, its wood surfaces intricately carved with scenes of the Laguna coastline, and a long fireplace with similar carvings dominated the wall across from it. Perhaps there had once been draperies or blinds, but I saw no evidence of any.

"Obviously, one doesn't sleep past sunrise," I observed.

Archie smiled, "Actually, you're wrong," and he pressed a button inset into the headboard that started a quiet whirring in the ceiling. Momentarily, four, gathered curtains of black, loosely-woven, linen lowered around the sides of the bed. The enclosure remained open at the top, so while diffusing light, the screen let in fresh air.

"Very Scheherazade. Probably also helps on a drafty evening."

"Like being in a cocoon. Put another log on the fire and settle in. I'll never have another house without one."

The twelve-inch, glazed floor tiles, each uniquely but complementarily patterned, had been fitted together in expanding, concentric circles, something that it is now nearly impossible to find craftsmen to attempt. The scattered area rugs looked Caribbean, which, considering where Danny had made his living, was likely. Everything looked original to the house, including the chandeliers, which were stemmed wrought iron.

I noticed a spiral redwood stairway in a far corner that was so gracefully suspended it seemed to be hovering in midair. "I assume that leads to the sundeck."

"Yes, and unfortunately, we have to go up there. If you don't get woozy from heights, I'll just stand at the top and direct you."

As long as it didn't suddenly sprout a rotor blade, I didn't care. I crossed to the steps and headed up. When I reached eye level with the teak rooftop deck, the sun had crossed the midpoint in the southwestern sky. There was also a noticeable increase in wind off the ocean which happens most afternoons near the cold Pacific. If I was going to be on time for dinner, I needed to pick up the pace.

Several groupings of redwood and wicker outdoor furniture of a considerably newer vintage were secured to the deck with eyebolts and cable. There was also a small, teak shed in one corner, where I assumed cushions and umbrellas were stored. I continued all the way up and surveyed the distant views. It wasn't difficult to understand why someone who was afraid of heights would be trepidatious. It was pulse-accelerating, more so with a stiff breeze.

"Look at the floor," Archie said. He was poking his head through the stairway opening and trying not to focus on anything but at me. The wood had aged a silvery gray, and I could tell by the wear pattern that it was old. However, because of the durability of teak, it was difficult to determine if it had been put down thirty years ago or three times that. But it had been expertly done, fitted perfectly and anchored with teak pegs spaced irregularly across the surface. Near the roof's edge farthest from the stairway, several planks had been removed and stacked neatly with a pair of cement blocks on top to keep them from blowing around.

I bent over the opening their absence created and saw gold printing below, spelling out what seemed to be the word PASS. I shifted to a better position and rubbed my hand along what I could now see were twelve-inch, green, glazed tiles of the same quality as the ones downstairs. Their surface was smooth to the touch, indicating they had not been exposed to the elements very long before being covered.

Finally, it dawned on me what I was seeing. The teak was concealing a tile representation of a craps table—what is commonly known as the Philadelphia Layout—only, in this case, rooftop-size and with the design baked into the glaze. Somewhere to my right would be the word LINE and spread across the rest of the area would be COME, FIELD and various numbers and combinations up to twelve. Consistent with the neon entrance, it had to have been Danny Dades-inspired, not to mention extraordinarily expensive. There was no arguing its dramatic effect.

I presumed there had also once been a giant pair of dice and corresponding chips for guests to amuse themselves while they partied. With no railings, though, I wondered how many distracted gamblers had gone one step too far in their exuberance.

"The tile with the P," Archie called out, "lift it."

The grout around the square was mostly missing, and I reached down and got my fingertips under it. The piece was cleverly hinged on the underside so that it would lay over onto the next square. I eased it down.

Below was a steel plate, but before I turned my attention to it, I examined the hinge on the tile. It was rusty and creaky and bits of oxidized metal had flaked off onto the surface below. It had sat untouched for a long time.

The steel plate turned out to be a lid with patches of brown wax residue on the seams. For waterproofing, I guessed. I felt along its forward edge, found a press latch and popped it. Recessed into the roof was a version of a safe deposit box about eighteen inches deep and twice that in length and width. A lot of space. It was also empty.

I glanced over at Archie. "Hector noticed a loose board while he was sunbathing. I didn't want a leak when the rains came, so I waited until it was too dark to see the drop-off and came up with a flashlight. I might also have put down a couple of House Specials first.

"I assume something was in the box."

"Yes, but it's better if I show you."

He could have done that downstairs and skipped the drama, but I was the one who had told him to start at the beginning. And in truth, no one would have been able to adequately describe jumbo craps in the sky.

Back on the main floor, Archie led me into a small library. The books shared shelf space with an assortment of third-rate, framed autographs, but the modern classics were all first editions, including a complete set of Ian Fleming. There was also a built-in, vintage hi-fi system that, like many of the books, would have come along after Danny. But the albums were some of the rarest vinyl ever pressed.

"This all comes in the deal," I said. It wasn't a question.

"Be my guest. You can have the relic in the garage too. The only packing I want to do is my toothbrush."

I followed him through a doorway and into a long hall that ran the entire back length of the house. The outside wall was floor-to-ceiling glass with vertical steel beams roughly every ten feet, creating alcoves that framed the view. The entire structure seemed to hang over a cliff, which was confirmed by the thick, plate glass panels set into the floor, through which I could see straight down into a long, narrow and very deep wine cellar that also had a glass floor. Beneath the wine cellar, the drama continued another several hundred feet, finally ending in a canopy of treetops. I had crossed swinging foot bridges in the Andes that were less dramatic.

"As long as there's something between me and the drop, height doesn't usually bother me," Archie said. "But this floor was way strange, so I had Hector throw a rug out here, just in case.

An Oriental runner covering several of the glass panels lay in front of a long, sturdy table in the nearest alcove. Identical tables were placed in the alcoves all the way to the end. Each of the others held a formidable piece of sculpture. This one, however, contained, not sculpture, but a collection of items I assumed were from the rooftop safe.

First were six thick, red leather journals, each held tightly closed by a vertical band of bright blue, still-springy elastic stitched into the back cover. The initials LLL in the same shade of blue were embossed on the upper third of the journal's face, and just beneath them, a tiny, silver flying bird was inset into the leather. About the size of a hardcover novel, they were clearly custom-made. I had never seen anything like them, but I had no doubt who the initials stood for.

I carefully fanned the stack. They were heavy and appeared to have loose notes, newspaper clippings and other objects inserted between their pages. The silver birds on their covers, though identical in size, were each slightly different in detail, meaning they had been crafted individually by a fine jeweler, not stamped out. I remembered seeing one on the ankle of a certain lousy swimmer I'd met.

Next was a bulky, twelve-inch, jewelry roll made of cranberry velvet and held closed by a pink ribbon with pink satin bulbs sewn into the ribbon's ends. I gently untied the bow. The velvet and ribbon felt almost new.

"Everything was wrapped in several thicknesses of extremely fine oilcloth sealed with wax," Archie said. "It's like it was put up there yesterday."

He was right. Aside from the slight odor of aging paper, everything was pristine. Inside the velvet roll were eleven, very delicate, silver bird bracelets or anklets of varying lengths. Again, the birds' details were individualized.

"At first I thought these and the ones on the journals were Sterling," Archie said, "but even protected, they should have been tarnished coal black. They're platinum,"

I'd left my jeweler's certificate in my other suit, so I took his word for it.

Just beyond the jewelry roll sat a pile of 11x14 glossies that looked professionally developed and, finally, a box of extremely fragile, onionskin typing paper. The box's top, which said Eagle Brand, had been removed and placed partway underneath to display the pages inside.

I read the title page then gently tipped the box forward so that several of the pages fell against my hand. I had expected them to be the same as my script, but when I saw the first-generation typing on watermarked paper and the residue of carbons between the sheets, a chill went up my spine. I usually reserve my emotions for private times, but holding the initial draft of Barrie Fontaine's story moved me in a way I hadn't expected.

I let the pages fall back into the box and stared at the top sheet again.

"I know it doesn't look like much," said Archie, "but trust me, it's important."

Mr. Hatt didn't know the half of it.

An Original Screen Play
Based on a True Story

BEVERLY HILLS IS BURNING

by

Lakeland London

June 4, 1935

The Writer is a Member in Good Standing of the
Screen Writers Guild of the Authors League of America

This Literary Work is Protected under the
United States Copyright Act of 1909

All Rights Reserved by Lakeland London

CONTACT:
Christopher Caplan
The Caplan-Hoving-Bronstein Agency, Ltd.
Beverly Hills, California

Every man who has lost a great love sees her all the time. A fleeting
glimpse in a closing elevator; her profile in a passing cab; a toss of hair

331

rounding a corner. No one, however, expects her to walk through the door in a screenplay. Especially, when you never knew her when she was alive.

I had come to know Barrie Fontaine in an historical sense, but this was more, far more. I felt guilty that my dead wife might be looking down at this foolishness. It's one thing to find a new love. A living one with whom to share the rest of one's life. But if I were simply lurching from one dead woman to another, what did that say about the exalted place in my heart Sanrevelle was supposed to be occupying?

In fact, is it even possible to have a romantic connection with no more dimension than cold type on old paper? With someone who was born before my father and whose eyes I can never look into? Someone I can never even meet? And what does it say about a man who seems to care more about ethereal fantasies than living breathing ones? As nonsensical as it was, Barrie had gotten under my skin and was burrowing around in there, looking for a place to stay. A place that had previously had room for only one other person.

I became aware that Archie was staring at me. "Are you all right, Mr. Black?" I didn't think the appropriate answer was, *Don't mind me, I'm just having a special moment with a dead woman*, so I turned my attention to the photographs.

Before the proliferation of personal cameras, men with the clunky equipment to memorialize private moments—often news photographers in their off-hours—plied the streets of every city. They were the first paparazzi, but their bread and butter didn't come from celebrities, rather regular people having a good time. No evening at Mocambo or the Trocadero was complete without a tableside glossy. Likewise, county fairs, parades and hardware store openings—any public gathering.

I turned several pictures over. Photographers usually imprinted their contact information on the back so customers could return for more prints—or more business. Many of these had been taken by a Woody Yates from Queens, who, not coincidentally, I knew was Barrie Fontaine's right-seater.

"I think this is Danny Dades," Archie said, handing me a shot. "He's in a bunch of them." The picture had been taken next to a busy craps table. A stocky, middle-aged man in a flashy suit and a flashier tie had his arm around the neck of an exceptionally handsome young man in white shirtsleeves and a black bowtie—obviously, a dealer. The man in the suit was grinning broadly and pulling the younger man's head aggressively toward him while he pointed a thick forefinger at the camera. There was a large pinkie ring on his extended hand.

The younger man was smiling too, but it was forced. He was trying to maintain some dignity by resisting the thick forearm cutting into his carotid. But he wouldn't have been resisting too hard. Casinos have never allowed cameras, so whoever this guy was, he had clout, further evidenced by the butt of the revolver visible inside his suit coat.

Archie laid a second picture on top of the first. This one showed Danny in a white dinner jacket with a rose in the lapel. It was nighttime, and he was standing in front of the chrome grille and dinner plate-sized headlights of a 1930s Lincoln coupe. A slightly-built man in a dark suit was handing Danny a set of keys, apparently presenting the car to him. Both were smiling broadly, but the presenter was more interesting than the gift. A very young, but very unmistakable, Meyer Lansky.

Archie didn't comment, so I assumed he wasn't fluent in organized crime chieftains. "And finally," he said, placing a third picture on my stack, face down.

I turned it over and felt my cheeks flush. A slender woman wearing white coveralls and flying boots was straddling an Indian Chief motorcycle in front of Highroller Hill. Her hair was pulled back in a ponytail, and she seemed to be laughing spontaneously, like you do at something unexpected. In case I needed help, her name was embroidered over her breast pocket.

Barrie

She was every bit as captivating as I'd imagined.

I waited for the initial rush to subside, but all that happened was that perspiration formed on my forehead, and my heart beat louder. "I've got a dinner date this evening," I said. "We need to finish our conversation."

Archie was suddenly very calm. "I think you should reschedule." He handed me a photograph of what looked like a large jewelry display case outside a storefront. A mob of people were filing by on each side, and an armed soldier stood at each of the four compass points.

Archie laid a second 11x14 on top of the one I was holding. It was a close-up of the necklace I'd taken off Valentine Jones, only now, the stone hanging from the others seemed too large to be real. Too large, in fact, to be attractive, except in a look-at-me sense. Even in black and white, I couldn't take my eyes off it.

"The Star of Havana," he said, "or if you prefer, the Crown Diamond." He was holding another velvet jewelry roll, identical to the one containing the platinum birds. He undid the two pink bows and let the roll fall open. It was empty.

CHAPTER FIFTY

Bronte Promises and a .25

I'd already asked Mac to join me for the Valentine Jones dinner. Not only is she good company, she has that rare quality of putting people on their best behavior. Even the terminally poisonous. She also diverts questions away from her many accomplishments to speak complimentarily about what others have done. Most importantly, Mac knows when not to talk, a fast-diminishing virtue. In short, she was perfect for this crowd.

"You're putting me in charge of a dinner for people I've never met?" she said. "Whoopee."

"Dinner's covered, we're just changing the venue. Your mission is to get the guests on the helicopters and charm them for seventy miles. T.T.'s got two Sikorskys standing by, and Symphony Express will handle the limos on both ends."

"Christ, Rail. These are show biz whack jobs. I don't even know who can sit with who."

"It's who and whom, but that's the beauty of my plan. They'll know you're a civilian, so they won't be expecting much."

"What a wonderful way of putting it. Let me write that down for my self-esteem class. Now turn up your hearing aid. If you ever 'who and whom' me again, Bub, next time you drop by for nookie, bring dirty pictures and your hand."

"I sense a very turned on lady. Now, please—pretty please—call Ross Dare and introduce yourself. He's rounding up your ducklings, and I've told him and T.T. not to mention the destination. Especially to Valentine."

"The more I hear, the more it's beginning to feel like a Lean Cuisine and *Antiques Roadshow* evening."

"I promise I'll make it up to you. A real promise, not my usual."

"Even the Bronte sisters walking tour?"

Oh, Jesus, not that. "Okay, even the Brontes."

The Highroller Hill dining room was in the back with a view through one of the canyons. I assumed this was because, after dark, there would be lights in the distance to lend drama. However, now that I was an oceanfront homeowner, I wanted to hear water when I ate—even when it was pitch black.

Unsurprisingly, Archie had no lift in his arms at all, so Hector and I rolled the heavy rosewood dining table and carried the matching chairs into the living room where we positioned them overlooking the waves far below. Hector had turned out to be nothing like I expected. He wasn't remotely fey but completely self-assured and with a physique like a decathlete. Archie clearly didn't run this relationship, which may have been why he hadn't fought too hard to keep him on his payroll.

Pressure didn't faze him either. He seemed to relish it and had Archie running around like the Nobel committee ass-sniffing a Commie author. He'd also bought enough halibut to feed Camp Pendleton, providing my Hollywooders weren't a card-carrying collection of protein poltroons. I did, however, refrain from mentioning who was coming.

Hector knew a restaurant in town that was closed for renovations, and after more of my dollars disappeared into the Laguna Beach maw, the owner agreed to send up his entire kitchen and wait staff. For a few extra bucks, he tossed in linens, dishes, and silverware. Flowers, Hector said, wouldn't cost anything. His brother had a connection.

Archie had told Hector I was the home's new owner, but he hadn't covered his being part of the deal. I had no question, however, that he'd welcome it, and after his exhibition of dinner party efficiency, I wanted him more than I wanted the house. I was only hoping I could afford his style.

Jhanya was expediting the paperwork, and Jake had already wired the money into escrow. "I could have gotten you a better price," she scolded.

"Then calculate your commission on the lower number."

"I'm not *that* upset."

Satisfied with dinner arrangements, I took the six red notebooks up to the master suite. Archie said there was more he wanted to tell me, but I stopped him. I wanted to discover it myself.

———————

Her handwriting was unusual but, once I got used to it, not a problem to follow. Like her screenwriting, her sentence structure was clear. The material covered years, but I limited myself to the portion covering her time with Barrie. I spent an hour skimming, but it would take a lot longer to stop replaying it in my head.

When I went back downstairs, Archie was on the phone, arguing with someone. I made myself a drink and wandered over to the front window. The sun was getting lower, and the breeze was continuing to pick up. I didn't envy anyone riding in a chopper tonight. Behind me, Archie shouted several colorful obscenities and threw the phone across the room.

"Somebody backing out of a deal?" I asked.

"The fuckin cops won't give back my necklace until there's a hearing. It's MINE! Just like everything else Danny Dades left. But that larcenous cunt's gonna go into a courtroom and lie her fuckin ass off. I got an injunction to keep her from auctioning the script, which I could prove I owned because I have the original. But now it's up to some Newport Beach judge what happens to the diamonds. MY fuckin diamonds! I have a little money, but what chance do I have against Valentine Jones and her million-dollar lawyers?"

Teddy had mentioned a small legal issue with the script. Apparently not owning something you were trying to sell qualified as small in the movie business. "Would it interest you to know Valentine is on her way down here for dinner? With her attorney?"

"Valentine's coming *here*?"

I nodded.

"With Marvin Oxford?"

"In the flesh."

Archie's face darkened, and I thought for a moment he might break into tears. Then I was concerned he might jump out the open window behind me. I missed on both counts. He left the room and came back with what I first thought was a novelty lighter. When I looked closer, it was a .25-caliber semi-auto so small and cheesy a Saturday night special would have been embarrassed to be seen with it.

After some fumbling, Archie managed to eject the tin, three-inch magazine and check it. "If she walks in here, I'm going to kill her. Oxford, too. And there's nothing anybody can do to stop me."

When he tried reinserting the magazine—backwards—I got up and took the gun away from him. "Archie, you're not going to kill anybody. Especially, not in my new house. And for the record, until today, I thought I was the one who owned *Beverly Hills is Burning*, so why don't you pour yourself another drink and start this story at the beginning. I have a feeling we're on the same side."

It was a rambling, emotional monologue that began with Archie's having gotten a call from Marvin Oxford that a major motion picture star was looking for a getaway place in Laguna. Then had come two, tough, in-person interviews followed by an onerous confidentiality agreement before Archie even heard the name Valentine Jones. Standard procedure, so far.

"But then that prick lawyer wanted a personal kickback of half my fee, which, because I couldn't use her name in my advertising or even tell people she was a client, I couldn't recoup."

God bless Marvin, I thought. This kind of unseemly overreaching would eventually bite him in the ass, but after his rant at the poker game about how Valentine treated him, they deserved each other. "You could have just walked away," I countered.

Archie looked at me like that was the dumbest thing he'd ever heard. "Are you crazy?"

That's why Hollywood people get a twisted view of their own

importance. Bad behavior is routinely reinforced by people who just want to breathe the same air. But I also knew that regardless of what the confidentiality agreement said, five minutes after he signed it, Archie had told the world who he was representing. Just like Marvin expected him to. And if Marvin went after him, not only would it cost his client serious legal fees and generate the exact kind of publicity Valentine was trying to avoid, but the kickback would come out in court. Hello, IRS. So whose ox had been gored?

"After Valentine bought her house, she invited me to a housewarming party where I met a lot of famous faces. She also put me on the screening list for her next picture. It was totally cool."

"And naturally, you thought you were friends."

"I really did. So, a few months ago, when I found Danny's stash in my roof, she seemed like the logical person to call. I knew what a script was, but I had no idea how to evaluate it."

"Put a pin in the narrative for a minute. What else was up there?"

He hesitated. "Like I said, the necklace."

"I've seen that. You accused me of stealing it, remember?"

"Oh, right. Sorry."

"What haven't I seen?"

"There was a gun. Not like mine. A really heavy one. Scary."

"A .357."

"That's what Valentine said, but I have no idea. She asked if she could have it, and I was glad to get it out of here. It didn't look very valuable."

So she was familiar with firearms, which, based on her pictures, I already knew. And now she had a magnum. "What else?"

"Some money."

"Don't go squishy on me, Archie. Not just *some* money. Barrie Fontaine's half-million."

He got defensive. "There was only a little over four hundred thousand. In these really old bills."

"Which had collector value as well."

"Probably, but I didn't know how to turn them around without a record of where they came from."

"So you used them to buy a King Air."

He nodded. "The down payment. You should have seen the dealer's eyes when he saw those bills. But now I'm totally fucked because the insurance company is denying the claim."

"Archie, you were drunk and high. You're lucky no one was killed. What did you think was going to happen?"

He hung his head, but I didn't have time for a self-pity jag that more than likely would turn shrill. "Let's get back to business."

He seemed relieved at the suggestion. "That night, Valentine was sitting here reading the script, when all of a sudden, she jumps up and starts acting out all the parts. It was weird. Like she'd become a bunch of other people. I don't think she even remembered I was here—she was that wrapped up.

"When she finished, she had this strange look in her eyes, and she grabbed my face and held it so tight it left marks. 'Archie,' she said, 'My whole life, I've been waiting for this part. I have to make this picture. I *have* to! Just tell me what you want, and I don't care how much it is.'"

Actors. Sometimes they don't know they're fucking with people's lives, but usually they do. I braced myself for what I knew was coming. Archie was so earnest I felt sorry for him. "Mr. Black, I didn't want anything. Not like she meant. If the script was going to be a movie, I just wanted to watch it happen. Be... how do they say it... part of the process."

"Let me guess, she offered you a credit."

What must have been his original enthusiasm had returned. "Co-Executive Producer, but she said she'd try to get the 'Co' dropped. God, I was so excited. If I let myself, I still am."

Magnificent. She'd woven the web in full view, but Archie didn't simply blunder in. Like a consummate mark being played by a consummate con artist, he'd actually asked her where to stand while she removed his blood. Bernie Madoff couldn't have done it better. "And because you were now partners, you let her take the carbon of the screenplay."

He nodded enthusiastically. "She was going to find somebody interested in financing it. Then we'd make a deal. Together. She said we'd call our company Jones-Hatt Productions."

I had no desire to make it worse, but he deserved some straight talk for a change. "Archie, Valentine Jones is the biggest female star in the world. Anything she walks through the door with, somebody is going to produce."

Now he looked sheepish. "I found that out when I got wind of the auction. She didn't own anything, and nobody cared. They cared even less that there wasn't an ending. They were just going to make one up."

What was it Teddy had said? *I just wanted Cortez to fix a few things and do some research to bring the third act together.* I try not to speak ill of the dead, but if I ever get another shot at Mr. Chessman, I'll slap the sonofabitch around for an hour no matter what shape he's in. Prick. No, scratch that. Producer.

I didn't want to get into a long dissertation with Archie about Valentine's studio deal and her family, so I closed with, "The reason nobody cared who owned the script was because whatever it would have cost to settle with you would have been spit compared to having a Valentine Jones picture."

He looked off in the distance. He ran a successful business. Now that he was thinking clearly, he knew it too. "Archie, this would be a good time to tell me about the crash."

CHAPTER FIFTY-ONE

I'd like to thank the Academy… and Gravity

Archie Hatt was smoking a joint as he drove. To his right, Valentine Jones wrapped her lips around a bottle of Jagermeister as she awaited her turn with the weed. As always on this stretch of highway, traffic lane-danced at heart-pounding speed. The quickest way to a fiery death in South O.C. is driving impaired on Laguna Canyon Road; the second quickest is driving it sober. The only reason the steep cut from high ground down to the sea doesn't look like two blacktop ribbons of Predator missile ejaculate is because environmentalists bitch until somebody shovels up the bodies.

Archie's tuxedo was slightly undone from an evening of hard partying. Valentine had partied just as hard but looked in considerably better shape in a tight black dress, silver Louboutins and platinum, flying bird anklet. She had the passenger side visor down and couldn't take her eyes off the Star of Havana and its sister-stones around her throat.

"I still don't know why you won't let me read the motherfucking notebooks," she snarled between slugs.

"I'm not getting into that again. I want to finish them myself first."

She went girlish and patted his leg. "I don't need the actual books, darling. Copies would be fine. After all, we're partners aren't we? *Producing partners?*" She made the term sound like she was cooing a baby. "How can I represent us if I don't know everything we've got?"

Archie hesitated and almost said yes. He actually had finished reading the notebooks, but they didn't have the ending to the story either. They went farther than the screenplay, intriguingly so, but not to Barrie's ultimate fate. But what was really holding him back was that he had visions of writing the rest of the script himself. He'd seen a lot of movies, and he was sure he could combine the endings of a couple he really liked for *Beverly Hills is Burning*. After all, he had great characters to work with, and everybody said he was the most creative salesman they'd ever met. He didn't see why he couldn't translate that to screenwriting. He might be new at this Hollywood stuff, but he knew he'd never get a chance to show what he could do if Valentine had the books too.

"Tell you what, give me a couple of weeks to get some other business out of the way then we'll sit down and read them together." By that time, he'd have something on paper. Surprise her with his talent.

Instantly, Valentine's demeanor changed. "You're a selfish fuckin asshole." She took a wild swing at his head with the Jager. Archie blocked it then nearly missed the wide, sweeping transition onto the 405. By the time he hit the freeway, though, he had the black BMW back up to 130.

The security guard at the general aviation gate into John Wayne was polite but ran Archie through the full checklist: ID, car registration, pilot's license, hangar permit and aircraft certificate, slowly photocopying each before handing it back. As Archie waited impatiently, the guard asked if he'd been drinking, then carefully noted Archie's lie on his daily log. The guard gave the impression of a guy who didn't like arrogant dicks with big cars and expensive planes who forgot him at Christmas.

The black and gray King Air was tucked in the rear of the Bowman Aviation hangar, its stairway extended. Archie drove the BMW past several parked planes and stopped next to it. Valentine popped the trunk and hauled out an orange and green parachute container, which she wrestled up the stairs to the cabin.

Archie yelled across the hangar to a man in blue coveralls. "Hey, buddy, get me a tow over here. And make it fuckin quick."

This elicited about the same hustle as the gate guard, with an added, "How about I break fuckin your face? And move that car outside. You can't park in here."

When the man in the coveralls finally disengaged the tractor, Archie leaned out the cockpit window. "I left instructions to be refueled."

The man shrugged. "Talk to accounting. You owe four grand."

"What bullshit," Archie shot back and slammed the window. He pushed the start button on the port engine before the man had cleared the plane, and the unexpected and dangerous move caused the guy to jump six feet. He waved his fist and shouted something Archie couldn't hear over the revving turboprop.

Archie flipped him off, started the second engine and taxied toward the runway. In the backseat, Valentine had her compact out but instead of makeup, the reservoir was filled with coke. She used the mirror and a razor blade to lay out a couple of lines.

As soon as the King climbed into the night sky, Archie terminated communication with the tower and slipped his headphones onto his shoulders. He looked back at Valentine who was just finishing the blow. "How about sharing?"

She handed him the compact and leaned her head back on the seat. "Don't be a pig. My hookup's out of town."

Archie nodded at the parachute. "You really intend to go through with this?"

"You ever see me handle a gun? Any gun? I've got an instructor who takes me to the range every week. I never want anybody to look up at the screen and say, 'She shoots like a fuckin twat.' Once I *feel* a part, I own it. You said Barrie punched out over North Laguna, right?"

"In a flight suit, not Dior."

"That's why I make movies and you sell shitty little houses in a shitty little town. In *Maximum Commando II*, I skydived in a bikini."

"Check YouTube, that was your stunt double."

Actress wrath bubbled to the surface. "Only because of the fuckin insurance company stopped me. I made that jump twenty times during training. Mine just weren't in the picture."

"Or from a plane."

"Fuck everybody, it's going to be all me this time."

"Is that you or Oscar talking?"

"Both."

Archie thought about mentioning that Burt Reynolds had ridden a Class 5 rapids without a boat, and McQueen, Schwarzenegger, Willis and Keanu Reeves had risked their lives multiple times without so much as a loud Best Actor shout from the Academy for doing it, but he let it pass. "Why don't you give me the necklace now? You're not going out with it."

"Not yet. I'm still getting to know Barrie. Diamonds capture emotion. Did you know that?"

Archie didn't know and didn't care. When he hit the coast, he banked south. "Let's find your car first. Everything looks different from up here, especially at night. They probably didn't tell you that in the simulator." He smiled when she told him to go fuck himself.

Seventy minutes later, Archie had made three dozen loops between the deserted beach of Crystal Cove State Park and the northern hills of Emerald Bay where Valentine's Mercedes SL sat on a dimly-lit ocean access path halfway between the road and the black water. It wasn't where Barrie had gone down, but that section of Laguna was all houses now.

The Jager was long gone, along with half a bottle of Ciroc he'd found tucked between the front seats. The coke had disappeared too, but that hadn't kept Valentine from putting her nose in the empty compact trying to find whatever buzz was left. She'd had the parachute strapped on for a while, but each time Archie descended to two thousand feet and started a countdown, she failed to open the door. After the most recent pass, he told her he was heading back to John Wayne, but she shouted at him to give her a little more time.

Without Archie's realizing it, the circumference of his route had expanded, until it was no longer a tight costal run but a seven-mile circle, reaching into the Pacific. Simultaneously, with the substances in his system, his altitude was now fluctuating wildly. Twice, he'd had to answer air traffic control's emergency calls and reassure them that he was just testing the climb rate of his new plane.

Some part of Archie's brain told him it was crazy to even think about breaking out the crank he had in his pocket, but he kept catching himself nodding off, and he was afraid it was only a matter of time before he lost consciousness. The first hit jolted him wide awake; the second made him feel like he could fly to all the way to the crescent moon in the southern sky.

Valentine almost came over the seat to fight him for the pipe, and he relinquished it and the lighter after one more huff for himself. He noticed she was still wearing the necklace, but he didn't care anymore. Combined with the altitude, the drug had him on a high he had never come close to.

Archie heard the Bic go on and off as Valentine took several deep hits. Then there was the rustle of clothing. When he looked behind him, she had her dress hiked up, her knees high, her panties off and was masturbating furiously. He'd never seen a woman do that before, and he was mildly curious, watching as she drove herself over the edge with a scream but still didn't slow down.

A moment later, the starboard engine sputtered and quit. The second didn't even bother to sputter. Valentine kept working on herself but shouted through clenched teeth, "Why the fuck is it so quiet?"

Archie knew something was wrong, but it took him a few seconds to grasp what it was. The adrenaline of fear pushed aside the drug, and if he could have gotten the parachute off Valentine, he'd have gone out and left her. Instead, he managed to pull back on the controls and gain several hundred feet of altitude before the King's nose began to roll over.

"Get the fuck out! Now!"

"What? Why?"

"Get the fuck out! We're going down!"

Even through her drug haze, Valentine understood that. She jerked the lever on the door down hard and hit the button to open it. It didn't move. "The fucker's stuck," she shouted, panic only inches away.

"Electrical's gone. Pull the emergency handle then kick it out."

The door blew open with a bang, and one side of the stairway broke loose and began slamming into the fuselage. The unexpected drag pulled the plane's right wing over, and whether she was ready or not, gravity slid

Valentine Jones into the night.

Archie heard her scream trail away, then he was busy getting off a mayday and trying to remember how to inflate the life raft.

CHAPTER FIFTY-TWO

Niblets and Sabras

I'd fought against interrupting because I wanted him to get the story out exactly the way he remembered it. Finally, he collapsed back in his chair. "You were damned lucky," I said, "but you know that."

"Part of me still wishes she'd drowned."

I understood. I wasn't so sure I didn't as well. "The house you sold her. Where's it located?"

The change of direction caught him by surprise. "In one of the coves. Considering who she is, it's not very impressive. Only twelve hundred square feet, but right on the water."

Ninety percent of people who buy a new house don't change the locks. I was betting Valentine wasn't much of a detail girl. "How many times have you been in and out of the place since your fight began?"

He reanimated in a hurry. "You mean without her knowing? That's unethical, not to mention illegal."

"How many times?"

His face twisted up, and he got defensive. "She told me to hang onto a key. You know, keep an eye on things. She's almost never there." I waited, and eventually, he got out, "Just once."

"What about the other times?"

"Okay, maybe there were a few more." His voice was starting to elevate. "But I didn't take anything, honest. I just looked around. I thought there might be something that could help me with the judge."

"Was there?"

"Not really, but the last time, I found the gun."

"Barrie Fontaine's .357."

"It was in the freezer. Inside a Ziploc with some frozen corn. I thought, who keeps a gun in the refrigerator?"

"It hadn't been there before?"

"No."

"Did you take it?"

"I was going to, but I didn't want it when I gave it to her the first time."

"Do you still have your key?"

"You can't be serious. I can't take…"

"Hang in there, Archie. You sold a house today. Things are looking up."

Archie punched a code into the private community's security gate. Valentine's house was one of three actually on the sand. It was also the smallest. We went down a footpath to the beach and came up the walk through a low picket fence with potted red flowers sitting on the posts.

There are no legal private beaches in California, so homeowners don't usually leave things out that can be walked away with—or vandalized. This horseshoe-shaped cove, however, was enclosed on both ends by sharp rocks reaching well out into the surf. The unwashed would need a boat or scuba gear to even get close.

The next door neighbor, a fit, forty-something brunette wearing a very small bikini over a killer tan was watering her little patch of lawn with a hose. When she saw us, she gave a big wave. "Hey, Arch, who's your friend?" She said *friend* like she was Frenching a popsicle and with a deep Israeli accent that, in my book, rated her exotic. I gave her my best I'm-not-a-burglar-but-I'm-still-dangerous smile.

"Hi, Ruthie. This is Mr. Black. He's looking for a house down here, and I'm helping him get an idea what to focus on."

"Well, hell, bring him over here, and we'll team up and drive that bitchy actress back to Hollywood so we can spend our days rubbing cocoa butter on each other. God knows, Mrs. Nassar won't notice." She tilted her head toward the third house. "Last time those blinds were open, Reagan still got applause at the Academy Awards."

Beautiful, clever and almost certainly *sabra*, which meant she could fire an M-16 and maybe drive a tank too. All my hot buttons. More importantly, it didn't appear she and Lady Jones got their nails done together, so my visit would go unmentioned.

"Now that I know where to find you, keep a candle lit," I called back. "What goes with Ruthie?"

"Anything you've got, honey. The last name's Halevy, and I'm in the book."

I filed that away. After all, I did live just up the hill.

From Valentine's well-kept yard, I wasn't prepared for the mess inside. It wasn't the remnants of some wild night but the kind of filth that accumulates over time. Fast food containers and old magazines flung carelessly on the floor. Clothes on every piece of furniture. Moldy plates and half-empty glasses stacked wherever there was room. I saw a couple of roaches and knew mice had to be there too. No wonder she didn't know Archie had been in and out.

"Hard to believe, isn't it?" he said.

"Why doesn't she have someone come in and clean?"

"Back when we were still talking, I asked the same question. I got this dead look, followed by, 'I'm a fuckin celebrity. If they don't steal—and they all do—first chance they get, they're selling me out to the tabloids.'"

If this was how she lived, she was probably right. I picked my way past some empty vodka bottles strewn along the hall and followed Archie to the kitchen. Since his last visit, the Smith & Wesson and the Niblets had gotten company. A tub of Breyers cherry vanilla, with the lid half off. "Looks like she's been around." I said.

"Valentine wouldn't eat a spoonful of anything that might put a pound on her precious figure. That probably belongs to the night security guy. He's got keys to all the houses, and he knows she's never here."

I removed the Ziploc and poured the corn down the disposal without touching the gun. I noticed the cylinder was full. Archie watched me but didn't say anything. I put the cold plastic bag containing the .357 in the back of my waistband and untucked my shirt so it would hang over the bulge. Now I had her prints on two things that could be connected to the Colosseum shootings. And the magnum had more stopping power than a pink pen.

I did a cursory search of the rest of the place and found little of interest. In fact, there wasn't much in the way of personal possessions at all. Just a few scripts with handwritten notes in the margins and a stack of publicity photos of her in black leather dispatching a mob of screen ninjas.

As Archie locked up, I wandered over to Ruthie's. She'd finished watering and was now lying on a chaise, adding to her tan. "I didn't want to leave without saying good-bye."

"Had enough of Vibrator Row already?" she smiled. I really liked that accent.

"Could I ask you a question?"

"Sure. Thirty-six C. And they're spectacular."

The accent suddenly took a backseat. Despite the icy steel against my spine, I felt a familiar stirring and was glad my shirttail was out—and long. Under different circumstances, I might have told Archie I'd see him later. Spectacular thirty-sixes are always in season. "I don't mean to pry, but does Miss Jones get many visitors?"

"That's not a real estate question. That's a cop question. Or maybe a PI."

"Neither, but you're partially right, it's not about real estate."

"You ever meet her?"

"Only in passing."

"Take it from me, keep passing. There's a lawyer who comes by every now and then. Marvin-something. Grim when he gets here, grimmer when he leaves."

"Anybody else?"

"Nobody I've seen. But if you're interested, I've got an emergency contact number. She didn't want to give it to me, but I told her it was a rule of the homeowner's association that if you lived alone, a neighbor had to have someone to call. Just in case. And it couldn't be some paid ass-kisser. It's not really a rule, but she's an actress, so what does she know?"

"Why bother if you don't like her?"

"I've read enough about Miss Jones's ugly behavior and trail of dangerous bedmates to know that sooner or later somebody's going come looking for something besides another gaze into those seductive brown eyes. When it happens, the tabloid bloodsuckers are going to hit this beach like Ike coming for *der Fuhrer*. I plan to lock my doors, run a thousand copies and slip them through the mail slot. Hold on, I'll get it."

She was gone only a minute while Archie waited discretely on the footpath. Despite what she'd said, I expected the name to be Marvin or one of her agents, perhaps even her grandmother.

I wasn't even close.

Michelangelo Scarpuzzi

"I recognized the telephone codes for the city and the country, but I looked it up to make sure," Ruthie said. "It's Sicily. Palermo, to be exact. You been there?"

"Yes, but not recently."

"You decide to go back, give me a call. I lingo the languo, or if you prefer, the other way around."

"I'll bet you do."

I waved Archie back to the car and took a slow walk up the footpath. I stopped above the houses and gazed over the Pacific while I punched the number into my phone. It was after midnight in the Med, so I could be getting Valentine's elderly father out of bed. Sometimes sleepy people can be helpful.

This voice wasn't sleepy. "*Pronto. Ucciardone.*"

I heard banging and talking in the background, so at the late hour, I assumed Ucciardone must be a restaurant. I speak passable Italian, but English often gets things moving faster. "Signor Scarpuzzi, please."

There was a long pause then, "*Momento.*"

I waited through the sound of a chair being pushed back and a couple of shoe shuffles. Then a much deeper voice came on. It was accented, but not Sicilian. Northern. Florence, most likely. "This is Capitano Conti. Who am I speaking with?"

"My name is Rail Black. I'm calling from California."

"How may I assist you, Signor?"

"I need to speak to Michelangelo Scarpuzzi. Can you please put him on. It's about his daughter, Valentine Jones." I decided to play all my cards. "The movie star."

The captain didn't sound particularly impressed. "Signor Black, you have been given very poor information."

"He's not there?"

"Oh, Signor Scarpuzzi is here, but he will not be coming to the phone. And we are very aware of Miss Jones; she has visiting privileges. However, there are no calls in or out of Ucciardone for prisoners."

I masked my surprise. "My apologies, Capitano. You are correct, my information is very poor indeed. Has Signor Scarpuzzi been there for some time?"

"Nineteen years, and if you call in nineteen more, he will still be here."

"If you don't mind, may I ask how long you have been at Ucciardone?"

"In this system, we are required to rotate every four years. I am due to be reassigned next month."

"So you would know if Miss Jones had visited her father in that time."

"Yes, twice, not long ago. Two weeks apart. He was not so good the first time, so she went to Venice and came back."

"Signor Scarpuzzi was ill?"

"Here we call it *demenza superiore*. I believe in your country, you call it Alzheimer's."

The picture was beginning to crystallize. "So when she came the second time, it was because her father was lucid?"

"Signor Scarpuzzi has days when he is exactly as he was when he was first brought here. Though, not so many anymore."

"Was Miss Jones alone?"

"The first time, yes. The second, there was a man with her. I am not permitted to reveal the names of visitors, but he is well-known to us."

"An associate of Signor Scarpuzzi."

"A man with many connections in your country." He paused, seemingly searching for the right words. "He is called when someone does not simply wish a problem to go away, but to go away… how do you say it… *con molto caos.*"

"With much commotion," I answered, thinking about people getting put in pizza ovens.

"Yes, much commotion. So everyone knows."

I should have been at least marginally surprised. But the cold emptiness I had felt the day of the murders had been all too familiar. Even then, I had suspected it. Then I had spoken to the duchessa who had, of course, known since the beginning.

Valentine's fury would have known no bounds when she learned Teddy had undercut her. Overnight, she had gone from aspiring mogul to employee—betrayed by her former lover and sold out by her family. The argument in Venice with her grandmother would have been titanic, but I knew the duchessa. Once she had made her decision, nothing would have swayed her, least of all a petulant actress. Not even one hurling threats, which she no doubt had.

I'd never know Valentine's exact words, but after our encounter, I could imagine their thrust. "Okay, I'll show the old bitch. I'll take away the only thing she loves. She'll hate me, but I'll be all she has left."

I wasn't upset that the duchessa hadn't told me. Even knee-deep in grief, Valentine was blood, and the Passavantis were Italian. No, that was wrong. They were Venetian, the heartbeat of Mediterranean intrigue and familial closing of ranks, long before there was an Italy.

A voice brought me back. "Is there anything more, Signor Black?"

"Can I assume there are tapes of everyone who visits Ucciardone?"

"Yes, and photographs taken on the way in and out. But I should advise you that the courts rarely grant access to them."

To anyone who's tried to navigate the Italian judicial system, they're still taking testimony on Mussolini's first divorce. But it wasn't important, I just needed to know they existed. "*Grazie*, Capitano."

"*Prego.*"

Archie was in the car, talking on the phone about a repossessed condo. I took his cell away and turned it off. He started to protest then saw my eyes. "It's time to talk, Archie."

"I thought we'd been talking."

"Not about the part you wish would go away."

His lip started to quiver. "I'm so afraid."

"There's no need to be. Not now."

"You don't understand. She's..."

"I know, Archie. So talk to me."

He put his head in his hands and leaned forward on the steering wheel. "I was supposed to be there. At Colosseum. Valentine called a few days before and apologized for all the things she'd said. She blamed it on the drugs. And *of course*, we were still partners. We'd sign our deal in the boardroom, and they'd present me with a check. One million dollars. The first of five. Just for the rights. I was going to get a piece too. From everything. Music, television... all of it. After the board meeting, there'd be a press conference and photographers. And they were talking to the *Tonight Show* and *60 Minutes*. God, I was so excited."

"What happened?"

"There was an accident on the freeway. Traffic was paralyzed. She kept calling. Hysterical. She said she was in the ladies room, and the meeting had already started. I was crying too. Then her phone went dead. A little while later, the news came on the radio about the shootings. And the reports just kept getting worse."

He turned and looked at me in earnest. "She did it, didn't she? She arranged for all those people to die." I didn't answer, and he began to sob, his shoulders heaving. "How can that bitch have done this to me? She wanted me dead too. I still can't believe it. She wanted me dead too."

I couldn't tell if he was feeling sympathy for himself as a possible victim of a greater tragedy, or if it was just about him. I had a good guess.

CHAPTER FIFTY-THREE

Uneaten Eggs and Varnish Remover

Matty Aspirins sat at the counter in the mostly-empty Brooklyn diner. Across the wide boulevard, the flower shop had been dark for over an hour, its CLOSED sign visible through the front door glass. The delivery van with the red roses painted on it was parked on the narrow side street next to the shop. It was sitting at an odd angle, as if it had been left in a hurry.

He checked the clock. Eight-fifteen. Closing time should have been seven, but he'd been sitting where he was since six-thirty and hadn't seen anyone lock up and leave. Matty dialed the shop for a third time. He listened to the ringing a full two minutes before hanging up. His brother still clung to his old answering machine which had to be switched on at night. It could be malfunctioning, but that wouldn't be like Dimitrios, who couldn't stand a burned out display light. Matty told the counterman to refill his cup while he went outside for a paper.

"You thinkin about eatin sometime tonight, buddy? I got a kid in college."

Matty slid a twenty across the laminated surface. "That get me a couple of eggs?"

The guy grabbed the bill and stuffed it in his shirt pocket. "How you want them?"

"Any way that'll keep you quiet."

Matty took his time working the vending machine until he saw a break in the traffic. He walked quickly across the six lanes. The flower shop's corner entrance was recessed, creating a display alcove that ran well back from the sidewalk. Matty crouched in the shadows, reached up and tried the handle. The door swung open, the bell at the top, ringing loudly in the stillness. He tossed his newspaper aside, took out his Beretta and went in low, moving quickly behind the cash register.

He waited while he became acclimated to the sounds. The whirring of the refrigeration system, the drip of watering lines, the riffling of papers from the breeze coming through the door. The hooked pole Dimitrios used to pull down the heavy blinds stood in a nearby corner. Matty used it to reach out and close the door, making sure to slam it extra hard.

Once the bell stopped ringing, the silence returned.

In the work area behind the showroom, the crippled girl who assembled corsages had taken a single bullet in her left ear. She was sprawled across the low table Dimitrios had built specially for her, her locked wheelchair preventing her from falling to the floor. The blood trail on her neck was coagulating, meaning she'd lain there a few hours.

Matty found the delivery boy in the restroom. He'd been shot through the door, probably trying to get away. The holes in the wood were small, most likely.22s, but too many for one shooter. The trapdoor to the basement was open, which it never was unless somebody was down there. Feeling exposed, Matty eased down the wooden steps, listening to them creak and prepared to throw himself down the rest of the way and start firing.

Dimitrios was taped to a chair. So was Iris, the bookkeeper. Both had been worked over with a knife before being shot in the back of the head. Dimitrios's ears were gone, and his eyes had been cut out. Iris's neck was slashed, and blood had run over her shoulders and down her arms.

Matty forced himself to turn away and went into the next room where Dimitrios kept an old wooden desk and filing cabinet. Both had been torn apart, the drawers pulled out and smashed, their contents littering the floor. Next to the desk, amid her junior high schoolbooks, lay Iris's daughter, shot through the face.

He'd known something was wrong when the envelope with his passports wasn't in his post office box. He'd even suspected the worst. But that didn't make it any easier. As a professional, he was also incensed. Nobody with any class shot cripples and kids. Fuckin wops.

The heavy wooden box stenciled CEMETERY VASES was under the stairs. He returned the Beretta to his jacket and dragged it into the room. Using the razor knife he found on the floor, he sliced the rope around the box. The knife's handle was slippery with his brother's and Iris's blood, and he flung it angrily across the room.

Matty burrowed under the vases until he found a thick leather pouch. He unzipped it, and four passports spilled into his hand, along with several thick stacks of banded, hundred-dollar bills. A wire transfer receipt from the Bank of Luxembourg was on top of one of the stacks. Dimitrios had written "Good Luck" in the margin. That would be the password to the numbered account. The balance was $2,657,445. He'd have to be careful. It might have to last a long time.

Matty discarded all but the Canadian passport and tucked the pouch inside his jacket, then using a pair of flower snips, he cut the gas line to the hot water heater. The rush of sweet smelling fumes quickly filled the room.

Upstairs, he found a can of varnish remover under the bathroom sink. At the same time, he took the delivery van's keys out of the dead kid's pocket. He splashed the remover over the workroom, taking care to soak the mountain of tissue paper used to line floral boxes. He then opened the back door and rolled a spool of red ribbon through it, watching it unwind until the empty spindle hit the street. The ribbon got the last of the accelerant. Matty stood on the sidewalk and lit it, watching the flame race on a line back into the shop.

He was almost to the intersection when the place blew. An enormous fireball mushroomed outward, tossing sheets of plate glass like autumn leaves and hurling the van into the boulevard. Cars skidded in all directions, but Matty somehow emerged unscathed and roared away into the night.

Montreal was seven hours north.

CHAPTER FIFTY-FOUR

Sweating Agents and Joe Cargo

My cell phone rang just after dark. It was Mac, speaking low. "I really want to extend my heartfelt gratitude for this enchanting assignment. The limo driver didn't get the memo about the address being hush-hush, and your batshit actress has now tried to jump out of the car twice. Who the hell is Archie Hatt, and why am I on my way to dinner with him?"

"I'll fill you in when you get here. How is she now?"

"I'm up front with the driver—who apologizes, by the way. We've got Miss Looney Tunes between Ross and Marvin, and they're trying to calm her down. She still looks like a wild woman, though, and there's no doubt in my mind, she's going to try to get out again. The guys I feel sorriest for are the two agents with her. They've called everybody but their moms asking what to do, and every time she looks at them she fires them."

"I owe you."

"Oh, you owe me, all right, and I haven't even gotten started on the helicopter ride. A week with the Brontes doesn't scratch the surface."

"Where are you now?"

"We just turned off the PCH, and we're on our way up a hill so steep it makes me want to pee myself. Thank God, it's too dark to see the edge."

"You're almost here. I'll be waiting out front."

"With a drink. And that's not a request."

"We've got something called a Highroller Hill Special. Five minutes from now, you'll have forgotten everything except how much you love me."

"For that, you better have one in each hand."

I stood outside and watched the headlights of the two super-stretches reach the top of the hill. They had to do some fancy backing and grinding to navigate the hard turn into the private drive, and the neon lit them up like the Vegas Strip. When they rolled up to the door, Mac was the first one out. "First altitude sickness, then blindness."

"Subtle, isn't it? And all mine."

She took a gulp of the drink I handed her and stared up at the expanse of concrete and glass. "You're kidding, right?"

Before I could answer, Valentine Jones leaped out of the backseat and headed down the drive as fast as her peach Jimmy Choos and matching micro mini would take her. I took a couple of steps in her direction, but a burly, bald man in the second limo stepped out and caught the world's most famous actress mid-stride.

She took a swing at him—a familiar move—but he absorbed her fist in one of his meaty paws and held it. She wrestled a little, then got very still. I couldn't see exactly what he did, but suddenly there was a squeaky little whimper followed by silence. A couple of moments later, they came walking up the blacktop together, she, a little unsteady, but not resisting.

Mac saw them coming and headed for the house. "This is where I came in. See you at dinner."

As they reached me, the guy extended his hand. "Joe Cargo. I understand you did a little soldiering, Mr. Black."

When we shook, I felt strength, but he didn't try to Marine Corps me, which my hand appreciated. "Word is you spent some time in the mud yourself."

"Good training for the picture business. Hope you don't mind, but I'm stag. Caught between girlfriends. Seems the older I get, there are fewer girlfriends and more betweens."

"Glad to have you—here and on the picture."

"Have you two met?" he asked. He moved his left arm, and Valentine took a step forward. He had his left hand gently on her waist, but that was all, and she separated from it when we shook. She gave no indication of wanting to run or of being afraid or in pain.

"Not formally," I answered.

I was surprised by her voice. Unlike what I was used to hearing onscreen and the profanity-laced hysteria during the parachute incident, it was almost demure. Certainly, it was soft. "You know my grandmother, don't you? That's what Teddy said."

"I do. I'm very sorry about your cousins."

I don't know what I was expecting, but from an actress of her caliber, a shrug wasn't it. Joe Cargo looked surprised too. "Who do we see about a drink?" Marvin asked, joining us and breaking the moment.

"Take the elevator. Hector will fix you up. Soon as I get the limo drivers set, I'll be in." Joe took one of Valentine's elbows and Marvin the other, and together, they guided her toward the door.

Ross Dare was standing next to the two agents, Ronnie and Lonnie Keck. Twins, not yet thirty. They'd probably started the day feeling pretty good about their careers. Now, they'd sweated through their suits and were unemployed. Ronnie was on the phone with somebody named Warren who was ripping him a new one loudly enough for the rest of us to hear. Then Warren fired him again—apparently to make sure we all knew how important he was.

Ross stepped forward and took the phone from the stricken guy. "Warren, Ross Dare." The other end got quiet. "Your two guys are terrific. I won't work with anybody else on this package. They've already got me thinking I should use C.C. for Howard Hughes when I was set on that Broadway guy over at WME. They've got some terrific ideas about Luciano too, which we're going to get into over dinner. How about I massage the budget to get your wife into the Cuba stuff? Audiences would love seeing her."

He listened for a moment then went on. "Yeah, the Dominican Republic, just like Coppola. Might as well imitate the master. I figure you'll want to be there, so I'll rent a villa for the four of us. It'll give us a chance to talk about getting some more pictures from you into the Colosseum pipeline."

Ross turned to the Keck boys and gave them a thumbs-up. "Candida sends her best to Yvette too. Saturday's fine for dinner. Bye."

There's nothing like watching a pro work. But Ronnie and Lonnie didn't much care about style points. I thought they were going to fight over who got to shine his shoes.

Then Candida Dare came into view, and I forgot everything else.

"Mr. Black, I'm so pleased to meet you."

I took her hand and felt her warmth, lost in the distinctly Brazilian way she said my name. Her voice was throatier than Sanrevelle's but all of the old familiarity came rushing back. First Barrie Fontaine, now this. Different, but part of the same whole. This sudden emotional uncertainty wasn't about either of them, though. It was about me. I was reaching for the unreachable because I couldn't find answers in my own life.

"Please call me Rail," I said. "It's been a difficult time, but Ross has been a real high point."

"For me as well," she smiled. "I'm too young to have heard your mother sing in person, but I grew up listening to her recordings. My father was in love with her voice. Probably the rest of her as well. You know Brazilian men."

She hesitated as if trying to find the right words, and Ross stepped in and extended his hand. "Ross Dare."

I took it. "A pleasure." He was a little over six feet, blonde, square-jawed and with a pair of piercing blue eyes that I doubted ever showed warmth. In another line of work, they'd have given him away. They probably did in Hollywood too. A killer was a killer.

"Before we left to come here tonight, Candida and I read about Sanrevelle on the Net. Are condolences correct so long afterward? I never get these things right."

"Thank you both. It doesn't seem like as many years as it's been, and condolences are perfectly acceptable. Hold on a sec, while I tell the drivers when to come back."

CHAPTER FIFTY-FIVE

Celery Sticks and Baby Glocks

Cocktails were in full swing, and people were giving themselves tours of the house. Valentine and Archie stayed on opposite sides of the room, but there was easy banter among the rest of the guests, and with more than one stiffly-starched waiter per person, the gathering was comfortably populated with food and drink. Just to make sure we had our servers' best personalities, I'd promised them a thousand-dollar-per-person gratuity if we didn't have any carryover drama from their regular workplace.

Hector had come up with beer-battered avocado wedges served with a Sriracha salsa that nearly blew the top of my head off. He coupled that with caviar mousse under buttery chunks of lobster, and people were going through the stuff like hod carriers at Golden Corral. All except Valentine, who had requested celery sticks and a shaker of salt substitute. If I'd heard her, I might have rammed a Ball Park frank and a jar of mustard up her ass, but Hector made the celery appear with a smile. Another reason to keep him. Like Mallory, he was a far better man than I.

I sought out Joe Cargo to satisfy my curiosity about his earlier handling of Miss Obstreperous. "If you don't mind, how did you get her under control?"

He rubbed his chin like he wasn't excited about the question. "Last year, she did a picture down in Panama. One night, she gets to pounding shots of *seco* with the stuntmen, grabs a set of car keys and goes flying off. It's an unwritten rule that stunt people watch over stars, so one of the guys who hasn't been drinking chases her on a motorcycle and sees her run down a kid walking along the side of the road. Naturally, Miss Jones doesn't stop, but when the stuntman finally catches her, he gives her the bike and takes her car back to the to the accident where he turns himself in.

"Everybody got lucky. The kid only had a broken arm, and the studio hustled Valentine out of the country before anybody could question her. Most everything else, a wad of dough made go away. The stuntman still had to serve some time, but since he'd tested sober, the lawyer got it knocked down from two years to nine months. He'll be home in a couple of weeks. We're all looking forward to the party."

"Sounds like a helluva of guy."

"I like to think so. He's my son."

I took a moment and let that sink in. "You're some kind of guy too."

Joe Cargo shook his head. "He was tough, now he's tougher. But I told our star she doesn't want me to walk off this picture."

Fear for one's hide. The last vulnerability of the morally bankrupt. There wasn't much left to recommend Valentine Jones for a place in civilized society. "Hungry?" I asked.

"Either feed me or show me where I can fry up some more of those avocados."

I waved to Hector, and fifteen minutes later, the best wine I'd never heard of and wouldn't have be able to order without having it written on my palm—an '83 Biondi-Santi Brunello di Montalcino Riserva—was flowing freely and chasing seared halibut, sautéed griolles and baby asparagus Parmigiana down moviemaker throats. At my request, conversation remained social only, and Mac and Candida were delightful at leading it.

Valentine picked at a couple of mushrooms and told one of the waiters to bring her a bottle of iced Belvedere. He glanced at me, and I held up my thumb and forefinger about two inches apart. Valentine gave me her own hand signal. By prearrangement, once coffee was served, Hector herded the wait staff to a room at the back of the house where they could have their own dinner. I didn't want to read about the business part of our discussion on some bottom feeder's website. I would have preferred Archie's not being there either, but I couldn't think of an adroit way to remove him then bring him back.

Under ordinary circumstances, Teddy would have been godfathering this process, and two-thirds of the decisions would have already been made. Those, however, had gone to the grave with him. A producer was the first order of business.

Academy Award-winners who can honcho a team and not ego-crush it are at a premium, I soon learned. Ones who weren't booked three years out, even more so. Marvin wanted to give us one of his clients who had a couple of nominations, but even I knew the guy had a drinking problem. Ross deftly deflected the suggestion by asking Joe Cargo what he thought.

"I'm no picnic," Joe said. "I shoot fast, and I expect everybody to be three steps ahead. When they're not, I eat asses." He looked at Valentine so his point wasn't lost. "I can't live with some artsy-fartsy who wants to spend half a day discussing my next setup."

"Sounds like you're asking for Sid Barron," Ross said.

"We've done half a dozen pictures together. I've never been to his house, and he's never been to mine, but we speak the same language. If it's awards you're looking for, though, I got zero, and Sid's right there with me. You want to make budget, we're six for six."

Valentine gave us a very ladylike, "No fuckin way."

I had no place in this, but Ross made eye contact with me, and I understood. If the money guy made the producer call, the debate was over.

"Then, Barron it is," I said to Joe. "And you and he can split any underage."

That was maybe a few million in potential bonuses, and he was surprised and grateful. "If there is, we'll share it with the crew, and you won't notice it onscreen."

"Cheap cocksuckers," added our star, but she was outranked and knew it. Marvin patted her arm. He knew actresses and their lawyers weren't ever in these meetings, and he wanted to preserve his place at the table. It was a lot easier to threaten people later when you'd been there at the beginning. Not to mention that as the architect of the aborted auction of a script his star didn't own, he needed to regain some goodwill with the power players.

The casting conversation was interesting for the first ten minutes, but most of the names Ronnie and Lonnie were throwing out, I'd never heard of. Joe Cargo, though, knew Hollywood chemistry, and Ross knew fees and availabilities. The most help, however, came from Candida, who vetoed a couple and suggested others based on what they meant overseas. Without my expecting it, Valentine chimed in with some good thoughts as so much of her boxoffice came from abroad.

The writer discussion was short. Teddy had already made that decision, and Ross had agreed. Cortez Detroit was the man. Marvin furrowed his brow, largely, I believed, because Cortez despises lawyers and always works a few slams into any movie he does.

Having read Lake London's notebooks, Dr. Detroit was going to have to find a way to tame the script while keeping it sexy. The picture was going to be an R anyway, but the sex had to be the kind you couldn't wait to get home to fantasize about. If it had people wincing and closing their eyes, it would hurt business. Cortez would hit the mark, or I'd suggest to Ross that we find a writer with a lighter touch.

I also wanted an author on the material as soon as possible. Publishing revenues would be enormous and establish an appetite for the movie. I wanted no holds barred on content there. The more salacious, the better. Harold Robbins didn't sell 750 million books describing communion—at least not the church kind. Depending on what Ross thought, it might also be smart to establish our own imprint. Books and movies are natural partners, and we might as well control that revenue stream too.

After we covered a few more things, I looked at Archie and nodded. He excused himself and moments later returned, pushing a serving cart piled with the red notebooks, the original script, the old photographs and the jewelry roll containing the flying birds.

"I thought you might want to see some of the things that brought us together," I said.

A hush descended over the table, and I noticed that everyone's eyes were now on the cart. Valentine stared a hole in Archie. Then, like he was demonstrating the features of a luxury home, he began explaining what each item was and passing it among his rapt listeners. "I've removed the elastic from one of the notebooks so you can see Lake London's actual words, but I ask you not to open the others," he said. "There are loose items between the pages that need to be catalogued. But if you're like me, just touching the covers makes you feel like Ms. London is reaching across time to introduce herself." He then went on to identify the people in the photographs—at least as far as he knew.

Watching others marvel at something you're a part of is one of life's great pleasures. Even Marvin was dutifully silenced, until he remembered he was a lawyer. "My God, it's Meyer Lansky," he said as he held the picture of Danny and Lansky with the Lincoln. "If we'd been able to show this stuff before the auction, the bidding would have started at eight figures."

Archie blanched, but I shot him a sharp glance, and he stood down. "Archie," I said, "why don't you give them a look at the Star of Havana."

He crossed the room and retrieved two photographs that hadn't been included in those being passed around. The other articles were forgotten as people craned their necks to get a look. When the necklace came into view, Mac, not a flashy lady by any stretch, sucked in her breath. Candida was mesmerized. That they were seeing it only in black and white made their reactions stand out all the more.

Joe Cargo held a photograph in each hand. "I can make the reveal of this a moment audiences will be talking about for a long time."

Marvin gave Valentine his best grin. "My dear, you're going to look ravishing in that necklace. You'll knock the role of Barrie Fontaine out of the park."

I had taped the magnum to the underside of the table. Now I removed it and placed it in front of me. I'd left it in the Ziploc and noticed a couple of kernels of corn were still stuck in the trigger guard. I liked the effect. I let everyone get a good look.

Valentine went instantly from ill-mannered bitch to indignant celebrity. "Where did you get that?"

"The Green Giant," I answered.

Archie got her full wrath. "You deceitful little faggot! I'll have your fuckin license for letting this cocksucker in my home."

"I doubt it," I said. "I was just retrieving what I own." I let that marinate a moment then inserted the saber. "Valentine, you will never be in a Colosseum picture. Not this one, not the next one, not ever."

There is deafening silence, then there is silence so complete you can hear a mouse whisper the next dimension over. As one would expect, it was the lawyer who found his voice first. "Over some bullshit gun? Get a grip, Rail, or find another business."

"Marvin, let me say this politely. Butt the fuck out. This is between me, her and a lot of dead people. Isn't that right, Miss Scarpuzzi? Of the Ucciardone Scarpuzzis."

In my mind's eye, I saw her skull begin to protrude through the skin of her face—the way it would when she was dead. I kept my voice level. "Earlier today, Mr. Hatt and I spent a productive hour with a small, but highly-regarded law firm here in Laguna. I now own the items that have just been passed around. Including this handgun. The one with your prints on it."

I gave that a moment to sink in. "I also control what happens to the Star of Havana. I don't think Mr. Luciano will be coming back to exercise his bill of sale, but we don't know if there's a descendant of Benedict Crown's who may have a legitimate claim. If there isn't, it will be auctioned for charity after the picture's finished, and I'll pay Archie ten percent of the hammer price."

Valentine seemed to be searching for some new epithet. While she did, I continued. "Tomorrow morning, the law firm will meet with the judge who is adjudicating the necklace dispute. The dispute you created out of whole cloth, Miss Jones. They will advise him that you have agreed to withdraw your claim because you are leaving the country for an extended period, and since there is a movie production pending that requires the diamonds, they will request an immediate dismissal. Marvin should be able to handle your end by phone."

Valentine's mouth opened and closed several times, then finally, "I have no intention of withdrawing anything, you motherfucker! You can't take this picture away from me. I'll murder you in the business. When I'm finished, you won't even be able to get a table at Taco Bell."

"Interesting choice of words, but as long as I'm writing checks, I'm betting people will still show up to make movies. You might also be interested to know that I had a conversation with the captain of the guard at your father's prison. They record everyone coming and going—and who they come and go with. But just to make sure you and I completely understand each other, why don't you take a look at a picture that's not part of the other collection. This one I took myself."

I pushed my phone across to her. Onscreen was the photo of the pink pen in Glenda Van Allen's shoe. "If you page through, you'll see it in a plastic evidence bag as well. Need I go further?"

She blew. "We're still sitting in my driveway, and that goddamn receptionist hands me her fuckin autograph book! I couldn't believe it when she told me that asshole, Teddy, gave her the okay. I looked for it before I left, but it must have still been in the car."

"No, it was under her. Where she fell. But she'll never know."

The rest of the people at the table were now staring at Valentine like she was an exhibit in a cage. A mutant you preferred not to share the same air with. Ross found his voice first, and it shook with anger. "Over a fucking *movie script*?"

"And a company," I said. "And to inflict as much pain as possible on the woman who took it away from her. No outsider ever knows what goes on inside a family, so there's probably a great deal more—real and imagined."

If Marvin stopped representing mutants, his practice would fold. Vendettas, he couldn't have cared less. He was seeing millions of dollars in fees evaporating, and his voice took on the flavor of honeyed smarm. "Rail, Rail, we're way over the edge here. Why don't we take a beat and pick this up in my office in a couple of days. I'm sure we can come to some accommodation."

I ignored him and continued staring at Valentine. "Also tomorrow,

Sheldon Spence, the top litigator in Minneapolis, will be filing a wrongful death suit against Colosseum on behalf of Francine Michelle Maloney. For those who need a *Playbill*, that's Teddy Chessman's twelve-year-old daughter. The one he never missed sending a check to, even when he was in prison. She's autistic, by the way. I intend to name you as Teddy's killer in the company's response. Marvin here, crack attorney that he is, will get you separated from the case, but the media won't care. Neither will the police after they turn your life inside out."

Archie was still back at Colosseum. He couldn't get his head around now having all doubt removed. "And I was supposed to be dead too?" he stammered.

When she didn't seem inclined to answer, I looked at her. "Considering what you've put him through, I think he's entitled to confirmation, don't you?"

Her eyes were on fire. "You seem to like the stage. Why stop now?"

"The answer, Archie, is yes. And in case the pros left one of her cousins or you wriggling, she was prepared to finish the job." I pushed the magnum forward. "With an untraceable gun. Then she would have put on her best movie star smile and given the media the bravura performance they expected. It was a sloppy plan, but Miss Jones is a brilliant actress, and, after all, this is LA. Only something went wrong, and suddenly, her seat in the ladies room got very warm. But like you have to be in show business, she was up to the moment. It's a shame no cameras were rolling, wouldn't you agree, Valentine?"

I saw Valentine's hand go to her lap. It looked like she was running it under her dress between her legs, but I hesitated, not thinking about a pussy holster. A second later, she was on her feet and pointing a baby blue Glock 26. It wasn't very big, but at this range, it didn't need to be.

The circular table was roughly eight feet across. I was two seats to Valentine's right with Marvin between us. Joe Cargo was on the other side of her followed by Ronnie, Lonnie, Ross, Candida and Archie. Mac was immediately to my right.

No matter how proficient a shooter you are, unless you're professionally trained and operationally experienced, your target acquisition arc is a very narrow field directly in front of you. Approximately, thirty-five to forty degrees, or in pie terms, a one-tenth slice. That's your best chance to kill somebody, and Ross and Candida were in that slice.

I stood to distract her. What I wasn't counting on was that she knew exactly what she was doing. She didn't even look over. She just kept pointing the Baby Glock where she had it. "Sit down, asshole, or the cunt with the accent goes first."

She hadn't racked the slide, but the hammer was back, so I had to assume there was a round in the chamber. If the magazine was full, she had eleven shots to get somebody. Or a lot of somebodies. I sat.

"What the hell, Valentine?" Marvin started to put his hand on her arm, and she elbowed him in the face so hard, his nose split wide open.

"Much as I'd like to compliment you for that," I said, "the cards have already been dealt, so why don't you sit down before you embarrass yourself more than you already have."

"Are you going to put me back in my picture? And return my necklace? Did you hear that? *My* picture and *my* necklace?"

"So you don't misunderstand me, I won't use any big words. No."

Once a marine, always a marine. Joe Cargo made his move. Valentine was faster. She pivoted slightly and shot him through the shoulder, knocking him back into his chair. She immediately returned her aim to Candida, her hand as steady as before. She'd had training. A lot of it.

The shot brought Hector on the run, alone. Apparently, the sound hadn't reached the servers having dinner in the back of the house. Valentine didn't turn but told Hector to stand where she could see him. I nodded, and he moved to a few feet behind the Keck twins, one of whom looked like he was about to faint. The other was trying to tend to Cargo. "I'll live," the director said, as he pressed a napkin to the wound, and the agent resumed facing forward.

"Valentine," I said calmly. "You can't kill everybody, and why would you want to anyway? No prosecutor's going to indict you for Colosseum. There's no direct evidence, and of the two people who could provide it, your father's *non compos mentis*, and good luck getting anything out of his associate."

"Don't bring my father into this."

I ignored her. "As for the three you did shoot, none of them will be testifying, and there are at least a dozen lawyers who could get you off on the circumstantial evidence. You're also famous, which in this town is like starting with a fan club, not a jury. So knock off the dramatics, and let's get Joe a doctor."

Marvin had stemmed his nosebleed. His voice was a little shaky, but he was still focused on his bank balance, not Joe Cargo's health. "Everybody at this table is going to have a version of what happened here tonight, and it'll get wilder the more they retell it. And once Ross gets on the phone and works some of that smooth, say-nothing-but-imply-everything crap of his, Valentine won't be able to get a mattress commercial. By pulling her off the picture, you're confirming the worst."

"Ross is his own man, but it could happen," I said. "That's why you'll tell her to leave the country. Eventually, she'll get rehabbed. They all do. But by that time, she'll only be fit to play grandmothers. Valentine's punishment is the worst thing that can happen to a movie star: obscurity... and loss of youth."

"And if I don't leave?" Valentine spit.

I smiled. "Bad things happen all the time. Even to movie stars." No one knew exactly what I meant, but no one thought it was an empty threat.

CHAPTER FIFTY-SIX

Peach in an Oak Tree

I hadn't expected the gun, and I didn't expect the shot. It caught Candida in the left cheek and tore through the soft flesh before exiting behind her ear. I don't know if it was because of the murder of my Brazilian wife, or if I would have reacted the same way if it had been Mac. But I did something I have been trained to never do when facing a dangerous adversary. I became enraged.

I cursed myself for threatening somebody who was pointing a gun at an innocent. Jesus Christ, I had been trained in hostage negotiation. Worse, I knew what had caused my stupidity, and it doubled my anger. It wasn't because Valentine was a woman. I'd seen enough deadly ones to know better. It was because she was a fuckin actress. Like that fuckin mattered. They don't even have a word for that kind of dumb.

Ross dove across his wife, shielding her from more shots. I pulled Mac to the floor and threw a violent elbow into Marvin's chest, sending him and his chair over backwards. It wasn't Marvin's night. As I lunged for Valentine, she fired twice more.

Her first shot missed, but the second tore through my side. It didn't spin me completely around, but it knocked me off stride and into the table. In that instant, she was gone, running hard up the stairway toward the bedroom. She'd kicked off her shoes, and she moved like a gazelle, long legs pumping and her tight, short dress riding partway past her unpantied posterior.

I tore open the Ziploc, grabbed the magnum and followed. It was dark at the top of the stairs, so I had to slow down to avoid being framed in the downstairs light. I moved as far up as I dared then dropped to my hands. I gave it a three-count, dashed the rest of the way on all fours and rolled into the blackness. I was impressed again. No shots to give away her position. I lay still and let my eyes adjust while I listened.

Nothing. Then, suddenly, she was running again. This time on the stairs to the roof. I felt my side. It was a through-and-through. Not much blood, and if the bullet had taken out something important, I would have already known.

It wasn't as windy uptop as it had been earlier, but the moon hadn't yet risen. I tried to pick out anything I could against the dark sky, but it was futile. My best hope was getting her to shoot. Working up my courage, I stood and walked the rest of the way up, ready to hit the teak if I sensed movement.

She finally made the mistake I wanted. The muzzle flash came from across the roof in the vicinity of the storage shed. I had given her a sideways target, and its narrowness caused the bullet to only ruffle my shirt. But it had been heart high. She was better than good.

From the ground, I squeezed off one shot. The boom and flame of the .357 was like battlefield artillery compared to the terrier bark of her 9mm. Whatever I hit shattered, but there was no scream.

There wasn't any place for her to run, but she'd been in this house before, so she obviously knew something I didn't. I heard someone else coming up the stairs, and told whoever it was to stop.

Hector's voice reached me. "There's a pair of shotguns in the shed, along with a trap thrower. She and I used to shoot clays on windy days when you couldn't tell where the sound was coming from. Archie doesn't like guns, so we keep them up here. Sorry, but I put them away loaded."

"Birdshot?"

"Yes, but there's a box of 12-guage in there too. For snakes."

I heard sirens in the distance. "How's Candida?"

"She's talking, but she's lost a lot of blood."

"Go back downstairs, and don't let anybody up here. Even if you have to tackle them. Cops included."

"You got it."

Just then, two blasts of shotgun fire broke the stillness. Hundreds of hurled BBs raked the deck. A few ricocheted into my shins, and though they hurt like hell, at that range, they weren't deadly. Immediately, two more blasts came. She'd now used both guns and would have to reload. And this time, it wouldn't be the lightweight crap she'd just fired.

I was through underestimating this lady. I gathered myself and ran straight at where I thought she would be. I was wrong. She had moved, taking her box of shells with her. By the time I realized she wasn't within arm's reach, she had dropped the shotgun and was raising the Glock. At this range, she wouldn't even have to aim. But in haste and adrenaline, she pulled the trigger too early, and the bullet splintered the teak at my feet.

I bull-rushed her and caught her in the chest with my shoulder like a linebacker. She still had her gun hand free and began hammering at my head. When she tried to get the Glock turned to shoot, I didn't let her. I dug in and whirled. Her arm hit the storage shed with enough force that I heard it snap. She screamed, and the gun clanked on the teak then clattered over the side.

She was still fighting, but I had control, and she felt like a wisp against my size. I released her, but not because I was finished. When I seized her throat with my left hand, my fingers nearly encircled her neck. With my right, I grabbed hard between her legs, feeling the holster and getting my fingers under the strap holding it to her thigh.

By throat and holster, I carried her to the edge of the roof. I couldn't see the ground, but I knew this was the steepest drop. Spittle was coming out of her mouth as she fought to breathe. She was kicking like a jungle cat, but I didn't feel it.

I put my face to her ear and whispered, "This one's for Glenda." Then I threw her as far as I could, watching her eyes come to the realization that she was about to die. She actually seemed to gain attitude for a second, then she became a disappearing peach fabric and tanned flesh bundle, heading toward terminal velocity. No popping nylon this time.

The ambulance took Candida and Joe Cargo. Ross rode with them. Candida was going to need some cosmetic work, but her wounds weren't life-threatening. Ross shook my hand before he climbed in back, and Candida managed a smile.

The paramedics tried to get me in the ambulance too, but when I refused, one got a cop to help load the stretchers while he cleaned my wound. "I'm gonna have to report you as a gunshot victim, which triggers a lot of paperwork," he said while I winced. "You need to have that looked at by a doc and get a tetanus shot anyway, so I suggest you haul yourself up to Hoag tonight. Otherwise, they'll send a couple of deputies around who won't ask what you want."

"Thanks for the heads-up," I said.

Despite the number of cops that kept arriving, the investigation wasn't much. There were a lot of witnesses, but everybody was rich or worked for somebody who was. The wait staff remembered their bonuses and went blind, deaf and mute.

Laguna Beach residents pay a lot of taxes to keep trouble away from their little ration of heaven—especially from violent trouble on the tops of expensive hills. To reinforce it, an assistant chief stepped forward and said the quicker this was over the better. That encouraged one of the men in blue to take a report on my wound without using the word gunshot and cut me loose to work out the legalities with my own doctor.

Archie said there were floodlights on the house that illuminated the hillside, so we all went into the glass-floored hallway while he turned them on. Valentine Jones was impaled near the top of a tree—an oak, I thought—that protruded out of the side of the ravine, hundreds of feet short of the bottom.

An upward-pointed limb had penetrated the back of her neck then reemerged through her face. She hung there like a rag doll, her shaved nether region and the stream of tattooed stars down her leg as exposed as the night I'd pulled her out of the Pacific. I saw a small sparkle near her foot and realize it was the flying bird anklet, reflecting in the glare of the floods. I thought she looked a lot better now, but maybe she'd been right.

Maybe she shouldn't have come to dinner.

One of the CSI people went down to the wine cellar to take pictures through the glass, and Hector said suggested everyone looked like they could use a cup of coffee. I followed him to the kitchen and asked if he'd like to stay on and work for me. He couldn't have gotten the, "Yes, sir," out any faster.

CHAPTER FIFTY-SEVEN

Cold Spaces and Stone Lions

I went back to Beverly Hills to wait out the media frenzy. It burned white hot as expected but didn't have legs. A famous actress with very few friends had gone off the rails and shot a couple of people—none seriously—then jumped off a roof. Drugs were strongly hinted at. Everybody at the dinner held their water, and after a couple of weeks of the usual fan hand-wringing, impromptu memorials around her star on the Walk of Fame and sleaze-merchant rush for the autopsy photographs, the Middle East belched another round of violence and some PETA model got caught moose hunting with a former governor. Just as quickly, the professional windbags and celebrity stalkers took their saliva elsewhere, and things got back to normal.

I fished J.C. Stinson's business card out of one of Lake London's red notebooks and stared at the number written on back: 000-333. I had never seen one like it, here or abroad, and I didn't think the passing of nearly nine decades was the reason.

Rabbit Suarez used to be a lieutenant with the LAPD Bomb Squad. If you never want to sleep soundly again, ask somebody like Rabbit what's being assembled in neighborhoods around your town. Men who do bomb work will tell you there are times they'd rather not get out of bed. Not because they're afraid, but because, some days, things just don't feel right. Those are also the days they hope they don't come up against some first-timer's half-assed rig with innocent lives hanging in the balance.

A few years ago, Rabbit drew both short straws. The bomb wedged into an elementary school bike rack blinded him, and a piece of shrapnel pierced a wall and severed the jugular of a second-grader. Survivor's guilt doesn't even scratch the surface.

Today, Rabbit runs a small shop in Studio City rebuilding phones, the trigger of choice for many professional bombmakers. You couldn't tell from his workmanship that he can't see, but like Rabbit says, when your life depends on something, you learn to do it in the dark.

My favorite charity, Blue Rescue, picked up the tab to retrofit Rabbit's house when he got out of the hospital, so even though he's not the warmest guy on the planet, he takes my calls. "What do you need?" he asked.

"I'm looking at an unusual phone number." I read it off.

He didn't hesitate. "It's a rogue, better known as a Kingsbury."

Even from Rabbit, I was impressed. "Okay, professor, teach."

"Coming from where we are today, it's hard to imagine how primitive phone service used to be. Every clown with a spool of wire was in the business, and if your neighbor had a different installer, you couldn't call across the street. Ted Vail, who ran AT&T, was buying up the mom and pops as fast as he could to create an integrated system, but then along came the G, who hate a good plan they haven't fucked up yet.

"Vail was a stick-it-up-your-ass kinda guy, but he had a Mr. Smooth on the payroll: Nathan Kingsbury. Kingsbury persuaded Washington to let Vail accelerate his buying, and in return, the Feds would get the right to help set rates. But even with the shackles off, absorption of thousands of independents was going to take time, so Vail also agreed to let anyone with a current phone connect to the AT&T system, providing they ran their own line to the hookup point. Translation: rich guys like you got reliable service, and Joe Six-Pack waited. The 000 prefix told AT&T Central Billing that that particular phone was a Kingsbury."

I didn't need help getting to the obvious. "Since the government wasn't fighting for millionaires' rights, Vail could charge the rogues anything he wanted."

"In the twenties and thirties, you coulda bought a Caddie for what some of them paid every month. So why does any of this matter?"

"The guy who built my home had a Kingsbury, and there's always been a rumor there's a hidden room somewhere. I might be putting two and two together and coming up with seventeen, but now you've got me wondering."

"You remember J. Paul Getty?"

"Of course. He got tired of having his house guests make international calls on his billions, so he locked off the regular handsets and installed a London pay booth in his foyer." He got skewered in the press, which he didn't give a shit about, and the freeloading was over. I sympathized completely. Been there and worse.

"And that was in the seventies. So imagine a time when Ma Bell could bang you for ten bucks a minute, and your maid had a boyfriend in Helsinki. A lot of phones lived behind moving bookcases or trick closets. Every now and then, some architect doing a teardown in one of the better neighborhoods finds one. If I'm lucky, he calls me."

I guessed that in Stinson's case, his biggest problem was Hughes, not the maid. "So how do I locate it if it's here? A voltmeter on the current lines?"

"Won't tell you anything. Entirely separate system. Describe the house."

For the next fifteen minutes, I ran through the details. He stopped me as soon as I mentioned the elevator. "It runs between the underground garage and your second floor bedroom, and you're the only one who has access?"

"Not by fiat, but in practical terms, yes."

"My bet is it runs somewhere you don't know about. Like the first floor or somewhere above the bedroom."

"It doesn't. I've got the original blueprints. And when I bought the place, I had everything gone over top to bottom so I didn't end up taking a surprise ride."

"The blueprints for a nuclear sub don't show the reactor either. And if you're really into fiction, Google up the ones for the White House."

I knew that, but I hadn't made the leap.

"As for your service people, did you just ask them to make sure the elevator was safe or to look for anomalies? Bombs rarely have an arrow pointing to them, either. You have to think about what looks, not just normal, but *too* normal."

"Now that you've made me wonder how I've managed to live this long, you have any suggestions?"

"If you were just an ordinary rich guy, I'd tell you to start pulling down plaster. But you're not. You've got connections. Use them."

It was 9:00 PM, and I was riding shotgun as T.T. Barcella sang *La Traviata* while he made circles over my neighborhood. A tech named Smitty was in the backseat, calibrating a pile of equipment attached to a thermographic camera and a bar of sensors riding under the helicopter's right strut. I didn't like being up there any more than I usually do, but the Kingsbury mystery had pushed my chopper aversion to a back burner. Smitty, who wasn't much of a talker—and even less of a diplomat than Rabbit—had already told me to stop asking questions, twice.

You normally get about five minutes of loitering over wealthy people's houses in a loud aircraft before your radio lights up from multiple law enforcement agencies. I'd told the authorities I wanted to look for a mountain lion that had been harassing my dogs. I don't have any dogs, but a mountain lion is always a possibility, so I considered it a white lie and not a felony. In a time of tight budgets, if I was willing to spend my own cash chasing off a deadly predator, the cops were willing to grant me an hour to do it.

To keep up the charade, T.T. was running a spotlight over my property and down the hillside in back. I might have also asked him to hit my asshole neighbor's windows a couple of times in retaliation for the golf balls he chips into my pool.

I had Mallory on the cell phone from the house, and he was not happy. "If it gets any hotter in here, the sprinklers are going to go off, and I'll be on my way to the Four Seasons." I felt for him. The windows were all closed, and the furnace was on high. We'd also built fires in the twelve fireplaces and turned on all the lights. Next month's power bill was going to put me in the DWP Hall of Fame and maybe get me featured in an Al Gore movie. The first, I can afford; the other, I can only hope.

Finally, Smitty announced that he was ready, and T.T. switched off the spotlight and began making slow passes a couple of hundred feet above my roof. I turned as far as I could in my seat to watch the monitor. Smitty had placed dozens of sensors throughout the house, and onscreen, the place lit up like the sun. As my eyes adjusted, the gradations became clearer.

After my conversation with Rabbit, I'd made a thorough inspection of the elevator, including propping open the door and overriding the safety switch so I could ride up and down examining the interior wall the entire length of the shaft. I also leaned inside the service portals above and below. If there was something unusual in there, I sure couldn't find it.

"How we doing?" I asked Smitty.

"If I see something, I'll let you know. In the meantime, shut the fuck up. And that includes the fuckin singing." I looked over at T.T. and saw him laughing. So much for somebody caring about the twenty grand this was costing me, but at least I could feel sorry for myself, sans Verdi.

"Damn it, I'm dying down here." Mallory complained.

"Tell him to keep moving along the interior walls," Smitty barked.

Even in the sweltering house, Mallory's body temperature was higher, and the contrast of his heat signature against the cooler spaces allowed Smitty to assess what was behind them. He reached over the seat and snatched the cell phone out of my hand. "Get in the elevator."

"Upstairs or in the garage?"

"Make an executive decision."

I turned and watched the muttering, red blob that was my houseman descend the back stairs and enter the elevator through the garage. "Leave the door open and take it up slow," Smitty ordered. I'd shown Mallory how to handle the override, and I watched the car begin to rise. Suddenly, Smitty yelled, "I said, slow, goddamn it!"

When the elevator reached my bedroom, Mallory started back down. About midpoint, Smitty shut off his monitor and began unplugging wires and packing up his stuff. I watched in silence until it was clear he wasn't in a hurry to say anything. "You want the rest of your fee or not?"

He looked at me through narrowed eyes. "It's in the back."

"The back of what?"

"Somebody turned the elevator around. The doors used to be on the other side, and there were three of them: basement, first and second floors. There's a cold space on the first floor behind the current shaft. Not large—about eight by ten feet with a twelve-foot ceiling. It's none of my business, buddy, but didn't you ever wonder why the fuck somebody would build an elevator that didn't open on the ground floor? When you come home with a quart of milk, what're you supposed to do? Schlep it to the bedroom then walk it down?"

All this time I'd been giving Stinson props for being a Lothario *par excellence*: luxury automobile to high thread-count sheets, no stops in-between. And he might have been exactly that, but he was also smarter than the current owner, because his milk didn't have to travel an extra floor.

I thought about how the elevator was positioned. In both the bedroom and garage, it would have been no problem, structurally or logistically, to have had the doors opposite their current placement. In fact, in the garage, it would have made more sense.

On the first floor, where the door would have once opened, now sat an alabaster sculpture of a life-sized male lion, a lioness and their cub, appearing to walk out of an African savanna into my living room. Set into the wall, it's a gargantuan piece, worthy of ancient Rome, with a full two-thirds of the animals inside the room and their three-dimensional savanna reaching up twenty feet.

Frankly, it's never been a favorite. It should be in the lobby of MGM. But I also thought it was original to the house, so I had the lions and their habitat painstakingly restored and left them in place. At Christmas, Mallory dresses the beasts in custom-made Santa outfits, which heightens their conversation value but probably lowers their dignity.

Now I realized somebody had added them after reversing the elevator. It was going be fascinating to find out what else I didn't know.

Getting through a wall of stone isn't easy, especially if you want to preserve it. Vito Indelicato and his son, Cristo, didn't even blink. "This is Old Country craftsmanship, Mr. Black. You ever decide to get rid of it, I know somebody who'll pay a million, maybe more." My fondness for Italian artisans immediately increased, right along with my appreciation of stone lions.

"We can do what you want with one cut, but that might damage the piece and interfere with stability. Give us a couple of days, and when we put it back together, you won't be able to tell we were here." I didn't bother to discuss price. If you've paid a master stonecutter lately, you understand.

When Vito and Cristo went home after the first day, they had turned the monolith into a vertical jigsaw puzzle, braced with steel rods. I stood and looked at it for a long time until, finally, my curiosity overcame my better judgment. I found a seven-foot pry bar in the Indelicatos' pile of tools, jammed the business end into one of the cuts and began working loose a 6x8-ft. section. It was the heaviest thing I'd ever moved, and I felt sweat running down my back as I fought for millimeters.

Even through the heavy plastic they'd laid down, I was tearing hell out of my black marble floor. The pros would have jacked it up and rolled it out. I wasn't that smart and should have stopped but didn't. Fully engaged now, I got a second bar and worked it into the other side of the section so I could go back and forth between them. It was probably the same technique that had built the great cities of antiquity, except I was allowed to stop for a cold beer.

When I had the block pulled out about three feet, I went down to the garage and got a large, Maglite LED, which is bright enough to reset your body clock. Leaning into the space, I played the beam behind it. Sheets of old plywood rose vertically on the wall, so I retrieved my trusty pry bar, squeezed into my hard-fought slit then made enough noise going through the plywood to bring Mallory downstairs in his robe and slippers.

"I'd offer to help, sir, but you seem to be doing a delightful job of running up the remodeling bill on your own."

I ignored him. "Look at this."

Mallory joined me behind the block and peered through the hole I'd made. It took him a few seconds, but he finally came out with, "Good God."

Rising twenty-five feet, twice what Smitty had predicted, was an open wall as if someone had completely stripped away the exterior of a two-story building. On the first level was a small office with a desk and a room filled with old filing cabinets. I noticed a period phone, but it was lying on its side, not connected to anything.

The upper floor was a single space, jammed tight with 1930s electronic gear, all neatly arranged. In the center of the room sat a rectangular table with a wooden banker's chair drawn up to a professional microphone, several notebooks and two sets of headphones.

The table's centerpiece was a telephone from the same era, and everything—phone, mic and headphones—was hard-wired into the electronic equipment across from it. I think part of Mallory's 'Good God' was triggered by seeing that the lights on some of the machines were glowing red, green and amber—like they were simply waiting for their operator to get back from a break.

Because of how tightly the space had been sealed, there was surprising little dust. Suddenly, my flashlight caught something that reflected back into my eyes. I elevated the beam and could see a tall, silver vase wedged between a refrigerator-sized receiver and a cabinet of gauges. I was trying to dial in my focus when Mallory said, "Sir, I think that's a cremation urn."

As it turned out, it was. Jilleen Cait Stinson.

CHAPTER FIFTY-EIGHT

Bad Men and the Mostest Famous

The office and file room were fascinating, and over the next several weeks, I would go through every slip of paper. But now, I climbed the small open stairway to the second level. It was all interesting, but I couldn't take my eyes off the phone. I took out my cell and dialed Rabbit. "I'm looking at something out of *Day of the Locust.*"

"Let me take a stab. Black Bakelite, round base, Bell logo on the dial and a spit cup."

I presumed spit cup meant the extension on the mouthpiece, and I tried to imagine the salesman's pitch. "Correct."

"You're in the presence of greatness. A Western Electric B1. Today, a pro could shoot enough juice through that motherfucker to launch a cruise missile."

"Comforting. There are two lines wired into it, each going to a separate piece of equipment."

"The line's been split, which back in the day was a real accomplishment. Describe the equipment."

I did, and there was silence on the other end. I thought for a moment that I hadn't gotten the details right. "You need me to go through that again?"

"Did some government guy build your house?"

"A lawyer."

"With important clients."

I confined my answer to, "One."

"Open one of the pieces. There's probably a latch on top. The front will drop down."

He was correct again except that the front swung away like a door. Inside was a reel-to-reel recording system, only the reels were as large as hubcaps. Wide celluloid was threaded between them through what I assumed were recorder heads. The second piece of equipment was identical.

"What's the tape look like?"

"No tape. I'm guessing 35mm motion picture film."

"With images?"

"No it's clear except for a pair of lines along the edge."

"Do they vary in shade or width?"

"Width."

"Somebody was using non-emulsified theatrical film to record straight audio. Very 1930s and a very sophisticated application for the time. I'd be willing to bet your machines are the only ones of their kind. Probably built by a sound expert working on the cutting edge or by a classified research lab. Either way, definitely not off-the-shelf."

I thought about Howard Hughes and how he had surrounded himself with forward-thinking engineers and the best technical men. There was no question in my mind where this had come from. "Can I play it without damaging the film?"

"If it had images on it, no. Time would have degraded the emulsion, and it would come off on the heads. That shouldn't happen with straight sound, but if these have been sitting for any length of time, you need to clean the film and heads first and lubricate the machine's moving parts." He walked me through the process, and I thanked him and hung up.

An hour later, Mallory and I had swabbed everything carefully with a weak solution of isopropyl alcohol and distilled water, brushed mineral oil where it seemed necessary and rewound the film. Mallory finished ahead of me and checked the cabinets next to each recorder. Both contained rows of dark olive, hexagon-shaped cardboard boxes the size of the reels. The boxes were fastened with matching canvas straps that buckled like a belt, and each was marked with a thick black, handwritten letter. Those in the cabinet on the left, an M; and on the right, an R.

I sat down at the table, put on the headphones that ran to the left recorder and took a breath. When I hit the PLAY switch, the ancient belts squealed for a moment, and the reels groaned, lurched then smoothed out. In my ears, a male voice with a hint of an Irish accent intoned "June 4, 1935, Mag Mell."

There was a scratchy silence, then a tiny female voice was talking. I strained to make it out, but even though I had the volume up all the way, she kept turning her mouth away from the receiver—like she was looking over her shoulder for someone who might find her on the phone.

She was also crying. "They took her, Mr. Stinson! They took her! Ma'am gave Barrie to the bad men!" Then she began to describe the trip to Palm Springs in heartbreaking detail.

After the tape ran out, I sat for a long time before I could bring myself to switch headphones and recorders. This time, when I heard J.C. Stinson's date mark, I braced myself. It couldn't have been more different.

"Hi, J.C. Ramona here." Her voice was upbeat, breezy, like superficial banter with a girlfriend. Only there was nothing superficial about what came next. "Before I get started, can you put an extra hundred in the bank? Sorry, but this girl just can't seem to stretch a buck. Okay, here we go. Had a heckuva time with Daddy tonight. Palm Springs. I'd never been! And you'll never guess who I was with. Give up? Madalynne St. Timothy! Can you imagine that? Little ol' Ramona Scroggins from Yankton, South Dakota sitting with the mostest famous star in all the world! Pinch me, somebody! Oh, yeah, this afternoon, I did some of the fun stuff too—with your ex-wifey and Daddy. I know you don't like to hear details, but whew, I'm still sore, and I've just got to tell somebody. Did you ever hear of putting a…"

I switched the recorder off, stood and handed the headphones to Mallory. "If you find yourself running out of things to talk about with Mr. Stinson, this should keep you busy for a few years."

As I made my way back to the living room and eventually into a glass of very red, very rich wine and an English Oval. I had to applaud my home's former owner for his thoroughness in keeping track of his enemies. I also levelled a measure of disgust about how he'd done it. I hope he'd felt some himself.

But Hooper was right. Script or no script, the story had survived.

CHAPTER FIFTY-NINE

Danny Plus One

BEFORE DAWN—JULY 8, 1935
PACIFIC COAST HIGHWAY, SOUTH OF LAGUNA BEACH

Danny Dades slowed the Packard to a crawl and levered the outside spotlight toward the shoulder of the road. The turnoff he'd marked this afternoon with a strip of white cloth tied to a stake had seemed impossible to miss, but he was beginning to think he had. When it finally appeared, he got out, pulled it free, tore away the cloth and threw it and the stake as far as he could in opposite directions.

Back in the car, he turned right and bounced over the dirt ruts in the direction of the ocean, which he was now able to hear. Several times, he turned to check that his motorcycle in the backseat wasn't about to push open a door and go flying out.

The government had recently purchased a large tract of the Flood Ranch, and the rumor was that it was going to be turned into the largest military base on the West Coast. Marines, they said. If that happened, it would make the costal land north of it, including Danny's, far more valuable once several miles of Pacific beachfront were eliminated from future southward development. It would also permanently buffer San Diego from LA, which was probably a plus for both.

He'd left Madalynne at Highroller Hill, soaking in the tub with a bottle of Chablis next to her. From his living room, he had watched the flames rise from Lake's place then die to a dull glow. And still no one had come. Investigators—when they were finally summoned—would find little to sift.

The second stake and cloth strip brought him to another stop, and he threw these away as well, then wheeled the car a hundred yards through the off-road scrub. He almost drove into the grave he'd dug, but half an hour later, Rollo was gone, and Danny was back on the PCH headed south again.

Lindbergh Field was a simple, two-runway regional airport, but it was home to an increasing number of long-distance flights as airlines took advantage of San Diego's near-perfect weather. Now, as dawn approached, even though the place was ablaze with lights, it was mostly silent. No planes yet, only a handful of people checking in for early departures.

Danny parked the Packard as far from the lights as possible, and with some difficulty, got the Indian out of the back. He wiped the tire tracks off the leather interior, checked for anything he might have left behind then pulled a packet of hundred dollar bills from his jacket. This particular stack had been one of the most waterlogged and had dried wrinkled and faded. He stuffed the bills into the gap between the passenger seat and its back. He knew someone would find them. He hoped it would be one of Luciano's people. This airport would be one of the first places they'd check.

He started his bike and rode slowly past the terminal. Inside, at the coffee shop counter, Price Galloway was shoveling down a mound of pancakes. At eight, he'd board an Aerovia Centrales flight to Mexico City, using a ticket in the name of Rollo Tripoli. From there, he was on his own, but with the ten thousand dollars Danny had given him for his trouble, it was a pretty safe bet he'd make his way back to Tijuana and blow it on tequila and hookers. Danny might even get lucky, and somebody'd stick a knife in him.

Either way Rollo Tripoli would become just one more drug dealer who took a powder with money that wasn't his. Luciano would turn the globe upside down looking for him, and when he came up empty, he'd quietly start a rumor that Rollo had screamed like a girl when he'd cut off his cock and stuffed it down his throat. Guys as important as Luciano always got revenge—even mythical—so others didn't get ideas.

Meanwhile, Danny would be managing Lansky's new place in New Orleans. The Little Man had said something about expanding in the Caribbean, and Danny was first in line to move up. It was shaping up to be quite a future.

He turned the Indian into the approaching sunrise, opened the throttle and thought about the little blonde actress awaiting him. She was always at her best when she was begging to be taken back.

CHAPTER SIXTY

Home

JULY 8, 1935
SOMEWHERE OVER THE CARIBBEAN

Tess Power awakened to sun in her eyes. She didn't know how long she had been out this time, but from the almost unbearable dryness in her mouth, she expected it had been a few hours. She'd been in restraints most of the flight, once Luciano told Novi to stop injecting her. Her arms were tied to the armrests and her bare feet to the frame of the seat in front of her. Another cord ran around the seatback, pinning her neck to it, and if she moved too much, the thug sitting behind her twisted it until she began to choke.

She'd expected Luciano to beat her, but he hadn't. He'd gone right to the knife. She had no idea what her face looked like, but she knew she wasn't pretty any longer. Her clothes had also been cut off, and she consciously avoided looking at her torso. Unfortunately, she couldn't do the same with her legs because she could see them each time the plane hit choppy air, and her head bounced.

The pain wasn't as bad as she thought it might be. She'd discovered that a knife doesn't hurt very much; it just scares you—really scares you. But once she forced herself to concentrate on other things, like redecorating the interior of the Trimotor, she only cried out once in a while. She got even braver when she saw how angry it made Luciano that she didn't beg.

Tess had to go to the bathroom, and she slurred her need through cracked lips. The words came out thick, and she didn't recognize her own voice, but

Luciano, sitting across the aisle, nodded at one of his men who got up and undid her bonds. She had trouble getting her legs working again, but as she rubbed them to get circulation restarted, it also reawakened the nerves in her behind. It hadn't been that long ago she had been sitting in a booth in Laguna that had been a lot more pleasant. Or so it had seemed at the time.

When she finally tried to stand, she almost went down then righted herself. The man followed her toward the rear where the restroom was, and she had to hold onto the seats to stay upright. When she got to the exit break, she numbly reached for another seatback, but there wasn't one there, and she stumbled and fell against the door. Her escort uttered a curse and picked her up, handling her like she had a contagious disease.

The man held the curtain of the lavatory and watched as she sat on the hard metal. She was beyond embarrassment, but she'd never been able to pee with someone looking. After a few long moments, he figured it out and turned his head, still holding the curtain open.

When she finished, she wanted to wash her hands, but nothing came out of the tiny spigot. She started to ask the man for a glass of water for her parched throat, but he grabbed her by the arm and jerked her out of the cubicle, pushing her roughly back down the aisle. It didn't matter.

She was aware that the engines had suddenly changed to a higher pitch, and she knew that momentarily, the nose of the plane would lift as the pilot ascended to a higher altitude. This was better than she could have expected. Somebody was clearly looking out for Tess.

She stopped abruptly, and the man almost ran into her. He put a meaty hand between her shoulder blades to push her again just as the plane began to lift. Timing it perfectly, Tess wheeled and kicked. Her foot hit him in the chest. It didn't catch him squarely, but the shift in gravity caused him to stagger backwards as he clawed at the air for purchase. There was none, and he went down and slid toward the rear of the aircraft.

Tess rushed forward. The exit door handle was in the up position just like she'd left it. She hurled herself against the steel, knowing that the outside air rushing by would be difficult to overcome. The door gave slightly, then the wind found the crack, and it whipped it all the way open and banged against the fuselage.

She was aware of men shouting, then she rushed into the void, marveling at the brightness of the sun and the blue of the welcoming sea.

Tess Power was coming home.

CHAPTER SIXTY-ONE

Buildings and Beers

Denise Spyrou was in the phone book; her mother wasn't. When I came up empty at the Gardenia, I swallowed my bile and dialed *Oblast*. It took some doing to find somebody who would even admit they knew Buka Pasternak then a slog through another Ukrainian hardhead to get her on the line.

"I hear you're having some real fun, Black." Her voice sounded like a bear with adenoid trouble, which meant she'd been drinking a lot of Horilka. "I just found out two of the people killed at your joint lived in West Hollywood. You're better for vacancy rates than a menorah shortage."

Engaging her would only give her license and make this take longer. "I need a phone number."

Denise picked up after only a couple of rings, and I could tell she'd been crying. I half-expected her to hang up, but she didn't."

"You heard about Zoe?" she asked.

"That's one of the reasons I called. I don't want you to think you owe me any confidentiality. If you believe telling the police about my being there will help them get the person who did this, please go ahead."

"But you haven't told them, which means you know it won't."

I didn't say anything.

"Will you make him suffer?"

"I'm not in the suffering business," I lied. "But I'll make sure he knows why I'm there."

"Thank you. You said that was only one of the reasons you called."

"Did your father ever mention anybody named Aspirins?"

She sucked in her breath, and I was afraid she might start crying again. "Is that who killed Zoe?"

"Possibly."

"My brothers told me a man with that name came to the shop. They thought it was a funny thing to be called, that's why it came up. We didn't usually discuss work, just meet for a beer a couple of times a week."

"Is that all they said?"

"No, there was more to the name. Matty. Matty Aspirins. They said my father wanted to sell him part of a building in Cyprus. I didn't know he owned anything there, but he kept a storage locker at the Gardenia, so I went through it and found a deed for a place in Pyrgos. I asked my mother, but she'd never heard of it either."

"Do you have the address?"

"Yes, and the manager's name."

CHAPTER SIXTY-TWO

Wine, Cheese and Gasoline

The Cashier was resting comfortably in the sunroom of Palazzo Passavanti. A fifteenth century ceiling mural depicting the final days of Christ and three hundred-year-old, gold-brushed furniture on inlaid, mosaic parquetry offered stark contrast to the twenty-first century hospital bed. The service had also sent a rolling I.V., but the Cashier didn't need it. His was a disease that ate only the mind.

A wheelchair sat against a wall in the adjacent hallway, but he didn't need that either. When he wanted to get up, or when the around-the-clock male nurses insisted, he could walk with no problem. Unfortunately, he was still strong in his arms and hands as well, so when being moved, he was restrained for his own safety as well as for his caregivers.

Initially, there had been considerable resistance from the police and judiciary about releasing an Article 41 prisoner to anyone but an undertaker. The law had been enacted exactly for people like the Cashier— men who pull the strings of organized crime in Italy and beyond.

While subordinate Mafiosi go into the overcrowded and generally lax facilities spread throughout the country, men like Michelangelo Scarpuzzi are sentenced to a segregated system of heavily-secured military stockades and dank fortresses usually far removed from large population centers and other prisons. Even the guards are drawn from a separate pool of corrections officers—men with no ties to Mafia-controlled towns and with no Sicilian relatives who could become targets for coercion or reprisals.

One Article 41 penitentiary, however, remains in the heart of the most visible and notorious city in all of organized crime: Palermo. Only a short drive from the birthplace of Salvatore "Charlie Lucky" Lucania, Ucciardone Prison, built in 1807, was used by Mussolini to torture Mafiosi, their wives and children. Later, it was commandeered by prosecutors to warehouse new generations of *Cosa Nostra* awaiting trail during the government's regular waves of crackdowns.

Today this *sanctum malus* houses the convicted godfathers, close advisors and financial masterminds of the most famous of criminal enterprises. But Italy is not like other places. Though most of these prisoners are serving life terms, some for ordering the murders of judges and prosecutors, they lounge in silk bathrobes and drink fine wine while they enjoy food prepared by their own chefs. When the weather is favorable, they play bocce through a haze of Cuban cigar smoke.

Periodically, a naïve politician will complain, and prison officials will take away the barbers and masseurs and visiting girlfriends until the media outrage has faded. But everything always returns—usually with an apology. The protesting politician? Most of the time, a visit from one of his fellow legislators is sufficient. Respectful accommodation keeps these two sides of Italian society orderly… and people alive.

There are three large suites of cells, or *grandi saloni*, at Ucciardone, where the most powerful of the powerful reside and hold court. For the past two decades, one of these three had been the Cashier. But now, he was gone. To Venice. To be cared for in his final days by a titled family to whom he was loosely connected through a bastard child.

No one in the Rome government or at Ucciardone had been taken in by this fiction of compassion, but several, high-ranking and much younger Mafiosi had recently been sentenced, and space was at a premium. So were medical resources for the old and infirm. And even seven decades after abolishment of the monarchy, nobility was still nobility.

Each evening at seven, as the Venetian sun turned the city to gold, one of the few permitted motorized gondolas drew up to the palazzo, and the Cashier was helped aboard by his burly attendants. Eventually, the Duchessa Passavanti joined them, always carrying a basket of food and a leather satchel.

After months of this routine, the neighbors no longer paid it any attention. Don't you know all the rich are crazy, they whispered. Why would the duchessa be different, considering her tragic losses.

Once the gondola left the palazzo dock, and the low growl of its engine pushed its occupants into the channel, the duchessa opened the basket and brought out a bottle of Sangiovese and an assortment of cheeses. These she shared with the man who lived in her sunroom and who sometimes ate and more often did not. They never conversed, and after an hour or so, the duchessa gave a nod, and the gondola returned home.

This day, however, the Cashier had been a restive patient. For the first time since arriving at Palazzo Passavanti, he knew exactly who he was, and he demanded to be told why he was in this house that he did not recognize. So, as he was prepared for his evening sail, he was in extra restraints.

And this time, instead of a cruise to nowhere, they continued around the Lido and beyond, until the gondola reached the open water of the Gulf of Venice. A few miles out, it was met by a barge. Without speaking, the gondolier and medical attendants ascended a stairway on the outside of the hull, leaving the elderly woman alone with the Cashier.

From the leather satchel, she removed a hundred-year-old *lupara*, the vendetta-settling weapon of Italian honor. She made no speech, asked no questions. She simply unloaded its twin barrels into the man who had taken her daughter and grandchildren.

As she was helped aboard the barge, another man stepped into the gondola and doused it with gasoline, then returned to the larger ship. Once aboard, he fired a flare downward.

From the aft railing, Duchessa Alegreza Passavanti, opened her bottle of wine, poured herself a glass and watched the burning gondola recede into the distance.

CHAPTER SIXTY-THREE

Godfathers and Omens

I'd been on movie sets before and found them, to be charitable, boring. Shooting pictures has been compared to watching grass grow. That's unfair to grass, which really hustles along.

I discovered my interest level had changed significantly now that it was my money running through the sprockets. However, Ross Dare made it clear our visit to *Beverly Hills is Burning's* first day of principal photography would be short and non-participatory. We'd shake a few hands then stand in the rear, watch one scene and disappear—without comment.

If the guy with the bankroll is on the set, actors start playing to the deep pockets. Not helpful for the art and worse for the budget. It also gives the director a case of the red-ass he'll make you pay for—one way or another. And nobody wanted to lock horns with Joe Cargo.

Our producer, Sid Barron, was as good as advertised. A wily veteran with a mane of white hair and the command presence of God's boss, he and Cargo had been driving make-or-break pictures in the speed lane for years. They didn't need help from me or my president—even though we probably had a lot to offer.

What I had done was loosen the schedule for delivery of the finished picture. The original plan had been to open Christmas Eve, but when I learned that would require cutting critical corners, I remembered a former Paramount president who also had a big-budget, R- rated picture that he'd bet the company on. *The Godfather* wasn't going to make its targeted Christmas release either, so Frank Yablans stared out across Central Park from the lofty heights of the Gulf+Western Building, ignored the fury of his bankers, his distribution execs and his chairman and selected March 22 instead—a time of year when nobody releases important pictures.

Then, as tends to happen two days the other side of winter, the entire country got smacked with snow, sleet, rain and high winds. But crowds lined up anyway. Hundreds deep in towns, thousands deep in cities. And when those shivering, drenched souls who weren't lucky enough get into the first shows were told it would be three hours before the boxoffice reopened, they didn't move. And it was a Wednesday night.

I didn't think *Beverly Hills is Burning* was *The Godfather*, and I didn't have Central Park to look onto, just the old Tower Records building on Sunset, but I like associating with winners. So I said a silent prayer and went with Frank. March 22. Now all we needed was snow.

The Brooklyn side of the East River still has a few warehouses that date to the early 1900s, and a little Hollywood magic had turned one of them new again. The discussion between the rabbi and Meyer Lansky would take place there, but first we had to get the rabbi to the meet.

A narrow, brick street containing a row of boarded-up storefronts had been resuscitated and dressed in pre-FDR signage. A pack of ragged kids were badgering a pushcart vendor while two men in rubber aprons unloaded a Tin Lizzie of ice blocks. There were even a few rats on duty, dining on a corncob in the gutter under the watchful eye of their wrangler standing just off-camera.

I didn't know where they'd found the shiny Pierce-Arrow with the all-white tires, but they hadn't taken the same care teaching the actor playing the rabbi how to handle it. The poor guy came careening down the street at full throttle, the car doing most of the driving. In his path, a hundred and twenty cast, crew, extras and rats watched calmly, seemingly unconcerned that their lives were in mortal peril. Somehow, our pretend Talmudist managed to wheel the wildly swaying machine safely past everybody as six cameras rolled.

As soon as he disappeared around a corner, Joe Cargo's deep voice rose above the company, "That's a take. Strike the set." Then Ross had me by the elbow and was guiding me toward our car. I knew Cargo was a one-take guy, but I asked Ross if maybe he should have shot the scene a couple of more times, just to be sure.

"Feel free to ask him yourself," Ross replied.

I took a look at the back of the wide bald head, thick neck and tattooed biceps—his shoulder now healed—barking at a PA. "Get the fuck out of my sight until you find me a ham sandwich." I decided that if one take was good enough for Joe, it was good enough for me.

I saw another PA indicate to Archie Hatt that he wanted to move his chair. The one with EXECUTIVE PRODUCER stenciled across the canvas back. The kid picked it up, and Archie followed him in the direction of the warehouse. It was going to take a lot of boredom to get the smile off that face.

As I got into Ross's car, I caught a glimpse of Wind Fortune arriving in her limo. After the Renaldo Zamora dead chicken crisis, our counseling sessions with Dr. Landau had started rockily, but a couple of months and more than a few tears later, the doctor suggested that she and Wind could soldier on without us. Since then, she had blossomed into an amazing woman and even roped her cosmetics company into establishing the Wind Fortune Crisis Center for Teen Girls. Everything was helped along by Jake's firing the agents, managers and assorted sycophants and taking over handling her himself. At a fee set by me.

I'd still been against her doing this picture, but Ross weighed in that he'd always thought she was the best person for the role, and Mallory, in that understated way he has, told me to stop meddling: "What the devil do you think she's been doing all these years? Selling Girl Scout cookies?" I left it up to Dr. Landau who gave her blessing.

Wind's first scenes weren't scheduled for another week, and stars rarely show up to watch other actors work. Apparently, this one didn't want to miss anything. Not even a broadside or two from Joe Cargo. I took that as a good omen—for the picture and the star.

As the driver helped her out of her car, I saw our writer saunter over. When Wind saw him, she beamed. Cortez beamed back, then they were in each other's arms—hair and makeup be damned. It was a further reminder that the only business I had in anybody else's love life was staying out of it. I made a note to apologize to both of them.

Ross interrupted my self-chastising. "By the way, knowing you were new at this, I took the liberty of seeing how much we could get for the picture if we sold it off. In case you got cold feet."

"Would the number make me happy?"

"Let's just say, you'd be whole with plenty left over."

"What about you?"

"I pencil-whip deals, schmooze assholes and kick ass all day long. I don't do it so I can walk away from what I sweated over. I love movies. And I think we've got a real shot with this one—and the company—if we stick with Teddy's plan."

"Candida agree?"

"She called this morning from Rome. She just closed the biggest presale for an action picture ever. She said to tell you that if you run, you're not the man she thought you were. Or the man Barrie Fontaine would have counted on."

I had to turn my face toward the window. Was it that obvious? "Like I said, Ross, you're the CEO."

CHAPTER SIXTY-FOUR

Old Cars and Old Scores

Ruthie Halevy was helping me redecorate Highroller Hill. It wasn't her forte, but Hector had some excellent ideas, and they were going through fabric swatches while they gabbed about a lot of Laguna Beach people I'd never heard of.

Mac had gone to China to play in a volleyball tournament. Afterward she'd stopped in Australia to see a surfer she used to be engaged to. She said she wasn't sure she'd done the right thing dumping him. I told her if that's what she thought, then she probably hadn't. She called once and said she and the surfer had rented a place in Gold Coast. They had a lot to talk about, and she thought it would take a few months. I was happy for her. Genuinely. And not just because I'd miss spending time with the Bronte sisters.

After a couple of my design suggestions were vetoed by Hector with unrestrained laughter, I wandered down to the single-car garage. If it hadn't been built with the house, it hadn't come along much later. Upkeep, however, had been non-existent. Narrow and forlorn, the wood was pitted and warped, the remaining glass opaque from blowing sand. The structure itself was rock solid, though. Archie had broken a window to be able to look inside then nailed a couple of boards over it. Carpentry wasn't his calling.

It turned out to be a chore getting through the door. The place had been shut up decades ago, and even after I sawed off the corroded padlock, the latch and hinges wouldn't budge. I finally got a tire iron from the Rolls and pried them off. They don't cast metal today the way they used to, and I felt something give in my back as the last one finally popped.

Between the dust, spiders and mice, the only evidence of a car were flat tires barely visible beneath the skirt of a tan tarpaulin. When I jerked the tarp free, it disintegrated in my hands. I coughed as I inhaled tiny particles of airborne canvas and swatted away an imaginary spider I was sure had gone down my neck.

If it wasn't the same car in the Woody Yates photograph, it was its twin. A '32 Lincoln V12 that had appeared black in the picture but was actually a deep maroon. Even compared to my Rolls, it was a prodigious piece of machinery and, backed into the cramped garage, appeared even longer and wider. I imagined Benedict Crown and Meyer Lansky cruising around Havana as I considered what Danny might have done to earn such a gift.

The salt air had had its way with the front bumper, but the grille, headlight trim and twin horns were in good shape. The untarnished orange on black California license plate read DD HH, which I took to mean Highroller Hill and its owner. In the days before vanity plates, it would have taken political influence to score them, but making sure a state power broker had a good time in Cuba—or perhaps just at Highroller Hill— would probably have gotten it done.

I had to squeeze sideways between the wall and car to inch my way to the driver's side door. In the process, I knocked loose a rusty rake that clattered to the floor and scared a snake that slithered over my shoes. I don't have a snake phobia, but having had one meander up my pant leg and take a nap during a mission where I couldn't move, I was pleased when I saw this one break into daylight.

The door handle worked, and I managed to get my hips then my shoulders inside the Lincoln. The interior was remarkably intact but smelled like the discard bin of a horse renderer. There was a key in the ignition, but I didn't bother trying it. I disengaged the parking brake then took out my cell phone and dialed the auto club.

The tow truck driver who dragged it to freedom warned me that the wheels might break off, or the axles could come apart. There was a lot of squealing of metal and four loud thunks as frozen bearings broke loose, but in the end, the eighty-year-old behemoth slowly ground her way to her first sunshine since the year they'd slammed heavy voltage through Bruno Richard Hauptmann. She didn't even blink.

After paying the tow guy and over-tipping him to stop his bitching about the drive up the hill, I opened both doors of the Lincoln, checked for residents in and under the seats then managed to pop the glove box. There were a couple unidentifiable rusty lumps inside along with half a pack of Old Gold Straights and a jar of Vicks that was still blue but that I didn't intend to sample.

The paperwork was crumbling, but enough had survived to show an ownership transfer from Consolidated News Services on Park Avenue to a Daniel Xavier Dades of Laguna Beach, California. It was the same company that had paid Barrie's salary. I also thought it interesting that Danny had been at least part Hispanic. Perhaps Cuban, which would account for a lot.

The trunk unlocked with a separate key from the one in the ignition, and I didn't see it anywhere. I checked the car again, then the garage, and came up empty. Rolls-Royce tools are manufactured from the same steel used in jet engines. You couldn't break one with a sledgehammer and all day to get it done. Jamming a long-length, flathead screwdriver into the Lincoln's key slot, I used my grip, forearms and what was left of my back to break free the latching mechanism and lifted the lid.

Eighty years it may have been, but a body is still a body. Danny Dades had become leather and bone, and constricting sinew had contorted his face into a silent scream. I was reminded of the prehistoric traveler of the Alps I'd seen in *National Geographic*, only this desiccated recipient of violence was wearing a blue silk island shirt festooned with pink flamingos over a pair of linen slacks and white canvas shoes.

Less decorative but more to the point were the three round holes in the back of his skull. Two of the mashed, soft-nosed slugs lay under him. I was able to confirm it was my home's former owner by the inscription on his diamond-studded Omega.

Danny,

Come to Rome soon.

AML

P

I wouldn't ever know who P was, but my money was on AML meaning All My Love. That Danny Dades' life had ended the way gangsters dispose of the foolish and the ambitious, I wasn't remotely surprised.

The only remaining mystery was who had ratted him out so that he ended up wedged in the trunk of a Lincoln with an aeriated cranium rather than tossing coins in the Trevi Fountain. Hooper's refusal of a copy of the script had bothered me when it happened. To be in awe of your father's talent and know his life story down to who he was sleeping with contradicted his disinterest.

I think Hooper just wanted to let the dust continue to collect.

Maybe there are a few writers who've never struggled, but most know the schedule of the dumpster pickup at McDonald's. Regardless of how big a house they eventually build, they never forget the gnawing in their belly and how to hold their breath while the landlord pounds on the door.

A fat wad of C-notes offered by a guy who's just rearranged your face isn't a choice; it's survival. Hoop deserved every dime. And if there hadn't been a payday, just violence? Well, he got to watch his son grow up. I'd make sure Hoop's name was featured prominently in the movie's credits.

On the plus side, if ever a piece of human scum had earned eight decades of turning to leather, Danny Dades was him.

I suggested Ruthie and Hector get us some lunch. Hector had been dancing around my Rolls ever since the house deal closed, so I handed him the keys and told him I liked the burgers at T.K.'s. A Laguna to Newport turnaround was good for at least an hour.

The tools in the garage were as old as everything else but still serviceable. I skidded down the side of the hill away from the ocean until I found I found a level spot. I cleared a small circle of brush then worked the pick and shovel until I ran into rock about five feet down. I was drenched with sweat but felt good. Even the earlier grab in my back was gone. Physical exertion has that effect, though I expected I'd be spending some quality time in the Jacuzzi.

I wrapped Danny in a sheet I swiped from the bedroom and lowered him into the ground without concern for gentleness or which end was up. I wanted to deliver some appropriate words, but my recall of Scripture isn't the best, and I didn't want to send him off with a mixed message. So I just said, "Good-bye, you piece of shit," which I think is from Psalms.

As I filled in the grave, I promised to raise a little hell in Highroller Hill every now and then, loud enough so he could hear it. Motherfucker.

CHAPTER SIXTY-FIVE

Gold and Ash

As I pulled out of my Beverly Hills drive on a bright fall day, one of the workmen outside the gate motioned for me to stop. I got out and walked over to where his partner was using a laser device to level a gold plate on the white stanchion to the right of the entrance. "Long as you're here, Mr. Black, might as well make sure we're doing it the way you want."

The only thing I'd had to go on was the description in one of Lake's notebooks, but the artists at Cartier had done an excellent job interpreting. They'd also talked me into a high-gloss, black acrylic instead of enamel to highlight the hand-engraved lettering in the eighteen-carat surface.

Mag Mell

Looking at it now, I wouldn't have wanted it any different. I realized that the house had been naked without it. "Perfect," I said. "Make it permanent."

"You got it," said the workman. "If you don't mind, what's it mean?"

"Heaven," answered the guy with the laser, his Irish as thick as the plate. "Only maybe a little better."

Yes, I thought. Perfect.

The silver urn was belted into the front seat beside me. Riding with it that way made it seem like we were doing this together. I talked to her about her

411

father—at least what I knew of him—and sometimes I just listened. She never spoke, but I could feel her presence.

J.C. Stinson had never visited me again, though Mallory says he's still around. So to complete the story, I asked a friend at the *Times* to track down his obituary. J.C. had last been seen off the coast of Oahu. According to reports, he was standing on the flybridge of his fishing yacht, firing a .45 at the incoming wave of dive bombers. The date: December 7, 1941. The yacht's name: *Jilleen Cait*. The witness didn't note if he was barefoot, smoking and wearing a Panama hat, but I suspect he was.

I selected Dana Point because there's a stretch of coastline south of the Ritz that's unsuitable for surfing and a half-hour walk from public parking—an appalling distance for Californians—so it's almost always empty. Even if you're intrepid, about all you're going to find there is beached sea grape, so it's a very peaceful mile and a half.

My friend, Jackie Benveniste, formerly of the State Department, and his significant other, Nancy, formerly of Hooters, have a place on the terraced hill overlooking this secluded piece of paradise. Their guard-gated community has a private lot just above the beach for residents and their guests. Providing your name is on the day's visitor list, and you can pass muster with the jackbooted security force.

I made it through without a strip search or having to toss a stiff-armed salute, but one of the mouth-breathers, whose nametag read Trigger, couldn't take his eyes off the urn. I offered to let him open it but said I needed time to take cover. His partner, Jed, didn't think I was funny and waved me through, but not without leaving a fat pair of palm prints on my hood.

I swung by Jackie's, fished the beach key out of the mailbox and parked overlooking the Pacific. I was the only car there, so I got out with the urn and sat on one of the benches for a while, enjoying the waves. There are usually dolphins meandering around, but today, there were none.

Then I saw something I had never seen this close to land before. A pair of killer whales not more than fifty yards offshore. They swam in circles for a while but didn't breach. I realized they were ushering a young calf through playtime. Without another soul in sight, Jilleen and I had them all to ourselves.

Eventually the whales dived and disappeared, and I took the steep path down to the beach. I'd checked the tide tables before leaving Beverly Hills and was right on schedule. The waves were picking up, and each successive series of rollers was moving an inch further onto the terra firma of California.

I picked a spot about twenty feet in and set the urn on the sand while I used a thick chunk of driftwood to trace

JC AND JC
FATHER AND DAUGHTER
TOGETHER AGAIN

The night before, I'd taken the business card J.C. Stinson had given Barrie and set fire to it in a glass bowl. It didn't take long to turn to gray and white ash, and I thought it fitting that some of the letters on the card were still visible. I crushed the residue into a fine powder, pried open the urn and joined it with Jilleen's.

Now, I gently poured the combined remains into the depressions of the letters and stood for a moment, watching the water advance. After a while, I moved to the rocks on the hillside and sat holding the empty urn while the tide against the setting sun gently eased the distant past out to sea.

Maybe someday, my own ashes will find Sanrevelle and our daughter, and we too will be together again.

CHAPTER SIXTY-SIX

Ray Charles

Matty Aspirins, wearing wrap-around Ray-Bans, sat on his balcony with a cup of strong Greek coffee and watched the fishing fleet lumber out to sea among the pleasure-seekers. The Cypriot had been right. Pyrgos was light years better than Miami.

He'd never seen so many women. They came in groups, pairs, alone. Vacationers, weekenders and day trippers from a thousand places around the Med, all looking for a few days or a few hours of uncomplicated food, uninterrupted sun and unentangled companionship.

He'd taken the second floor of the Cypriot's building for three grand a month and told the manager that when the Cypriot showed up at Christmas they'd make a longer-term arrangement. He said he was laying low from his ex-wife's lawyers and duked him an extra ten large to keep his mouth shut. The guy had practically spit up on himself. Now even the housekeeper wasn't allowed to knock on his door. Matty had a few months to figure things out.

An Athenian doctor and his gay lover had the first floor, but they were rarely there. The only thing Matty didn't like were all the Arabs around. He didn't care about their politics as long as they stayed out of his face, but they were the noisiest fuckers on the planet. And they had this thing about hanging speakers outside, so you had to listen to their fuckin music too.

Matty had just gotten back from his third trip to Switzerland. This time the doctors said they weren't going to be able to get any more glass out of his face. They'd removed twenty-seven shards, including more from his eyes, and there were still some left. Most would work their way out over

414

time; the rest would be buried with him.

The retina in the eye that had taken the laser was permanently damaged, but as long as he wore dark glasses, the halos were tolerable and didn't affect his sight. Walks on the beach had brought back his strength, and all in all, he considered himself lucky.

He hadn't gotten the same enthusiasm from his people in New York when he called and told them he was finished. While he was at it, he said that he owed them for Dimitrios. "We talked about whackin you two years ago. Should have," came the response.

But Matty knew he wasn't worth the trouble to hunt down. The way the business worked, his name was already ancient history. Whoever came behind him wouldn't go out on his own terms, but that wasn't Matty's problem. It was a more disposable world.

"Hey, Ray Charles," the thickly accented voice cut through his reverie. He looked down to the street and saw Gabriel, the teenager who delivered fresh fish and vegetables to the housewives. Matty didn't cook, so he never bought anything, but he let the kid sit on his balcony and smoke while he practiced his English, which seemed to be getting worse.

"Capital of Tax-AZZ is Dal-AZZ," Gabriel called up.

"Not even close. Austin."

"No shit, Shylook."

Matty just shook his head. "Why don't you give it up? And get me some Marlboros, will you? I'm gagging on these Greek fuckers."

"I bring next trip. Hey, the *pousti* doctor rented his place for month. Three dudes from Argeeteeny. Maybe *poustis* too. You up for a little fuck in the ass?"

"Argentina, you dumb fuck." Matty tossed the remainder of his coffee over the railing, but Gabriel was already trotting away, laughing. He stopped and turned back, waving a wad of cash. "They have big party tonight. Say bring much women, so maybe not *poustis.*"

Either way, better Argentine *poustis* than Arabs, Matty thought. Quieter. Maybe he'd check out the party. See what Gabriel managed to round up.

Matty was up before the alarm went off. It was the first time he'd set it since he'd arrived in Cyprus, and he'd had trouble figuring out the French instructions. He still had a headache from the Retsina, but the half-dozen Excedrin he slammed down would help.

It had turned out the Argentines weren't *poustis*, and the women at the party had been beyond his wildest dreams—especially the one called Dariea. She'd fucked him then licked his cock until he had to tell her to stop. She'd put him off when he tried to get her to come upstairs, but as drunk as he'd been, that had probably been a good thing. Today, they were going to float around on the Argentines' boat, and she could lick all she wanted. He felt himself getting hard thinking about it.

When he got to the dock, Gabriel was already there, loading the idling yacht with more food and booze than a dozen people could consume. The kid broke into his best grin when he saw Matty. "Ray Charles gonna get him some POOZZ-ay. Floatin and fuckin all day for sure. Maybe all night too."

Just then, the young Argentine they called Renaldo came out on the fly bridge. "Hey there, Matty. Thought the Retsina might have done you in. Come on aboard."

Matty climbed the stairs and stepped through the raised rail onto the afterdeck. "Some machine. Looks like every bit of seventy feet."

"Eighty-two. I like to feel something with balls under me. "Let's get going. The girls are going to meet us about a mile past the breakwater."

Something in the reptilian part of Matty's brain stirred. "Where're your buddies?"

Renaldo gave him a wide grin. "I told them they were on their own today. I was gonna surprise you, but what the fuck. Last night you said you could handle a boat, right?"

Matty nodded. "Nothing complicated, but yeah, I had a thirty-foot Chris back in the States."

"Dariea says you like to see a couple of girls go at it. Shit, who doesn't? Well, she's got a younger sister, and apparently, they do things to each other that'll make the top of your head blow off. The plan is for my lady to get in with me, and the three of you can figure out if you want to follow us or head off on your own. That is, if I can keep my date from wanting to join in."

Matty's face broadened into a smile that just kept coming. Jesus, he thought, I shoulda retired years ago. "No shit. How young's the sister?"

"She didn't say, but hey, it's the Med." He let it hang there. "Why don't you grab us a couple of beers while I get this thing into the channel. Then we can sit in the sun and consider the possibilities."

Matty went through the door into the salon and felt the cool of the air conditioning. Maybe he'd check out the staterooms, get the feel of things.

He found the fridge and felt the engines engage and the boat move away from the dock. He opened a beer for himself and put one on the counter for Renaldo.

As he turned, I stepped into view. "Hi, Matty. Sorry to spoil your day."

THE END

ACKNOWLEDGMENTS

Laying brick is hard. Farming is backbreaking. Busting through a door in the middle of the night with your gun leveled not sure what's on the other side requires a commitment most of us will never have to measure in ourselves. Entertainment dealmaking and writing books pale in comparison. I am deeply appreciative to be able to lead the life I do.

I have never lacked for self-motivation. If I wanted something, I worked to get it. But as I put a few years, successes and failures under my belt, I learned something. If you don't have people beside you who won't waver when the waves get high; who will encourage you to do even the most unpleasant job, not just to completion, but the best it can be done; and who will grab you by the lapels when you need it, then you can't do anything. Not even something like writing books. The following is for those who stood alongside me.

Writers never know if what they've written is good or borscht. Some salve their fear of the latter with alcohol, others by never reading reviews (so they say) and a few by hanging around with people who regularly tell them they're an American treasure. After writing my first novel, Doug Grad, then a senior executive at HarperCollins, read it and made a multiple-book deal with me. Without Doug, Rail Black might never have become a reality, and *City of War, Wildcase* and *Beverly Hills is Burning* would exist only in my imagination. I am very lucky. However, no one has yet told me I'm an American treasure.

Motion picture agents are different. Their job is to keep you realistic, a word few in Hollywood can spell. These agents are tough, smart and driven—the three things doing deals in this town demand. For that, I thank CAA's Tony Etz and Matthew Snyder. Soft spoken, but hardly soft.

I also want to thank the real J.C. Stinson—the man who wrote *Sudden Impact* and Clint Eastwood's signature line, "Go ahead, make my day,"— for granting me leave to use his name, personality and slightly modified doppelganger as Howard Hughes's attorney. And most particularly to Angela Stinson, J.C.'s lovely wife and the ultimate Stinson decision-maker. I hope I made her day.

Special thanks goes to John and Sue Benjamin of the Shuttleworth Collection in Old Warden, UK for providing me with photographs of the lone, extant, original de Havilland 88 Comet aircraft, the *Grosvenor House*. Also a special thank you to Michael Ovcacik for his photographs of the *Grosvenor House's* cockpit. Without John and Sue's taking their time and Michael's fine work, I would not have been able to get Barrie Fontaine up and down. I do, however, apologize for the crash.

To my good friend, the screenwriter, Dennis Hackin, as supportive a friend as anyone will ever have, I offer not just my thanks but my lifelong appreciation. And to the Honorable Judge James Zagel, Homer Hickam and Gayle Lynds who are always available to share a moment and a kind or critical word, my gratitude runs deep.

I would also like to issue a special thank you to Robert Bidinotto, a first-rate journalist and author who took the time to write about me.

I created Rail Black, but he has several godfathers and godmothers: Mace Neufeld and Stephanie Austin who have been there from the beginning; Bob Turner, the kind of man one hopes his sons will emulate; and most of all, Kathy Morgan, the tough dealmaker with the best laugh on the planet.

I would like to thank my family for their encouragement and support. The only thing less exciting than watching a writer work is listening to him talk about what he's written. New earplugs have been ordered.

A special thank you also to Clive Cussler, who sent me off into the world of novels with kind words I can never forget. I deeply appreciate it, Clive.

I would also like to thank Robert W. Enzenauer, MD, MPH, MSS,

MBA and current Professor and Chief of Ophthalmology at the Children's Hospital of Colorado. Not incidentally, Dr. Enzenauer is also Brig. Gen. Enzenauer, and he has been most generous with his time.

Acknowledging people you will never meet may seem unusual, but here it is mandatory. Somewhere right now, huddled against the cold or baking in the sun, often wet, shivering, hungry and exhausted but thinking of nothing but their mission, are the bravest of the brave: the men of Delta Force. There will be no parades when they come home, except the ones their families give in their living rooms. Theirs is a quiet honor. I thank them for my freedom. And for that of all Americans.

Finally, I want to acknowledge my late father, Ralph Russell, a master showman and theatre impresario who never used the words art and motion picture in the same sentence but who knew how to milk the last dollar out of two hours of film. We had a sometimes strained relationship, but he was the man who sat me down in a theatre seat when I was still too young to talk and let me watch every picture that went across a screen.

I'm still not smiling about tarring a theatre roof in ninety degree heat, or scraping gum off acres of cement floors with a can of carbon tetrachloride and a putty knife, or picking up things I'd rather not remember from the parking lot of a drive-in. My attitude also hasn't changed about wearing a tuxedo and selling tickets and popcorn while my friends were out on dates, but I've decided not to file a child labor suit. The meager paychecks with the *It's-a-family-business-and-you're-family* excuse? Well, some things need a little more time.

Neil Russell
Beverly Hills, California